CONFESSIONS

OF THE

SECOND BORN

Also by Kastie Pavlik

<u>Children of the Morning Star Series</u>

The Arrival Reawakened (1)

Confessions of the Second Born (2)

Last Born Daughter (3)

Eternal Light Descendant (Final)

Additionally

How to Make Lemonade

Praise for *Last Born Daughter*

Prepare to have your heart ripped, because that's how Ms Pavlik rolls and I love her books for that.

~Ruth Miranda, Heir of Avalon & The Blood Trilogies

...a compelling world that will draw you in and make you cheer for your favourite characters – then break your heart when you realise not all will survive. It's a masterfully crafted tale of love, loss and sacrifice, perfect for fans of vampires, myth, legend, and paranormal romance and suspense.

~Serene Conneeley, Into the Mists & Into the Storm Trilogies

Thrilling...devastating, but satisfying. A riveting read you'll have trouble putting down.

~M.K. Deppner, Photographs of October

...I dread and thrill in equal measure for where Pavlik will take us. So much hangs in the balance, and with an ending to Last Born Daughter that left me in stunned silence, this series still has so much more to come.

~Julie Embleton, Turning Moon series & Voyager Chronicles

Praise for *How To Make Lemonade*

Beautiful prose and an unexpected story...Ms. Pavlik delivers unique twists and leads the reader through the darkness toward the light...or does she?

~M.K. Deppner, Photographs of October

I simply could not put it down...I was left replenished, satisfied, my thirst slackened by this fresh glass of lemonade!

~Ruth Miranda, The Preternaturals Series

CONFESSIONS OF THE SECOND BORN

Children of the Morning Star Book 2

KASTIE PAVLIK

CONFESSIONS OF THE SECOND BORN: Children of the Morning Star Book 2

Revised Edition

ISBN-13: 978-1-7376818-1-6
Library of Congress Control Number: 2021917773

Printed in Fairfield, Ohio
The United States of America

Revision based on the original edition
"Confessions of the Second Born"
© 2018 Kastie Pavlik
ISBN-13: 978-1-72169-200-2
Library of Congress Control Number: 2018908987

Editing Services: Magpie Press
Original Photographs and Illustrations by: Kastie Pavlik
Map created with Public Domain images
Public Domain source map credit to Ian Macky
Email: *kastiepavlik@gmail.com*
Instagram & Facebook: *@kastiepavlikauthor*
www.kastiepavlik.wixsite.com/author

...EVIL IS A CONSEQUENCE OF GOOD,
SO, IN FACT,
OUT OF JOY IS SORROW BORN.

EITHER THE MEMORY OF PAST BLISS
IS THE ANGUISH OF TODAY,
OR THE AGONIES WHICH 'ARE'
HAVE THEIR ORIGIN IN THE ECSTASIES
WHICH 'MIGHT HAVE BEEN.'

~EDGAR ALLAN POE, *BERENICE*

TABLE OF CONTENTS

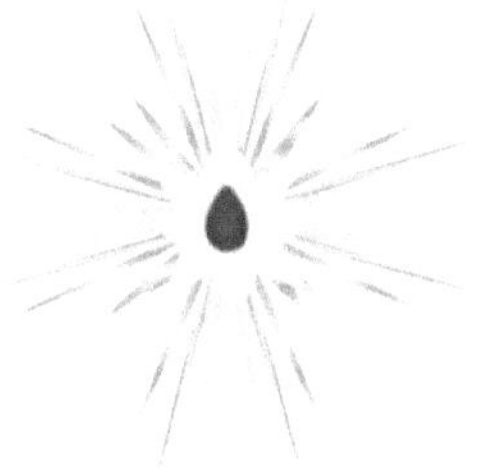

Chapter One: Heralding the Red Horse

I

Orison Crossing, Illinois, Summer 2006

If not for the sun's midmorning perch, he might not have seen the white glint in the alley. The boy would be at the candy counter, parting with the meager dollar bill in his pocket. Instead, he gripped his handlebars with colorless fists.

In a daze, he stepped off the pedal and into the street. He didn't hear his bike crash on the sidewalk. His heart thundered too loudly as curiosity pulled him closer.

It was a hand, waxed the hue of death, jutting from the trash. The boy jolted and fought the urge to flee, blindly scrabbling over the building's brick and mortar façade for support.

He'd never seen a dead body before.

He ducked into the alley and inched the tip of a sneaker-laden toe beneath the hand's black plastic covering. Time slowed to a crawl. His pulse drummed away all thought as he lifted his foot.

It wasn't the man's pallid, dull skin, his lifeless eyes, or even the stench of death that tightened fear's grip. No—it was the two bloody crusts, the puncture wounds on the man's throat. The boy leaped back.

He must have cried out.

A shadow loomed over him. Hands landed on his shoulders. The boy caught his breath. He peered over his shoulder, expecting to see a soulless monster.

But it was an old man in worn coveralls. Tired eyes met the boy's horrified gaze. The old man nodded. He'd seen them, too.

As the old man's arms lowered, he yelled, "Someone get Walter

1

Hodges down here, *right now!*"

A man jogged over, phone in hand, eager to help. He swore and turned away, hyperventilating as he dialed 911. "T-there's a-a *body*…"

His voice disappeared as other people scurried over, asking questions all at once. They would have trampled the boy had the old man not tugged him onto his dusty boots. Clearing his throat, the old man threw his arm out and spoke in a voice as grim as the lines splitting his face. "Stay back! There's marks on his neck. He's been *bitten*."

The boy gaped at the old man. Then the whispers began, one word drifting from mouth to mouth: *vampire*.

The boy panicked. Tears flooded his vision as he burst through the crowd. He covered his ears and squeezed his eyes shut. He didn't want to hear it. Hear them say *his* name.

The sidewalk vanished from beneath his feet. He threw his hands out and screamed. As the terrifying sound ricocheted down the alley, a strong arm encircled his torso and caught him in midair.

The crowd fell silent.

It was stifling.

Trembling, the boy opened his eyes.

He was crouched before him—the friend of Death who had never actually known him. The man who had walked the line of time without aging a day for longer than the old timers could remember. The sunlight bathing his alabaster skin did not deceive him. The boy knew the rumors.

Publicly, the man was Eric Ravenscroft, attorney at law and philanthropist at heart, but privately, in a world ruled by whispers, he was the vampire of Orison Crossing, and that made him the crowd's primary suspect.

II

Ten-year-old Tommy Ellis wore the unmistakable scent of death. Eric set the boy on his feet, straightened the ball cap over his choppy, carrot-orange hair, and wiped his cheeks dry.

Smiling despite the tightness in his chest, Eric knelt on the sidewalk and gently grasped Tommy's shoulder. He peered over his sunglasses into the boy's eyes until they dimmed.

"Don't worry, Tommy," Eric whispered. "I am not the one who did this. Forget what you saw. Go home. Your mother's off. Be with her."

Eric pushed his sunglasses up. Light returned to the boy's gaze. Tommy beamed a wide, toothy grin and ran across the street to his bike, waving and yelling, "See ya later, Mr. Ravenscroft!"

Eric somberly watched him pedal away. Children's minds were too fragile to manipulate, but this was not a memory a child should have.

As he stood, he surveyed the crowd. The whispers weren't new, but he'd never been scrutinized by such accusing eyes.

People instinctively stepped out of his path as he approached the old man. Weston Faust, a dairy farmer who lived on the outskirts of town, nudged his chin at William Jamerson's makeshift grave. "There's holes in his neck."

Eric clenched his jaw. Bill had been a member of the Flock, which made him off limits to the Vampiric Nation. He shook his head and patted Weston on the back.

Turning to face the crowd, he said, "I am well aware of what you think you know about me. But don't trust hearsay. I am your friend, your neighbor, and a benefactor for this town—my hometown."

People fidgeted, looking away or staring at the ground, anything to avoid eye contact. Eric turned back to Weston. "Walter's on his way?"

The old man nodded.

"I'll be in my office," he said quietly. "I want to help Judy however I can—let him know."

Winston nodded again.

Eric walked past one squirming person after another and was almost clear when a burly fellow with an unruly mane blocked his path. In a gruff, insinuating tone, the man said, "I know what you are. You did this. Bill was *my friend.*"

"Did you witness his murder?" Eric asked in an icy voice, leaning in close. "Tell me what you know, Berg. Speculation won't hold up in court. Besides…" He dropped his voice even lower. "If I truly am what you fear, is it wise to confront me like this? Do you really think these *people* could save you?"

Berg flinched at the blackened fire behind Eric's sunglasses. "I-I d-didn't see a-anything. I-I swear!"

Without moving an inch from Berg's face, Eric loudly announced, "If anyone wishes to discuss the matter—like a civilized person—my door is open, as always."

Long seconds passed before the burly fellow mumbled an apology.

Eric sidestepped him just as a car door slammed. Heavy footsteps thudded against the sidewalk behind him and a thick voice boomed off the alley walls.

"What have we got here?"

"Mornin' Walter." The old man clasped the Chief's hand. "Gertrude Ellis's boy found him. Looks like Bill Jamerson—with marks on his neck."

Walter's face snapped up and he turned at the waist, locking eyes with Eric. Mentally cursing his timing, Eric grudgingly returned to the alley and offered Walter a firm handshake.

"I have another unit and the coroner on the way. Any idea where Bill's wife is?" Walter asked.

"When I met with them yesterday, she mentioned a doctor's appointment for their youngest child," Eric replied stiffly.

"Yesterday, huh?" Walter looked skyward and huffed. "Well then—"

He stepped back and turned with his arms outstretched. Making a sweeping motion at the crowd, he yelled, "Listen up! This is a crime scene. Unless you want to sleep on a hard cot tonight, take twenty very large steps back. If you aren't across the street, you'll be cited for interfering with a police matter."

He gestured at the old man. "You too, Weston. I'll take your statement once we secure the scene. Did you touch anything?"

"Nope, but Gertrude's boy lifted the bag with his foot."

"Good grief." Walter sighed. "I gotta have another talk with that kid. He's too damn curious. Go on and stand over there, please."

Careful to face away from any lip-reading eyes, Eric quietly said, "Tommy won't remember anything, Walter."

The Chief huffed again and rubbed his forehead. "You didn't—" He shook his head. "Of course you did."

Eric didn't reply.

Scratching his ear, Walter grumbled, "I suppose it'd be understandable that the shock alone would make him forget. Thanks for that spin."

Walter looked over the growing throng. It'd already tripled in size. "As if it isn't complicated enough. You know who they suspect."

"Yes."

"Is it what they think?"

"Possibly."

"Could it be your brother?"

"No."

"Well, do you—" Walter lowered his voice. "You said he's a dignitary—can he find out who did this?"

Eric stiffened. "Conduct your investigation. I'll do what I can."

As he turned to leave, Walter asked, "How's our girl?"

"Fine." Eric took a step and paused. "Is that all?"

"It's just—" Walter paused and cracked his knuckles—a nervous reaction to pushing past Eric's *we're done talking* tone. "I think announcing her return might be *useful*. A distraction?"

"I'll take it under advisement." Eric stalked from the alley before the lawman offered any more suggestions.

Orison Crossing was his haven, a place of lazy, sunny days and quiet, peaceful nights. People were kind and caring, the community safe and enduring. The Schaffer's "murder-suicide" of 1975 and the 1988 arson of the Sunset Grove Parish withstanding, the town had been relatively quiet since the 1930s.

He clenched his jaw again. Death was his devious and inescapable companion, with trickery and debauchery hidden up his sleeves, holding a sickle in one hand and a scythe in the other.

Eric peered beyond the large, block letters on his office window, and marveled at the beautiful young woman chatting with his secretary. Death was a crafty bastard with a touch that tended to stick, but it couldn't hold onto *her*.

Eric entered the lobby vestibule and the accusing eyes disappeared. He pulled the next door open. The accusing voices faded. *She* was there to consume his reality. A radiant pixie with honey hair and alluring gray eyes, her essence a drug, her aura unlike anything he'd ever known.

She'd *died* to bring peace to the Vampiric Nation.

And Bill was murdered to shatter it.

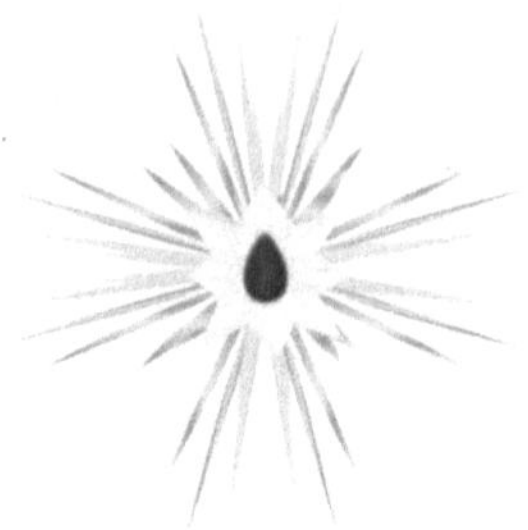

CHAPTER TWO: THE PRICE OF PROTECTION

"Good morning, ladies." Eric tossed his sunglasses onto Molly's desk and folded Paresh into his arms. A question lingered in her uncertain eyes. Eric dotted her forehead with a kiss. "Everything is in order at the cottage."

Relaxing against him, she gazed outside. "What's going on?"

"Small town curiosity." Gently ushering her into his office, Eric said, "Give me a minute with Molly, okay?"

Chewing on her lip, Paresh hesitantly nodded and shut the door. Eric grabbed a notepad off Molly's desk.

"What are you doing?" she asked, warily watching him scribble on the pad.

He gave it to her face down. "Don't read it out loud."

She cautiously picked up the note and then dropped into her chair, hand covering her mouth. "Oh my God."

"Walter will be here soon," Eric said. "Please begin the transfer process of my cases to Ken and Karen—permanently."

Molly looked up so fast her glasses slid to the tip of her nose. "What do you—"

Eric pushed her glasses up and took her hand.

"Given recent events," he began in a gentle voice. "I cannot stay in the public eye. You have been a good, loyal friend and that won't change. You'll just have more time for yourself—which you deserve, especially after the other night."

For a long time, she stared at him, too dumbstruck to speak. Then, as her eyes glistened with moisture, she faced away. "Y-yes. Of course. I understand."

Eric pulled her up and peered into her eyes. "No, you don't. But you will, I promise."

He nudged her to his chest. The sobs she'd so valiantly tried to hide gushed forth into his shoulder.

"I-I was just *so worried*. You…you were all *bloody*. Seeing you like that—" she choked out. "I know I'm not supposed to ask—but first that, and then you told me to stay away, and I didn't hear from you for three days, and now Bill—"

"Oh Molly," he whispered, hugging her closer. "I've been so selfish."

A muffled, "No, you haven't," came from his shoulder.

"Yes, I have. You deserve answers. But, I need to talk with Paresh before Walter shows up."

Molly raised her head and brushed at the damp stain on his suit jacket. "I'm sorry. I-I don't know what came over me."

"You're always there for me. I should be there for you, too. We're friends, right?" He wiped tears and mascara smudges from her cheeks, and offered a somber smile. "Everything will be okay."

She snatched a tissue off her desk and blew her nose, nodding halfheartedly. Shaking graying hairs from her eyes, she sighed and reached into his jacket.

She pulled out a the slim case and handed it to him. "You forgot your *spectacles*, again."

He grinned and slid the silver frames onto his nose. "I don't know how I ever survived without you."

"Me neither." She dabbed her eyes and slapped at him to go away.

Obediently heading for his office, he said, "Thank you, Molly. For everything you do and the secrets you keep."

☽ ☀ ☾

Perched on the suede sofa that divided the office, Paresh stared at the LCD television with her hands folded in her lap. It was the same way she'd sat the night he'd told her his truth.

"It's more entertaining when the TV is on," he said softly.

Her gaze drifted from the screen to him. "Something's wrong. I can feel it."

"I learned the hard way not to keep things from you, so I promise I won't try to shield you anymore." He grabbed a bottle of water from the refrigerated sideboard, and then shrugged out of his jacket and sat beside her.

Tired lines creased Paresh's forehead. "You can't keep blaming yourself. Neither of us knew what Lucien had ordered. It was Destiny."

"I still should have told you everything. No reason in this world or the next excuses that." He tossed his jacket onto the recliner and set the bottle on the coffee table.

Tingling heat penetrated his sleeve as her fingertips swept over his arm. "You desire to protect the people you love. Share that burden with me. You're stuck with me forever, you know."

"I can't imagine my life any other way," he whispered, brushing honey-colored locks off her shoulder. He lightly stroked her throat. A muscle beneath her eye twitched. "It's not any better?"

"Not as frequent."

"No one's ever survived Lucien's bite. And you lost so much blood." Eric pulled her into his arms. "I wish I knew what to do."

She leaned against him. They sat in silence and stared at the blank television awhile.

Eventually, Eric asked, "Remember my clients from yesterday afternoon?"

"The Jamersons?"

He nodded. "The father, William, is dead. His body was found in the alley two buildings down by the son of one of my hostesses at The Greenery."

She sucked a breath in and sat up, pressing her hand to her mouth. "How?"

Before he could answer, a realization spun him into a silent daze. Few vampires knew about Paresh and the Second New Age. Which meant—

Paresh grabbed his hand and searched his face, worried lines bridging her brow. He sighed and squeezed her hand.

"Your blood was only supposed to be distributed to the Elders and the VaSH Commanders and Officers. If they're the only ones who know—" Eric wiped his face. "Oh God, Bill's jugular was *clearly* punctured."

"He was *bitten?*" Paresh asked, eyes wide. "What does that mean?"

Grimly facing her, Eric replied, "Whoever killed him either sits on the High Council or commands the Vampire Shadow Hounds. They *wanted* us to find him."

Exhaling a forceful breath, Eric ran his hand through his hair. The tightness in his chest turned into a weighted pit.

"On top of that," he added, "everyone thinks *I* did it. Even Walter was alarmed that I met with Bill yesterday."

Paresh threaded her fingers between his. "They can't honestly believe it was you."

"I sit at the heart of the unknown that every human instinctively fears. Darkness, spiders, mice—fear is a powerful force."

"But you didn't kill him."

Eric shook his head. "Doesn't matter. How many people kill spiders and mice based solely on fear?"

Paresh opened the water bottle and sipped in thought. "Do what Walter said, then. Use me as a distraction."

"That's not fair to y—" Eric turned sharply toward her. "You *heard* that?"

Paresh gnawed her lip. "Kind of. It was hollow and muffled." She shook the water bottle. "Like I was underwater. And it didn't last long."

"But you heard him." He tucked a lock of hair behind her ear. "Your alteration is nothing like mine. It's like when Lucinda was pregnant. I was gone while the baby grew and changed her body, but when I finally saw her, so round and radiant, she never looked more beautiful."

Paresh smiled wistfully. "Lucinda was lucky to have someone who loved her so very much."

Eric cupped Paresh's face and kissed her. "I'm the lucky one." Warmth sliced through the dread in his chest as he caressed her cheek with his thumb.

He kissed her again, gently at first, and then deeply, long, and lingering. Her fingers stroked his neck and twisted through his hair. They parted with their foreheads touching. Eric traced her lips. Her breath moved over his skin. He closed his eyes. "God, I love you."

He felt her lips turn up and heat flooded his core. Her aura enveloped his whole body as she lovingly massaged his neck and said, "I am forever yours."

☽ ✳ ☾

Eric sighed. "I don't want to do this."

"Is it so horrible?" Paresh asked. "I miss him."

"You are bonded to him like a daughter." Eric's icy eyes darkened to deep navy. "I hope you never see the version of him that I know."

"He's changed," she said gingerly.

"Maybe God can forgive and forget, but Jonathan doesn't deserve that. Especially not from me." Eric pulled a black case from his pocket.

Inside, layers of velvet cushioned the Star of the Vampiric Nation. Eric pushed a long silver prong inward until it clicked. When he pulled his finger away, a droplet of blood pooled to the surface.

"I wish he'd just carry a cell phone," Eric grumbled as he set the pin and case on the coffee table. He licked the blood off the already healed wound and looked up to see Paresh hungrily eyeing his finger.

Blushing, she knitted her hands between her knees and stared at the table. He gently kneaded her shoulder in an effort to get her to look at him, but she merely bit her lip and squeezed her eyes shut.

"It'll feel more natural, in time," Eric said. "It's okay to——"

Molly's voice buzzed through his intercom. "Mr. Ravenscroft, I'm sorry to interrupt, but there's a Mr. Lucien on the line, insistent that you're expecting his call."

"*Mister* Lucien?" Paresh curiously followed Eric with her eyes as he approached his desk. "*On the phone?*"

"I'll take it, Molly," Eric said.

When Eric answered the handset, the Arch Elder's apathetic voice said, "What do you need?"

"Jonathan."

"He's on sabbatical."

"On sabbatical?"

"Do you intend only to repeat me?"

The chill in Lucien's voice frosted Eric's ear. Shaking it off, he clenched his teeth and replied in a tight voice, "One of your hunters attacked a member of the Flock and left the body for discovery. He was one of my clients and I——"

"One of my hunters?"

"Or an Elder. Who else knows about us?"

Long seconds passed.

"Damn near everyone in this town saw those bite marks! Who killed him?" Eric demanded. "Say something!"

"We shall deal with it here."

Another blast of cold air followed and the line clicked off. Eric slowly cradled the phone.

Paresh leaned on his desk anxiously awaiting a recap.

Slightly dumbfounded, Eric sat back and said, "Lucien said they will 'deal' with it."

"But why did *he* call? Where's Jonathan?"

"On sabbatical." Eric tossed his hands up. "Whatever that means."

Picking up the picture frame on Eric's desk, she lovingly looked upon her parents. "Hopefully finding his penitent heart."

"Maybe," Eric said, more dismissively than he intended. He retrieved his pin from the coffee table. Tucking it into his pocket, he crossed to his office door and opened it as Molly was about to knock.

Caught by surprise, she stammered, "W-Walter's here."

"Send him in." Eric left her in the doorway and returned to his desk. Molly waved the Chief in and pulled the door shut.

"Morning, Walter!" Paresh sat in a chair opposite Eric's desk as the lawman sauntered over. "How're you doing?"

"Mornin' hon. Wish I could say I'm doing better, but that's the job. How are you feeling?" Walter set his hat on the sofa before easing into the chair beside Paresh. "Eric said you've been ill the past few days."

"I'm a little better today."

"Glad to hear it. Those travel bugs can be nasty little suckers, but you're in good hands."

"What have you learned?" Eric asked curtly. Whether planned or not, he did not enjoy being toyed with at Jonathan's—or Lucien's—whim.

"Sometimes I forget who I'm dealing with," Walter jokingly whispered to Paresh. To Eric, he replied, "I think we should speak privately, Counselor."

"She knows about Bill. Go ahead."

Paresh nodded sadly.

Walter shook his head, but began his report. "There are two punctures in Bill's throat, like Weston said. A preliminary estimate shows the spacing matches human canines, but there's no bruising for the cuspids. There's no blood at the scene and it seems that his attacker wanted him to stay dead: there was a dagger in his heart. The handle is solid gold, with a carved crescent moon embedded with rubies."

"Why a dagger?" Paresh asked.

Sharing a grim look with Walter, Eric said, "The bite was staged for discovery, but likely real and capable of infection—so they staked him."

"You sound a little too certain of that." Walter's voice was quiet. "Did you learn something?"

"I've reached out, but don't have answers, yet. It's just the most likely scenario."

"That's not the only reason I'm here." Walter heaved a big sigh. "Judy said Bill never came home last night."

Eric's chair creaked as he leaned back and faced the ceiling. "My alibi is beside you."

"I appreciate that, but I'm not there, yet, old friend. I need to know what happened yesterday. To fill in as much about his last moments as I can. I know their eldest son, Blake, was arrested last week over some missing tools from a neighbor—"

"And they called to retain me since they couldn't post bail and he was sitting in jail awaiting arraignment." Eric sat forward. "But that was the morning Paresh came in, so I had Molly refer them to my partners."

Walter produced a pen and notebook from his pocket and began writing. "Mm-hm. So why did you meet with them yesterday?"

"You know Karen and Ken can't afford to reduce their rates like I do," Eric replied. "I'd been covering their fees until I could intervene. They got Blake released on his own recognizance and filed a motion to dismiss the charges. Yesterday was the earliest convenience for me to talk with Blake to ensure the dismissal will be granted."

Walter fumbled with his pen. He knew quite well about Eric's "talks."

Eric met Walter's speechless stare with a face of stone. He and Paresh's father, Andrew, had worked diligently to eliminate serious crime from Orison Crossing after the gruesome happenings in 1975. That meant employing a skilled and a generously compensated police presence, as well as a heavy reliance on Eric's influence—a power the Chief wasn't above using, despite seeing it as a moral taboo.

"I spoke with the victim by phone and arranged for Blake to return the tools with apologies," Eric said dryly. "Blake agreed and will perform labor and yard services for his neighbor until school resumes. He has learned the errors of his ways and will be a productive citizen henceforth."

"Yeah, I'm sure," Walter mumbled, his attention returning to his notes. "Then what?"

"Judy and the kids left. Bill stayed for a drink—you know he loves that Kentucky bourbon I keep on the sideboard. He vented and thanked me a few times, and left about thirty minutes later, just before five. Paresh and Molly were in the lobby. They saw him leave."

Paresh nodded and pointed in the direction of the alley. "He walked out that way."

The Police Chief glanced at Eric. "Was he drunk? Could he have passed out in the alley?"

"I don't know how he wound up in the alley."

"Well, how much did he have to drink? Was he drunk?"

"He had a strong helping—three fingers—of single barrel, neat. He was in good spirits and coherent when he left."

"And when did you leave last night?"

"At five o'clock."

"Where did you go?"

"The Greenery."

Walter let out an exasperated huff. "I hate talking to attorneys. You don't offer more than what's asked. This isn't a deposition, damn it. You know where I'm going with this! Give me something I can work with!"

Eric contemplated his friend. "I took Molly and Paresh to dinner. Sarah Weaverly can attest that we were there for about an hour. The sun was still up when I brought Molly back here to her car. I didn't notice anything unusual. Then, Paresh and I returned to my house, where we stayed in for the remainder of the night.

"This morning, Paresh and I picked Molly up at her house around six-thirty. Molly then drove my car to the cottage and dropped me off. She and Paresh arrived here shortly thereafter."

"And you were alone at the cottage?"

Eric's eyes darkened. "Yes. I *am* still responsible for the property. I tended to a personal matter and walked into town. I came upon Tommy running from the scene right before you arrived."

Ebony strands fell over Eric's glasses as he pinched the bridge of his nose. He closed his eyes, awaiting the next question.

Walter snapped the notebook shut and tucked it into his back pocket. "I'm only doing my job."

"I know." Eric sighed. A warm hand slid over his arm, absorbing the tension from his muscles and lifting the pit in his chest. An affectionate tingle followed, winding into his heart. He glanced briefly at Paresh before apologetically saying to Walter, "This situation alarms me more than I'd like to admit."

"Yeah, me, too." Walter started to rise, but Eric motioned for him to stay.

"Wait. There's more."

Walter sank uneasily into the chair. "With specifics?"

Eric shook his head. "I'm sorry. No."

"Do I even want to know?"

Again shaking his head, Eric removed his glasses and set them on his desk. "I truly doubt it—three nights ago, about a dozen vampires were in Sunset Grove, along with my brother."

Walter blanched. "A dozen vampires..." he repeated. "*Here?*"

"My understanding is that they all left, but...anything more is speculation."

"*Why?*" Hard lines creased Walter's face.

A light touch on his shoulder turned Walter's attention to Paresh as she said, "It had nothing to do with this town."

"The hell it doesn't!" Walter retorted, straightening his spine. "Pardon my language, but I've got a dead man two buildings down that would argue against that statement if he could."

"N-no—" Grimacing, Paresh doubled over, clutching her throat.

Eric rushed to her side and grabbed her hand. "Close your eyes and take deep, even breaths until it passes."

His gaze shifting from Paresh to Eric, Walter grew even paler and inched up in his seat. "Oh no. Ohh *no!* What have you done? Is *that* why she hasn't been feeling well?"

"It's not…like that," Paresh groaned through clenched teeth.

"It's complicated," Eric said quietly, worried eyes centered on Paresh.

"Un-complicate it for me then," Walter demanded.

Paresh took in a long breath that trickled out as her hands dropped into her lap. "Eric only wants to protect you—"

"Now look here! I may not understand everything in this world, but it's *my job* to ensure the safety of this town. And if that means you tell me something that puts my life in jeopardy, then so be it! How am I supposed to deal with *that,*" Walter yelled, pointing toward the alley. "If I don't have all the facts?"

Paresh whimpered and grabbed her throat again.

Protectively folding her to his chest, Eric turned grim eyes to Walter. "What would you do, as a man of the law, if you knew of the people who disappear or die every day because of the things you don't understand? How could I forgive myself if you died because of something I told you? There's nothing you can do. You are better off not knowing."

"And that's a decision you're just going to make for me?" Standing, Walter jabbed his index finger on the desk. "I've known you for more than forty years and I've never asked questions. I trust you and it's time you started trusting me. Your world is crossing into mine and I have a town full of people who want *you* in jail. If I don't get answers to clear your name, a wild mob with guns and stakes *will* appear on your doorstep."

Snatching his hat, Walter stalked toward the door.

"Please don't leave angry," Paresh pleaded breathlessly.

"I'm sorry, Paresh, but it's time Mr. Ravenscroft learns he can't control everything."

"He learned that the hard way three nights ago."

"Well I don't know anything about that, now do I?"

"You don't understand—"

"Let him go." Eric tightened his embrace as Walter slammed the door behind him.

"He should know," Paresh whispered.

"Can he handle knowing that a dozen people died that night?" Eric stared at the door, stroking her hair. "That Lucifer—who does actually exist—possessed Nicole and killed both of us, *and* David? That your resurrection brought salvation to an entire race, but put your life in greater danger? That Bill's death may only be the first of many?"

"He accepts you, and you are one of those things he can't comprehend."

"I killed two men."

"They attacked you." Paresh cupped his cheek. "It's his life to risk."

Eric closed his eyes and leaned into her warmth. He sighed. "Okay," he whispered. "Let's see how Molly takes it first and then I'll talk to Walter. But, I really don't think knows what he's asking."

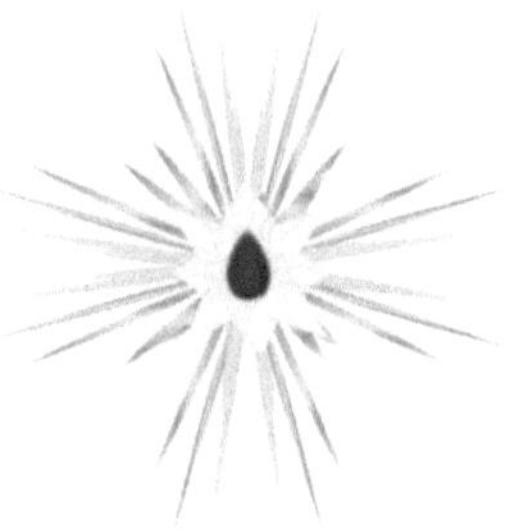

CHAPTER THREE: THE FALL OF THE HOUSE OF RAVENSCROFT

I

Eerie blue veins snaked across the blackened electronic casement. A thunderous peal followed, and then the wind came, an angry banshee warning of violence and fury. Thick drops began to fall.

Outside, the Arctic's Midnight Sun ruled over Devon Island in Nunavut, Canada. But, within the Arc of True Blood, the programmed weather simulation reflected Jonathan's mood.

Lucien's eyes burned into his back. The Elder had been watching him from the dome's outer ridge, safe from the rain's reach, for some time now. Jonathan blinked slowly as cool water berated his face. He stared up at a crescent moon and stars instead of a gloomy, overcast night.

His life was in turmoil, his body ravaged by feelings of guilt and self-loathing, and his mind consumed by the pain of empathy. But, the moon was still there, his only anchor of time in a reality spanning three thousand years. Once a silent companion, now it told him immortal did not mean eternal.

"Reveal your sins to Lucien and seek his guidance to save your soul."

Those words, spoken by the Archangel Gabriel through Paresh, clawed deep gashes into his psyche that refused to heal. His soul was free to suffer the consequences of his actions, and the cold captivity of a thousand years was no comparison for the agony of love. It formed the basis of every emotion. It altered the way he viewed the world and the sins of his past. He saw himself differently and he despised it.

He closed his eyes and focused on the raindrops, anticipating each splash on his skin. He let his breath out painfully slowly until his lungs burned and his pulse drummed in his ears. Even that couldn't silence

Paresh's voice.

Lucien stood directly behind him now. Jonathan bowed his head. *Everything* had changed.

Lucien's voice was quiet. "Time does not stop for us."

"That is twice now in a matter of days you have said that to me."

"What does it mean to you?" Lucien stepped closer. His aura softened the barrage of droplets and chased the chill from the air. The scent of vanilla incense followed, covering the smell of dank earth that always came with the rain.

Jonathan watched water pool around his leather shoes. "To trust you before time runs out."

"Then follow the Archangel's order as given through the Sacred Vessel."

Jonathan wilted as he let out a despondent sigh. "What do you want to know?"

"Tell me how you met him."

Jonathan thought back to 1847. How that crystalline blue, and the impeccable purity of innocence, had mesmerized him as nothing else ever before...

☽ ✵ ☾

A gentle breeze caressed his face. Its touch soft with a hint of autumn's chill. Carrying tantalizing notes of sweet pine and woody oak, it should have been crisp and fresh.

But it was putrid.

He stood on the porch of a small town general store after leaving the Arc of True Blood with no set destination. Lightly fingering the Vampiric Star on his lapel, Jonathan contemplated the warm bodies crowding the street. His thirst was usually too powerful for such temptation, but the acrid air made his stomach roil.

Filthy humans and manure, he thought, yearning for the days when they'd ignorantly thought the world was flat. Their incessant need to reproduce had spread them to nearly every continent.

Disgusted, he opened an exit portal into Animus Hollow with the Vampiric Star. The Hollow's endlessly rolling white haze separated Heaven, Earth, and Hades, and allowed him to travel between them. As he turned to step inside, he caught a flash of crystalline blue.

The vibrant color pierced the crowd's drab hues from across the road and rooted him. He closed the portal. It was a child—the epitome of delicious innocence.

His teeth prickling, saliva gushed into his mouth and crimson flooded his view. The boy was maybe five years old, staring at him—no, *through* his humanoid façade, at the hunter in wait, enticing the beastly bloodlust that lurked beneath.

Clenching his jaw, he tried to swallow the uncontrollable hunger clawing at his throat. A spark fired in his gut. His teeth cracked under the pressure of his jaw. His gums ached and his lungs burned as his heart raced faster and faster.

They're still blue! his mind screamed, on the brink of delirium.

Eyes locked on two dots of bright blue in a sea of blood red, Jonathan forced himself to take measured breaths. His pulse began to slow and his lungs ballooned with much needed oxygen.

No one had seen through his barrier in centuries.

The shield of his aura's dense layers left only an unearthly charge in the air that prickled the nape and riddled human skin with goose pimples. And yet, that boy, dressed in a velvet jacket and short pants, had chased the beast with icy eyes that rivaled the arctic wind.

Jonathan shuddered. In those eyes, he saw the reflection of a demon looking back at him.

The boy jumped into the street and disappeared. Jonathan stepped off the porch and closed his eyes, all too conscious of the dust and dirt settling onto his trousers and shoes, and the bodily odors and skin oils sinking into his clothes and hair as the crowd instinctively parted around him. He focused through the distracting stink, and filtered out the excited chatter about the town's new name: *Orison Crossing*, the blacksmith's rhythmic clanking of metal on metal, and laughter and music in the tavern.

Light footfalls led him to a delicate trail of rose and violet perfume thirty yards ahead. Jonathan's eyes snapped open.

A woman stood there. Thick, opulent hair spilled from beneath a white bonnet, and a lace shawl draped her shoulders over a bright, rose-red frock. Decadent silk and the over-pronounced bustle of her gown set her apart from the bland cotton crowd—as did the boy at her side, staring at Jonathan with that mesmerizing color.

The crystalline blue shifted to a point over Jonathan's shoulder. Horse hooves clopped against the district's wooden planks as a gleaming black carriage trimmed with gold turned the corner.

Jonathan grunted impatiently and leaped to the roof. Agitated by his true blood essence, the horses whinnied and stomped, and forced the driver to yank on the reins with both hands to stop beside the woman.

His pallid skin and tailored clothing belonged to a man of high stature, not a servant. He shot a concerned glance at the boy, who stood on his tiptoes to reach the latch. They shared the same straight nose, smooth forehead, and angular jaw, and both combed their hair neatly to the side. The driver was the boy's father—but his eyes were dirt brown.

Holding the door for his mother, the boy looked up at Jonathan, his brilliant orbs stabbing like daggers. Reeling backward, Jonathan pressed his fists into his eyes.

"*What are you?*" Jonathan yelled, falling to his knees in agony. He heard the carriage depart, and the pain faded as its distance grew. When he opened his eyes, only a thin layer of crimson was left. Growling, he shoved off the roof to the next one and the next, pursuing them on high until he reached the northern edge of town.

Dust and rust-hued leaves swirled in his wake as he hit the ground and dashed into a small grove. He lost sight of the carriage until the trees opened into a field. Harvested corn stalks crunched under foot. The coach was ahead, creeping toward a house on the hill east of town.

Jonathan cut behind the carriage, spooking the horses as he passed. Frustrated at being locked into a semi-altered state, he waited at the edge of the yellow, two-story house's property for the carriage to arrive. Two dark-skinned people greeted them. The male opened the carriage latch and the female assisted with their wares. The father climbed down and took the mother's hand as she stepped out.

The mother's countenance was haunting, even to Jonathan. Composed of dull earth and stone, humans lacked the vampiric race's radiant additions of gems and polished metals, and yet her eyes embraced the sun with a sapphire's internal fire. Gleaming, onyx hair contrasted milky skin, and regal, chiseled features rivaled those of any female true blood.

Still, only human—

The boy jumped out and flashed his soul stealing eyes as he ran past. Jonathan pursued until he saw the boy's destination: a small shack behind the house.

Primitive things, Jonathan thought, leaning against the house. Humans had made decent technological strides over the centuries, but they had yet to acquire indoor plumbing.

As the mother chatted with her servants about the town's new name and the business district's flourish, Jonathan's gaze drifted over the property.

A curved marble slab in the far corner caught his eye. A lamb rested atop the arc's zenith. He sauntered over, stopping at the white picket fence guarding the small plot. His feet were not permitted to touch any sacred soil, even that of a family cemetery.

"Laura Francine Ravenscroft," Jonathan read. "Died January 20, 1842, aged six years, four months, and twenty-one days."

"That's my big sister," a young voice quipped. "Mama said she went to Heaven to be with Jesus."

From the corners of his eyes, Jonathan glanced down. He hadn't heard the boy's approach. "What's your name?"

"Eric James Ravenscroft," the boy replied.

Once again engaged by those crystalline orbs, an image began to form in Jonathan's mind: a man with hair as black as the night and eyes of the clearest blue. Except for those differences, it was like looking into a mirror. The man's translucent, alabaster skin made Jonathan realize that the boy was deathly pale.

The man in Jonathan's mind, with his tall, lean, and muscular frame, would make the perfect companion to erase a bored and restless existence. Lucien and the Elders meditated to assuage their carnal instincts, but his thirst was too strong to banish by thinking it away, and he required more physical activity than the dome—or Lucien—could provide.

Jonathan smiled, a devilish grin, neither warm nor well intentioned. "Eric, you say?"

Eric nodded slowly, riveted on the elongated teeth previously hidden by Jonathan's lips.

Jonathan's smirk widened. This extraordinary boy would know those ivory protrusions intimately in time.

Perhaps he'd even survive a little nibble. The words rang through Jonathan's mind, swiftly growing into a feverish goal—despite his lethal reality.

"Well Eric," he said, pointing at the headstone, "I'll make sure you never end up like your sister."

Peering over his shaded lenses, Jonathan captured the boy's gaze. It took an unusual amount of energy to dim the light there.

"That's a good boy," Jonathan whispered at last. "Now, forget me and run to your mother."

The boy obediently ran to the house.

"Run, little Eric Ravenscroft," Jonathan said with dark satisfaction. "One day, you will be a man with no faith, and you will become mine. That's a promise I'll carve in stone and sign in blood."

☽ ✳ ☾

The rain had stopped. Silence and sorrow reigned.

Jonathan shoved his hands into his pockets and faced Lucien. "Eric has no idea—no idea at all—of the pain I've caused him. And you have no idea of my sins against his family and our laws."

"You are discreet," Lucien replied, tipping Jonathan's chin with lingering fingers.

Their eyes locked. For a long time, neither spoke.

Lucien lowered his hand. "How did Eric lose his faith?"

Jonathan gestured at himself and halfheartedly replied, "I destroyed his life."

Lucien waited quietly, so Jonathan added, "A name change on a property deed revealed that James secretly owned a plantation in Kentucky with a hundred or so slaves. The abolitionist town was infuriated, which made it easy to spread another rumor that Ravenscroft's daughter wasn't born from his wife."

Jonathan wagged his finger. "But not from a slave. That'd be too predictable. I whispered about a woman bent on blackmail, which forced him to destroy the evidence.

"They knew Laura had died from scarlet fever, but their rage was deafening—even to the doctor who treated her. No—to them, James Ravenscroft had murdered his daughter for the sanctity of his image."

Jonathan feigned a dramatic sigh. "And of course, his wife had known all along, spending his ill-gotten money, raising his bastard child, hiding his horrendous lies—even Eric was shunned from school. The church barred them from services. Every one of their friends turned their backs on them."

Rolling his eyes, Jonathan groaned, "James made it all *so easy*."

"Oh?"

"He and Victoria, and their servants, had helped dozens of slaves escape through the Underground Railroad. In fact, three were hiding in the secret dugout under the porch when I met Eric. Wanted posters had to exist somewhere, which meant bounty hunters did, too. I whispered the address into the ears of a few couriers and—"

Snapping his fingers, Jonathan said, "The hunters showed up with the entire town as witness. James Ravenscroft was a monster who had sold the slaves out for profit.

"The citizens rallied and ran the family from town, and officials seized his assets. No one intervened for fear of tarnishing their own

21

reputations, not even his good friend, Thaddeus Hawthorne, who was an attorney who traveled the circuit with Abraham Lincoln."

Jonathan quieted. "I underestimated that man."

"Was Thaddeus a colonel then?"

Struck by the curiosity in Lucien's voice, Jonathan hesitantly answered, "Lieutenant colonel—retired. He was promoted when he re-enlisted for the Civil War."

"A high rank. Access to governmental influence. Friends with the man who would become president. Had you exerted any influence over him, you would have broken our law."

Jonathan's head bobbed in agreement. "I was careful. The Hawthornes snubbed the Ravenscrofts of their own accord and left a social scar that never healed.

"The Ravenscrofts fled Orison Crossing and lived as squatters, doing the odd job here and there for anyone who would take them. But, eventually, they returned to the outskirts of town where James bargained with a farmer to build a small shack on his land in exchange for labor and limited wages. Even little Eric and his mother worked the fields and tended to the animals, day in and day out, working hard for a meager life.

"It was going so well, but no matter the hardship, James and Victoria's faith never faltered. James was a beaten man, but as long as he had his family, he would not forsake his god. There wasn't much left that I could do."

Jonathan half-laughed. "And then Victoria got sick. She hid it well. Pushed herself to work until she choked up blood, chilled by day and fevered at night, worn out by fatigue.

"Finally! A reward for my labor. The disease consumed her until there was nothing left. There were tears and blood, and plenty of heart-wrenching pain as father and son mourned their loss."

Jonathan's gaze dropped to his feet. "I did that to him." His voice was somber. "Eric's mother died in his father's arms right in front of him…and that was essentially the last day James Ravenscroft ever acknowledged his son's existence."

II

"Hold on, back up! Eric had a sister?" Paresh asked, mid-bite.

She and Molly were in The Greenery's greenhouse, which Eric had closed to the public. Two half-full glasses and a bottle of pinot noir sat between them, accompanied by wedges of chocolate cheesecake on

22

almond crust. Sarah Weaverly, the restaurant's manager, had prepared the dessert solely for them.

As Molly nodded, Paresh pointed to her plate with her fork. "This is delicious!" Cocoa and chocolate liquor tantalized her taste buds trailed by a smooth, creamy finish.

"Sarah has a magic touch with food." Molly glanced at the heavy double doors as though expecting to see Sarah there. With a sigh, she watched the subtle currents of water weaving through the concrete floor. "Everyone in town loves her desserts."

Hoping Paresh missed her melancholy tone, Molly said, "But, yes! Her name was Laura. I only know because Grandpa found her birth and death certificates. Eric was about a year old when she died from scarlet fever. She was six."

"How sad! Do you think he remembers her?"

"I don't know. He told me he grew up in poverty and lost both his parents when his mother died, but he doesn't talk about much prior to meeting Thaddeus."

"I suppose some things are too painful to remember," Paresh said. "Even for him."

An awkward silence fell between them. Tapping her fork against her plate, Paresh gnawed on the inside of her cheek. Finally, after a drink of wine, she flashed curious eyes at Molly.

"Why did your grandfather research Eric so much anyway?"

Molly smiled. "He was a high school history teacher and, every year, he asked his students to write about Orison Crossing's history. Well, one student's paper had a few discrepancies and a name he'd never seen—one that matched the rumored surname of the mysterious man living with the Hawthorne family.

"He couldn't confirm the anomalies with official historical records, so he set the paper aside and held the student after class to ask about the sources listed in the bibliography."

Molly squeezed her eyes shut and tapped her head with her index finger. "Oh, what was that kid's name?"

Molly snapped her fingers. "Aha! It was one of the Fausts! They've been farming here since before Orison Crossing existed. Um, oh, what was her name?" She closed her eyes again and muttered to herself, "Doreen? No…Dora! Dora Faust!"

"Who? The student?" Paresh eagerly leaned forward on her elbows.

"Oh, I don't know the kid's name." Molly waved dismissively. "Dora was the source referenced in the kid's bibliography. Here, let me start over—the student was a Faust who used family records for his paper. The afternoon after Grandpa asked him about them, the kid brought in a bunch of old diaries.

"Dora was his great-great-great—" Molly paused, counting to herself, "four, so one more—great grandmother, but she was a young girl, maybe ten or twelve, when Orison Crossing was incorporated and the village plans were drafted.

"The Faust family wasn't extensively wealthy, but they owned a lot of farmland and sold some off to Thaddeus to form a few of the residential districts. Dora was the only girl in a family of six boys, so she was rowdy. She wound up everywhere she shouldn't and had her nose stuck into everything else.

"She founded the *Daily Sunset* in 1861. Prior to that, she kept diaries and wrote about everything from her daily chores and the books she was reading, to spying on the boys at the swimming hole and various happenings around the area.

"There were lists of names: landowners, district planners, politicians, architects, engineers; it was a literal who's who of the 1840s and 1850s. And there were two prominent names: the Hawthornes, as the founding family, of course, but the other name existed nowhere in official records, no matter how hard Grandpa searched."

Paresh held her breath in anticipation.

Molly lowered her voice. "According to Dora, James Ravenscroft was a well-to-do, generous man who was handpicked by Thaddeus to oversee the village planning. All of those old buildings downtown?" Molly swept her hand in the business district's direction. "*Eric's father* was the engineer that turned a strip of buildings on a dirt street into the core of a proper town. *And* he incorporated the railroad that Thaddeus wanted."

Paresh sat back, troubled. "But how can that be? Eric said he was poor. He never mentioned any of this."

Molly nodded and raised her eyebrows. "*Exactly*. And it wasn't just his dad! Thaddeus held a contest to change the town's name from Hawthorneville to something more suitable. Eric's mother, Victoria, had the winning entry. The town was formed from a large portion of Sunset Grove after it had been cleared for farming, so she chose 'Orison' to honor the parish in the forest, and 'Crossing' for the railroad."

"So the Ravenscrofts are just as important as my family? Why is there no record? Has Eric kept it hidden?"

"I don't know, but Grandpa didn't doubt Dora's account because she was spot on with everything else. All the other names show up in the records. In fact, the man listed as holding James Ravenscroft's position is Orson McFadden and the honor of titling the town goes to his wife, Betty, for the same reason Victoria listed."

"Did the diaries say why?"

Molly shook her head with a sigh. "Grandpa skimmed a few at first, and then started to dig in, but the next day, the student took them back. Grandpa spent years trying to get the Faust family to let him borrow the diaries again but they refused.

"He jotted down everything he could remember and scoured historical documents. He didn't get far, but Dora's list included the children, so he did find Laura."

Molly paused barely long enough for a sip of wine. "I now know that Eric destroyed his birth certificate, but he never pulled his military service record—and, of course, my grandfather found it. When he saw that Eric's body was never recovered, he became obsessed with the man living with your family—the 'man who time forgot.'

"He spent every spare moment researching Eric's cavalry involvement in the Western Theater of the war. He'd take me to the cemetery to see Eric's headstone, and told me all kinds of stories as I grew up. Because of that, I felt like I knew Eric before I ever met him."

"So that's why you accepted his truth so easily on that trip." Paresh shook her head in awe.

Taking a deep breath and nodding, Molly said, "Yep. That was actually Grandpa's leading theory, though he was reluctant to believe it himself. He kept his off-the-wall ideas mostly to himself. He didn't want people thinking he'd lost his mind."

"So at some point, Eric's rich family fell into poverty, his mother died, his father became an alcoholic, and history erased them." Paresh swirled the ice in her water and lifted the glass to her lips.

"That's right." Molly sighed and sat back, watching the sun's reflection shimmer across the pond. Ripples broke the glassy surface when koi popped up to gulp air.

"It's unimaginable," Paresh whispered, following Molly's gaze. "The tragedies in his youth, the war, losing Lucinda and his son, and watching my family die. I can't fathom losing everyone you care about over and over."

Molly started to agree when a familiar voice said, "I make for interesting conversation today."

Standing at the heavy doors, Eric's expression was neutral, but his eyes lacked their usual friendly glint. Molly hung her head.

Eric grinned. "You know it's true. I'm *fascinating!*"

He approached the table and gently squeezed Molly's shoulder. The friendly spark was back. "Why don't we lighten things up? Sarah said you were raving about her best dessert yet."

Eyes swelling with tears, Paresh jumped up and ran to him. "I love you so much!"

Embracing her, Eric kissed the top of her head. "Molly shouldn't tell you things that will make you cry, especially when you've been drinking wine."

Molly shot him a halfhearted smile that flattened before reaching her eyes. "How'd it go with Walter?"

"As expected. He's sending a car over to Simon's to file an anonymous missing persons report." Eric helped Paresh into her chair and ran his hand through his hair. "He's having a hard time with some aspects of that night."

"Should I talk to him?" Molly asked.

"He'll come around when he's ready. Give him time." Eric grabbed a chair from the next table and joined them. "How far did you get into the Ravenscroft saga?"

Molly gave him a sheepish look. "I'm sorry we were talking about you."

Eric waved his hand. "Everyone in town is talking about me and few care to get their facts straight."

Sarah appeared with a goblet of garnet fluid. "I'm hearing your name a lot today, Mr. Ravenscroft—in many *hushed* conversations."

With a grin meant to reassure her, he replied, "I'm a popular guy." He took the chalice and set it on the table. "Is business down?"

"Not really. If we've lost any local traffic, it's been offset by people from the city. We'll only see a minor dent in the books, if anything."

"Thank you, Sarah." He gave her a dismissive smile. Once she closed the greenhouse doors behind her, he asked, "So, where were you?"

Paresh quietly asked, "Why don't you ever talk about your childhood?"

Despite his neutral façade, the intensity with which he contemplated his drink betrayed his true feelings. He put the glass to his lips and drank slowly. Then he sat back and folded his hands in his lap.

"I can take most things in my life in stride," he began slowly. "But, there are some things better left buried by time. Somewhere in my youth, my father's life went horribly wrong. And he loved my mother so dearly that losing her left him drowning in despair so dark and deep that he forgot me and died from a broken heart."

He paused, contemplating his drink. The silence was thick and uncomfortable. He pursed his lips and nervously scratched his head.

"I…I earned our keep on a farm belonging to the Fausts. I tended the fields and cared for the animals to pay for the one room shack they let Father build on their property. I did extra chores for small meals and meager wages. Coins my father stole." He paused again, his eyes darkening as he clenched his jaw. "I worked from morning to night while my father drank and got thrown out of the tavern."

"I'm so sorry!" Paresh slid her hand onto his thigh. "You were so young…I shouldn't have asked."

Black hair fell over his glasses as he shook his head and covered her hand with his. "I was young, yes—but I do know what happened, what kind of man my father was."

To Molly, he said, "When I learned about your grandfather's research, I bought Dora's diaries from Weston."

A wistful smile lifted his cheeks. "Dora was a sweet girl—my very own guardian angel. Mother died when I was nine and Dora was fourteen. She gave me leftover biscuits from breakfast and boiled chicken eggs. She'd sneak away from her chores to share her lunch and help me finish afternoon jobs early so she could teach me lessons or read books with me. She even mended my clothes and stole hand-me-downs from her brothers. Thanks to her, I had shoes—real shoes."

A chuckle fell from his lips. "Isn't that odd? Shoes were such a luxury."

He sighed. "One day, I was in the barn and overheard Dora arguing with Farmer Faust—no—*begging* him to throw my drunken rat father into the gutter. That I shouldn't pay for his sins. But taking me in meant hiring a laborer with proper wages and having an extra mouth to feed.

"Farmer Faust knew what Dora did for me and never stopped her as long as it didn't cost him money or interfere with her chores and schoolwork. The Fausts always put their own welfare above all else, even in the face of another's suffering.

"Only Dora was different." Eric took a long drink. "When Father died, I was no longer Farmer Faust's problem. He gave me a week to save money and move on, or he'd take me to an orphanage.

"I was thirteen. I'd be put to work regardless of where I went, so I used that week's feed and delivery run to beg for money around the county seat's courthouse, and that…that was the day I met Thaddeus."

He again contemplated his drink as though seeking an answer to an unasked question.

"Dora's diaries…" Hesitant to continue, Molly asked, "That's how you learned about your father?"

A glimmer of darkness surfaced in Eric's eyes. "I'd like to believe my father was a good man. My mother cherished him, after all. But everything I've read indicates not. And those very things led Thaddeus Hawthorne to extend his gesture of good will to me that day."

Eric glanced up sharply at Molly. His voice was gentle, but his words were firm. "It was not a purely selfless act. It was driven by guilt. Born from a brutally cold shoulder in the interest of self-preservation during a friend's darkest hour. I will not discuss this further. It is a period of my life that is done, and not one that I care to remember."

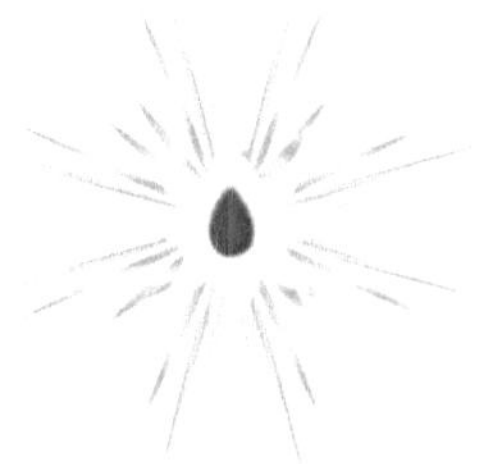

Chapter Four: The Wraith Reapers

I

Hidden by his aura, Jonathan spied the father watching his son sleep. A crackling fire heated the small room, barren save for a small woodpile in the corner and two makeshift cots of cloth-covered hay near the hearth. Rough-hewn blankets draped the tiny body there. Had the night been colder, the wretched bag of bones would have slept in one of the barns instead of their drafty shack.

Jonathan had been pacing—each foot landing without disturbing the dirt floor—for some time now. It was 1851, marking the boy's tenth birthday and nearing a year since the mother's death. The disease had consumed her to a haggard shell of skin-covered bone, and now she withered in a rudimentarily marked grave out back. The father, James, had mourned at the tavern, and little Eric had worked until dark, making the day typically unremarkable.

The pain of intangible sorrow could not be grasped or seen, yet it tugged on the father's heart with a merciless grip. The fiery poison that burned his throat couldn't melt the ice encasing his soul, and as it drowned in firewater, it dragged him into the depths of Hell. The once prosperous world of Ravenscroft had crumbled.

Jonathan's narrowed eyes settled on Eric.

Why do you hold on? he wondered, recalling the boy's nightly prayers for his mother and father. His mouth split into a wicked grin of sharp teeth and malice befitting a demon handcrafted by the Devil. No answers to little Eric's prayers would ever come—he would lose his faith and mature into the powerful man Jonathan desired.

"But not soon enough," Jonathan muttered, frowning at his scuffed shoes. The boy lived in filth, covered to his ears in dirt before the sun poked over the horizon. The rancid stench of poverty had become all too familiar. It clung to Jonathan's hair and skin, and survived long, hot soaks in the arc's bathhouse.

"*You smell of manure and hay.*" Lucien's lone observation had disgusted Jonathan. He'd returned to the bathhouse and flayed off most of his flesh before feeling clean enough to return to his master's side.

As though scolded by those distant words, Jonathan hung his head. Kicking at the dirt in frustration, Jonathan quelled a yearning to taste the sweet, youthful sustenance pumping through that boy's body. Little Eric had become a tether—

Movement caught his eye. The father had narrowly avoided falling into the hearth while staggering to the woodpile. Sparks flared as he tossed in a log and stumbled over to Eric.

The boy murmured as James knelt and smoothed hair from his forehead with rough fingertips. Looking much older than his thirty-one years, the father sighed and bowed his head. His body quaked as he buried his face in his hands.

"I'm so sorry, Eric," he choked out, wiping his palms on his pants. He grabbed the bottle by his cot and hurled it at the fire. Thirsty flames lapped up the whiskey spilling from its lip.

Slapping his hand to his forehead, James collapsed against his cot. "I let her die…and you suffered all alone. What kind of father am I?"

Tears dripped from James' dusty skin and left a trail of dark spots on the floor as he crawled to his son. He held Eric's hand against his cheek. Jonathan squatted in front of James, trying to gauge the intentions veiled within his drunken stupor.

"Tell me everything will be fine, Eric. Tell me you forgive me, that your mother forgives me." James dropped the sleeping boy's hand and sobbed. "But how could you ever?"

Tugging at his hair and tattered clothes, he whispered, "Look at me. I was James Adam Ravenscroft. What did I do to deserve this punishment? Those vicious lies? Why did God take my wife, my job, my money…my *family*? Oh! Victoria. Laura. Er…Eric…"

He shook his fists at the ceiling. "He's just a child. He did nothing to deserve this life. *Nothing!*"

James choked and curled into a ball. "You don't deserve this," he whispered, staring at Eric with a tormented gaze.

Jonathan's eyes narrowed to slits. "I will not permit you to rejoin the Flock!" he growled to himself.

"I'll make it right. I promise I'll make it better!" James cried. "I'll do it for you—for Victoria. She'd be so disappointed in me, but I'll make her proud again. I failed her. I can't fail you, too."

Jonathan padded in silence to the corner. The father's constant alcoholic haze barely allowed suggestive whispers to float through, and even then, Jonathan was lucky if they rooted. That wouldn't be enough this time.

"The boy looks a lot like his mother," Jonathan said aloud.

"*Wh-what?*" James cried, his body rigid as he eyed each dancing shadow. "*Who's there?*"

Jonathan paced the wall opposite the flames. "Doesn't he remind you of your dead wife?"

Shooting up, James tripped over his feet and clumsily darted in circles. "*Who's there?*"

Jonathan drew in close to blow into his ear, "*You killed her.*"

The man spun around and accidentally smacked Jonathan's hidden hand.

Shoving James down, Jonathan accused in a deeper voice, "*You killed her.* He blames you. She blames you." Jonathan leaped back and settled into another corner, heard and felt, but unseen.

Jonathan's prey stood and whirled in wild circles, shrieking, "*Who's there? Where are you? What do you want with me?*"

An icy voice slithered between Jonathan's lips. "When he opens those crystalline eyes, don't you see her staring back at you?"

Dropping to his knees, James glared at the ceiling. "What do you want from me?" he cried. "Why do you torment me so? I was good man! I was a good m—"

"Does a good man turn his back on his son? You gave up. *You never fought back.*"

"No one would help me! I had no choice! I had no…*choice*…they didn't believe me…" James stared blankly into the corner.

"*You had no choice?*" Jonathan mocked. "Liar! You knew they were lies, but you did nothing more than stalk off like a beaten dog. You brought your family to Hell. You sent your wife to Hell. You abandoned your son. He lives in Hell." Jonathan crossed the room soundlessly, regarding the pathetic lump of humanity with genuine disdain.

"It wasn't true. None of it!" James wailed, slamming his fist into the ground. "*Why are you doing this to me?*" He lifted his face to the ceiling. "Why do you torment your children?"

Jonathan's wicked laugh filled the room. "You think *He* would speak to *you*? You have forsaken Him."

James sobbed into the dirt. Face ghastly pale, eyes haunted, he muttered, "He has turned His back on me as I have turned mine on Eric."

The boy moaned and rolled over. James crawled to Eric, begging, "Please forgive me. None of it was true. None of it, but I did nothing—"

Jonathan leaned over James and sneered, "How can he forgive you? You killed his mother. His only friend in the world. Then you forgot him. You aren't a good man. You're selfish. *You don't deserve him as a son.*"

Jonathan jumped back as James grabbed at the voice in his ear. "I lost the love of my life! God stole her from me!"

Circling him, Jonathan taunted, "No, *you* killed her. *You* didn't fight hard enough and *you* brought her to the pits of Hell. You killed her and he despises you for it."

"*Stop it!*"

A cruel smile turned up Jonathan's lips. He hungered for the vulnerability James exuded—to sate his thirst by drinking from that defeated man. But, Jonathan needed Eric to witness his father drowning in humanity's weaknesses to defeat his faith.

"He really does look like her. Don't you see her face when you look at him?" Jonathan asked in a sickly sweet voice.

Tears streaming down his cheeks, James shook his head, but then he dropped his nose to the ground and rammed his fist into the dirt. "Yes! Damn it, yes! I look at him and see her face, and remember watching her die. Seeing her dead in my arms…I can't remember her any other way and *I can't stand it!*"

Jonathan laughed, an evil sound that stripped James of any remaining resistance. "You hate him, don't you? That he looks like her. That she spent so much time with him."

"Yes, yes, *yes!*" James cried into the dirt, pounding the floor with each emphatic agreement.

"Drink your pain away." Jonathan's wicked grin seeped into his voice. "Eric hates you. He's still hiding wages from you. He wants to leave you here alone."

James faced the direction of Jonathan's voice. "He's what? But his spot's been empty for months."

Jonathan laughed again. "You selfish fool. He stopped digging holes. Check the feed sack under the main house's porch. Go on. Take his hard earned money and erase your pain."

James shuffled to the door. He hesitated when Eric whimpered in his sleep.

"Drink your pain away," Jonathan repeated with mock sympathy.

James slipped into the night, leaving Jonathan alone with the boy.

"Only a few more years until I rid you of that bothersome man. A demon's face will stop that weakened heart of his, and when you find his body, you will feel true despair. Then you'll lose that faith you stubbornly cling to."

Grinding sleep from his eyes, Eric sat up. Upon seeing his father's empty cot, he turned a stone-cursing glare to the door.

Glancing back at Jonathan's shadowy perch, Eric drew his legs up. "I haven't seen you in a while," he said in a flat voice, facing the fire.

"Well, I can't trust that drunkard to do his job," Jonathan replied, frustrated that Eric could still see through his barrier. "You're an investment and I can't claim you if you don't survive. When you are older, I will take you away with me."

"You said that last time." The response was emotionless and cold.

"You shouldn't be able to remember that." Jonathan closed in wearing an expression of wicked malcontent. Erasing Eric's memories took far too much energy to fail so easily. "I'll try harder this time."

As Jonathan's unearthly aura began sifting around the boy, Eric said, "You are Death."

"In a manner of speaking, I suppose you are correct," Jonathan agreed in a low voice, adrenaline surging throughout his body at the boy's fearlessness. "Vulnerability is nothing compared to a strong will."

"The weak die." Eric swiveled and centered his crystalline orbs on Jonathan. "Does that mean Death is weak?"

"Oh, I am far from weak." Jonathan's vampire eyes dropped to the pulse in Eric's throat and pressure mounted behind his teeth. He licked his lips. The room was turning red. "Far, far, away…"

Packing all his power behind one forceful directive, he met Eric's gaze and commanded in a raspy voice, "Look away and forget me, *now*."

Defiant blue pierced his crimson view.

"How can you resist me?" Jonathan demanded.

Eric's heart pounded through Jonathan's aura and pulsed against his body. Gnashing his teeth, he lunged and pinned Eric on his back.

"How can you accept death, but stay faithful to *Him?* He gave you this life!" Jonathan yelled. The boy didn't flinch, not even at his fangs.

"God is all I have left. Mother and Sister are with Him. Why would I fear joining them?"

"You little—" Jonathan growled, impaling the cot with his growing claws. "Look away and forget me!"

Jonathan's engorged eyes ripped into the boy's unwavering crystalline depths and a sudden, wicked peace settled over his heart. "I understand now. I'll reap some benefit tonight."

He sneered, an evil grin that shot chills into his target's heart, and in one, swift, forceful motion, he grabbed the boy's wrist and sliced it open. Eric cried out, fear finally creasing his young face.

"S-stop!" Eric frantically tried to yank free.

Jonathan mocked, "I thought you were ready for death. Isn't *He* watching over you?" Jonathan rose, effortlessly lifting the boy and dangling his bloody wrist over his mouth.

A single, glistening drop led a steady stream of succulence to his tongue. Jonathan closed his eyes with a moan. Nothing about Eric was normal, not even the ecstasy invoked by his young innocence.

Ethereal ripples coursed over Jonathan's body as temptation ravaged his mind like madness. Surely, he stood at the event horizon of an endless free fall. Such pure rapture bypassed his defenses and awakened the beast. Its hunger roared off the walls of his heart.

Eric's wrist slid closer, the warmth of his skin caressing Jonathan's lips. "More…" Jonathan moaned, his teeth prickling with anticipation.

A dangerous growl rose up his throat. Logic finally sparked against carnal hunger. His eyes snapped open, and with a gentleness that belied his strength and desire, he lowered Eric to the floor. He turned slightly and tucked the boy out of sight behind his back.

Eric scurried to the far wall, sobbing and holding his bloodied arm. Jonathan's shoulders trembled as a horrible sound shook the little house.

A sigh too joyous to come from such a monster trailed Jonathan's laughter. "I understand it now." Without turning, his aura shot behind him and dragged Eric back to him. "This power—your power—I can use it."

Trapped by the air itself, Eric could only stare into the dilated and bloodshot eyes that whipped around and bore into him as a deep, raspy voice slid between teeth stained with his blood. "Sleep now and forget you ever saw me."

Eric went limp as the last syllable passed between them.

"This has been entertaining," Jonathan whispered. His aura lowered Eric to his pathetic bed. "You won't see past my barriers again—not until I'm ready to claim your soul. Goodnight, Little Eric Ravenscroft. Don't let the bedbugs bite. That's my job."

He pulled a small ceramic vial from his pocket and ran a thin line of ointment over Eric's wrist, erasing the wound. Jonathan turned away, licking at the blood drying on his lips, and settled into a corner to watch Eric sleep.

☽ ✳ ☾

The air dripped with regret. Staring at the pebbles beneath his shoes, Jonathan emptily finished, "Three years later, I gave James a fright his heart couldn't take. I sent him to Hades, doomed never to see Victoria again. I ruined him in life and in death—"

"So that is the connection," Lucien interrupted.

Jonathan shot an annoyed look over his shoulder. "Were you even listening?"

"Of course," Lucien said. "I am intrigued by what bonded you to Eric. His blood must have altered your lethal protein's physiology and aligned it to the biorhythm of his DNA, which allowed you to infect him later."

"Well that's just fantastic," Jonathan snipped. "What if that night had never happened? I would've killed him?"

"Yes," Lucien said nonchalantly, "but you weren't meant to kill him."

"Then why am I here?" Jonathan kicked a rock. "To relive his pain? To feel the suffering I inflicted upon him? Because Gabriel said so? Why should I feel like ripping out my own heart if it was all part of *their* grand plan?"

Anger blazed in his eyes as he turned to face Lucien. "Tell me! What does this accomplish?"

Jabbing himself with his fingers, Jonathan said, "Surely I have sunk further than the hand of forgiveness can reach. Lucifer's minions have a better chance at redemption."

He hesitantly touched Lucien's chest. "I am the Second Born, created with a ruthlessness that doesn't even exist in *your* heart."

"Perhaps He is not as quick to turn His back to you as you think." The night barely touched Lucien's whisper.

Jonathan's glare faded. A despondent sigh floated past his lips and his hand fell to his side. "It can't be that simple."

"You always follow orders. What makes this different?"

"I don't understand the reasoning."

"Reasons have never mattered."

"I only follow your orders."

"Consider it an order from me," Lucien said. "Even at your darkest moment with Eric, you adhered to our rules and kept the beast from taking control."

"You think that was my darkest moment with Eric?"

"During his human years."

"Why are you here?" Jonathan whispered. "You hate the rain."

Turning his back to Lucien, he splayed his fingers and held his palm up to the moon. Studying his unblemished skin, stretched taut over the veins and tendons of his hand, he said, "My skin has earned the mark of time, the wrinkles that come with a vile heart. He should not have taken mercy on me. I'll never change."

"He disagrees with you. But, it is your decision."

"Why are you here?" Jonathan repeated softly, glancing over his shoulder in search of something—a gesture of warmth or reassurance. He saw only Lucien's silvery, stoic visage.

"There's been an attack in Orison Crossing."

Every muscle tensed. "Paresh?"

"No. Eric's client. Left for discovery."

Even as relief washed over him, Jonathan's chest felt hollow. Lucien hadn't come out for him. "I'll contact Alex. The Crimson Guard—"

"I've already dispatched Raven and Donovan."

Jonathan turned with a furrowed brow. "The Wraith Reapers aren't bodyguards."

"They perform security detail for the High Elders during Winter Solitude and you trained Raven, which makes her the optimal choice," Lucien replied. "No VaSH Hunter can match Eric's strength to protect him better than he can protect himself."

Reflecting quietly, Jonathan lifted his face to the moon.

"I issued a kill order," Lucien added. "The Crimson Commander would not accept that so easily."

"Alex would justify incapacitation and capture. I agree with your decision, of course," Jonathan replied, his voice lacking conviction.

"You and Alex work well together," Lucien said, his voice as soft as the moonlight reflecting in his quartz crystal eyes. He slid his hand up Jonathan's arm to his shoulder. Warmth flared in Jonathan's chest. "No other VaSH Commander would so willingly allow you to control his squad. You and the Crimson Guard are better suited to the issues here."

Jonathan's eyes lingered on Lucien's petal pale lips. The blue hue of his skin gave them a lavender appearance. He drew in a deep breath and let it out slowly, closing his eyes to collect himself.

"I understand," Jonathan said. "Did Eric call? What did he say?"

"The body was from the Flock and was discarded in public." Lucien drew closer. His fingers slipped up to Jonathan's neck. His breath brushed Jonathan's cheek.

"What do you intend to do about it?" Jonathan asked with an

expectant sigh.

"I intend to let you handle it," Lucien whispered, his aura cooling as he dropped his hand.

Jonathan's eyes opened slowly. Lucien was walking toward the outer rim. "But you—"

"The hunters are on their way. Speak with Eric and Alex, and account for your pack." Lucien paused, but did not look back. "You trained her to be merciless. Act swiftly, lest you find yourself counting severed heads in place of able bodies."

II

Crickets and cicadas serenaded summer's warmest evening yet. Rich indigo color arced over the forest canopy, and twinkling stars adorned the endless black abyss that followed. Beneath Heaven's dazzling fabric, Eric sat on the cottage steps, his gaze rooted on terra firma.

With childlike wonderment, Paresh had jumped up to catch fireflies only moments ago. She'd stopped about twenty yards away when a dense orb of chartreuse light gathered her up in a slowly rotating, luminescent cloud. Ebbing with the fluidity of water, it moved with her, floating backward or forward on gossamer air currents in tune with her movements. Tucking her hand to her chest, she brought the beating flutter in close, as though in an embrace.

Giggling, she raised her arms high above her head and twirled in circles. The fireflies spiraled upward in a flurry of twinkling light and cascaded out at the zenith like a fountain of water spray. Slowing, she lowered her arms parallel to her swirling skirt, and the cloud converged in unison to become a veritable glowing vortex.

Her skirt swayed as she stopped and reached out to one glowing body. As it landed on her fingertip, others gathered around it and formed a small ball of flickering light. She stared in awe, lost in the magical moment.

Suddenly, the ball scattered and rejoined the larger, rotating cluster, and the scent of spiced cologne delighted her nose. Strong, capable hands clasped over her belly. Warm lips caressed her nape.

"You're so beautiful. Make love to me." Eric nibbled on her ear.

She relaxed against him. "Someone might see—"

Kissing along her neck, he mumbled, "There's not another soul for a mile in any direction." Fanning his hands to her hips, he held her against his aching body.

She exhaled a moan as she grasped the back of his neck and leaned into him. He nudged her around and took command of her mouth.

Standing on her toes, she returned Eric's feverish kiss with a hunger of her own. Burning heat swelled beneath her ribs and ignited her pulse. Every impassioned kiss, each heated breath, Eric's tantalizing scent, his racing heart——

His body spoke to hers of a need she was only too willing to fulfill.

Sliding across his shoulders and down his back, her fingers tingled at the feel of solid muscle beneath his shirt. She yearned to feel his naked strength against her skin.

She tugged the fabric free at his waist. Eric loosened his embrace, and his impassioned kisses and moans spurred her on to the buttons. Nearly ripping his shirt open, she shoved the fabric down his arms. It crumpled on the grass like a white sheet.

Her hands and fingers danced freely over his chest, swept down the hard ridges of his abdomen, and traced a line around his belt. Caressing a path up toward his neck, she explored the contours of his back and then buried her fingers in his hair. She broke free of his mouth to kiss along his jaw. Another masculine moan fled into the night as Eric's hands dropped to her waist and he faced the sky, exposing his throat.

She kissed him there, lingering and savoring the heat of his pulse on her lips. His hands tightened on her hips and his heartbeat quickened. An excited quiver raced across her cheekbones and pressure mounted behind her canines. She exhaled breathlessly and threw her head back as awareness opened her body to the night like a newborn blossom.

Beyond their circulating orb of twinkling companions, the moon burst forth, huge and bright, streaked and pitted with more detail than she'd ever seen. Stars blazed with fiery, prismatic light, and the canopy leaves gleamed like polished malachite.

She could pinpoint each cricket chirp and cicada drone, and the fireflies' near-silent flutter had become a steady hum, like a fan on a hot day. A car engine rumbled beyond the forest, and the cottage's grandfather clock steadily ticked the seconds.

Beautiful as it was, the melody of night was a mere backdrop to the rhythm of Eric's heart. Of the blood swishing through his veins. She sighed happily and closed her eyes, content to listen.

She took in aromas of freshly cut grass and earthy, wild mushrooms, the rose garden's delicate perfume, and the sweet nuttiness of pollen farmed by bees that day, and detected organic compounds in the air's water vapor that betrayed distant rainstorms.

Her skin jolted with electricity as Eric's fingers slipped beneath her shirt, throbbing in tune with his heart. She wrapped her arms around his neck. The usually prominent bergamot and musk in his cologne hid behind a more intriguing note, one of pheromones and raw masculinity. Reveling in the complexity of his scent, she kissed his throat and licked the salt of his skin from her lips. As his arms tightened around her waist, she kissed a path to his collarbone. The feel of cool metal made her lean back and open her eyes.

Rainbows of light streaked off the silver cross he wore. His skin, always nearly luminescent, now absorbed and reflected the moon's vivid, silvery-blue light. For a moment, she thought of Lucien, but then memory swept her back to the spiritual plane and an angel swathed in the palest of blues who shone brighter than a star.

"Gabriel," she whispered, lightly touching the holy trinket as she slid her palm down over Eric's beating heart.

Marveling at how the night's light frosted her ivory skin like fresh snow, she whispered, "This is heavenly."

Smiling up at Eric, she added, "I love this feeling. So in tune with everything. With you. Here."

The love and longing in Eric's eyes stole her breath. If not for the rotating chartreuse cloud, she might have thought time had stopped.

"You are beyond beautiful," he finally whispered. "This is your element. Where you belong. Where you shine."

Kissing her gently, he folded her into his arms and lowered her to the grass. Enveloped within his aura, her body tingled as affectionate, unseen fingers slid beneath her clothing and stroked every inch of her skin. She felt naked before him, open and vulnerable to his every desire. She cupped his face and kissed him, sliding her tongue along the elongated canines that were slowly descending from his upper jaw. An excited whimper came from her throat, which he met with a hungry growl.

Rolling her onto her back, he ravished her mouth and pushed her shirt up. She stretched her arms above her head with anticipa—

A chill stiffened his aura. The cloth slipped through his fingers. His entire body went rigid, and his eyes, fixed on a spot of grass beyond her cheek, grew darker and filled with blood.

"Wh—"

Pressing a finger to her lips, Eric gave her a solemn look. The forest had gone silent and the fireflies had disappeared. An unsettling energy prickled her nerves.

Eric jumped to his feet and ran across the clearing.

Paresh sat up and tugged her shirt down, her heart threatening to beat its way out of her chest. She'd felt that strange energy once before—in a moment of absolute terror.

Whatever was out there had revealed itself deliberately, and as she watched Eric disappear into the shadowy forest, she thought about the murderous rogue vampire, and the fact that she was alone, at the cottage, again.

III

Using his momentum to boost his strength, Eric charged into the canopy's inky curtain and curled his fist around throaty flesh before the hooded figure could duck or dodge. He pulled the figure forward and then thrust back, flinging it deep into the forest.

The ebony clad body slammed into a thick maple with a sharp *crack*. Slicing through splinters of bark and frenzied leaves, Eric caught the figure by the throat and pinned it against the trunk with a ruthless grip. He aimed his left hand with dagger-like nails at the intruder's heart.

"You *are* good." Youthful and feminine, the voice's genuine admiration lacked any concern.

Shaking the shadows from her face, she flashed a grin of snow-white teeth and sharp fangs, and revealed the exquisitely refined countenance of a true blood.

With a glint in her darkened, swollen eyes, she added, in a deeper voice, "But, *I'm not the only one.*"

As her eyes flashed over his shoulder, Eric's blood ran cold. Tightening his grip, he turned his head. Through the dense foliage, he saw Paresh standing where he'd left her—exposed and defenseless in the clearing. She was oblivious to the figure emerging from the tree line behind her.

His breath caught in his throat.

"Think you're *good enough* to reach her in time?"

Eric growled and jerked the female forward to slam her harder against the tree. The forest floor trembled. Leaves rained down. The scent of blood spilled into the night when her head cracked on the trunk. She whimpered and went limp. But Eric was already racing toward the clearing. He heard her body drop as he crossed the tree line.

"*Paresh! Run to me!*" The other vampire was directly behind her.

IV

"Bonsoir."

Paresh's eyes widened as the whisper floated past her ear. A masculine form, cloaked in black, stepped into her visual field. She tried to scream, but a lump in her throat blocked her voice.

Ashen-hued fingers gently held hers as the man dropped to one knee. He lowered his hood, revealing shoulder-length, dark brown hair and luminous skin. With a friendly smile, he kissed the back of her hand.

"Enchanté, Mademoiselle. Je m'appelle Donovan." Wrapped in darkness, but as pale as the moon, he was as handsome as Eric or Jonathan.

He dropped her hand and bowed his head, and then a steel arm appeared around Paresh's waist, whisking her behind a familiar column of moonlit muscle. Eric's aura and voice seethed with lethal intent. *"Who the hell are you?"*

Paresh peered at the vampire. "I think he was speaking French."

The vampire met her eyes with a grin that revealed partially elongated canines. "You are correct, milady. We are fluent in all human languages, including those of archaic or extinct tongue. I am Donovan, First Officer of the Wraith Reapers. It is an honor to meet you at last."

"The Wraith Reapers?" She stepped to Eric's side, but he blocked her from moving closer.

"He's a VaSH hunter," Eric said. "A true blood."

"Ah! Correct, sir!" Donovan's smile grew as he tossed his head back to shake wavy strands from his face. Silvery light bathed his skin, yet his chocolaty eyes defied the monotone world and gleamed with the golden luster of a tiger's eye stone. "We are on a mission of the greatest importance! Lord Lucien the Eternal, himself, sent us upon learning of the attack in your village."

"Us?" Paresh stepped past Eric's arm.

Eric tossed his chin over his shoulder. "His partner's back there, unconscious about thirty yards in."

Donovan sobered. "You knocked her out?"

At Eric's glare, Donovan relaxed and smiled. "I'm impressed. No one ever bests Raven." His voice was smooth without a care. "And she's not my partner. She's my Commander."

Grinding his teeth, Eric snarled, "I don't give a damn who the hell she is! Lucien had no business sending vampires here without consulting me first!"

Clearly stunned, Donovan parted his lips but said nothing.

A soft, feminine voice rang out from the forest behind him. "Our lord sent us on express order to protect you during this investigation. We are but his servants to the end, loyal to his will, whatever that may be."

The woman stepped from the shadows and knelt beside Donovan.

Bowing her head, she placed a gloved hand over her heart and clutched the other into a fist at her side.

"I am Raven Hawkings, Commander of the Wraith Reapers. This is my First Officer, Donovan. We are the best of the VaSH. You have nothing to fear."

Long lashes hooded Raven's spirited eyes as she traced the muscles of Eric's chest and abdomen. "I'm sorry we, ah, interrupted your *business*."

She laughed softly. "I realize I am fortunate you didn't kill me, and, as I didn't want to risk death again, I figured I'd circle 'round here to introduce myself properly."

Eric stepped toward her, scowling with demon-like rage. "Lucien didn't say he was sending anyone."

Raven stood and lowered her hood. The huntress appeared to be only slightly older than Paresh, and possessed her lineage's regal features and partially elongated teeth. However, a choppy bob of bright pink hair, eyes that shone like sapphires, and ears lined with small gold and silver hoops made her resemble the singer of a punk band rather than the Commander of an elite hunting unit.

"Sir Jonathan was to contact you."

"Jonathan is on sabbatical," Eric said tightly, nudging Paresh behind his back. He glared at the hunters, challenging them to push him.

"Goody Raven," Donovan said, his grim voice matching his expression. "We should settle until he confirms our orders."

"Aye, agreed." The Commander dropped to her knee. "Please contact Sir Jonathan or Lord Lucien. We'll maintain our post until you are satisfied."

She held up both hands and then slowly reached into her cloak where she withdrew a thin and slightly curved wedge of metal about three inches in length. Tossing it at Eric's feet, she said, "Lord Lucien ordered me to give you this communication device. Wear it as so—"

She indicated the metal strip lining her lower jaw. "It converts the vibrations in your bones to words. Activate by voice command or touch to open a channel to your contact."

Ignoring the device, Eric fiddled with the Vampiric Star he'd hastily tucked into his pocket earlier. A few minutes later, his cell phone rang.

Fixing his eyes on Raven and Donovan, he coldly snapped, "Yes?" After a moment of silence, he demanded, "Describe them."

Eric's stare flew over the hunters to the black forest. "Where the hell are you? Lucien said you were on sabbatical."

Another moment of silence passed before he replied, "Of course I'm under suspicion! What do you expect?" His gaze shot impatiently skyward as he listened to Jonathan's moody response.

With a huff, he interrupted, "There was a weapon involved—a dagger with an insignia on the handle. A crescent moon with rubies."

Raven and Donovan's heads both shot up.

Eric's eyes narrowed. "Jonathan, what's the significance of the crescent moon?"

Anger lit Eric's face ablaze. "The Crimson Guard?" he growled. "You brought those bastards here and now one of my clients is dead!"

He ground his teeth and snarled, "I am not thrilled that Lucien took it upon himself to designate bodyguards for us. Ask him how safe we're supposed to be when I knocked the *Commander* unconscious on arrival."

Hanging up on Jonathan, he shoved the phone into his pocket and pointed at Raven. "Orders confirmed. Tell me about the Crimson Guard."

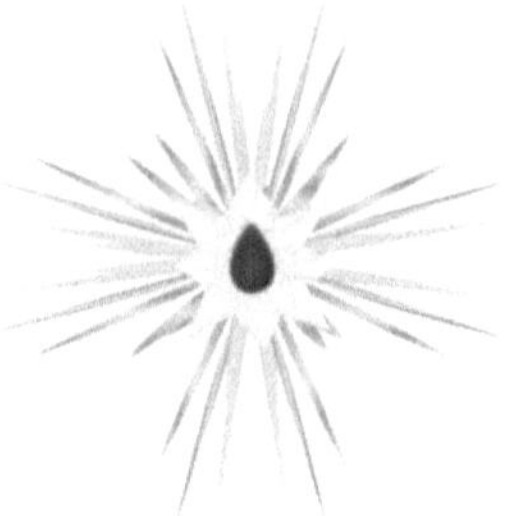

CHAPTER FIVE: THE HAND OF A RONIN WARRIOR

I

Shadowy ribbons stretched across Raven's face as she locked eyes with Eric. "First, with all due respect, I chose not to evade your attack. It was not a matter of not being able to do so."

"Mend your damaged ego on your own time," Eric growled.

Balling her fist over her heart, she bowed her head. "You deserve reassurance in my abilities. I do not fail my missions."

"That remains to be seen. Answer me."

"Aye, sir," she replied. "You have some knowledge of the Crimson Guard?"

"I know it exists."

An icy edge cleft through Eric's aura. Squaring her chin and shoulders, Raven replied, "The Crimson Guard is the largest squad, and specializes in capture, detainment, and protection. It's technically ranked second, behind my squad, but its honorable stature earns the most respect. It frequently splits into two divisions, with the First Officer, Seneca, taking command of the main squad, while the elite form Sir Jonathan's pack—"

"His pack," Eric interrupted with disgust. "Always with him. Of course they were here that night."

"Aye," Raven said, maintaining the rigid posture of a soldier as she stood. "And Seneca's division was here, as well."

Paresh peeked around Eric's arm. "But, I only saw a small group in the forest."

"That was the pack. You only saw them because the Commander, Alexander, dropped their barriers. The strongest officers stay with him when they split." Raven's voice softened as her attention settled on the girl. "However, in this case, they were guarding Lord Lucien."

"So, where were the others?" Paresh asked.

"Hidden," Raven replied. "Lord Lucien's departure from the arc was an unprecedented, grave risk. Lucifer could have severed the Vampiric Nation's head and submerged us into chaos by killing the First and Second Born alongside our Servator and final hope for salvation."

Sliding around Eric's arm, Paresh stood beside him with confusion wrinkling her face. "But what about the High Council? The other Elders?"

"Mere true bloods with titles," Donovan grumbled.

Eyeing her First Officer, Raven said, "For a thousand years, the First and Second Born ensured our survival. *That alone* secured our loyalty and discipline. Without them, there would be no solidarity, only anarchy and ruin."

"Our nation would crumble." Donovan rose and dusted off his knee. "All VaSH officers and Elders know that only Sir Jonathan may succeed Lord Lucien as Arch Elder."

"*Jonathan?*" Eric shook his head, imagining Jonathan at the helm, freed from Lucien's reins, his savage thirst set loose. "He'd break every rule in the Treaty in less than a day."

"Aye. Sir Jonathan succeeds Lord Lucien." Raven confirmed her officer's quip without acknowledging Eric's comment.

Gripping Eric's arm like a scared child clinging to a blanket, Paresh asked, "So then, the Crimson Guard protects Jonathan like an Elder? They keep him safe?"

A faint sigh dropped from Eric's lips as his knotted muscles loosened under Paresh's touch. Filled with worry for Jonathan, her aura hungrily devoured his negative emotions and left behind only calm. He planted a kiss atop her head and caught Raven's expression softening.

According to Jonathan, the huntress was quite capable and trustworthy, but Eric knew the liar in Jonathan too well. He returned a guarded stare and Raven stiffened.

Raven nodded at Paresh. "Aye, milady. Alex has a special affinity for Master Jonathan. It is an honor to be his shield."

"Sir Jonathan may not sit on the High Council," Donovan added, "but he is our elder. Like Lord Lucien, Sir Jonathan severs heads at the slightest infract—"

"Enough!" Eric's eyes fiercely drilled into Donovan before falling softly on Paresh. He threaded his fingers through her hair and she released his arm, revealing the bruised outlines of her hands and ten bloody punctures.

"I-I'm s-sorry," Paresh stuttered, tugging her shirtsleeves down to cover her lengthened nails. Her cheeks flamed red as she dabbed at the tiny wounds.

"It's okay. And so is Jonathan." Eric tucked Paresh under his arm and faced Raven. "Forgoing *unnecessary* details, security was tight that night?"

Again eyeing her First Officer, Raven replied, "Apologies, sir. Aye. Alex and the pack came with Sir Jonathan, as usual, but not before I informed him of Lord Lucien's intent. I then ordered Seneca to mobilize the Crimson Guard to escort our lord here. Without Sir Jonathan's knowledge, the squad regrouped. Seneca oversaw perimeter detail while the pack covered Lord Lucien."

"And chased me to Grandfather Wisdom to die." Paresh shuddered.

Raven shifted uncomfortably, her eyes and mouth grimly set. "That night haunts Alex."

"Splendid to know the Sandman is torturing more than just her," Eric replied tightly.

"It is genuine—" Raven replied as Paresh said, "It was meant to be."

An awkward silence followed, echoed by the forest's unnatural stillness. Eric sympathized with Raven's position. Saying anything to soothe Paresh would insinuate a VaSH Commander's reluctance to follow orders: a disrespectful and punishable challenge of Lucien's decision.

"While the Crimson Guard was here," Raven said at last, "I remained at the Arc of Mourning Eidolons with the other squads on high alert under the guise of an *unknown* threat."

"All hunters were accounted for, so we can eliminate them as suspects," Donovan added.

Eric's eyes narrowed. "Perhaps at that time. The murder occurred last night. Where was everyone then?"

"The High Council convened a session with the Commanders and First Officers in the early evening," Raven replied, "and I subsequently ordered a mandatory meeting to go over security specifics pertaining to the Second New Age. Few hunters are unaccounted for at that time."

Donovan's face was as solemn as his voice was quiet. "Goody Raven, one hunter left early to return here."

"Who?" Eric demanded.

Glaring at her subordinate, Raven reluctantly answered, "The Crimson Guard's Commander. Alex."

This time, silence dropped like a weight. Eric had caught both the emotion in Raven's voice and the expression on Donovan's face as his gaze sank into the grass.

"Will your feelings for Alex interfere with your duty?" Eric demanded.

"A traitor must die, no matter who it is." Raven's voice was quiet, but her determined expression left no doubt about her allegiance. A sudden fire lit her eyes. "*My* squad kills rogues who threaten the Nation, without mercy, and, as I said, *without fail.*"

Paresh gasped. Eric tightened his hold on her and swept his free arm out to the side. "Then do your job and eliminate him!"

The huntress shook her head. "I must respectfully refuse."

Donovan's face jerked up. "You what?"

Raven swept Donovan's legs and shoved his shoulder into the ground, and dropped to her knee beside him. To Eric, she said, "You may share Sir Jonathan's rank, but Lord Lucien's orders supersede all and he was adamant that we stay by your si—"

"I don't think Lucien was entirely forthcoming about this situation with you," Eric growled. Despite Paresh's essence, angry spires shot through his aura.

Raven turned a lofty gaze his way. "I can't leave, but I'm not powerless." She tapped the communicator. "Chavnia, Jocathian. Alex is the target. Contact me immediately when he is in cust—"

"*What?*" Raven demanded.

After another moment, she ordered, "Hold your positions." She tapped the sliver of metal again. "Seneca, as High Commander of the Vampire Shadow Hounds, I hereby relieve Alexander of his rank and authorize you to assume full command of the Crimson Guard. You are to apprehend and detain him immediately as a suspect of treason. I will not hesitate to deal with insubordination in the strictest manner possible. Notify me once Alex is in custody."

Raven met the anger simmering in Eric's eyes with cool determination in hers. "Alex is meeting with Sir Jonathan at Snowblood Square. Seneca will seize him as soon as they are finished. It is imperative that I speak with you privately. *Now.*"

When Eric silently locked eyes with Raven, Paresh gently tugged on his arm. "Let's go in. All this talk about killing and death is too much. I need a break."

Closing his eyes with a frustrated sigh, Eric covered Paresh's hand with his. "This has been so hard on you," he whispered. He glanced sharply at Raven. "The keys are in the door. Let yourselves in."

Respectfully bowing her head, Raven yanked Donovan to his feet.

Eric watched them go until the door shut behind them. Searching Paresh's eyes, he asked, "You seemed like you were feeling better, like you were finally comfortable here again, before they showed up. But now…we don't have to go in."

"It's fine," she said, sweeping down to retrieve his shirt and the communicator from the grass. "I'm just tired and that makes the bite hurt more."

"I wish I could take your pain away." Eric cupped her cheek.

She nuzzled his hand. "I need to sit down and not think about this right now." She glanced off to the side. "Please, it's catching up to me, that's all. Don't worry."

He pulled her against him and held her head to his chest. Closing his eyes, he took in deep breaths and blew them out slowly, allowing the tension to drain from his muscles and fully erase his demonic façade. Heaving a sigh, he said, "I won't take long. And we'll sleep in tomorrow, I promise, okay?"

"Okay," she mumbled. "But can we sleep at your house tonight?"

Clenching his jaw, he held her tighter. "Of course. We can stay anywhere you like. Someday soon," he whispered, looping his arms around her waist, "we'll make new memories here that you'll look forward to remembering."

She leaned back and lightly stroked her throat with a vacant look in her eyes. "We already have."

"I love you," Eric said.

She nodded and tugged at the shirt in her hand. With a weak smile, she held it out and helped him dress. As she slid the buttons into place, he watched with concerned eyes, feeling helpless and very unlike the Sacred Vessel's "Anointed Strength."

"I love you, too," she finally replied, fidgeting with the hem. She tucked the sliver of metal into his pocket.

Before she could turn away, he ducked down and stole a kiss. "It's going to be okay. Everything is."

Lacing her fingers through his, she bit her lower lip and led him to the cottage. The hunters were perched upon the stone hearth when they entered. Paresh sat on the Victorian sofa opposite Donovan and Eric motioned for Raven to follow him.

"If you need anything …" Eric lightly squeezed Paresh's shoulder.

"I'll be fine." She turned a tired smile to Donovan.

The hunter flashed his elongated teeth in a charming grin and respectfully bowed his head. All evening, their actions, steeped in the mannerism of knights and kings, had defined the strict code of honor that had governed them since the dawning of Christianity.

But, they're still killers, Eric thought, with the realization that a code broken by someone entrusted to protect the Second Born meant nothing at all.

☽ ✳ ☾

Raven trailed Eric down the hall. When a *click* indicated a door closing, Donovan's chin tilted up. Seconds stretched into minutes while he and Paresh regarded each other.

Finally, his brow furrowed. "Are you feeling okay? You're paler now and your pulse is erratic."

Her hand fluttered to her throat. "I-I'll be fine. These attacks don't last long."

Without disturbing the air, Donovan appeared beside her, ceramic vial in hand. "This ointment relieves pain and mends wounds on humans instantly. I don't know if it'll work, but it won't hurt."

She smeared the oily substance between her fingers, judging it with a grimace. It smelled like herbal mint tea, but its olive color and slimy texture gave it the appearance of something coughed up during flu season.

"It's not as gross as it looks. The moment it touches your skin, the pain should vanish. Here, let me." He lightly massaged a dollop onto her throat before she could object.

She melted at his touch—warm and gentle—a soothing contrast to the burning pain. "Mm…"

"There you go," Donovan whispered.

Closing her eyes, she leaned her head against the sofa's wooden frame and took a deep breath in. She let it trickle out, contented.

"Keep this with you." He pressed the vial into her palm and lingered a moment before returning to the hearth.

"Wow," she whispered. "I feel so much better. The mint is wonderful, so energizing. Thank you."

Donovan offered yet another respectful bow of the head with his fist clenched over his heart. "Anything I can do for you surely isn't enough, milady. I am honored to serve you."

Energy bubbled up from somewhere deep inside and escaped as a giggle. Donovan looked up, grinning. "I suppose this all seems a bit silly and archaic, doesn't it? But, it is how we've lived for a long time."

"I'm sorry. I don't mean to laugh. It's not silly, just *so* formal. And maybe a little archaic," she admitted, holding her thumb and index finger out as a measure.

A nostalgic smile lifted her cheeks. "It's really not much different from growing up with Master Jon. Just strange to be on the receiving end."

"Your bond with the Second Born is enviable. Only Lord Lucien knows him so intimately."

"I miss him. He was always there, like a father. And now, he's this all-important man. Only, he's not even a *man*, really, but something else altogether, and leagues above me."

Donovan contemplated her quietly.

With a defeated sigh, she looked down at her hands in her lap. "When I think about how much my life has changed in the last week, it's overwhelming. I wish Master Jon was here, but I suppose he's too busy for me now that his *assignment* is done."

"Ah," Donovan said with a half-laugh. "I'm sure he doesn't see it that way, but I can't speak for him. To me? You are the crisp, white flower that only blooms at midnight, the brush of warmth on a cool autumn night, the fire that burns inside a perfect diamond."

His eyes gleamed as he panned the room with his hand. "More beautiful than a million full moons. Far beyond our worthiness to bow to as our queen. You are our mother, our rescuer, the giver of new life. No one is too busy for you. You are the one who is leagues above us—*all* of us."

Suddenly feeling his lips against the back of her hand, she gasped and instinctively pulled away. She hadn't seen him move, yet he was kneeling before her.

"Century after century we waited for salvation, never certain we'd see it. You gave us life. I'm proud to be here. There is no more honorable a way to die than to do so defending you."

Rocking back on his heels, he cocked an eyebrow, and rolled his hand up and away from his chest. "In through the nose, now."

When had she stopped breathing? She sucked in precious air. Tears blurred her vision. She'd never thought about *them* living that long, waiting day after day for *her* to save them.

"Come now, don't cry, milady." Donovan leaned forward with both hands on her knees. "The Almighty could have wiped us from existence, but He saw something in us, something worthy of redemption, and sent you. It's a good thing."

Paresh sniffed. "I know I'm the Sacred Vessel, but I hadn't given my purpose much thought. It's a bit—"

"Overwhelming?" Donovan finished with a warm smile. "Last week you didn't know we existed and thought you were a normal human. It's understandable."

Wiping tears from her cheeks, he added quietly, "I've never comforted anyone like this, but it feels natural. I loved you the instant I received your blood. It…it's like it imprints you on our hearts and gives us a calmness to help us understand it."

"Th-thank you." She blew out a shaky breath. "I thought I was okay, but then Bill died…and I have a feeling that something bad is going to happen."

She paused and hesitantly asked, "Would you walk with me to Grandfather Wisdom, the tree in the southern clearing?"

"Of course, milady."

She caught his chin as he began to bow his head. "Okay, but this has to stop. I don't want to feel like King Arthur's wife anymore. Can we drop the formalities?"

"Ah, the Knights of the Round!" Donovan exclaimed in a hearty, rolling British accent, jumping to his feet. With a wink, he pulled her up from the couch. "Very well, *Miss Hawthorne*, although I'm not sure Queen Guinevere is the best analogy here. I don't want Sir Eric to think I'm swooping in as Lancelot."

"Oh, right." Paresh blushed.

"But! I shall be your knight until the End of Days!" Grinning, Donovan ducked out of his cloak and swung it over her shoulders. The wool carried the spicy scent of clove oil. Beneath it, Donovan wore a long-sleeved black shirt, equally dark jeans, and silver-tipped, black cowboy boots.

"Raven," he said in a low voice. "At Lady Paresh's request, I am escorting her into the forest to visit Grandfather Wisdom. Please acknowledge confirmation." After receiving an answer on his communicator, he led Paresh to the front door.

Pulling the cloak tight despite the evening's warmth, she hesitantly stepped outside and mentally chided, *you're acting like a child using blankets to escape a nightmare.*

Joining her on the flagstone path, Donovan stuffed his hands into his pockets. "Your pulse is all over the place, again."

Paresh wound the wool around her fists. "I've been trying so hard to act like I'm fine, but you can tell just by my pulse that I'm not, can't you? Which means Eric has known all along, doesn't it?"

He nodded. "Is the bite that bad? We have treatments at the Arc of

Mourning Eidolons that might help."

Shaking her head, she said, "That's not it. It's going back there. To where *it* happened. My memories are so vivid."

"You don't have to go."

"But I do. This is my home and I've waited too long to return to have it tarnished."

"Your determination makes you stronger than you think." He paused in thought. "What you've been through would have left any human permanently scarred. You don't need a brave face."

"What I went through would have left any other human dead," she mumbled.

Donovan grinned. "Ah, yes, of course. I suppose then it's a good thing you are not an ordinary human."

"And then there's that. What am I? Not human. Not vampire. What?"

"Hm …" Thoughtfully scrunching his face, Donovan tapped his finger against his lips. "Perhaps you are like the fictional dhampir that humans invented. You're the closest thing to a halfling this world will ever see, unless, of course, you and Sir Eric can bear children."

The fabric slid through her fingers as she absently flattened her palms against her belly. "Children?"

"I didn't mean to imply that you are with child, milady," he said hastily. "But is it that scary a thought? True bloods can infect, but we'll never know the wonder of creating new life."

"N-no," she stammered. "I-it's not that. I hadn't realized…I'll never have children."

"I'm sorry." One hand landed on her shoulder as the other brushed his forehead. "I'm not doing much to ease your concerns."

She licked her lips and sighed, and Donovan returned his hands to his pockets. He gazed around as though searching for a lighter topic.

Finally, he faced at the sky and said, "Few things are more beautiful than the moon illuminating an unblemished sky full of stars, even if you can't see them as clearly here as you can from the arcs."

He quickly added, "Pollution, you know. A thousand years ago, it didn't matter where you stood. When the sky was clear, it was clear."

Paresh bobbed her head and followed his gaze. "The sky was clearer in Kansas, too."

Donovan's eyes glittered with excitement. "Then you get it!"

The genuine smile plastered on his face prompted a chuckle despite her mood. "I guess you enjoy stargazing when you aren't hunting, huh?"

"All true bloods do," he said. "We weren't created to enjoy this world, not the way humans were. Perhaps that's what we envy most. Humans take nature for granted. But it's the truest gift."

A flick of his silver-tipped toes sent a rock sailing across the clearing. His wistful eyes reflected the stars.

"Some are bitter, of course. That *is* why we're here. But, what I mean is…" He paused, scratching his head in thought. "Well, *listen.* The crickets and frogs. The animals and the bats. I don't know if it's your essence, or your blood changing me, but I finally feel connected to the living world. It's awesome."

"Awesome," she echoed. The word sounded so odd rolling off his lips. But, he was right. She closed her eyes and listened to nature's symphony.

Moonbathing toads inflated and deflated their croaking throats, the orchestra's percussion section. Crickets were on strings, strumming their bodies rhythmically, and bats were the woodwinds with air skimming their delicate wings. Much like patrons wrestling with candy wrappers, opossums and skunks rustled as they foraged for food.

Nature was at peace. It lifted her soul.

She started to smile, but the darkness suddenly squeezed all life from the night and summoned a memory of breathing shadows and a raccoon with a racing heart. A silver blade reflected the moon's light and limned an arc into her heart. She stumbled backward, clutching her chest, gasping.

Donovan instantly stopped beside her, bracing her shoulders with his arm. "What's wrong?"

"I—"Terror popped her eyes open wide. The forest's black silhouette bulged. The shadows within teetered and swayed like the cloaked figures that had caused that raccoon's fright. The instinct to run lit her nerves on fire.

"*Oh God,*" she groaned, grabbing her head. Her vision swam with dizzying ripples. Somewhere, deep inside, she knew she needed to fight the panic. But, she could feel *it. It* was out there. *It* wanted her.

Death.

Her voice shrieked, ragged and raw, within her head.

Get up! It's behind you!

It's ahead of you!

She was surrounded. The world was spinning. Her feet were twisting.

Which way?

Straight!

But he's ther——

Too late.

Darkness rushed up hard and fast. Sharp pain shot into her palms as the impact jolted her entire body—

"*Hey!*" Donovan yelled, tugging on her shoulder. Concern flickered like fire in his golden gaze and drew her in like a moth.

The world stilled. Her mind went quiet. Paresh looked down. Her jaw quivered. Tears seared her eyes. A knot lodged in her throat.

She was on her hands and knees. In the grass. At the edge of the forest. In front of the southern trail.

How?

Thick tears splashed her palms as she examined them. No blood. No dirt. No debris. No pain. She looked up.

The black forest was gone. Moonlight trickled through the shining treetops, painting the trunks indigo and silver. She choked on her sobs and sat back on her legs, grinding her hands together, struggling to understand.

"Wow," Donovan whispered. Uncertainty and darkness skewed his features with odd, shadowy angles. "You—you just took off. I mean—"

He blew out the breath he must have been holding. "Wow. That…*that* was intense."

Wiping her eyes as new tears formed, Paresh whispered, "I'm sorry." She buried her face into her hands and choked. "This…feeling won't go…a—" she hiccupped, "—way. I'm so…pathetic."

"I don't think—" Donovan quieted and then swore under his breath.

"I'm supposed to save your race and I can't even face *a tree!*" she wailed, throwing her hand at the trail.

Kneeling before her, Donovan smoothed damp strands of hair from her face and dabbed her cheeks dry with his sleeve. He studied her with sad eyes. "You aren't pathetic," he said at last. "You were traumatized."

He held out his hand. "And you're not alone. I'm here."

Swallowing the lump in her throat, she hesitantly accepted his hand. "O-okay."

Her eyes burned as they rose together. She locked her jaw, determined to imprison her tears.

"You're shivering. Here—" He swaddled her within the cloak, which had fallen off during her flight.

She clutched at the wool with pale knuckles and stared at her feet. Willing them to move was futile. Even though the path was there, and she could see it clearly, she couldn't take the step.

A firm finger tipped her chin up. "You are stronger than you think."

Bracing herself, she huffed and swallowed, and nodded firmly. They crossed the forest threshold.

Donovan was quiet awhile, for which she was thankful. She needed to keep her mind blank. If she opened the floodgate, her thoughts collided, alongside her emotions: fear, embarrassment, shame. And then, the pain of Lucien's bite would follow, a fiery torrent in her veins.

"I know what happened to you," he said at last, his voice low and somber. "I read the report. Hell, I heard it straight from Alex."

Donovan tugged a leaf off a low-hanging branch and twirled it between his thumb and forefinger. "That doesn't mean squat, though, since I don't know how it was for *you*. I can't empathize."

She didn't respond. Couldn't.

"But still, I wanted to tell you…I envy you."

"Huh?"

"When I was watching you earlier—with the lightning bugs—it was mesmerizing," he confessed. "Your memories may be soured by that night, but you belong here. You and this world speak the same language. This place, that tree included, loves you, and I think those little flies were trying to show that Gaea—Mother Nature—cares about you."

She nodded.

"And I don't—can't—understand that, either," he added. "Technology fills our arcs with gardens and weather simulations, but it all lacks the subtly of the natural order, the Earth's pulse, that spirit of the organic that cannot be synthetically reproduced."

The leaf slid from his fingers. She watched it seesaw back and forth until it landed on a patch of dirt.

"I've heard your arcs are amazing," she said.

"The Arc of True Blood is our shining grace, more stunning than the Hanging Gardens of Babylon—or so I've heard. I'm not old enough to have seen them in person."

She eyed the pale hunter—his youthful face etched with thoughtful wrinkles, index finger scratching his temple automatically, awkard in his effort to comfort her. She lightly touched his hand and whispered, "Thank you, Donovan. I appreciate what you're doing."

He nodded and squeezed her fingers.

"So, uh, how old are you?" she asked.

"Ancient." He smiled, held his arms out to the sides, and turned in a dramatic circle. "You've got a bona fide antique here! Lucifer created me in 40 A.D. when Caligula was the Roman Emperor."

Paresh was speechless. He'd lived so long. Next to him, she was a naïve child.

"I devoted the first half of my life to eradicating humans in a war against a god that most of the world didn't believe in. And then that god replaced the Great Holy War with a dream I've never even seen."

Paresh could only gape at Donovan, at a veteran of the greatest war the world had never known. "But you said Caligula was the emperor. How did society function during such a brutal war? I mean, the Romans captured all of Europe."

"Ah! That's the altered history you know." He pretended to zip his lips. "I am not permitted to reveal any truth prior to 1000 A.D. That was a conditional sacrifice to keep our memories intact. We didn't want to forget why we wanted this life."

Gnawing on her lip, Paresh tried to imagine such an epic erasure. A memory surfaced of Lucien's crystal eyes, where she'd seen centuries of blood and war swimming in his pupils. "Was it worth it?"

"I don't know." Tilting his head back as though studying the dense canopy, Donovan ran his hand through his wavy hair. "Maybe we didn't know what we were asking for. But it doesn't seem like it should be this chaotic. That I should be hunting a *Commander*."

He glanced at her. "I didn't mean to drag the mood down, again. This is all so—"

"Overwhelming?" she interrupted with a smile.

He chuckled and nudged her with his elbow. "I was going to say 'new,' but how about that? We understand each other!"

Bumping him back, she said, "You know, for all our differences, the same event changed both our lives."

"You happened." He made a thoughtful sound. "We're finally in the Second New Age and I'm besieged by emotions I don't understand."

He quickly added, "But! I can focus on my duties. I'm a great multitasker. I promise I can protect you and be struck dumb by love at the same time."

She laughed and sputtered out, "What?"

He again scratched at his temple's invisible itch. "Love! I don't know anything about it! I mean, humans care for each other. They know love. And now, suddenly, my heart *hurts*. Physically. All I can think about is one woman and my chest aches because I'm not the only man in her life."

He gave her a questioning look. "Why does it do that?"

"Uh…" Already at a loss for words, he stole whatever thought she had by stopping and cupping her cheek. The golden flecks in his eyes burned like embers.

"Sir Eric is lucky to know his soul mate so earnestly and completely."

With a sigh, he released her and studied his palm. "This body is two thousand years old and has known many pleasures in battle and bed, but now my infant soul suffers the heartache of a grown man. We weren't designed for the complexities of personal relationships."

Paresh quietly composed her thoughts.

"I've lived a sheltered life," she started, "so I don't know the answers. But, you're right. Love is painful. I've lost love that I'll never get back. And, I've found love that I'll never let go. The heartache is how you know what you have, or that you had something worth missing."

"Ah! 'Tis better to have loved and lost!" he said with a throaty rumble, lunging forward in a poetic stance.

"Than never to have loved before."

"'At all.' Tennyson would probably like to have his words remembered correctly!" He straightened and swatted the air dismissively. "But I get it. When you find love again, the pain makes it more fulfilling."

"Yeah." Paresh gnawed on her lip. "When I lost my parents and thought Eric had abandoned me, I felt like I'd never know love like that again. My parents were dead, but Eric was still out there, somewhere. I missed him every day."

Her gaze dropped to the twig-covered path. "But I was also so angry with him that I didn't want to see him. I think I might have hated him."

She whispered to herself, "I can't imagine hating him."

Donovan regarded her with gentle eyes. "Did I made you cry again?"

She shook her head with a wistful smile. "The moment when I felt his arms around me, that love rushed back and was fuller and richer, and it was the most wonderful thing."

"True bloods never cared for each other. For a moment of mutual, intimate pleasure, we were partners in bed, nothing more."

"That's so cold." Paresh folded her hands over her chest, clasping the cross Eric had given her. "Do you know you love this woman because it feels warm?"

"Not exactly—" A knowing smile crept across his face and he glanced at her through hooded eyes. "With love comes jealousy, another powerful force. I can't imagine her with any other man."

Fidgeting with the cloak's hem, again, Paresh hesitantly asked, "It's Raven, right? And Alex? Do you think…would she choose him over us?"

Donovan's body tensed—briefly. He slumped back lazily as though cushioned by the air. "Nah. Goody Raven walks the straight and narrow, and always follows orders. She knows which one of us truly cares for her." He nodded at the break in the trees ahead. "Is that the clearing?"

Her stomach lurched and knotted, and her feet grew heavier than stone. They'd arrived faster than she'd expected. Memories ravaged her mind: demons dancing in fire, figures cloaked in red, glinting silver daggers, and Eric, pinned against the ground, helpless and desperately screaming for her life.

Her uncle's brown eyes flashed open, reflecting flames of madness and blood, and chased every ounce of warmth from her body. She shivered and tried to cry out, but her voice was frozen.

"Hey! Come on! Not again!"

Donovan's voice sounded so distant.

"Paresh? Paresh! Come back to me!" He snapped his fingers in front of her face, gaining her focus for an instant. She'd stepped into the clearing and he'd grabbed her hand. "You shouldn't—"

His voice faded and, somehow, she was suddenly standing at the base of the behemoth: Grandfather Wisdom, the giant silver maple that ruled over Sunset Grove. She saw herself there, ghostly, bloodied, and limp, hanging from leather restraints. Shadowy whispers echoed, "*Run, Paresh, run! Run to Eric!*"

All the breath rushed from her lungs. Tears scorched her eyes. Burned lines down her cheeks.

"*Run!*"

A swatch of moonlight brushed Grandfather Wisdom's furrowed trunk and washed away the image of her broken frame, and the serenade of night burst forth protectively around her as if to swallow the voices.

Catching her breath, she was vaguely aware of Donovan lingering outside the clearing. "I've always loved this tree and found peace here. Now all I see is pain and death." She closed her eyes.

"I should have waited for Eric," she whispered, wishing she hadn't hidden her demons from him. She sighed and opened her eyes. As she touched the tree's rough grooves, warmth pulsed into her fingertips.

A gaping hole appeared and formed a vacuum that sucked her fingers into the trunk. She cried out, trying to pull away, but a luminous, paraffin hand shot out and jerked her into the black void. As the hole closed behind her, she heard her own scream ricocheting off the trees.

II

Raven slapped a small disc above the door and smoothed her finger counterclockwise around it. A steady, barely audible hum filled the room, deepening in frequency as the disc's circular edge began to glow. With a quick pop, rays of electric-blue light shot out parallel to the walls and raced through the corners to wrap the entire room in a neon grid. The lines sank into the surfaces and disappeared, and the buzz went silent, leaving behind the seemingly unimportant disc as the only evidence that a barrier even existed.

"The button will give us privacy and let us hear them," Raven said.

Eric closed his eyes and listened for Paresh's pulse. It was steady, proof that she felt safe with the vampire hunter.

"Why the sudden urgency?" He opened his eyes to see Raven on bended knee, chin tucked, eyes down. "I'm losing patience with the bureaucracy of your tradition. I am not Lucien or Jonathan. You can speak freely."

"My lord, I was truthful in saying that you and Master Jonathan share the same privileges; however, I neglected to detail those privileges. To let my First Officer know more would compromise my mission."

Eric's internal alarm prickled. "If you can't trust your First Officer, I sure as hell don't want Paresh alone with him."

"His trustworthiness is not in question." Raven rose and paced the width of the room with her head cocked before stopping to paw through highboy's drawers. "Donovan protects High Elder Lord Corben during Winter Solitude and I trust him with my life. That, alone, should mean something."

"If you really trust him to that extent, he would know what you know. He's your second in command."

"Aye, milord. But, not many will accept taking orders from someone of human origin, and your life is already at risk by being the Servator. Few know that you and Master Jonathan are now lords of the High Council, equal to Arch Elder Lord Lucien in every way."

"W-what? Lucien said we were equals, but I didn't expect that," Eric retorted. "What is he thinking? I don't know anything about your ways."

"I cannot say." The pink-haired woman flattened her palm against the pale green wall.

Narrowing his eyes, Eric impatiently asked, "What are you doing?"

"Searching for a Cimex Drone."

"And that is?"

"A bioengineered listening device used for long-term surveillance. It's adaptable and mobile, and resembles a larval bug that can burrow into hard surfaces or hide in soft materials."

For a few minutes, he watched her put her ear to the wall and knock every few inches. "Do you expect to find one?"

"No, but I didn't expect to hunt a VaSH Commander with full access to our arsenal or knowledge of our situation, either. We have a scanner for these stupid things—"

"Who else did Lucien tell?" Eric sat on the edge of the bed and wiped his face with his hands.

She craned her neck to see him without turning. "The Commanders and the High Council, including the traitorous Elder."

"So you know about that, too, then. Does Lucien know who it is?" Slicking his hands through his hair, he rose to pace between the door and the chaise lounge. The tightness in his chest was back.

"Aye, sir, but he's not disclosed that information quite yet. Lord Jonathan aside, only Alex and myself are privy to the full story."

Eric groaned. "You were ordered here and the Crimson Guard was ordered to investigate the Elders."

"You understand the situation quite well." She sounded impressed as she moved onto the southern wall. "They're gathering intel on the Elders and the Fallen Host's involvement."

"The Fallen Host?"

"The angels who fell with Lucifer during the Great Holy Rebellion. They've tried several times to mobilize against our empire, but cannot penetrate our defenses." She searched a nightstand and found nothing, so she crawled over the bed.

"But they're angels—"

"No, they're demons, but that's a technicality that is irrelevant." She met his eyes with a mischievous glint in hers. "Lucifer gave us the strength and skill to battle against the Heavenly Host. We are more than capable of holding our own against his league."

She hopped off the bed and poked through the other nightstand. "Lucifer may have created Lord Lucien with less strength than he alone possesses, but he was *His* most powerful angel. Our Eternal Lord proved quite formidable against the archangel battalion during the war. You should understand given that you share the Second Born's DNA. He's nearly as strong."

The drawer creaked as she closed it. "Any true blood who takes exception to your humanity should keep that in mind!" She laughed and offered a coy grin. "They'd be right shocked when you shredded them to a bloody mess!"

Eric watched her with puzzled eyes. The huntress bore little resemblance to the creature he'd attacked in the woods. "You're different now."

"I was *born* different." Shrugging, she plopped down on the foot of the bed. "I adapt easily to changes in hierarchical associations. Lord Lucien suggested you might prefer a more casual interaction."

"Lucien's offering advice, now?"

"Starry night! That'd be something to see!" She laughed again. "Believe me, sire, it was an order."

The knot in Eric's chest began to loosen. Raven's light and airy aura lacked the spiritual scarring that had affected other true bloods after centuries of warfare. It reminded him of Paresh's innocent naivety, which was not a quality he expected to find in the VaSH High Commander.

"Then drop the 'lord' and 'sire' titles, too." He sat beside her. "Call me Eric or Mr. Ravenscroft."

"Which do you prefer?"

"Raven," Donovan's voice interrupted. "At Lady Paresh's request, I am escorting her into the forest to visit Grandfather Wisdom. Please acknowledge confirmation."

"Do you object, Eric?" Raven asked, gauging his response.

"You trust him with your life?" He met her scrutiny with wary eyes.

"Yes, but more importantly, I trust him with hers."

"It's fine." Eric sighed and wiped his face once more. Raven's assurances did little to alleviate his anxiety over leaving Paresh with a stranger.

"Confirmation acknowledged. You may proceed." Upon seeing Eric's conflicted expression, she said, "I can belay that order."

"I trust Paresh's judgment. She likes him." He rose and crossed to the window. "My ignorance of your ways and weaponry got her killed once already. I don't want it to happen again. Not that you can possibly understand."

"Actually, I am the closest you will get to a true blood who can understand." Raven glanced at him in the vanity's mirror and caught his eyes gleaming at her over his shoulder.

The urge to run to Paresh swelled like a balloon in his belly when he heard her pulse suddenly jump erratically. Eric ground his teeth and turned toward the door.

"Give Donovan a chance," Raven requested politely. "She will always have a strong ally at her side, but it can't always be you."

Glaring at the huntress, Eric mentally conceded that she was right. This was their life now. He listened awhile longer before asking, "Who are Chavnia and Jocathian? And why did you order Alex's squad to capture him? I don't care how loyal you true bloods claim to be to Lucien. I question Seneca's willingness to capture his own Commander."

Raven turned to face him. "Chavnia and Jocathian are my hunters, and for reasons unknown, they've been reassigned to stand by High Elders Lady Ambrosia and Lord Corben."

The note of irritation in her voice gained a visual query from Eric that he knew she saw and chose to ignore. "Our sister squad was the next available resource. Seneca will detain Alex, believe me. *She* is loyal to her Commander, but she will also do damn near anything to get that title for herself."

"You're a ruthless lot, aren't you?" Eric mumbled to himself.

"Seneca disagrees with Alex's pacifist ways. She'd rather be a Wraith Reaper. We're given the High Council's most controversial orders—one misstep or poor decision can reap eternal fire on the entire Nation."

Eric leaned against the window frame. Paresh and Donovan were in the clearing. Raven appeared beside him.

"I can't see any VaSH Commander as a pacifist, let alone someone in Jonathan's favor," Eric said.

"Alex was a noble man with a good heart." The leather fibers in Raven's glove ripped apart as she clenched her fist. Her words struck the air like a sword. "Attacking a member of the Flock is a coward's way to fight, and no one expected it from someone as mild as him, which makes it the perfect start to what they hope to achieve."

"Civil war." Eric's eyes mirrored her grim stare. "I was expecting a direct attack."

"He's watched you with Master Jonathan for more than a century. He knows what you're capable of. You charged Lucifer without an ounce of hesitation, in a vastly depleted state. We've never seen *anyone* do that." Her voice softened with a note of awe. "To be honest, we have no idea what the limits of your bloodline are."

"Yeah, well," he said dryly, "as valiant as it seems, I charged into my death for the second time."

He tensed and grabbed the window frame. Paresh had stumbled backward holding her chest. His heart skipped a beat. "What's wrong?"

As he turned for the door, Raven held out her hand. "Wait! We've both heard what she's said to Donovan tonight. If you go to her now, you will nullify every effort she's made to keep you from worrying about her and every effort you've made to let her believe you haven't seen it."

His chest rising and falling rapidly, Eric clenched his jaw and glared into Raven's eyes. "I am her Anointed Strength. I should be the one next to her right now, not some stranger!"

Movement in his peripheral vision drew his attention to Paresh dashing madly toward the southern trail with Donovan chasing after her, calling her name. *What the hell is going on out there?*

He turned again for the door, but Raven blocked his path. "I will go around you or through you. Your choice," he warned.

Raven nodded at the window. "You know better than anyone what it's like for human emotions to battle vampiric alteration. You may be her Anointed Strength, but she wants to fight this on her own. If she wins without your help, she will be stronger for it."

Stepping to the side, Raven added, "You can't fight this one for her, but it's not my place to stop you."

"Damn it!" Eric turned restlessly. Outside, he saw Paresh drop to her hands and knees at the path. Her heart was beating faster than he'd ever heard. Donovan seemed confused as he knelt beside her. Her chest-heaving sobs made Eric's heart feel like it was in a grinder. The window frame creaked under his grip.

"It's not the alteration that's got her right now," Eric said tightly. He huffed heavily and balled his hands into fists. Blood dripped from where his nails dug into his palms. "She's remembering what you bastards did to her!"

"Donovan's good at what he does," Raven said, gently covering Eric's fist. "If she's in danger, he'll let us know."

Eric whirled around, nearly delirious as Paresh's panic infected his aura across the distance. He knocked Raven's hand away. "The last person she needs comfort from is another vampire hunter! The one you're after? *He did this to her!*"

Taking a reverent step back, Raven reached into her pocket and produced rings with black stones. "Let's follow and then double back ahead of them. Neither will ever know."

Eric snatched up a ring, disgust icing his words as he said, "David's men were wearing these damned things. I couldn't hear a sound they made."

"Hilja rings are mobile sound barriers."

He glanced up sharply and slid the larger ring onto his middle finger. "*I am well aware of that now.*"

She placed the smaller one on her pinkie. The onyx centers emitted a soft red glow. "They activate when the interior surface makes contact with skin."

"Why can I hear you?"

"In close quarters, the barriers cancel each other out. If we were farther apart, we'd have to use communicators. Lord Jonathan and Lord Lucien can tweak the ring's performance with their auras, so I presume you can, too."

Eric eyed the ring. "I doubt I'll be 'tweaking' anything soon. Let's go."

Following in silence, Raven waited until Donovan had successfully distracted Paresh to say, "You are more than capable of protecting her; I know that. Lord Lucien sent us as a line of defense as we investigate, especially if Lucifer returns. Defeating him would take Lord Lucien and Lord Jonathan, together, at the very least, but we could put up a hell of a fight in the meantime."

"He can distract her. She needs it. I do not," Eric replied, his voice curt and his attention clearly focused on the path ahead and the voices traveling back to them.

Raven absently stroked the bruises that hadn't yet healed on her throat. "I'm not trying to distract you. I was truthfully surprised by the strength in your arm—you threw me so effortlessly. I've never taken a hit like that, driven by such raw power, and I spar with Lord Jonathan. Your aura, too—"

She flattened her palm against her chest. "It took my breath away." Earnest sapphire eyes met his. "I watched you dash across the clearing. I had plenty of time to dodge you. But in close combat, I'd never react fast enough."

Eric's fuming silence stretched thinner between them. Raven looked upon the waning moon with regret. "I didn't mean to sneak up on you. But, I'm not a voyeur and I was curious about your abilities. It's important to me that you know my missions are never this disorganized."

The southern path was ahead. Donovan and Paresh were getting closer to the second clearing. Eric quickened his pace and muttered, "There goes your pride again."

"You were a soldier once. Running a sloppy ship hardly reflects well on me."

In the silence that followed, Donovan and Paresh's conversation carried back to them. Eric quickly looked over at Raven. "Did you hear Paresh's question?"

"Aye." Raven's words were hesitant and soft. "Like Donovan, the Sacred Vessel's blood has affected me, and I, too, am somewhat conflicted by these emotions. However, it seems to have come with a measure of control—a side effect, if you will." She paused and lifted her chin. "My feelings for Donovan and Alex will not interfere with my duty, I swear it."

"I am quite familiar with the power of love. Don't underestimate it."

"I promise to take it to heart, my lord," Raven said with a respectful tilt of the head.

"Donovan doesn't like Alex much." Despite his mood, Eric was curious about the hunters' dynamics.

"They've always had a rivalry and it's never been about me."

"Then why?"

"Donovan is the oldest true blood not sitting on the High Council. Not only was he passed up for my position, but also Alex's and the vacant Elder spot—"

"Why?" Eric interrupted.

"Lord Lucien wanted those in line for eldership to serve under the VaSH High Commander to hone their skills."

"Not tucked away in an arc under protection?"

"If they can't perform their duty to him in battle, they don't deserve to sit beneath him. They aren't Elders, yet, and there are always others to take their place."

"He really is coldhearted."

"Perhaps, but he holds our nation together."

Tilting his head back, Eric watched moonlight trickle through the leaves above. "Are you in line for the High Council?"

"Never will be. I am the youngest surviving true blood and have already gone higher in the ranks than I ever should have gone. It's a long story that's not important right now. Let's just say that I have true justice in my heart and—

"*What?*" Raven slapped her hand against the communicator on her jaw and her aura charged the air with alarm. "*Shit! No!* Hold your position! He's in my realm now and has forfeited his right to capture!"

"What happened?" Eric demanded, feeling his stomach drop.

Raven's darkening eyes shot him a sharp look and she started running. "Alex escaped into Animus Hollow and his energy signal landed *here*—"

An unnatural scream echoed through the night. It froze Raven in place. Eric shoved past her, frantically yelling for Paresh even though he knew he was already too late.

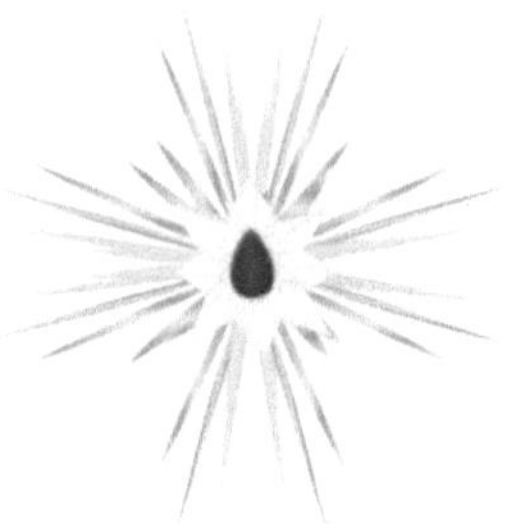

Chapter Six: Death and Rebirth

Lucien smoothed his kimono around his knees as he knelt at the low table and closed his eyes to seek solace in a level of silence unknown to the Realm of Man. Chaos threatened to destroy his nation and the enemy was moving faster than anticipated. The dawning of the Second New Age had changed everything.

For thousands of years, his cold heart had given him the advantage of strict logic, untarnished by emotion. But now he relied on the barriers shielding his residence to hide a troubled mind and heart. His race had found both hope and discipline in his confident, stoic nature; he could not permit a new emotion to change that. In Greek mythos, Atlas had carried the weight of the world, but that had never included the Vampiric Nation's bloody burden. That was for Lucien to bear alone.

He inhaled deeply, expanding his lungs until sharp pain riddled his chest. A restrained airflow streamed between his lips. He began the cleansing exercise by slapping his hands together, taking another deep breath, and raising his hands above his head. He exhaled slowly and evenly as heat coiled between his palms. Like a magnet, it attracted the negative energy that had battered his aura for days.

One at a time, he relaxed every muscle from his forehead to his toes, breathing deeply as gravity pulled his arms downward. When his elbows met the tabletop, his hands slid apart leaving only his fingertips touching. He pushed the air down to the table's surface, swept his hands out to the sides, and shoved his palms to the floor, where the negative energy was released from the bonds of hostility and fear to be recycled by Earth's renewing spiritual essence.

As heat dissipated from his palms, he emptied his lungs with a final huff and opened his eyes. A ceramic teapot and cup sat before him. His hand was on the pot's handle when his shoji screened entrance skidded open.

Jonathan kicked off his shoes and hurried in. "Alex is gone."

"Oh?" Steam wafted from the cup as Lucien poured crimson liquid from the pot. "Grab a cup and drink with me."

"Lucien, he's the one they're after. I need to go."

"I need you here." He brought the cup to his lips.

Jonathan briefly squeezed his eyes shut and shook his head, throwing his hands up. "You don't understand! Inside Snowblood Square, I gave him permission to investigate the scene—before Raven started lopping off his hunters' heads, as you implied. But when I came out alone, Seneca was there and immediately started barking orders into her communicator about tracing Alex's energy signature, and she warned Raven that he was headed her way. He's the one, and I let him go!"

"Raven has given Seneca command then. The Crimson Guard remained at post?"

"Yes. Raven ordered them to tend to their mission here."

"Very well." Lucien took another sip with garnet-stained lips. "Grab a cup."

Dropping to his knees, Jonathan slammed his fist onto the table. "Aren't you listening to me? He's after Paresh!"

Lucien's eyes flashed over the cup's rim. "She is in capable hands. They don't need you."

With an angry grunt, Jonathan rose and returned a moment later with a cup in hand. He slid it across the table and glared at Lucien as he filled it.

"Let Raven and Donovan do their jobs." Lucien lowered his eyes, concerned they would betray the emotion he'd been unable to hide from his voice.

"They should have their whole squad assembled," Jonathan grumbled as he accepted Lucien's offering. "I don't agree with your decision to divide them."

"Then counter it."

Jonathan met Lucien's challenge with an obstinate stare. Frustration twisted his aura and the air began to thicken. Relenting with a huff, he snapped, "I would be a fool to interfere. You are never wrong."

"She is Eric's charge now," Lucien said quietly. "How can you hope to save her when you are so unwilling to save yourself?"

The cup cracked in Jonathan's hand. "Physical prowess cannot save me, but it can save her."

"So you would kill an ant with an anvil that could crack open as easily as that teacup there? The little ant would scurry through the debris."

Lucien folded his hands into his lap. "Physical prowess means nothing if you are too blinded by guilt to think clearly. You must take care of yourself first. Only then will you have the strength to call yourself her protector."

Blood dripped between Jonathan's fingers. "I should be there for her while I can be instead of here babbling like a needy child. My fate is done."

Lucien brought the cup to his lips. "You want redemption, but are reluctant to accept the second chance afforded to you. Gabriel sees something that you cannot, and until you see it, too, I can do nothing for you."

"Gabriel sees it, huh?" Jonathan rolled his eyes and emptied his cup with one swallow. Blood dribbled from the cracked vessel and stained his shirt. He regarded the crimson blossoms with bitter indifference and a grunt. "That fool can't see anything beyond the blood I've bathed in. There was a time when I thought I walked in Death's shadow, but he was actually walking in mine. There's a reason I'm Lucifer's favorite and the Archangel has gone as dumb as he is soft if he hasn't realized that."

"It is your choice." Raising the cup to hide his mouth, Lucien feigned a dramatic sigh. "But I find your bitterness most unbecoming, my beautiful Jonathan. Surely you do not expect that Paresh will be the only one to miss you?"

☽ ✳ ☾

Tiny flames nipped at Jonathan's nerves. "Lucien—"
Staring at the blood on his hands, Jonathan shook his head and whispered, "I don't think I can do this."

"You last spoke of how your plan went awry during Eric's teenage years. You had underestimated that man, Thaddeus."

In the silence that followed, Jonathan reluctantly continued, "That man got in my way. Eric loved him like a father."

"'Thou shalt not useth thine influence over humans in positions of military, political, or other great power,'" Lucien quoted from the commandments laid out in the Treaty of the Lasting Peace.

"I know the rules," Jonathan replied dryly on his way to the sink. "He kept his military and political ties until the very end, so his son, Lucas, was outside my reach, as well."

After washing his hands, Jonathan presented a new cup to Lucien. As the Elder tilted the pot over the rim, he said, "Never mind that they were of the Flock, of course."

"Of course," Jonathan said emptily, accepting the filled cup.

"Lucas was born after you altered Eric, correct? Did you have any interaction with him before then?"

Jonathan ran his finger around the cup's rim, his gaze trained on the blood inside. "You really want to know it all, don't you?"

"They're your confessions. Don't you think they should be presented clearly?"

"Fine." Jonathan sighed. "Nothing much happened aside from his love affair with Lucinda, the Colonel's daughter. I allowed him to form that attachment so I could use it later to destroy his faith——"

Eyes the color of burnt ash pierced Jonathan into silence. "I hope to hear you were not involved with her death."

Jonathan held his hands up. "I had nothing to do with it. Lucinda and Darien Ravenscroft were meant to die, and Eric, alone, was the only obstruction. I vow it. No games."

Lucien's eyes lightened to orbs of purified silver. "No insatiable cravings or difficulties hiding yourself from him?"

"None," Jonathan said. "After drinking his blood, it took little effort to shield myself from him. Well, except one night while his cavalry unit was on patrol."

Taking a drink, he relished the warmth and flavor of the blood sliding down his throat. "It was my fault. There was a full moon that night and I dropped my guard. I let the horses get too close, and one reared up and threw its rider. It was strange—Eric looked straight at my location in the trees, as if pulled by my presence. One of the others headed my way to scout the area, but Eric ordered him to hold position and jumped off his horse to investigate personally."

Jonathan set the cup on the table. "I couldn't chance Eric seeing through my barriers again, so I hid to observe his aura up close. It had darkened around the edges. He was almost ready."

"You were so close. Why didn't you take him then?"

Jonathan smirked. "What kind of a question is that? It would have been a violation. Besides," he added with smug confidence. "I knew I'd win eventually, and the wait made victory much sweeter."

Lucien began clearing the table. "There's my Jonathan, sounding like yourself for the first time in days. That arrogance in your voice, the fire in your eyes..."

Balancing the cup on his palm, Jonathan leaned back on his elbow and stretched his legs out beneath the table. Nostalgia prompted a smile as he studied the exposed beams in the ceiling. "I had little to do with what demoralized him in the end. It was the war. I've often wondered if he would have lost his faith without my interference."

"He only joined the military because of the Colonel."

"But his father had been friends with him. Eric may have idolized him and joined anyway."

"And he would've had an affluent life and family awaiting his return."

"Perhaps——"

"They needed you. You couldn't have altered him otherwise." Lucien rinsed the pot at the sink.

Jonathan sat up and inhaled the tantalizing ribbons wafting from his cup before setting it down. "I'll never forget when Eric lost his faith. It'd been a desperate few weeks for his unit. They were nearly out of food in an area that sympathized with the Confederacy, and just when they thought their idea to raid the enemy's supplies had worked, *bam!*"

He slapped his thigh. "The Confederates ambushed the wagon train and had no intent of taking prisoners. Injured men crawling on their bellies were easy targets. The smart ones played dead." He finished his drink and tossed the cup to Lucien.

"Eric was behind one of the wagons and black energy was swarming around him." Jonathan scoffed. "As if I'd give him away."

He smacked his palms together and one hand flew forward. "Two shots rang out. There was something musical about it, like it was meant to catch my attention: wind whistling over leaden projectiles speeding toward his chest. Tearing into his flesh. Shattering bone. Eric's impending death."

As he spoke, his outstretched hand circled back to thud into his sternum. He flailed and feigned falling to the ground. "A pair of smoky wings materialized behind him as he fell and the Fallen swallowed every ounce of his faith. Oh how my heart raced!"

He thumped his chest rapidly and grinned. "The air was thick with his blood. I could taste it. I physically ached to bite into his throat, to feel his skin on my lips. But, I also wanted the sweetest possible glory. To savor my win. I restrained myself and chased off the low-level collectors with my aura. They were reaping with no interest in one soul over another and fled like scared scavengers. They had no idea how special Eric was. Then again, neither did I."

Jonathan propped himself up. "I suppose if Lucifer had known——"

"If he'd even seen Eric," Lucien interrupted. "He would have instantly recognized the Host's involvement and destroyed him."

Rolling onto his back, Jonathan tucked his arms beneath his head and quietly contemplated the ceiling. "I suppose you're right. After witnessing Lucifer with Paresh, he would have seen to it personally."

"What would you have done?"

"I don't know that I would have released my claim—even to him."

Towel drying the cups, Lucien asked, "You would have faced Lucifer, and death, for a human?"

"He was mine," Jonathan said with a stiff lip and a sense of stubbornness. "And besides, Lucifer wouldn't have killed me. He is far too proud of my thirst—"

"You are overconfident and fortunate he did not kill you the other night."

Jonathan dismissed Lucien's concern with a flick of his wrist. "I don't think he'd kill either of us and lose the chance to turn us loose on the world again."

Lucien regarded him with an emotionless face, and for a time, neither spoke. Finally, the Elder returned his attention to the dishes and placed them on a countertop bamboo tea tray. "That may have been true before the Second New Age, but now he will target us as threats. Had you attempted to save Paresh or Eric, he would have struck you through the heart without pause, and I would not have futilely risked the Crimson Guard to save you. Our selfishness was born from his, which will always surpass ours. Never forget that."

Jonathan solemnly conceded his agreement with a nod.

"That displeases you?"

"No." Jonathan sat up with a sigh and smoothed his hand over his hair. His gaze dropped to the bloody stains on his shirt. Aware of Lucien watching him, he removed his jacket and unbuttoned his shirt.

Lucien disappeared behind a long canvas screen splashed with watercolor cherry trees in bloom. He returned with a towel and clean garments as Jonathan was pulling off his undershirt.

"So what, then?" Lucien asked at last, handing him the towel and nudging his chin at the blood that had seeped through Jonathan's shirt.

The towel was moist and warm. "I don't care how Lucifer sees us and I don't expect anyone to stand against him to save me. I didn't like watching her die. That's all."

"Paresh is alive. That should be enough."

"You're right, of course, and it is."

"You say the words, but your voice does not believe them."

"Maybe it's not that easy."

"Come now." Lucien's voice was soft as he crouched before Jonathan.

"You're upset again. I do so enjoy the spark that flares in your eye when you talk about Eric."

"Lucien," Jonathan whispered, dropping the towel as he searched his master's face.

The Elder retrieved the towel and dabbed at Jonathan's chest. "For a long time, I had to imagine how marvelous Eric must be to infatuate you so." He folded the towel and placed it on the table. "No one else spurs such passion: not Endymion, not Alex…not even *me*. I expected to be disappointed when I met him, that my imagination would surpass the worldly beauty that had such a hold on you."

Jonathan sat up, holding his breath. "And?"

Lucien's eyes lifted to his face. "I wasn't disappointed." He caressed Jonathan's cheek and exhaled forcefully. "You fight the sins you must confess, while I am the one in denial."

"I don't know—"

Smoothing the back of his finger down Jonathan's throat, Lucien whispered, "You have a bond with Eric that transcends physical attraction, and I'm standing on that cusp with you now, trying to understand it. I must remain a coldhearted pillar, but with you, I…"

"Lucien," Jonathan whispered with anticipation. "What cusp? What are you saying?"

"I just want something that I can never have." There was a melancholy note in his quiet voice.

"But you can have anything you want." A pressure Jonathan didn't understand built within his chest. "This doesn't sound like you."

"Exactly." Lucien tossed the shirts into Jonathan's lap and stood. "So the Fallen were about to steal Eric's soul—"

"Wait!" Jonathan jumped up to catch Lucien's arm. "What were you trying to say?"

"Don't mistake a moment of weakness for anything more," Lucien said coldly, jerking away. "I am not a soft man and I never will be."

The words clutched Jonathan's heart in an icy grasp that froze him in place. The tight feeling around his heart shrank from the sting of rejection. He couldn't accept that. He wouldn't. His aura exploded with hot, livid anger.

For so long, he'd been restricted, constrained by the Nation's rules and Lucien's apathetic persona. But for a brief moment, he'd felt the nostalgia of their early years, when they'd reveled in killing and pleasure in near equal measure.

He glared at Lucien's squared shoulders and the silver hair that rigidly fell down his back. Before the War, Jonathan would've sidled over and brushed those silky strands aside to let his lips roam Lucien's neck and Lucien would've responded to him.

But that was then.

"Damn it, Lucien! I never saw you as a 'soft man.' Our lives are finally getting interesting again and you're withdrawing more than you did after the Treaty was signed!" Jonathan growled as he whisked the garments from the floor. "The only thing that's changed is the bureaucracy that *you* created. Stop hiding behind it!"

Lucien didn't move or reply.

Jonathan tugged on the undershirt. "You want to know why I'm so passionate about Eric? He's never boring! He's never kept secrets, he's trusted me when he shouldn't have, and he's talked with me even when he was angry with me. I have killed off his family and—no! Hell! I've tried to kill him! And still he talks to me, calls me his brother, and—"

Lucien peered over his shoulder with a suggestive, rounded cheek.

"What the hell are you smiling about?"

"The spark is back," Lucien said, resuming his stoic façade.

Jonathan threw his hands up and sat on the tatami mat. Huffing as he shoved his arms into the clean dress shirt, he shook his head and grumbled, "This is ridiculous."

"The Fallen were about to steal Eric's soul…"

"Yeah, yeah. And I wasn't going to let them have him." He paused to glare at Lucien's back again as he tugged his cuffs straight. "This is pointless. Even if you do need me, I'm not sure I want to be here."

"Jonathan," Lucien said in a quiet voice. "I do need you."

Buttoning his shirt, Jonathan grunted and sullenly said, "Once the collectors fled, I held Eric against my chest. In his eyes, I saw a void empty of faith edged by all the fear and sadness he'd withstood in life. He'd been valiant and strong through his bleakest moments, never giving into despair no matter how badly he wanted to—"

Lucien's aura stiffened. He grabbed the towel off the table without turning. "But?"

"Nothing." Jonathan watched Lucien dispose of the towel and wondered for the first time about the night Lucien saved Eric. Perhaps Paresh's blood had roared like a fire to melt Lucien's icy core. Perhaps it had plunged Lucien into as much chaos as he'd felt himself.

Keeping his thoughts to himself, Jonathan leaned back on his elbows and said, "Eric looked exactly like the man I'd envisioned. The light in his eyes was dimming, but something stopped me from tearing into his throat. It was like a calming peace, a moment of serenity that sated my thirst and snuffed my desire. I gave him a choice. Death or life."

Lucien knelt at the table. "You couldn't force his destiny on him."

"I suppose that's why I didn't keep him with me, as well, even though I'd wanted to watch his alteration. Suddenly, the thought of watching over a human filled me with disgust, so I took him home to his wife."

"Did you notice anything about the fetus inside her?"

"No. I was only with her long enough to command her to speak of his return to no one. I should have realized Gabriel would interfere: she didn't speak of Eric's return, but wrote of it in a letter to the Colonel."

Lucien chuckled to himself. "The Great Second Born, foiled by a human woman and her guardian angel." When he realized that Jonathan was staring at him, his smile thinned into a line. "What?"

"You laughed."

Lucien straightened his spine and let a slow breath pass through his nose. "How did you handle Eric's love for his wife?"

Studying the woven fibers in the tatami mat, Jonathan silenced the questions stacking up in his head. "I didn't. In fact, I didn't approach him again until the night he stole that bloody chicken."

Jonathan forced a smile and rolled his eyes. "There he was, the man I'd been feverish for, such a pathetic sight, clinging to a headless, half-plucked corpse as a lifeline. But then, I realized—he was alive, and *I* had changed him. He'd beaten me...*a human*. I both loathed and lusted for him.

"He was near a small ridge of trees wearing a bloodstained shirt and trousers. He was leaner than before, so his clothes were loose. Without human blood, his skin's pallor was dull and he reeked of vulnerability. I had to know—how would he control the beast? His hunger? Would his thirst drive him into the house for something better than a *chicken*?"

Rolling his eyes again, he met Lucien's emotionless gaze. "No. He fell to his knees as though he knew what he was. It seemed like resigned acceptance, not surprise or anger."

"A quiet, willful child with abilities that baffled even you—he was always different. He made his choice."

"He was obviously too weak to be a physical threat," Jonathan said. "But his power over me had never been physical. I was anxious as I looked into his blackened eyes. A stunning sliver of crystalline blue glistened there like the ice shines under the arctic moon. But, there was no spell to fall under. Our hierarchy was at work and I was his master."

Jonathan sighed.

"Or so I thought. Why did I expect Eric to be an ordinary fledgling? The more forceful my commands got, the more defiant he became. I held him on the ground laughing at his attempts to escape and told him he could never win. He'd made a vow. He belonged to me. But a fire burned in him that I couldn't understand. I may have altered him, but he still wasn't mine."

Stretching his arms overhead, Jonathan stood and moved toward the panel that led to Lucien's private courtyard, the largest in the arc. He slid the shoji screen open.

The soothing sounds of running water, croaking frogs, and the gentle, rhythmic clanking of a bamboo fountain greeted him as he stepped onto the deck. Down the steps, a stone path led to the pond where an elevated granite slab seemed to float. A low, blocky table sat upon it, flanked on each side by cushioned mats. A waterfall fed the pond, and beside it stood a cherry tree, brimming with showy white blossoms that never faded. Lace leaf Japanese maples in crimson and bright green wept before clusters of bamboo shooting up from the rocky landscape.

The first rays of a simulated sunrise beamed over the fence's caps. Jonathan's heart sank as he sat on the deck. "I wish the moon was out."

"It cannot always be night." Lucien appeared beside him, gracefully folding his kimono as he knelt. "The sun must rise."

They were quiet awhile. Waterfall aside, the only movement came from the koi as air bubbles rippled across the pond's mirrored surface. It was too still.

Jonathan uttered a directive. "Command code zero, zero, two, arc simulation adjust air effects ten knots."

Leaves began to rustle and small branches swayed. The cherry tree's petals loosened into a dainty flutter of spring snow, scattering a delicate perfume into the breeze. A dash of warmth brushed his cheeks as he inhaled the sweet aroma and the earthy scent of the pond's algae.

"You've disturbed Lady Rainne's morning meditation," Lucien said with a trace of humor.

"That amuses you?"

"You are particular about your environment."

"I'm entitled to what I want," Jonathan replied stubbornly.

"Generally, yes. But not always." Lucien's eyes were closed. He took in deep, even breaths with his chin raised to the breeze.

"I suppose not," Jonathan quietly conceded.

"What happened that night?"

"You already know."

Lucien silently waited.

Jonathan begrudgingly said, "Eric was so panicked; his pulse was pounding hard. I parted my lips to taste victory and felt his blood pulsating through my aura. I had to have him! I ripped open his shirt and he arched against me—"

Jonathan absently touched his cheek. "—and then I was up, screaming and clawing at my face like it'd been scorched by the sun."

Half expecting to see blistered skin and blood, Jonathan looked at his fingers. "He was wearing a cross! How? Why? *What made Eric Ravenscroft so damn special?*"

Dropping his hand to his lap, Jonathan said, "Eric wasn't mine. *And* he posed a great risk to us. I returned here bearing that holy mark."

"I remember."

"Then why?"

"A report is not the same as a confession. Now I know of the consuming desire you felt."

"Eric was there," Jonathan retorted. "It's hardly a confession."

"You aren't confessing to him."

Jonathan clenched his jaw. "Maybe I should be."

"No." Lucien took a deep breath and exhaled slowly. "So after you returned here, I requested that you bring him to me, at a time of his choosing, and to keep watch over him until then. I am sure you attempted to persuade him many times, correct?"

"Not at first," Jonathan grumbled. "I watched him for a while. When his wife died, anger gnawed on his heart and sent him back to the war that had destroyed him. He joined the Colonel and sated his thirst at last."

Grinning wickedly, Jonathan added, "And sate it he did."

"You find joy in that when you should feel regret?"

Lapsing silence lifted Lucien's empty eyes. "Well?"

"What regret?" Jonathan snapped. "I had nothing to do with it. He inherited my thirst. I wanted to see if he'd embrace his true nature or not. If things had gone differently, he might have returned with me then. Of course I'd find joy in that."

Lucien's gaze skimmed the courtyard. "Eric killed indiscriminately during the war, but he wasn't on the battlefield that night. He was fortunate I didn't convene the High Council to take action against him."

"Fortunate? You suspected what he was, even then." Jonathan followed Lucien's eyes to the sun rising over the far wall. "Maybe I found pleasure in it then, but Eric took innocent lives. If he hadn't regained control, his fate—and ours—would have changed forever."

"You grinned when you said it."

"What do you want from me?" Jonathan demanded, glaring at Lucien. "I feel physically sick for the pain I've caused Eric, but I refuse to be shamed for actions he took on his own. Maybe it's not something we'd think our Servator would do, but he did, and the person I was then enjoyed it. *You* would have enjoyed it. He was beautiful and calculated until the beast forced his human eyes to open."

Jonathan leaped up. "I'm sick of this. Being condemned for grinning at a memory and playing 'what ifs.'" He tugged the shoji screen open. "I told you I'm not going to change. The darkness in my heart belongs to Lucifer. How can I win against that?"

Lucien's quiet voice trailed him as Jonathan stormed inside. "If you truly believe that, I'd expect you to be in league with our enemy."

"Believe whatever you want," Jonathan retorted, crossing the central room and throwing open the screened entrance. As he grabbed his shoes, hurried footsteps crunched the rocky path beyond the gate.

A blond female in a crimson tunic and white capri pants burst through the gate and raced up the wooden steps. The urgency on her face, and the fact that she'd skipped VaSH protocol at Snowblood Square, seized Jonathan's heart in a vice.

He called to Lucien. "Something's wrong. Seneca is here."

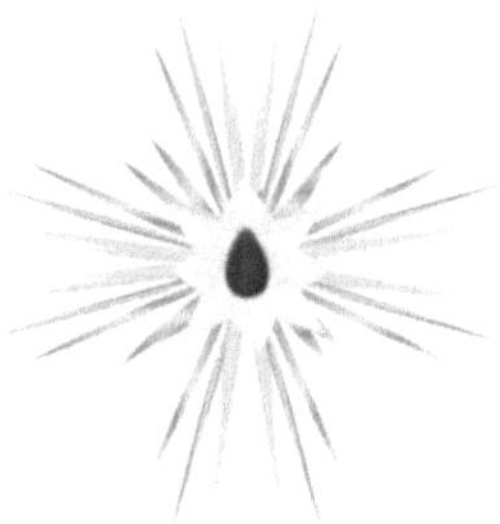

CHAPTER SEVEN: FROM DARKNESS

I

The silent vacuum was devoid of feeling. No rush of air. No tug of gravity. And yet, she fell. The starlit wings enveloping her body were so blindingly bright that only their white, feathery tips stood apart from the blackness. Her tears glittered like diamonds as they splashed the feathers trailing her descent into endless pitch.

A muffled, masculine voice travelled from some distance away, strange and warbled, as though distorted by time and space. She closed her eyes and focused all her energy on that voice. He was shouting…and he was angry. The voice faded and an image appeared that she could see only with her eyes shut.

A man and a woman were there, along with someone beyond her sightline. The scene sharpened to reveal a heated confrontation between the hidden person and a man with auburn hair tied back with a crimson ribbon.

"Master Jon!" she cried in a silent voice.

A flash of metal zipped out from the hidden person's hand followed by bloody spray. A crimson bloom rapidly grew on Jonathan's left side. Clutching the wound, he dropped to his knees.

"No! Master Jonathan! No! No…please! No!"

Darkness tunneled her peripheral vision.

"Please…don't!" She tried to reach out to Jonathan, to touch him, but he was too far away.

Jonathan looked up with a weak smile and fell forward on a blood-soaked palm as the scene faded into blackness. Back in the void, her voice came alive, shrill and shredded.

"No! Jonathan! Come back!"

She frantically clawed and kicked at the wings and the silent darkness. The more she fought, the tighter the embrace became.

"*No! Master Jon! Come back! Don't leave me alone!*"

"Paresh! Paresh! Stop!"

"No! He can't die! He can't!"

"*Paresh!*"

"No!" she wailed, hot liquid stinging her eyes. "*Master Jon!*"

"Paresh, open your eyes! Wake up! *Please, wake up!*"

Finally, the voice registered. A voice from home. A voice she loved. She opened her eyes.

"Eric!" Flinging her arms around his neck, she cried into his shoulder, "It—it was so awful! *Awful!*"

"Shh, it's okay, I've got you," he whispered, smoothing his hand over her hair. "You're safe now."

Holding her to his chest, he rocked back and forth until her sobs began to subside. She was quiet awhile before she sniffed and looked up.

Cupping her face, Eric stroked her cheek with his thumb. "What happened?"

Shaking her head, new tears welled. "I…I don't—"

"It's okay. It's okay." Eric kissed her forehead and pulled her close. "Donovan said you screamed and collapsed when you touched the tree."

"Collapsed? N-no, that's not—" Paresh swallowed hard. She shot an anxious look at Grandfather Wisdom. "That t-tree—"

"It's okay," Eric repeated. "Tell me what happened."

"A hole appeared in the trunk and a hand reached out. It tugged me inside. And then, I was falling through a large, black space that had no beginning and no end. Wings were around me. And then I saw…I saw Jonathan's—" She buried her face into the crook of Eric's neck, too scared to say it aloud.

"Raven." Though quiet, Eric's voice was firm. "Return to the cottage and contact Seneca with orders to check on Jonathan's welfare."

"Right away. Donovan—"

"Of course, ma'am. I won't leave her side." His voice was serious.

"I must have worried you so much," Paresh whispered.

"Now, now," Donovan said, stroking her hair. "We're here to take care of you."

She sniffed again and glanced at the hunter. Donovan gave her shoulder a gentle squeeze and smiled.

"He's right," Eric said. "And I know that Jonathan is at the arc right now where he's very well protected."

She blew out a shaky breath. "O-okay."

"Can you tell me what you saw?" Eric wiped away her tears. Concern filled his eyes.

"Someone stabbed him. There was a lot of blood and then he fell to his hands and knees."

"Did you see who did it?" Donovan asked.

She shook her head. "There was a woman there with light brown hair and someone else I couldn't see—that's who killed him."

"How many female VaSH hunters have light brown hair?" Eric asked Donovan.

"It's a boring color, so maybe a handful."

"Anyone on the Crimson Guard? Someone close to Alex?"

"She's not close to Alex, but is tight with Seneca: Minerva, the second-in-command when the Crimson Guard divides. Right now, with Seneca in command, Minerva is the acting First Officer and Co-Commander."

"Of the squad that failed to capture its Commander." Eric's voice was grim. "Anyone else?"

"A few others. Ariel and Anemone with the Chthonic Knights, but Anemone dyes her hair blue. Shareilia on the Silent Vespers and—" He closed his eyes in thought.

"Raven. Her natural color is brown." He quickly added, "Not that I think it's her."

"Nor I," Eric replied. "Paresh?"

She shook her head. "The woman had shoulder length hair, mussed up, not a bob."

"Hm." Donovan stroked his chin with his index finger. "There probably aren't many VaSH females that will match that. I'll contact Skyvania at the Arc of Mourning Eidolons to have her scan the ranks to see how many hits she gets from the Nation as a whole."

"Can she be trusted?" Eric asked.

"Oh yes. She is a sympathetic friend." Donovan touched Paresh's arm. "How do you feel?"

Paresh rested her head against Eric's shoulder. "I want to go home and sleep."

Eric tightened his hold. "Go ahead and close your eyes. I've got you."

As her eyelids lowered, she heard Donovan ask, "Do you think Alex was behind..."

His voice trailed off as exhaustion edged Paresh into her subconsciousness. The angry voice was there, shouting behind a shadowy veil, but she drifted beyond it into blissfully forgettable darkness. When she opened her eyes, she was still in Eric's arms, but he was sitting on the cottage steps, talking with Raven and Donovan.

"Hiya, sweetie," Raven said with a smile. "Sir Jonathan is well. Spitting fire, apparently, but well. Seneca saw him herself at Lord Lucien's quarters, so—"

"She didn't call on him from Snowblood Square?" Donovan asked. "She can't enter Lord Lucien's residence."

"She did as ordered. Don't concern yourself." Raven looked Paresh over. "Do you feel better?"

"A little, I think. And that's good news."

"We'll return to my place tonight," Eric told Raven. "What about you two?"

"We're with you." Raven swept her hand toward the carriage house and Eric's car. "Shall we?"

Eric contemplated her for a moment. "You and Donovan scout ahead on foot. We will follow—"

"Wait a sec," Paresh interrupted. "Before I fell asleep, Donovan asked if Alex was responsible. Didn't they arrest him? Shouldn't we be okay?"

Sharing a gloomy look with Raven, Eric shook his head. "They missed him. Jonathan gave Alex permission to investigate the use of his squad's dagger. He left straight from the meeting, so Jonathan didn't know anything until he saw Seneca waiting for him."

"Does that mean he's here? *Alex. Is here?*" Paresh felt panic nesting in her gut. The forest seemed black again, with shadows waiting to leap out and grab her. "No, no…"

Eric's jaw bulged at the hinge. He and Raven stared at each other with an intensity that distorted the air.

Without turning, Raven said, "Donovan, scout ahead of us and do a thorough perimeter check at Eric's house. Go now."

"As you command." Bowing to Eric and Paresh, Donovan disappeared down the flagstone into the forest's inky swell.

"I will stay close to the car," Raven said to Eric. "Donovan and I will maintain contact, and can regroup at any point."

Nodding his approval, Eric replied, "Give us a moment. Wait at the carriage house."

"As you wish," Raven said with a reverent nod. "The button is active, if you'd like privacy. I'll check on you in ten minutes."

"Very well."

Eric carried Paresh into the master suite. The disc flashed blue when he closed the door, prompting a quizzical look from her.

"It's the sound barrier Raven put up earlier," he explained.

Eric laid her on the bed and hovered above her, smoothing her hair and gliding his finger around the curve of her ear. "I was so scared I was going to lose you again," he whispered. "I wish I could take your pain away as easily as you take mine."

Holding his hands against her cheeks, she mumbled, "I love you."

He touched his forehead to hers and closed his eyes. "And I, you."

"What else is wrong?"

He sighed. "Something Lucien said has me thinking about what happened at the tree."

"Am I going to see horrible things every time I touch it?" She whispered the question with an involuntary shiver.

"I don't know," Eric said, sitting up and brushing his fingers through her hair. "That tree is special. I've always felt at peace there, but you changed it—made it better—when you were a child."

"I remember," she said with a soft smile. "It was always tranquil there, but when we were together, it was like being tucked into my parents' bed on a snowy day with the fire going, or lying in grass warmed by the sun beneath a crisp sky dotted with white, puffy clouds."

"Like home?"

"Like home."

"But only when we're together." Eric's hand paused. "Lucien said it's a spiritual nexus that you'll feel anywhere as long as we're together, but it will always be strongest here, because it opened at the moment of your birth. That's what makes this place feel like home."

"I remember. You told me after they left that night."

Eric's fingers resumed their journey through her hair. "Yes, but I think there's more to it. I think Gabriel is watching over you and communicating using the tree."

"Then why do I always see death? Why can't I see something good, like you, or our future together?"

"This *is* our future. We've been thrown into the center of a millennia-old war. Maybe Gabriel is offering you a chance to change things."

Paresh sat up. "The first time, I saw my death and I couldn't change that. I was supposed to die."

Eric wiped his brow at an apparent loss for words. Paresh hugged his arm and leaned her cheek on his shoulder. "Maybe Gabriel's preparing me for what's to come."

Tears welled in her eyes. "I don't want Jonathan to die."

"I'll do everything I can to ensure his safety. I promise." Eric caught her tears before they rolled down her cheeks. "How about if we go—"

His cell phone rang. Glancing at the display, he muttered, "Speak of the Devil."

He held the phone open at Paresh's ear. She hesitantly asked, "Master Jon?"

"Pare!" Jonathan sounded relieved. "Are you all right?"

"Oh thank God!" Paresh cried, grabbing the phone. "I was so scared!"

"You shouldn't worry about me," Jonathan replied. "I'm fine. You're the one we must protect."

"Everyone keeps saying that—"

"Because it's the truth." Jonathan quieted. "You are important to us—to Eric—and to me. Do you understand?"

She nodded and smudged new tears as she stifled a sniffle and croaked, "I miss you."

"I miss you, too, Pare. We'll see each other soon," Jonathan said. "Right now, I need to talk to Eric, okay?"

Paresh nodded again. "'Kay." As she handed the phone to Eric, there was a knock at the door.

"My lord? It's been ten minutes," Raven said from the other side.

"Lord?" Paresh asked Eric, confused as he waved off the phone and went to the door to check in with Raven.

Paresh put the phone back to her ear. "He'll be back in a sec. Promise me you'll take care of yourself."

"I will, Pare. Cross my heart," Jonathan replied.

"*And hope to die, Second Born?*" Paresh asked in a suddenly musical voice that was as beautiful as it was unnatural. "*Do not forget. You are a bridge between this girl and her Anointed Strength; your life is more important than you know. I am your judge and I am watching. You must try harder.*"

II

Paresh offered a tired smile in response to Eric's wide-eyed shock as she handed him the phone. Before he could speak, she said, "I'm pretty sure you're right about the tree."

She swung her legs over the side of the bed and leaned on her hands with her head hanging between her shoulders. Exhaustion hemorrhaged from her aura. Eric wondered when it had gotten so bad. He was surprised she could keep her eyes open.

"Jonathan, hold on." He dropped the phone on the nightstand and offered his hands. When she took them, he felt her siphon his energy.

"I know I'm the 'Vessel' and all," Paresh said, "but being hijacked by Gabriel? I can't take anymore tonight."

Eric tucked her close and flooded energy into his aura for her. "Do you want to wait with Raven in the living room while I finish up?"

She nodded and shuffled toward the door. The button flashed blue when the door closed behind her.

Eric grabbed the phone and sighed.

"How is she, really?" Jonathan asked.

"Not well. She's trying to hide her pain, but the attacks come several times a day, and her memories are…terrifying. She had a panic attack with Donovan on the way to see Grandfather Wisdom—"

"Which gave her a delightful vision, I hear," Jonathan interrupted, sounding concerned for the first time in Eric's life.

"She was hysterical when she woke up…and I…I couldn't do anything for her," Eric replied, sinking onto the bed. He absently ran his hand through his hair. "She's beyond exhausted. We're going back to my house tonight. She doesn't want to be here."

"I'm worried about her."

"You aren't the only one."

"Can you still entrance her?"

"I'll try if she can't sleep tonight."

In the silence that followed, Eric listened to Paresh describing Molly to Raven until Jonathan said, "She's in the final stage of alteration. Solid food won't sustain her, and her bones can't produce enough blood to replenish what she uses. You know what this means."

"Yes." Eric rose and stared out the window. The moon hung low over the canopy. "She's having trouble with it."

"She needs to do it or she'll get worse."

The intensity in Jonathan's voice warmed the cold spot he occupied in Eric's heart. "I know. Have you made any progress on your end?"

"No, unfortunately. Any sign of Alex?"

"Not yet. Raven sent Donovan ahead as a scout. Why did Lucien reassign her hunters? We could use them here."

"What's this? The fearless Eric Ravenscroft wants more vampires in his precious little town?"

"There's the Jonathan I know," Eric said dryly. "I knew he'd appear sooner or later."

"No…" Jonathan's voice trailed into something that resembled sadness. "I share your concern. Lucien put the Wraith Reapers and

Crimson Guard on security detail. Raven and Donovan were assigned to you and Paresh, and her hunters and a portion of the Crimson Guard are guarding specific Elders as they would during Winter Solitude."

"Why can't someone relieve the Wraith Reapers so they can regroup?"

"Lucien wanted them specifically. I don't know why and——"

"It's not your place to question his order?" Eric demanded. "Because apparently it is, *now*."

"I trust his reasons and we both have faith in Raven and Donovan's abilities."

Eric clenched his teeth and growled. "If anything happens to Paresh——"

"I will not allow it," Jonathan replied. "Anyone who lays a hand on her will not survive the consequences. I will see to it myself."

"You'll be behind me, I guarantee it."

"I wish I had opened my eyes earlier to see you as you truly are," Jonathan said.

"What is that supposed to mean?"

"That you've been exactly what I wanted all along and I never sa——"

"I thought we were past all this," Eric spat.

"I don't mean it like that." Jonathan sounded remorseful. "I should've seen you for what you are instead of something to possess, that's all."

"Oh."

"Eric?"

"Yes?"

"I've been talking to Lucien…"

"Yes?"

"Do you remember that night? In the Confederate camp?"

A chill trickled down Eric's spine. "*What?*"

"I was there. I saw what you did."

The fire of anger sparked everywhere at once. "Of course I remember it!" Eric snarled. "*It's not something I'll ever forget!*"

An awkward silence fell between them. The hall clock seemed overwhelmingly loud in contrast to the women's soft voices.

"What in Hell's name does that have to do with anything?" Eric growled. "You don't bring that up and then——"

"You thought you'd kept it hidden from me all this time. It must be difficult to learn that someone else knows your other darkest secret."

"Damn it, Jonathan!" Eric swore. "I'm finished with your games!"

"No games! I…" Jonathan's voice faded. "Can't you see I'm not like that anymore?"

"I find it hard to believe that you'll ever change."

An anxious sigh passed through the earpiece. "I need perspective—advice—from you. You understand me, my thirst. I know it because I saw it, that night."

Eric fumed in silence.

"So tell me why?" Jonathan asked in a quiet voice. "They were your enemies in war. Why didn't you kill them all?"

☽ ☀ ☾

Moonlight sifted through the clouds and the naked forest. If he were human, the night would seem calm and quiet. But, with his new body, alone in silver-limned darkness, it went beyond the winter night's air whistling through the Virginian forest. It was the rippling creek at the camp's southern edge, magnified until he felt icy waters on his feet. The whinnying horses, whose nervous cries had become relieved sighs at his absence. Every discussion, each uttered word, traveling clearly to his ears as though he sat amongst the Colonel's men as they ate meager meals of hardtack and beans around fires that crackled with such clarity he visualized every popping ember.

He'd buried Lucinda a week ago. Then joined the Colonel and returned to a life he'd lived for years. But, everything had changed. Every day was a struggle. The pulse of the camp called to something hidden within him. Something dark and instinctive—a hungry beast that clawed at his heart and veins, demanding to be sated.

Relief only came by concentrating on the auditory wealth of his surroundings. On anything but that pulse. For hours that night, he'd lain in his tent, identifying sounds to distract his mind and hone his senses. Then the scratching of pen against paper had conjured an image of a featureless man in nightdress scrawling a letter home. In that unknown soldier, he'd seen himself, pen in hand, hunched over his prose with hair falling into his eyes. For three years, he'd written to his beloved at every opportunity, comforted by the memory of her face and the worn letters beneath his pillow each night.

No matter how long his life lasted, he would never see her again.

He had risen with a mournful sigh and set off on foot to clear his mind. He'd been walking for twenty minutes and the sounds of camp were still sharp. He trudged deeper into the forest until the sounds finally faded.

If only escaping memory was as easy.

Men in his previous unit had spoken about how distance and time stole all but the basic features of their wives' faces, and others claimed no memory at all. He'd felt fortunate to remember the afternoon sun shining like gold in Lucinda's hazel eyes, the way her lips curved up more on one side when she smiled, and how her chocolate-brown hair twisted the wrong way despite her efforts to train it otherwise.

Now, he only saw her lifeless eyes and his dead son slumped on her breasts. Time had trapped him at her side where the midwife's urgency and his own desperation had charged the air as blood pooled at their feet.

He welcomed amnesia.

Leaning against a tree, he closed his eyes. It was quiet. For a long time, he stayed there, observed only by the crescent guardian of night, wishing this moment of solitude could soothe his grieving soul.

Then the cold breeze carried something decisively out of place—whispers. They were faint, far ahead of him.

Haunted by Lucinda's deathly countenance, he walked toward them, making no sound on the dead undergrowth. Other noises filtered in behind the whispers. The Confederates had set camp on the forest's opposite edge and sent two soldiers to scout for enemy camps—much as he had done with his unit prior to his "death."

Anger churned his sorrow into a pillaging fire that demanded retribution. The beast was awake. Lucinda's dull, empty eyes lifted from their bloody son and beseeched him to contain it. Her lips parted, but out came an evil sound that twisted her face into that of the smirking, auburn-haired demon. His blackened eyes stole the air from Eric's lungs and ripped away part of his soul forever.

He fell against a thick oak, trying to force the image away and catch his breath. But the barrage worsened as the scouts drew closer. Each drawled sentence fueled uncontrollable flames. Clutching at the beast's vice-like grip on his heart, he squeezed his eyes shut. Violent chills rocked his body. Dizziness crashed in merciless relentless waves.

A human-shaped shadow crossed the blue-hued ground. Images flashed in his mind. The slaughter of his comrades in Arkansas. The Confederates who'd refused to take prisoners in this so-called "gentleman's war." Men who had killed only to kill. The Confederacy had sent him home to watch his wife and child die. These scouts were a mockery to his very existence.

His cheeks tingled and pressure mounted behind his teeth. This time he relinquished control—his body wanted it, craved it. Something within him finally felt alive again.

Pressure gathered in the hinge of his jaw, as though the bone itself was stretching like taffy. He squeezed his eyes shut and slid to the ground. His canines descended and sharp points dipped behind his lower lip. As the pain faded, he opened his eyes to a new world. The colorless void of night was gone. It was like a cloudless day at noon—awash in crimson.

Strength surged throughout his being. Sounds were crisper. The soldiers' hearts pounded against his eardrums. He could count their breaths. Shadows were a bare whisper. The edge of a gun poked around one tree. The sliver of an arm appeared behind another. He could smell their adrenaline and taste their sweat. Both made him hungry.

The tree's bark cracked under his hand as he shoved off. Feeling completely unlike himself, he stepped into their path and relished the way each snapping twig made their pulses quicken. They ducked behind trees before they came within view, but he knew where they were.

Metal slid against leather as a soldier pulled his gun from its holster.

An unearthly energy he'd felt once before surged around him. He expected to see the smirking auburn devil, but it was only him and the soldiers. The energy swelled from within, flooding him with power and a desire for blood. He stopped in plain sight.

The men jumped out. The left held a revolver, and the other, a Sharps carbine rifle. "Get your hands up!" yelled Revolver.

A wicked grin stretched across Eric's face as he raised his hands and continued his approach. "They're up."

"Hold it right there!" yelled Rifle.

Eric laughed. The foreign and devilish sound visibly shook both men.

Revolver cocked the hammer. "Something funny, boy?"

Eric made a wide arc with his arms. "This is a beautiful night." He shot them an unsettling smile. The strange energy charged them.

They dropped their guns. Their fear leeched out as choked gurgles. Rifle's pants darkened in the crotch.

"Hmph," Eric grunted, standing before them. "You call yourselves soldiers? I am but one man and you fall apart?"

Grabbing Revolver by the throat, Eric whispered into his ear, "You can cock your gun to take a life but can't face death? Scum like you doesn't deserve to live!"

Eric snarled and bit into Revolver's jugular. Satisfied moans vibrated his vocal cords. The warm flesh cushioning his teeth was as addictive as the nectar rushing over his tongue.

He snagged Rifle by the collar before the coward could flee. Blood dripped from Eric's chin as he dropped Revolver, who landed with a dull *thud.*

"I was a sergeant once," Eric said in an icy voice. "Shot my own men in the back for running. You wouldn't be the first deserter I've killed."

He stared into Rifle's eyes until they became empty pools of mud. "But you only kill to kill."

"Kill to kill," Rifle repeated in monotone.

"Worthless. Every last one of you." Eric rolled his eyes, which returned conscious thought to Rifle. "Will you beg for your life, you pathetic Confederate?

Terror trained Rifle's eyes on Eric's bloodstained mouth and held his answer captive.

"No matter." Disgust twisted Eric's words. "Why should I afford you an opportunity you don't see fit for your enemy?"

Eric arched his brow at the man's pants. "Your bladder is weak, but your heart is strong."

He yanked on Rifle's collar and plunged into his throat. When he was finished, the man's corpse formed an unnatural puddle next to Revolver.

"*Pitiful!*" Eric screamed, kicking them both in the ribs. "I died at the hands of cowards like you!"

Animalistic growls echoed off the trees. Bark exploded as he smashed his fist into a maple's trunk, staring at the corpses, simmering with rage. They had stolen his life, taken him from everything he loved, from everyone who had loved him. There was nothing left for him. Not even death.

He threw both bodies far into the forest and faced the sky with closed eyes. New strength coursed through every muscle. His body sang to the night. He wanted more.

The clatter of their camp was sharper now. There were so many of them. He wondered if he could kill them all. Or, if they could kill him. He grinned. "Fine either way."

The stench of their latrine hit his nose long before he saw their campfires or the first row of crimson-tinted tents. He strolled into camp, lifting his arms to the sky.

"I am a rarity in this world," he announced.

Soldiers scrambled to their feet, cursing and shouting warnings to each other. Eric stopped before a terrified cluster of men ensnared by his aura. He licked the blood drying on his lips and winked. "I want a fight, so you have to wait."

Turning, he faced the men rallying their guns behind him. He pointed at each one, briefly distracted by the length of his blade-like claws. Studying his hands, he said, "I am honorable enough to give you fair warning and a fighting chance, but I'm hardly a gentleman. Run away, like the cowards you are, or stay and die, like the fools you are. Either way, it's more than I was ever affor—"

A shot rang out.

Black powder hit his nose before the lead ball pierced his skin. It burned, but hardly hurt. A vermilion flower rapidly bloomed on his white shirt. Pushing his finger through the hole in the fabric, he felt his soft tissues working the metal to the surface as the wound healed.

He shook with laughter as he held the projectile between his fingers and dropped it. He charged the shooter, grabbing him beneath the jaw with one hand while the other shoved down on his collarbone.

Chilling screams ripped through the night as the shooter's skin stretched taut over veins and arteries, and tendons and muscles, and tore like fabric at the seam as bones snapped beneath the surface. A collective cry ran through the terrified camp when Eric bit into the shooter's throat. And then…everything went stagnant.

Eric licked his lips and squeezed the shooter's throat until the man's head drooped at an unnatural angle. Dropping the corpse, Eric coldly spat, "You, on the other hand, have no honor." His gaze shifted to the others. "And you, as well, are not gentlemen."

A group of five men, clad in long johns and varied attempts at proper dress, recovered from their shock and rushed him, lashing fists and feet. Eric caught one by the waist and thrust him backward into a fire. One flew over his head and landed on his neck with a sickening crunch. Eric tossed a third high into the air. Horrid, unnatural shrieks accompanied the thud of the soldier's body landing as his femur snapped in half and skewered his thigh in a spray of blood.

Grabbing the throats of the remaining two, Eric flashed his teeth. One man whimpered.

"You are weak!" Eric growled. "Those who fight in war should be prepared to die!"

He heartlessly crushed their windpipes and dropped them. They writhed on the ground, clawing at their throats as they suffocated.

"You pitiful wretches! I'll kill you all!" Eric screamed, swiping the air with his daggered claws. Most men had backed away. Some still had guns pointed at him.

"Cowards. Aiming at an unarmed man. Ha!" Lunging, he yelled, "I barely had a chance to shoot the men who killed me. You'd better be quick on the trigger!"

Forming a spear tip with his fingers, he killed the closest man with a fatal blow to the heart. The men to either side fell to the ground with their organs spilling from jagged gashes across their bellies. The last man dropped his gun and put his hands on his head. The chevrons on his jacket were the same as the ones Eric had worn.

"N-no! P-please!" the sergeant pleaded, falling to his knees, curling his fists at the base of his throat.

"I was once like you, but begging didn't do my men any good." Eerily calm, Eric's voice clashed with his hungry stare. "They were ambushed. Massacred. The wounded? Shot in the head. Mutilated. Scalped by your sympathetic forces. They were better off playing dead than trying to escape."

Eric moved to grab the sergeant's throat. A halo of fiery white light enveloped the hapless sack's entire body, so blindingly bright it forced Eric to back away, and put the man out of his reach.

As the halo faded into a faint glow, Eric seethed. The beast wanted to bathe in the blood of every man there. It roared within him, *Tear them all to pieces!*

"What are you holding onto?" Eric growled. "Show it to me! Now!"

Fighting against the beast's urges, Eric snatched the object from the sergeant's hands. It was a golden locket.

"Angela!" the sergeant cried, feebly reaching for the trinket.

A black and white photograph of a young woman smiled at Eric when he opened it. Her blond curls slowly loosened into dark waves that twisted the wrong way at the part, and her thin smile grew fuller and curved up higher on one side. Her small, round eyes stretched into large, honey-glazed almonds that shone like the sun.

Eric's heart skipped a beat. "Lucinda?"

A loosely formed mist rose from the locket and materialized before him as a ghostly embodiment of the woman he loved. She stood intimately close and stroked his cheek, her fingers tender and soft, like he remembered. Feather-light lips dusted his mouth.

He dropped the locket.

"I love you, my darling," Lucinda whispered, her fingers tracing the chain around his neck to the cross pendant. "But this isn't you. Eric Ravenscroft is stronger than the beast."

She pulled the cross from beneath his shirt and held it out in her hand. "You must have faith, my love, my husband, dearest Eric."

The instant he reached out to her, he jerked back, yelping. She was as hot as a boiling kettle. His eyes widened at the cross-shaped burn on his palm, black like a brand. The holy trinket was made from wood; how had it done that?

"This becomes the beast," Lucinda said, nodding at the mark. "Not my husband." She gestured for him to take the cross from her hand.

Clenching his jaw, he hesitantly reached out again.

"This becomes the Flock. You must decide your path." Lucinda's smile was a ray of light that cut the darkness and silenced the blood-thirsty beast.

Instead of burning him, the cross sparked an internal fire that razed his anger and lifted peace from the ashes.

Lucinda's smile stretched into her eyes. Plump tears fell upon her cheeks. "I love you, my darling."

He reached for her hand, but she was as thin as air. As she mouthed goodbye, her form reverted to mist and streamed into the locket.

As though the golden piece was playing a recorded memory, Eric saw the sergeant in full dress with a sack in one hand, hanging his head to hide his tears. The woman closed her eyes and bid the sergeant farewell with a loving kiss, and then turned away to hide her own tears. Both knew they might never see each other again. It was a familiar scene. Lucinda had worn the same expression during his departures.

"Who is she?" Eric asked quietly, retrieving the locket from the ground. Lucinda's face was no longer there, only the smile of the sergeant's woman.

"A-Angela. M-my wife," the sergeant stuttered, scurrying away from Eric's approach.

Looking up from his bloodstained fingers, Eric surveyed the camp. Everyone—living and dead—wore either a faint, white halo or a dusty, black cloud. The force in the light was warm, like his wife, while the darkness exuded hate, as he had moments ago.

He contemplated Angela's photograph. Lucinda was right. He was a man, and a good one at that, not a barbaric beast using revenge to sate its thirst. They were all casualties of war, in one sense or another, whether alive or not, and that had nothing to do with losing his wife and son, or the fate he had chosen for himself.

Turning on his heel, Eric tossed the locket to the sergeant. "Give your men proper burials. It looks like I am a gentleman after all."

☽ ✳ ☾

"The war saved me that night," Eric said. "Each soldier was prepared to kill and to die, but there is a difference in killing for a cause and killing in cold blood. I had a choice: succumb to the beast and become a monster, or empower my humanity and fight for morality. My destiny may have been determined at birth, but I had to decide my fate, and that critical moment showed me where the paths led."

"A choice," Jonathan replied. "It always comes down to that with them, doesn't it?"

"I hope this helps you, Brother."

"I won't tell Paresh." Jonathan's voice barely registered.

"I appreciate that."

"Eric?"

"Yes?"

"Do you think there's hope for me?"

Eric paused before answering. "We all make mistakes. Hope and forgiveness exist for everyone. No amount of darkness can swallow the light of truth to hide what you seek."

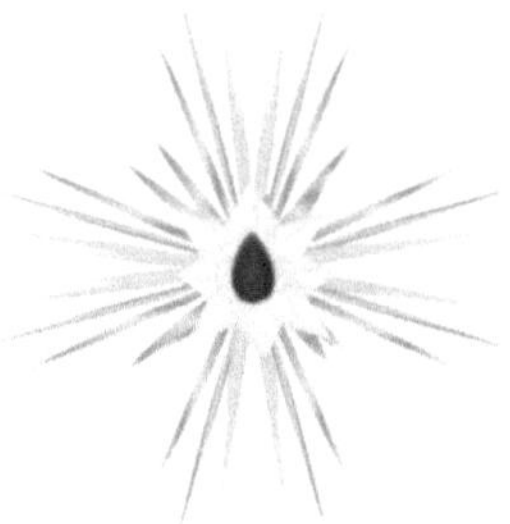

Chapter Eight: A Crimson Shadow

I

A shudder ran through her. Her breath was warm and uneven against his throat, and her aura raked his bare skin with unseen, lightning-hot claws.

Squeezing her eyes shut, Paresh whispered, "I can't!"

"Try again." Eric skimmed her ear with his lips.

She hesitantly parted her mouth. Desire and hunger flooded her aura as her breaths came faster. Her nails dug into his back. Her thighs tightened around his waist.

"You can do this," he urged, gently holding her head in place with her teeth against his throat.

"Feel the heat on your lips," he coaxed. "My pulse on your teeth. It's there, right there, waiting for you."

"No," she whimpered. Her aura shifted, cold and rigid, as she wiggled out of his grasp. "I can't! Please, don't make me!"

"Shh…it's okay. It's okay." Eric kissed her with each whispered assurance.

She fell back against the pillow and clung to him. She nervously rubbed her forehead. "I'm sorry."

"It's okay." Eric caressed her cheek, thankful that she couldn't see his face to know that it really wasn't—not with fully formed fangs and her levels of weakness and fatigue.

Hunger pangs, achy joints, and muscle spasms were inevitable—and the least of his worries. Her immune system was losing its battle against Lucien's lethal protein. Her nerves and connective tissues would deteriorate, and that would kill her faster than starvation.

"How do you feel?" he asked.

"Better." She traced his collarbone with her fingers. "Being with you and touching you makes me better."

"Siphoning my energy will give you a boost for now." He planted a kiss on the tip of her nose. "The rest will come naturally."

Sliding her tongue along her fangs, she stared into the blackness beyond his head. "I suppose."

Stroking her hair, he said, "It *will* get easier. When the time comes, you'll want to do it."

"I believe you." Her smile seemed forced and tired. She nodded at the door. "We should get up. Molly will be in for a shock if we don't catch her first."

"It's a bit early, yet." He withdrew from her and lay on the bed beside her. "I promised you could sleep in."

"Mm." Paresh rolled onto her side and tucked in close. She twisted the sheet around her fist and pulled the fabric up to her chest. "I wish we never had to get out of bed."

Grinning, Eric dropped his gaze to the plump swell of ivory above the sheet. He tapped her hand down to reveal her breast. As he murmured his agreement into kisses trailing down her neck, the barrier's absolute quiet reminded him of the vampire hunters in his house. He had no idea what was happening beyond his bedroom door.

II

The house always felt abandoned. Too still and too dim, with a hollowness that amplified noises and riled the darkness. She set her keys down on the media table and cringed at the loud *clack!* She focused on the only light seeping in over the sink, where stained glass washed the kitchen blood red. The shadows seemed undisturbed.

She sighed and plucked Eric's jacket off the ottoman. She folded it over her arm. The house was too quiet. Eric rarely slept and was usually in the shower when she arrived. After a night spent wrestling more with her sheets than sleep, she'd awoken and left earlier than usual. If not for the car in the garage, she might've thought he'd stayed at the cottage.

She smoothed her hand across the black fabric draping her arm and lifted her lips in a smile befitting the crimson tinted blackness. Until dinner the night before, Molly had thought Paresh emerged from her ordeal emotionally unscathed, but she would slap her hand on a Bible and swear in court that the air around the girl had grown colder after Eric suggested going to the cottage.

Paresh's reaction made Eric's irises darken, and that made Molly realize that her meager words of support were useless. How could a simple human help divine beings face a world beyond comprehension?

With a troubled huff, she tossed his jacket over the back of the sofa and sat on the arm. She loved them both dearly, but Eric was her family and she hated to see him worried.

No matter the role, I hope I'm in the future awaiting you, she thought, slumping into another sigh.

"My! What a solemn sound from such a pretty lady."

Jumping up, Molly whirled around to the source of the jovial, masculine voice. Her heart pounded the breath from her lungs as a form shimmered near the kitchen barstools and slowly materialized.

A man appeared, tall and slender, dressed all in black with shirtsleeves pushed up to his elbows. Dark eyes glinted against pale skin as he flaunted a smile of unnaturally long teeth and stepped toward her.

"You're early." He glanced at his wrist even though he wasn't wearing a watch.

Backing away from the man she knew to be a vampire, she stumbled and landed on the ottoman. Paralyzed by his inhuman beauty and mesmerized by his lustrous eyes, she could only gape at him as he knelt before her, took her hand, and sniffed her wrist.

"Charmed to meet you, *Molly*." He flipped her hand and kissed the backside. "I take it you've never met a true blood before?"

An iridescent sheen flashed across the surface of his hooded eyes. When her heart skipped a beat in response, he grinned. Pressing her palm against his cheek, he said, "I'm as real and harmless as your Eric."

Feeling the firm structure of his face under skin smoother than she'd ever touched, she heard herself whispering, "Who are you?"

"Aha!" Leaping back, the vampire folded down to one knee in an eloquent bow and announced in a hearty voice, "So glad you asked! I am Donovan, First Officer of the Wraith Reapers, sent on express order from our eternal lord to protect our fair maiden!"

"Do excuse his flair for the dramatic. My First Officer loves an audience." The feminine voice was dry in tone and came from the shadowy hallway. "'The world is a stage' is his daily mantra."

Molly slid off the ottoman and backed up until she hit the door. Pressing her palm to her chest, she stuttered, "T-two? Eternal l-lord? Wh-what's going on?"

Donovan faced the disembodied voice. "Well?"

"No answer when I knocked. He must have the button fully activated and I'm not going to barge in on them."

"*What is going on here?*" Molly demanded.

"We were to stay cloaked until Eric apprised her of the situation." The woman's voice now came from a glimmering shadow near the dining table.

Donovan flashed a smile at Molly. "Oh come on, you know I have a weakness for pretty ladies, Raven."

"Tsk." The shadow sighed as it formed into a young woman. She, too, wore all black, distinctly more militaristic and less casual—her pocketed jacket hugged the swell of her breasts and her cargo pants disappeared into combat boots. Bobbed hair shone like a pink halo and the same shadow piercing quality graced cornflower blue eyes.

"I must ask, once again, that you excuse him." The woman rolled her eyes and shot an agitated look Donovan's way. She walked over to the lamp on the media table. "Perhaps we have worked together too long."

Donovan swatted the air. "Now, now, Goody Raven, if that were true, you'd have much more realistic expectations of me."

The woman yanked the pull chain. In the light of the single bulb, she approached Molly with an extended hand. "I'm Raven Hawkings, this joker's Commander. It's an honor to make the acquaintance of anyone in Eric's high esteem."

Interpreting the slight tilt of Raven's head as a sign of respect, Molly hesitantly shook her hand. "Molly Sims." She glanced at Donovan, who had jumped up to sit on the bar-height countertop. "Are Eric and Paresh in danger?"

"Not anymore," Donovan announced, swinging his legs.

"You're taking my order too far! Knock it off!" Raven ruffled her hair and grumbled, "He barely follows my orders on a good day."

Molly was still holding Raven's hand. Flustered, she let go and fidgeted with her glasses. "I-I don't understand."

"There's a potential threat against them," Raven said.

Molly grabbed the doorframe for support and squeezed her eyes shut. "You mean after the other night. And Bill. They're still…*what?*"

"You poor thing." Raven gathered Molly together and guided her to the armchair. "I don't know what I can tell you."

"Eric tells me everything." Molly glanced from Raven to Donovan.

"So you know he died a few nights ago?" Donovan looked down his nose to judge her reaction. "Killed by *the* Devil?"

Irritation blazed in Raven's eyes until she saw Molly nod. "I see, then. And do you know what the implications of that are?"

Again, Molly nodded. "Eric descends from what you consider noble blood and he's part of what's going to save your race. The Servator?"

"Ah!" Leaping down, Donovan clapped his hands. "You are so feisty and delightful!"

"Stand down," Raven ordered. "She isn't like us. Give her a moment."

"I meant no disrespect," Donovan said, pouting as he eased onto a barstool. "It's rare to find such an interesting human, you know."

To Molly, Raven said, "Protocol dictates how we treat our nobles, but, knowing Eric as you do, it shouldn't surprise you that he and Paresh requested that we—"

"'Lighten up,' I believe was your order, right, Goody?" Donovan quipped with a smile.

"—address them casually," Raven finished tightly. "So I advised my First Officer to act at ease, which he is quite delighted to do."

Molly stared at Raven a moment. "Okay, I understand that. But this 'potential threat,' it…it involves Bill's death, doesn't it?"

Raven sat across from Molly on the ottoman. "Aye."

"Molly?" Eric's worried voice bellowed down the hall an instant before his bare-chested form jogged into the room. "You're so early today." He knelt before her, taking her hands in his, searching her eyes.

"I couldn't sleep."

"I should've called you last night," Eric said.

"It's okay." Molly squeezed his fingers. "You and Paresh are safe."

He contemplated her before nodding. "Raven and Donovan have treated you well?"

"Oh yes," she replied. "It's been interesting."

"What have they told you?"

"That they're here to protect you and Paresh because of Bill's death."

"Yes. Yes, that's right," Eric said. "Just in case, I'd like you to stay with Paresh until this is resolved. Raven and Donovan will keep you safe, too."

Raven's fist thudded against her chest. "As you command, of course."

Donovan nodded somberly, apparently less at ease in Eric's presence.

"What about Walter?" Molly asked.

"You know his pride." Eric shook his head. "I've made him aware of the risks. That's all I can do."

"Good morning, everyone." Tying the sash of a pale blue silk robe, Paresh smiled at Donovan and Raven as she walked over to Eric and Molly. She pulled the older woman up into a hug.

"Don't worry," Paresh said. "Eric will do what he can to protect Walter."

"Oh Paresh." Molly patted the girl's back. "You're such a sweetheart.

You have the weight of the world on your shoulders and here you are comforting me."

"How do you feel this morning?" Donovan asked quietly, his eyes fixed on the table.

As Eric and Raven both looked up for the girl's answer, the air around them changed—charged with nervous anticipation.

Paresh didn't seem to notice. Her hands dropped to her sides as she smiled at Donovan. "Better. Thank you."

"What happened?" Molly asked, unsuccessfully trying to catch Paresh's hand as she turned away.

"I had a nightmare," Paresh replied, heading for the kitchen.

In the silence that followed, Molly studied the others' ashen-hued faces, each as unreadable as stone as they watched Paresh paw through the refrigerator. They seemingly hadn't expected that answer. Molly wondered if Paresh was lying to her, to them, or to all of them.

Forcing a smile and swallowing her worry as she had done for so many years with Eric, Molly joined Paresh in the kitchen. "You didn't eat much at dinner. Let me fix you breakfast."

"Thanks, Molly." Paresh took an apple from the crisper drawer and glanced at Raven. "Did Alex appear last night?"

"No, milady. All quiet."

As Paresh rounded the counter, Donovan hopped off the stool and peered at her with narrowed eyes. "Your pulse is stronger today. No more pain?" He stroked her throat with his thumb.

"Good so far. It'll be a while before I completely recover—" She touched her throat and stole a peek at Eric. He looked disheveled and fresh out of bed, but his eyes shone with keen awareness.

"You will in time." His stiff smile failed to hide the concern in his voice. For a long time, he and Paresh gazed at each other in silence.

Raven cleared her throat. "So, what's on the agenda today, boss?" Her chipper tone changed both the topic and the mood as she swiveled on the ottoman to face Eric. "I need to test the saliva sample and retrieve the dagger."

"I have a meeting with the mayor this afternoon—that you will not be attending," Eric said, pointing a stern finger at Raven. "Hide somewhere close, if you must—out of sight. You can take care of your tasks when I stop by the police station to check in with Walter."

Turning the apple in her hands, Paresh timidly asked, "Eric, can we go back to Grandfather Wisdom? Before you go to the office?"

"You want to try again so soon?"

"Since I'm feeling better." She nodded. "Time's not going to wait out my memories, and if you're right, I need to figure this out before my nightmare becomes reality."

III

In the distance, a lone crow's caw reverberated with the gusto of an entire murder. A tree branch snapped and leaves rustled. Donovan envisioned glossy black plumage slapping the clear blue sky. Such an intelligent creature surely took pleasure in the wind caressing its wings while gaining momentum with each downward thrust.

Feathers and air. Darkness against light. Pleasure with a spirited touch. The mental imagery was a welcomed respite to his current reality where time was nonexistent and the complexities of life had been reduced to nothing. The creature glided from his audible range and the world returned as it existed for him.

"To death and new beginnings," he whispered with a lazy smile. Snug on a grassy patch beneath a gnarly oak, Donovan lay on his back with his arms tucked under his head.

He cracked an eye open. In the clearing, woodland animals frolicked in the sun's blistering light. Beneath the canopy, where shadow reigned, Raven sat on the hood of Eric's car, the grim line of her lips matching the crinkles over her brow. Molly was propped against a tree, reading in anxiety-laced silence.

"Why don't you take your own advice and cut loose a little, Goody?" Donovan asked.

"I'm uneasy. And stop calling me that," she grumbled, tossing her jacket onto the car's roof.

"It's been over three hundred years. I think it's stuck by now, *Goody*." Donovan's appreciative eyes passed over her tight-fitting black cami. "Stop fretting, little mouse. They'll be fine. We're close enough to hear a commotion but far enough to afford them privacy. At least we aren't cooped up inside the cottage."

He shrugged. "But I suppose I'd still get to share the company of you lovely ladies. You can glare at nothing or read the same page repeatedly wherever we are." His lips formed a lopsided grin when their curious ward ducked upon realizing that he'd seen her peeking over the book.

"I don't care about that," Raven replied sullenly with sagging shoulders. "Something isn't right. Alex should have moved by now."

"Maybe he didn't come here."

"Seneca followed his energy signature. He's here." After a moment of silence, she tapped her ear and closed her eyes. "Aye, he's out there. The Cataclysm does sing a rather distinct song."

Closing his eyes, Donovan tuned out the forest's buzz and focused on an out of place metallic chime. Adrenaline shot into his heart. The burst enhanced his abilities to pinpoint the sound's location less than a mile due west. Without revealing the excitement coursing through his body, he quietly said, "At least he's not with *them*."

"Aye."

No longer trying to hide her curiosity, Molly dropped the book into her lap. Raven held out a hand in her direction. "Sit tight and don't worry, 'kay?" She flashed a wide grin and lifted her sunglasses to wink. "This is what we do. Donovan will take care of you. I'll be right back."

As she leaped off the car and dashed west of the carriage house, Donovan relaxed with a sigh. "There she goes again, stealing all the glory. Alex won't be a threat much longer."

IV

"Why do you want me to find you?" Raven muttered. "When you know what I must do?"

Alex didn't reply despite leaving an insultingly easy trail to follow. He had to be close enough to hear her. For three miles, he'd led her through thick undergrowth into the denser, western side of the forest. The hawthorn trees were particularly annoying. As she blocked a branch from swiping her cheek, its long thorns raked her palm. She wiped the blood on her pants and stopped.

It was unnervingly silent. The terrain ahead sloped down into a dried up creek bed, and the trees were spaced farther apart, with sprouts of leafy green in between. Sunlight trickled through the foliage, but the air was so thick with animosity that darkness loomed where none actually existed.

He took me out of Donovan's range, she noted mentally before asking, "What're you up to, Alex?"

No answer.

Scrutinizing the treetops, she withdrew the daggers sheathed on her thighs. Interconnected scythes and a flowery interpretation of the Vampiric Star formed her squad's insignia on the daggers' golden hilts. Rubies dotted the spots where each scythe's blade met its handle and the center of the star where the handles crossed.

For a fraction of a moment, a millisecond of reality, her mind turned from the forest. The Wraith Reapers' icons of death incarnate stood opposite the Crimson Guard's distinction of nobility and loyalty: a crescent moon draped with golden threads, tipped in adoration of the Vampiric Star, with slanted rubies kneeling before their nation's glory.

"Now it means nothing!" She whirled in a circle, staring down every shadow. "You have tarnished the nature, the symbolism, *the very name*," she cried, "of your squad with your cowardly act!"

She tossed the daggers up and caught them by their blades, slicing into her palms to slick them with her blood scent. Rolling forward, she threw one high off to her right side. She landed on her knee facing that direction with the other dagger aimed and ready. "Hello, Alex."

"What the hell, Goody? Damn it, I got my hair cut yesterday!" he whined. "I think you took a good two inches off!"

"Then I missed by about six." The second blade zipped on a lower trajectory, carving an effortless path through the trees. "I meant to get you between the eyes."

A resounding *thud* shook the ground as Alex landed in front of her. Grunting in frustration, she slowly stood and raised her hands. His revolver, loaded with exploding silver bullets, was pointed at her head. But she was more concerned with the hand hidden behind his back. There, he palmed the Cataclysm, a razor-sharp, whip-like weapon that he wielded with deadly precision. It snaked through the air and chimed on the wind as it sliced through its victims as delicately and lethally as a ballad sung by the angel of death.

"Had to even it up, didn't you?" Rectangular, garnet-tinted lenses hid eyes that were greener than a sun-kissed fern frond. He loosened his hold on the revolver and dropped a chunk of blond hair.

"That's what you get for ducking." She sized up the blunted tips of his spiked hair and shrugged. "Looks like one side is a bit off, but whatever."

He grinned and patted at the stumps with the revolver. "Don't get any ideas about fixing it. My guy does a much better job than you—"

Before she could twitch, Alex trained the gun back on her nose. His aura was stiff and weighted by a wariness that he was trying to hide behind his usual aloof demeanor. But Raven knew he was never as absentminded as he seemed.

"You should tip him extra. You're looking extra yummy." Raven winked and took a quick inventory of Alex's red and black uniform. His pockets appeared to be quite well stocked despite his rapid departure from Snowblood Square.

"Yeah, well, it makes a difference when someone isn't trying to take off your head, you know!" He laughed and scratched his head without changing the gun's aim or lifting his finger from the trigger.

Still more worried about the hidden weapon, Raven's cool eyes scrutinized his muscle movements as she lowered her hands. "So what brings you out here, Alex?"

"I'll thank you to keep those up, if you'd be so kind," he said in a serious tone, nudging the gun and his chin up at the same time. His sleeveless, form-fitting shirt exposed the tightening muscles in the arm behind his back. "Don't think I don't know all your tricks. I don't want to kill you, but I will if it means my life or yours."

"Oh, that's cold." She pursed her lips and shook her head as she lifted her hands. "What happened to honor and the old way of things?"

"The old way of things no longer suits our society."

"Aye, that's become quite evident, hasn't it?" She shot a meaningful glance over her sunglasses. "Old friends and new alliances, huh?"

He nodded. "The old way of things has us locked in this stalemate."

"Stalemate? Try checkmate. I'm not armed." Raven started to lower her hands again.

Alex threw his head back with a laugh. "Checkmate, my ass! You always have a trick up your sleeve! Now keep those hands up. No more warnings." The slightly squeaky and humored tone was present, but his voice had deepened and taken on a grave edge.

"No more joking around, I suppose." With a sigh, she flattened her palms on top of her head, forced to wait for an opening to grab her double-bladed combat scythe. Alex would strike faster than the half second she needed to grab it from the pocket that stretched down her right calf. "So, let me ask again, why'd you drag me out here, Alex?"

He cocked his head. "How easily do you suppose I could plant one of your daggers on a body? Seeing as how I have two of them now?" Metal chimed as he hinged the Cataclysm on his belt. Displaying her weapons in the previously hidden hand, he said, "You like to throw these things around. How long do you suppose it would take Lord Lucien to order your head along with mine? Want to guess? Or just find out?"

"You call him 'lord' like you have any right!" she spat, glaring at him as a surge of adrenaline shot into her veins and began to change her body and deepen her voice. "For you, of all true bloods, to fight this low and dirt—"

"You think you have it all figured out, don't you?" He twisted to the side and arched forward, and two silver flashes flew by her ear.

Pink hair and a sliver of metal fell to her shoulder. Seconds later, her daggers embedded into a distant tree with heavy *thunks*.

"Now we're even," he said, flicking his hair.

"Not quite; you got one of my hoops. Looks like I get to claim one of yours!" She dropped to the ground and lobbed a dirk, pulled from her boot, at his face.

Alex turned into a whirlwind of dust and debris to dodge the attack. The explosive report of his firearm echoed off the trees. As the bullet zipped past her cheek, the wind chimed in perfect sync with a high-pitched metallic whine and cold steel sliced through her left arm. Yelping in pain, she clutched a gushing wound instead of her weapon's handle.

"Shit! You bastard!" she yelled, staring in disbelief at the blood pouring between her fingers. The Cataclysm's return path came lower to whip its victim's legs. She jumped straight up and grabbed hold of a thick branch. Her bloody right hand dipped into her pocket again, but slipped off her weapon when Alex severed her perch.

"I only wanted to talk, Raven," he said, circling her as she crashed to the ground. His sharpened canines gleamed like polished ivory as the sun kissed his paraffin face. For a man who preferred non-lethal measures, he was exquisitely radiant before delivering a deathblow. "I already told you—I know all your tricks. But you don't know all mine. The Second Born may have trained you, but I've sparred with him countless times, and you have no idea what getting pushed that hard can make you do."

"Training? *I* don't know? *You watched him beat me!*" Raven clenched her teeth. Blood streamed down her arm. "And now you use the Cataclysm on me? On *me?*"

"Don't blame me for defending myself. What did you expect?" Alex nudged his gun at her wound. "Do you really think I'd go up against Lord Lucien's *Precious Little Raven Hawkings* without an ace up my sleeve? You get a hold of your Deathscythe—I die. And that's not about to hap—"

Alex's face snapped sideways in surprise as a dark, growling form sprang from the bushes. He and his assailant disappeared down the embankment, snarling like warring beasts. A blossoming plume of dirt and leaves hid all but the sounds of a violent battle between creatures not meant for the Realm of Man: preternatural growls, gnashing teeth, and the ripping and tearing of claws meant to strip flesh from bone.

Raven quickly gauged her wound. The Cataclysm embedded silver debris in its victim, which, to a vampire, meant delayed healing and, to a vampire hunter, improved the odds for a lethal hit. The blade had grazed the bone. She was losing too much blood.

"Bloody stars," she cursed, biting her lip. It felt like a fiery worm was burrowing into her arm, and she didn't have time to apply ointment or even a crude patch. A dark form was flying directly at her and closing the distance fast. She dropped low. Donovan's body slammed into the tree behind her.

Get him before he can kill anyone else! She lunged with extended claws. Then she felt the cold barrel of a gun against her forehead.

"Don't," Alex growled. Furrows etched his smooth forehead, and part of one lens had fallen out of his sunglasses, exposing an angry, engorged eye. "You stay put, First Officer."

"You can't escape, traitor!" Donovan hissed.

"You have a bad habit of meddling. Raven should have put you in your place long ago!" Alex readied the Cataclysm to strike.

As he was about to flick his wrist, Raven whispered, "I wouldn't." The points of a double-bladed scythe pricked the nape of Alex's neck.

The tension in their auras twisted the air between them. Raven lifted her chin and glanced down her nose. "Checkmate."

Poised to unleash deadly attacks, Alex looked from Donovan's smug grin to her face. "Unarmed you said?"

"You have an ace; I have a trick." She shrugged. "Sparring only gives you time to react. Training gives you time to learn, and he *trained* me to be the best. So. I. Am. Now, lower your weapons, former Commander Alexander of the Crimson Guard. You are hereby taken into custody for treason and the high crime of stealing from the Flock."

"Think what you like, but it's not the same and you don't have the clear upper hand here. I'm quicker on my trigger than you are on your blade." He smiled, a wicked maw of sharp, bloodied teeth. "I think you'll be lowering your Deathscythe. And I'll take my leave for now."

"You should count yourself lucky that she hasn't killed you already!" growled Donovan.

"She hasn't saved your life yet. Stay quiet, because I promise that you will die before either of us." His uncovered eye was trained on Raven. "So how about it? Live to fight another day or take your chances in the here and now?"

Raven relaxed her grip. The Deathscythe's blades fell away from Alex's skin. At the same time, he carefully dropped the hammer on his revolver and pulled the barrel from her head. The Cataclysm stood ready to strike Donovan.

"A little insurance," Alex said with a wink, stepping back. "Can't trust that First Officer of yours, you know. He never has been good at following orders."

Raven smirked. "I won't capture you next time."

"I didn't expect you to *try* this time." Holstering the gun, he said, "I'm almost disappointed, really. I always enjoy a good romp with you."

"Maybe you should find it flattering."

"Or maybe it's the first crack in your unbreakable façade, my dear Raven." The fondness in Alex's voice clearly bit at her. "The old way of things is dead, indeed."

"Just go," Raven whispered.

Alex tapped the switch on his wrist. "My dear, dear Raven," he said quietly, thumping his palm against his chest as he shimmered out of sight.

"How can you let him go like that?" Donovan demanded, jumping up to her side.

"Where's the woman?" Raven countered, catching his arm before he could pursue.

"Hidden and safe."

"And Eric and Paresh?"

"At the tree, as far as I know. I heard the shot and came running. This side of the forest is saturated with the scent of your blood."

Raven nodded absently. Donovan couldn't have heard the shot or made it there that fast if he'd stayed at the carriage house as ordered.

She flinched when he touched her arm. "I can't believe he got you. You're slipping."

"That wasn't an Alex I've ever seen—he was like a cornered beast." Raven stared at the spot where Alex had disappeared. "Eric and Paresh are alone at Grandfather Wisdom, and he knows it. Let's go."

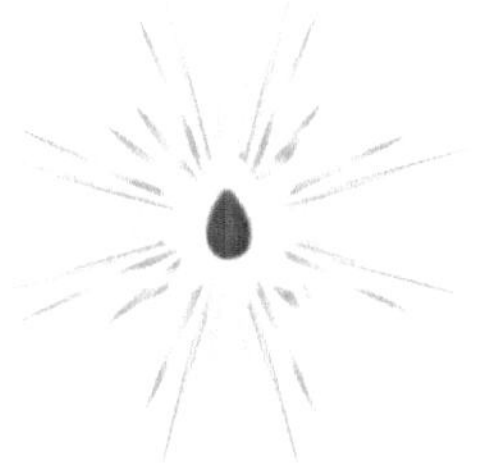

CHAPTER NINE: CROSSING THE DIVIDE

I

The ghostly hand beckoned from the void. Accepting its pale fingers, Paresh glanced over her shoulder. The hole to her world was already tunneling. As she watched her empty body sag into Eric's arms, she cried out. But her voice was thread thin across the spiritual plane. "Eric!"

His eyes shot up as though he'd heard her. But then the hole closed and bound Paresh to the void's vortex of silent pitch. Glowing wings shrouded her astral body, trailed by thick and lustrous feathers. Haloed with the sun's brilliance, yet dusted with the moon's pale light, they possessed qualities of the air and cosmos like a physical intangibility. An embodiment of harmonic contradictions.

Gabriel whispered to her, his voice musical and light, dipping into valleys and peaking over mountains, skimming plains to surf oceans. A complimentary balance to Mother Nature's majesty.

He'd previously spoken as simply and clearly as a human. But now, his words were muffled, as though he had covered her ears.

He wasn't talking to her.

I don't understand! Please, show me! Show me what you want me to see!

Weight tugged at her eyelids. Jonathan appeared, sheathed in darkness. The scene slowly cleared, and Paresh saw him in fully vampiric form, bearing a demonic scowl that shot chills into her heart. The brown-haired woman materialized, too, twisted on the ground behind him, in a pool of blood.

Metal scraped metal and crimson spray trailed a singing flash of silver. Jonathan fell to his knees, again clutching a gory wound in his side. Blood poured between his fingers—a scarlet river that fed the congealing puddle below.

No! Master Jon!

Bracing against her silent screams, Paresh tried to turn and face the assailant. The scene was fading fast. She couldn't look away from Jonathan—from his smile—as he looked up at her.

Master Jon! Don't leave me!

Incredible, rising heat distorted Jonathan's face, and then a fiery, sable cloud rushed in, burning Paresh's throat and eyes. A city formed before her, set aflame and shaken apart by growls surely formed from the belly of a monstrous behemoth. The air melted under intense pressure and buildings crumbled amid the screams of the tormented. Clawing at her throat, Paresh gasped for air, but instead sucked down thick, black smoke.

A male figure stood at the epicenter, tugging on heavy chains crossed over his chest. Slender in form and unnaturally tall, his skin burned like a candlewick and his screams were too horrendous to bear.

Upon seeing her watching him, he quieted. He showed no emotion. No pain. He was as expressionless as a rock smoothed by ocean waves, except for his eyes, which glowed with a blue flame that stabbed her soul. With a burst of strength, he ripped free of his restraints. He fell to his knees and vanished into a flourish of flames.

The shaking stopped and silence draped an inferno that consumed all it touched. Bright light shot up from the epicenter into the heavens—not as a beam, but as a pair of colossal wings, like those of a hawk. They stretched unendingly until time stopped and froze the flames.

In that moment, Paresh understood peace in chaos. It was unnaturally still and deceptively serene. She felt warm and safe—exactly how she felt when wrapped in Gabriel's wings.

She almost smiled.

But then, time reset and the hellish world returned. Fires roared, growls shook the earth, and tormented wails filled the air. She flayed skin from her throat as smoke snaked down her airway. Her vision tunneled. The flames were so close. The sweat on her skin boiled.

She tried to open her eyes, but her tears had soldered them shut. Somehow, after gasping in nothing but ash, she managed to choke out a scream.

Invisible hands jerked her into the bottomless void. Gabriel's wings tightened their embrace. No longer contained, her sorrow howled through the abyss and heavy tears cut a glistening stream through the trail of feathers.

Soft words glided to her, full of the musical prowess befitting such a heavenly voice. *Poor child. The wings of Hawkiel's light are not your burden; my heart mourns that you bore witness to them. Mourneth not the afflicted. Redeemeth them from the hand of the Morning Star and saveth a nation. That is all you need know.*

Gabriel's voice eased the pain gnawing on her emotional pillar. She took a deep breath and squeezed her eyes shut. Tears rolled down her cheeks.

"I don't understand, and I don't care! Why must Jonathan die?" she croaked out, her throat burnt and raw.

In the grievous silence that followed, Gabriel's wings faded to crystal transparency and her heart grew heavy. She jolted in place as gravity's center shifted and dropped her into a world of light—the Realm of Man—the reality ruled by Death.

II

The instant Paresh touched the tree, her spiritual essence left her body and crossed the dimensional divide. Eric tucked her body to his chest.

"Paresh," he whispered.

"Eric!" Her voice sounded miles away.

He stroked Grandfather Wisdom's coarse bark. Traces of her aura lingered there. He flattened his palm and bowed his head, reluctant to break his only link to her soul.

Paresh's eyes snapped open. Leaping from his embrace with a limberness befitting a woodland fairy, she landed before him on pointed toes. Supported by mere blades of grass, the sun illuminated her hair like a golden halo and the air shimmered at her back like two pairs of flitting wings. A holy blue flame burned in her eyes, and, when she parted her lips, her voice was far too lovely and unnatural for anyone in the physical world to behold.

"Eric the Anointed, Strength and Protector of the Sacred Vessel. Cast off your worries; she is well."

It took Eric a few seconds to understand what he was seeing. He wondered if he should kneel or bow—offer some form of respect—but then heard himself saying, "Tell me what you would have us do, Archangel Gabriel."

"So direct, you are. Impatient, even. Much like your brother." Wearing an expression of curiosity, Gabriel cocked Paresh's head in contemplation. "No, not impatient. Anxious."

"I want to help her."

"As do I."

"What is she supposed to do with the visions you give her?"

"She sees what she chooses to see. I show her the road; she chooses the path."

"I don't understand."

Gabriel smiled and gazed down into Paresh's hands cupped at her bosom. "When this one's soul was sparked, I was the first to hold it and marvel at Destiny's grand plan. It was no bigger than a marble, easily lost in the folds of my wings if not for the brilliancy of the life that burned within it—within *her*."

He met Eric's eyes. "We are beings created from love incarnate who care for all of God's creations equally. However, with this one—" He hugged Paresh's body. "I loved her the moment I met her and vowed to watch over her with all my power."

"I still don't—"

A finger silenced Eric's lips.

"Impatience it may be after all." Shaking Paresh's hair from her shoulders, Gabriel glanced at the sky.

"So long it's been. So very long ago, I was charged with watching over a nation soaked in innocent blood. For that reason, I cannot meddle in matters concerning its future. They alone must determine their fates; I can only observe the consequences and try to maintain the balance in this world. And, alas, though it saddens me so, she is a part of what I cannot influence. Yet, I help her where I can."

"So you open the door and hope she walks through to find something useful?"

Gabriel nodded. "Yes! Yes! This world is little more than a figment of imagination suspended on a pendulum swinging through time. As long as it maintains momentum, it continues to swing, but if the balance is broken, it stops. And that leaves the Almighty with little recourse."

"Is the balance in danger?"

With a soft laugh, Gabriel replied, "The balance is always in danger, child. God created this world to survive on its own with the guidance of His Heavenly Host. Fibers of light and fibers of dark intertwine with freewill, shifting every second. Humans keep this world going; it's at their whim that the fibers bend and twist into the lives they lead. And just as we are there to guide them, there are others to lead them astray. You cannot have good without evil. When the world was new and nothing bad existed, the natural order of things corrected the course on its own."

"The serpent."

"Very good. The Morning Star to be precise—always shining as God's favored one—grew jealous of His desire to share His divine love with His new creations."

"So this war, the war that Lucien fears—"

Gabriel shook Paresh's head. "The fibers stretch eternally in every direction. At any moment in time, we can see how one action might affect another hundreds of years into the future. To be sure, the path can always change; nothing is etched in stone—such absoluteness is taboo in any natural order. However, current events are blurring our vision."

"Then Paresh—"

"Is the only one with whom I may share my vision, though I have no control over what she sees. I feel grief and sadness when her eyes are closed."

"She loves Jonathan and doesn't want him to die."

"Ah yes, that one. Only he controls his fate. He knows what he must do; his impatience interferes."

"He doesn't see himself as worthy of forgiveness," Eric replied.

"I cannot offer further help. The hand of forgiveness is within reach; he must choose to grasp it. No one is beyond redemption, not even the Morning Star. Lucifer is simply too stubborn to admit defeat."

Paresh grimaced and Gabriel's light dimmed.

"She must return now." His voice came from every direction at once. "Fare thee well, Eric the Anointed. Take care of our little one."

The blue flame in Paresh's eyes extinguished, leaving behind tiny pupils devoid of conscious thought. She fell limply into Eric's arms. Lowering her to the grass, he stroked her cheek and counted the seconds before she finally stirred.

"Jonathan," she moaned. "Don't, please. Don't…"

Eric buried his face in her hair. "Everything's going to be all right," he whispered. "I promise you, Paresh. We'll save him. And find peace."

III

Jonathan swept his hand through the reflecting pool, scattering sunlit ripples over the surface. *Like that's going to erase what you see in your own eyes. Stop looking at yourself.*

He fell back onto his elbows with a sigh and dropped his foot into the water, kicking a sparkling arc that splashed down near the center. He did it again, too preoccupied to care about ruining his ancient—and handmade—Italian leather wingtip. After all, his Italian cashmere jacket was water-stained and crumpled in the grass, and his trousers were doused. He was tired of *caring* and disgusted at feeling that way.

"Stop running and you might not feel so restless." Behind him, Lucien was silhouetted by the simulated sun.

"I'm not in the mood to talk," Jonathan mumbled.

Lucien slipped out of his sandals. Lifting his kimono, he stepped into the water and then folded and tucked the silk fabric protectively. Sitting perpendicular to Jonathan's back, he replied, "I am aware."

Soothing vanilla wafted over Jonathan. He loved Lucien's scent. Closing his eyes with a self-deprecating groan, he shook his head. How could he possibly know if he *loved* anything?

"You want to go to her," Lucien said. "And yet, you don't."

Through hooded eyes, he admired Lucien: his striking lines, the ivory tips that glinted beneath luscious lips, the way his slender throat blended into the noble posture of his shoulders and back. The sun kissed his pale blue skin as gently as the moon did, and highlighted pointed ears that poked through frosted silver locks.

He's so close, Jonathan thought. *He's here. Right here. I could just—*

Jonathan let his elbows slide out from beneath him and leaned back. He held his breath for half a heartbeat and nestled his head into Lucien's lap.

"My Jonathan," Lucien said quietly, sweeping his fingers across Jonathan's forehead. "I dislike seeing you this way."

Jonathan closed his eyes, murmuring incoherent appreciation. Lucien's caress travelled across his brow, around his eye, along his cheekbone, and then brushed the tip of his nose before gliding sensuously around his mouth. Soft locks grazed his face as Lucien's tender lips pressed against his.

Cupping Lucien's cheek, Jonathan arched his neck and returned his kiss. Drifting down to Jonathan's nape, Lucien tugged the crimson ribbon free and then threaded his fingers through the length of Jonathan's hair. He murmured an order to Arc Cyber Control, "Command code zero, zero, one. Arc simulation dimness adjust twenty-two hundred hours. Waning crescent moon, thirty-degrees, east."

Through cracked lids, Jonathan watched the sun sink along the western edge, swiftly trailed by haunting oranges and rich indigos that darkened to star-spangled pitch as the moon ascended its perch.

"You're smiling," Lucien said. "You would have it rain now."

"You don't like the rain."

Lucien's fingers danced across Jonathan's forehead. "I would stay, if it would please you."

"No—"

"I've pushed you too hard." Lucien straightened and stared over the grassy hills beyond the pool. "What do you *want* to tell me?"

"Whatever you want to know."

"My wants do not matter. Gabriel delivered the message to you and gave you power over your own fate."

"Lucien, I—"

"What do you *want* to confess?"

"Lucien." Jonathan tried to sit up, but his master held him still.

"Stay. This is nice."

Jonathan caught his breath as heat flared in his chest. Letting the air trickle from his lungs, he said, "Earlier, I didn't mean the darkness in my heart belongs to Lucifer."

"He put it there."

"But it's mine to battle."

"Control is no longer an issue. The Servator has sealed away our beastly instincts. You refuse to believe."

"I know my thirst."

"Were you ever enticed by Paresh's blood?"

Jonathan recoiled internally. "I'd never touch her like that."

"Purity such as hers could drive a sated beast mad, and yet you were unaffected, even when you drew her blood samples."

Jonathan was quiet.

"You control your thirst."

"A thousand years ago," Jonathan said, "Alex chose pacifism and rehabilitation, and stifled his urge to kill. Maybe he cracked when he received her blood."

"Does it sadden you to see him act—"

"Like me?"

Lucien smiled. Briefly. "Strangely?"

"I suppose. But if someone as gentle as him can fall—"

"Who can fall is irrelevant."

"That's not my point!" Jonathan slapped the pool's glossy surface. "Why *me* over someone like Alex who would rather save life than take it?"

"You possess unparalleled rank and freedom—"

"Lucky me," Jonathan mumbled. "My birthright won our Second New Age and yours threatens to destroy it."

Lucien stared into the distance. His voice was low and quiet when he finally spoke. "The Elders are displeased with my decisions. I have not behaved within their expectations."

"Since when do you care what they think?"

"I don't," Lucien said with the barest hint of a grin. "I've interrupted the Fallen Host's plan. Lucifer is ignorant of my evolutionary growth."

Glinting mischievously, Lucien's eyes narrowed. "He misunderstood my order to kill Paresh, *and* he failed to notice I was there. He's distracted, which gives us an advantage, for now."

"But—"

"Alex made his choice," Lucien interrupted. "Now, you must decide to make yours."

Plucking at the water, Jonathan whispered, "I should confess to Eric."

"I forbid it. Selfishly unloading your pain onto him doesn't change the present or future, only the way he sees the past, and you."

"And how is that?"

"As a brother."

Somehow, nostalgia warmed Jonathan's heart beneath the weight of his guilt. "I waited for months after the Confederate slaughter to approach him again, you know. Eric no longer resembled the pathetic creature that had drained the blood from a headless chicken. He was magnificent, a war machine on the battlefield who struck down anyone who fired upon the Colonel. But at night—"

Jonathan sighed. "Those crystalline eyes stole the moon's luster and fevered for the men in his camp. I needed more than watching. I craved his blood, his naked flesh."

"You went to him?" Lucien asked.

"That's when I began our nightly visits. He was distrustful, of course, but self-restraint and a 'friendly' ear got him to warm up to me, eventually." Licking his lips, Jonathan paused.

"Oh, but he was so much stronger! I wanted to fight him again. And I wanted him to want it, too. I fantasized about him wanting me as much as I wanted him. It drove me mad. Impatient. It's like what you said about Paresh's purity—my delirium grew from denying myself what I sought most."

"And so the games began," Lucien said.

"Those humans. So undeserving of his devotion. Lucas used him and passed him to his son, Nathaniel, like he was a possession to give away." Jonathan flung his arm bitterly out to the side.

"Why does it continue to bother you so?"

"They treated him like a dog." Jonathan's jaw bulged. "He was born from my noble lineage. They should've groveled at his feet."

"And yet you did nothing to make his life better. You left him vulnerable to a sun that scorched his skin and burned his eyes when we've had protective shields, creams, and lenses for centuries."

"He was supposed to find a better world when he came back with me!" Jonathan insisted. "If I'd given him our conveniences then, he never would've wanted to explore my offerings!"

"So you devised a way of interfering that stayed within our rules."

"The cycle was never going to change. Eric has my thirst, but not my restless nature. He's happy as long as he has purpose."

"A reason to exist is more than we've ever known."

Lucien dunked his fingers into the pool and held them over Jonathan's forehead. As the cool droplets splashed his skin, Jonathan inhaled deeply and gazed over the hills. This hidden side to Lucien stirred a heat in him beyond what he'd known before.

"I want to start in 1908," Jonathan revealed softly.

"Doesn't Eric know what you did to Nathaniel and his wife in 1908?" Lucien asked.

"He does. But it forms the foundation for everything that follows." Jonathan sought understanding in Lucien's eyes.

"Proceed."

"First—Lucas, Lucinda's half-brother, fathered the Colonel's only grandson, Nathaniel. So, understandably, Nathaniel was in a position of power. He held investments in hotels, restaurants, railways, and government. But, he was self-indulgent and greedy. It wasn't political. My involvement risked nothing to the Nation."

When Lucien nodded his agreement, Jonathan's gaze lifted to the moon. "Nathaniel threw lavish parties with his wife, Elizabeth, as a constant fixture at his side. Flaunting the tiny waist and large bodice that came with a tightened corset, she was a decoration of lace, sequins, decadence, and pearls. She coiled men around her fingers or scooped them up from puddles at her feet. When she held out a cigarette, a dozen lit lighters appeared. Her need for male attention made her a lucrative lure for Nathaniel's hesitant investors—or politicians. He indulged her every want.

"But when she announced her pregnancy in 1904, suddenly her only job was to birth Nathaniel a healthy heir. He confined her to the estate. Restricted her to *female* friends and staff. No men. No parties. She was hardly an afterthought when he left for his nightly excursions. He'd abandon her for months at a time when the railroad in Las Vegas presented a wealth of mining opportunities. The women in her circle grew bored and stopped visiting. Her servants were her only companions."

"Until Joshua was born and family tradition gave you an opening," Lucien said. "The infant stayed with his mother."

"The fact that Eric wasn't human didn't matter—he was a male, in the house, alone with Elizabeth. It was too easy. Whispers breathed life into marionettes, and the game began."

☽ ✳ ☾

Chiffon ghosts flowed loosely between stationary panels of crushed red velvet framing the windows. Their gossamer fingers intimately stroked Jonathan's thigh and took on humanoid form. But no one noticed. Not even Eric.

Jonathan focused on him, a challenge to sense the other predator in the room. *Why have you not developed the skills my lineage affords? You could detect the VaSH's cloaking devices by now, let alone my aura!*

Empty and expressionless, Eric's face mimicked a once jagged rock smoothed by beatings from the sands of time. He didn't even twitch when Jonathan kicked off the wall and it creaked in protest.

Earlier that evening, Nathaniel's paranoia had peaked, and now Elizabeth was caught in the dull gray that was his shadow. Folded up on the bed in a white nightdress, she cried into her hands, a colorless doll awaiting destruction.

A day's worth of russet-hued beard growth and rage twisted the social elite's features into those of a scowling vagabond. Nathaniel's brow cut a single, angry line across his face as he whipped a finger at Eric, standing in black behind him.

"You think I don't see how you look at him?" he yelled. "*I see how every damn woman in this house looks at him!*"

Eric looked detached. Bored. Perhaps wondering why he was there.

Your vampire blood wants to walk away, but that damn human heart of yours cries for that woman, doesn't it, Brother? Jonathan approached Eric with a sinuous shape curving his lips. *Without me, you will never see how insipid your life has become.*

As though sensing Eric's moral battle herself, Elizabeth slapped Nathaniel hard across the face, crying, "How dare you not believe me! How can you accuse your own wife of such things?"

Two pale fingers stayed the hand Nathaniel raised to retaliate. The human glared over his shoulder at Eric. "You're here to protect me, not stand there and watch! Do your job!"

"No." Eric's eyes dropped deliberately. Nathaniel's followed to three-year-old Joshua, wrapped around Eric's leg after stumbling into the room seconds earlier. "My job is to protect *him* and he has no need to see you strike his mother."

Nathaniel ripped free and rubbed the red outline on his wrist. "*Don't think I don't see how she looks at you.*"

"Then you see that I do not share the same look with her," Eric said without looking up as he stroked the child's hair.

Elizabeth's eyes widened as she blanched and sank into her feathery bed. Tears spilled down her cheeks as she nervously stared at her palm.

Nathaniel shoved his nose into Eric's face. "Who do you think you're talking to? Where do your loyalties lie, anyway?"

The chill in Eric's eyes forced Nathaniel back a step. "I took an oath to your grandfather to protect his descendants. My loyalty lies with him."

Nathaniel tugged at his jacket and straightened his spine. "Very well. My wife is mine to handle as I please. You will not interfere again. Understand?"

Their deadlocked gazes—one ablaze with fury and the other unreadable—lasted agonizingly long seconds. Eric finally scooped Joshua into his arms and turned to leave. Only then did Eric's jaw tense and his eyes flash in quiet anger.

Jonathan followed, holding his breath. Time was a universal constant, but this bare fraction plodded by excruciatingly slowly as Eric put one foot in front of the other. He didn't once acknowledge Elizabeth's silent, desperate plea as she watched him in the vanity's mirror.

Jonathan finally appeased his lungs with a thin stream of air once they crossed the threshold into the hall. A grin bent his lips when Nathaniel slammed the door and something crashed against it.

A malicious laugh clawed at Jonathan's throat, though he dared not let it escape. Elizabeth must have thrown the vase from her nightstand. A scream, followed by a floor-shaking *thud*, indicated Nathaniel's response, and the fact that Eric kept moving made Jonathan's grin grow even wider. *Did she throw it at her husband or at you, Brother?*

At the end of the hall, Eric stiffly opened the hidden panel that connected the family to his basement living quarters and descended the dim stairs. The human child, tucked to his vampiric guardian's chest, fell asleep quickly in the underground darkness.

Eric, however, sat upright—a living statue. Jonathan knew a violent battle waged beneath that beautiful, stoic façade. Taking his usual seat in the corner chair, Jonathan relished the hell Eric's human heart endured all night as Nathaniel "handled" his wife two floors up.

☽ ✺ ☾

Eric rose at morning dusk, returned Joshua to his room, and toured the grounds with the first security shift. The beast within Jonathan squeezed its fists with all its might, twisting and crushing his organs without concern for the pain. Jonathan wasn't sure he cared, either.

Eric still belonged to Nathaniel.

Unlike his brother, Jonathan was not a creature torn in two. His true, uninhibited temperament was about to swallow the logic that controlled his civilized persona, unleashing a monster that lived in the realm of nightmares.

He needed a release.

Storming the length of the mansion, he crossed from Eric's stairwell to the servant's stairs, daring Eric to sense him despite the damage it would do.

"*You're so bloody oblivious!*" Jonathan growled aloud, stomping his way to the second floor. Grinding his teeth, he marched past the guest suites and the veranda overlooking the foyer. In the family's quarters, a delicious scent drew him to Elizabeth's door.

Cloaked by his aura, he slipped inside.

In a room shattered by violence, the woman slept on her bed, once a haven of pillows and lush fabrics, now stripped bare save for a pillow and the sheet clutched in her discolored hands. Blood stained the mattress, some spots small, and others large and patchy. Sooty streaks stained her cheeks, and deep red and purple hand-shaped outlines marred her arms, wrists, legs, and throat. The cylindrical shape of the bluish-purple knot bulging above her right brow matched the profile of the bedpost. Every inch of exposed skin bore some type of scrape or bruise, but the worst was her left eye—angry red and black, and swollen shut. Two crusty trails of dried blood led from the corner of her mouth—one down her chin and the other across her cheek to her earlobe where plump drops and blackened tears had stained her pillow.

Strangely, Jonathan's tension drained. Leaning against the door, he watched her for a long time.

His reach had been too narrow.

When Elizabeth woke, in the one eye that could open, he saw an opportunity he'd be foolish to ignore. Contrary to her fragile appearance, Elizabeth Hawthorne was not a woman easily broken.

In the weeks that followed, she kept to her rooms, refusing entrance to her staff, the nanny—even her son. Only at night, while everyone but the night watch and Eric slept, did she venture out. Always stopping first to sweep her fingers through her sleeping son's hair, she roamed the halls and gardens like a ghost searching for its soul.

All the while, her constant, demonic companion dropped suggestive whispers into her ear as effortlessly as one of the Fallen, and in that voice, she found her strength. In her willingness to listen, Jonathan found his path to victory.

When Nathaniel left on another month-long trip to survey mines, Jonathan issued a final whisper to rig his marionette and promised to give her a deserving audience. He resumed his nightly discussions with Eric while Elizabeth turned her charms to the night staff.

Four years of isolation had not stolen her power over men. Most of the bruises had faded, but ruddy shades of brown and pale green still tinged her eye. Purple eye shadow and maroon rouge brought new life to the last betrayal of Nathaniel's beating—enough to spark a man's need to rescue a distressed damsel.

That unlucky soul turned out to be Cooper, a recent hire aptly nicknamed "Rusty" due to his red mop and beard. Hopelessly ensnared by his employer's wife, he became unwittingly—though not unwillingly—embroiled in a love affair founded on a plot for murder.

As each night passed, Eric grew quieter and more withdrawn, and Jonathan's anticipation soared to unknown heights. As it churned with his impatience and unrequited desire, he feared Eric might sense friction and suspect his involvement. But, as usual, his brother's obsession with human loyalty and morality blinded him to the truth.

"You'll never realize on your own that I'm the puppet master, *Brother*," Jonathan whispered to himself. It was the night before Nathaniel's return and Jonathan had released his aura on the grassy hill west of the house. Eric's silhouette appeared in the distance.

Even you have a pre-written role. No matter what you try, I will not permit you to waver. Your very predictability makes it so easy.

Eric climbed the hill and sat beside him, his enticingly sweet and spicy scent wafting over Jonathan. Eric's lips parted without forming words. Silence lapsed.

Impatience nipped at Jonathan with sharper teeth than usual. Part of maintaining control meant forcing Eric to speak first, but his scent…the moonlight dusting his porcelain face…his pulse—the glorious swishing in his veins—

Jonathan cleared his throat. "Trouble in Hawthorneville, Brother?"

Wiping his face, Eric shook his head and gazed at the stars. "You've heard everything I've heard." His voice possessed a faraway quality, as though speaking to the heavens without expecting a reply. "I cannot let her succeed."

"Nathaniel's not your ward anymore," Jonathan said bitterly.

"I can't ignore a threat to Nathaniel simply because I have Joshua now. Nathaniel would have been my nephew—my son's cousin. I promised the Colonel to protect his descend—"

"'I promised the Colonel,'" Jonathan mimicked, his patience racing away uncontrollably. "*Oh! You sicken me!*"

Eric's jaw gaped as Jonathan faced him and snapped, "Did you expect me to wait forever?"

Visibly struggling to make sense of what was happening, Eric peered at Jonathan like he was caught in the light of a speeding steam engine. Gradually, his eyes narrowed and an accusation formed on his tongue.

Jonathan cracked an unsettling grin and rolled on top of him, holding him flat against the grass. "Do you get it now? *Brother? Do you?*"

"*You!* You set her up!" A sliver of crystalline blue encircled Eric's otherwise darkening eyes. Sharp, gleaming tips jutted from beneath his lip. "*How could you do this?*"

"The moonlight looks so glorious on you when you're angry." Skimming Eric's ear with his lips, he whispered, "They are petty and greedy, and brought this upon themselves. I am not permitted to influence what is not already there. Open your eyes and you will see."

"Get off." Eric was icily calm.

Jonathan rolled onto his back. The stars glittered in the clear night sky. "You can't win. I will have my prize."

Eric vaulted up and sprinted to the mansion. Folding his arms beneath his head, Jonathan sighed. "The stars will shine and the Earth will spin. And you, *dear brother*, are as equally predictable."

Eric's distant form disappeared into the rear service door. Jonathan grunted. "Hmph! Will you force your will onto her?" Laughing quietly, he wagged a finger at the prisms above. "Oh, no. That's not morally correct."

Jonathan's lips formed a lopsided smirk. "You will not free that woman. She stands willingly in my open palm. You've already lost."

Later, in the predawn hours, Jonathan returned to the grand house. The inevitable was about to happen and he already knew how it'd play out. As expected, Eric entered Elizabeth's room and placed three suitcases beside her bed. Unseen, Jonathan crossed his arms and propped his foot against the wall as Eric shook her awake.

"Leave," Eric said hollowly. "I will protect Joshua, but you can never see him again. This is the only way."

Rubbing the sleep from her eyes, she grumbled, "And where would you have me go that my husband wouldn't find me? *This* is the only way."

"You will not succeed."

Glaring at Eric, she sat up. "I suppose if I refuse, you'll stand by and watch like the lecherous pig you were *that* night, hm?" A delicate foot dipped from the sheets and kicked over the suitcases. She pointed at the door. "I will not sacrifice my son to you or that monster. Leave my room. You have clearly shown that you have no business here."

☽ ✳ ☾

Nathaniel's train was due at the Orison Crossing Terminal at six-thirty that evening. Forced to face his loyalties, Eric hid Joshua with his nanny in the detached servant's quarters and then left with the chauffer in the newest modern convenience: the automobile.

Petroleum-fueled engines had rendered onsite horses obsolete. After investing in racehorses in St. Louis, Nathaniel had repurposed his stables as carriage houses for a small vehicle fleet. The noxious gases were just as offensive as manure—but, without the easily spooked beasts there to betray his presence, Jonathan could wander more freely.

"But soon that won't matter," he muttered, pacing the foyer's marble floor. "This is the last night—"

A car's headlamp flashed the walls. Butterflies dove into Jonathan's belly. Giddy with excitement, he settled into the corner where he could see both the entryway and the twin stairs leading up to the second floor veranda.

The French doors swung open and Nathaniel burst in, his cheeks already flushed crimson. His mouth formed a cruel void as he let loose a massive, wall-shaking roar.

"Cooper! You rotten son of a bitch! Get your ass down here!"

Stomping with the force of a man ten times his weight, Nathaniel started up the east stairs. A face peered from the shadowy second floor hall. A pale shroud, Elizabeth ducked down the west side. She froze in horror when her husband's finger flew in her direction.

"And you!" His eyes narrowed over a thin smile. "See how far you get."

She nervously looked at Eric as he stepped into the foyer. Not acknowledging her in the slightest, he steadied his gaze on Nathaniel. Elizabeth scurried past him and broke into a hard run, looking back only when Rusty's first scream rang out. She tripped and hit the pavement. Blood streamed from deep scrapes on her palms and knees.

Ah! Such sweet perfume!

Jonathan slipped out behind her as she whimpered and picked herself up. Eric shut the French doors and passed by without noticing him—as usual—but his scent snuffed Jonathan's annoyance. Beneath his layers of bergamot and raw masculinity lay the aromatic side effect of blood-boiling anger.

Oh, it'll get hotter before the night is over, Brother!

Jonathan hopped off the terrace stairs and trotted after Eric. They were out of human range to hear the screaming in the house as the woman desperately begged the estate guards to open the gate. Jonathan and Eric, however, could clearly envision fists and feet swinging amid violent sprays of blood.

Wringing her hands, Elizabeth shrank in on herself when Eric arrived. He pushed an iron bar to swing the gate open. "She is not a prisoner in her own home."

The woman darted to freedom. Eric turned back toward the house with determination in his eyes. Jonathan ground his teeth. It was time to regain control of his marionettes.

Five minutes later, Elizabeth trudged through the gate in a trancelike state. The mansion's open French doors shone as a beacon through the veil of Jonathan's persuasion. Elizabeth saw nothing else, and no one saw or heard her coming until the instant she stepped into the foyer and he relinquished his control.

"Oh God, Rusty!" She clamped her hand over her mouth, eyes rooted on her bloodied lover's body. Nathaniel loomed over him, kicking him repeatedly in the stomach and face. The red-haired sap flopped loosely, unconscious and barely alive. Elizabeth sank to the floor. Nathaniel's face swiveled to her.

Eric had been leaning against the west banister, physically present, but mentally elsewhere—until Nathaniel moved for his wife. His eyes focused and his muscles tensed.

"Eric, take Joshua into the city for the night. Your services will not be needed here," Nathaniel said.

His jaw bulging, Eric didn't move—at first. But then his eyes darkened and his aura spewed forth suffocating air around Nathaniel.

"*No!*" Jonathan growled. He ran up the stairs and into Elizabeth's room, returning to the second floor veranda in seconds.

Nathaniel's collar was balled in Eric's fist and his eyes were dim. Tight words slid between Eric's teeth, "*You will not—*"

The impact of metal and leather against the marble floor broke Eric's concentration. Light returned to Nathaniel's eyes. Jonathan leaned over the railing, pointing at the two suitcases he'd thrown into the foyer.

"W-What the...?" the brute sputtered, unwittingly mirroring Eric's stunned expression.

Jonathan smiled and held up the third case, tapping it several times. He winked at Eric and unlatched the case. Bound stacks of cash tumbled out.

"A gift, Mr. Hawthorne," Jonathan announced, "from Eric to your wife, offered this morning."

Jonathan dropped the empty case and leaped over the railing, landing an instant before the case narrowly missed the heap once called Rusty.

Anger flashed in Eric's dark eyes. "*What the hell are you doing?*" He shoved Nathaniel aside to get to Jonathan.

Sidestepping Eric, Jonathan taunted Nathaniel. "Look in the others." He pointed at each case. "That one's stuffed with more cash and that one's full of personal affects. And to think, they denied anything was going on—"

Eric tackled Jonathan. "*Don't you say another word!*"

Laughing flat on his back, Jonathan pushed against Eric's shoulders. "He even promised to keep her safe from you!" Facing his brother, Jonathan innocently asked, "Now why would you do that, Eric?"

Eric's fist smashed into Jonathan's cheekbone, and repeatedly swung up and came down harder. But each blow only made Jonathan laugh harder.

"*You did this!*" Eric screamed, his voice alien and rough.

"Ooh," Jonathan cooed. "The Hawthorne dog barks at last! I can see your teeth! Are you finally off your leash?"

"*You did this! Why? Why!*"

"*Why?*" Jonathan mimicked, catching Eric's fist. Anger lit his nerves as his body took on its demonic form. "Because it's been sixty-years! You are mine. *Not theirs!*"

Kicking Eric off, Jonathan jumped up, but Eric immediately tackled him. The moment they hit the marble floor, Elizabeth cried out.

Eric glanced up at Nathaniel who was straddling her with his hands squeezing her throat. Jonathan swept his arms out, knocked Eric down against his chest, and rolled to reverse their positions.

Calmly and deliberately, Jonathan said, "They are only human. They are meant to die, and at one time, we were meant to kill them. You don't belong here."

Eric grimaced as he wrestled with Jonathan's words. His body went lax and his head fell to the side. "I can't—" Eric choked on the whisper.

"You can." Jonathan relaxed his grip.

A low, guttural groan built deep within Eric's throat. His abdomen went rigid and the noise escaped like an animalistic roar. Swinging his face up, Eric glared at Jonathan with bottomless, blood-engorged eyes. He slammed his head back against the marble and yelled, "No! You did this! Not them! How could you?"

Jonathan brushed Eric's ear with his lips. The taste of his skin…a wave of delirium threatened to consume him. "Because you act like a beaten dog in a gutter! Only you don't sulk off to heal. You return to this thug and it sickens me! You share *my* blood. Can you comprehend that? You, dear brother, outrank the Elders. You are *royalty*."

Squeezing his eyes shut, Eric sucked in a breath and shoved Jonathan off with a burst of energy. He leaped to his feet and kicked Jonathan hard in the chest in a fluid and shockingly powerful motion.

Jonathan slid across the marble floor, the wind knocked from him. Clutching his chest, he choked on his own blood and felt bones move freely beneath his hand. Broken ribs. An unattached sternum shoved dangerously close to his heart. One wrong move would make it a lethal skewer. As Eric yanked Nathaniel up by his shoulders, Jonathan saw a shadow shimmer at the door.

"Don't you dare come for me, Commander," Jonathan growled. "I've waited too long to see him like this. Retrieve the child."

Both dazed and awed by Eric's prowess, Jonathan leaned forward on his palm while using his other hand to splint the bones puncturing his lungs. He craved to watch Eric rip that man's heart out, but he'd never been injured like this.

His bones snapped and scraped as they remodeled and healed, but the sternum wouldn't reconnect until it was back in place. It had cracked near the ridge, leaving his collarbone and shoulders intact. Staring at the blood dripping from his mouth into a puddle on the floor, he mentally sorted through a shortlist of options.

Bracing himself with his abdominal and back muscles, he lifted his hand from the marble and stabbed his chest with a lengthened claw. Taking measured, shallow breaths, he managed to snag the sternum. Shifting the angle of his hand, he pulled it away from his heart. As relief washed over him, he grew aware of Nathaniel screaming at Eric. A sharp pain followed as he overcorrected and accidentally shoved a healing rib into his right lung.

Jonathan gritted his teeth. Blood gushed up his throat. He spit out a mouthful. The breast bone was reconnecting on the left side, at least.

He angrily looked up at Nathaniel who was thumping his chest like a great jungle ape.

I almost died because of you! Jonathan screamed in his head.

"…were given to me!" Nathaniel yelled. "Bought and paid for by my father, and you accepted his payment, and mine for Joshua! Don't ever forget that!"

Nathaniel's fist slammed into Eric's jaw. The brute reeled with a jarring cry, cradling his hand to his chest. "Holy shit! What the hell are you made of?"

"Oh, I cannot *wait* to kill you," Jonathan seethed beneath labored breaths as Eric replied, "Yes, I protect your son as a promise to your grandfather—and to earn payment received under that agreement."

Sickening! All of you!

Still splinting his chest, Jonathan grimaced and stood. Elizabeth scampered unnoticed up the stairs. Nathaniel raised his other fist at Eric, nostrils flaring and jaw grinding. Jonathan turned away, disgusted.

He slipped out the open French doors. Alex met him immediately, cloaked and hovering like a mother hen. "The angels never even hit you that hard," the Commander said, trying to investigate the wound through Jonathan's shirt. "You can't take another hit to the chest."

"I won't. It'll end soon." Jonathan waved him off. Given the gravity of his wound, his entire pack was probably ready to pounce despite his order not to interfere.

"The boy's in place," Alex said.

A woman's scream tore through the house, followed by a sickening *crunch* outside. Through the foyer doors, Jonathan saw Nathaniel fall to his knees, vacant eyes aimed at Rusty's body, as Eric climbed the stairs.

Jonathan grinned expectantly at the railing of Elizabeth's balcony. When Eric appeared, his gaze drifted over the woman's corpse sprawled on the gravel below to the child in the bushes. Joshua had risen slowly, his horrified little body tightly wound, eyes wide and quivering, mouth open in a silent scream.

Jonathan patted the boy's head with bloody fingers. Thick tears ran down Joshua's cheeks as his chest heaved to release a piercing shriek.

Eric's eyes were dark and empty, and betrayed the vampire blood that refused to do the bidding of a human heart. He'd finally stepped over the dividing line. His humanity had lost.

Lowly whistling to Alex and his pack, Jonathan strode down the drive. "I win," he said. "Let's see how long this stoic purpose of yours lasts in the Realm of Man now, *Brother*."

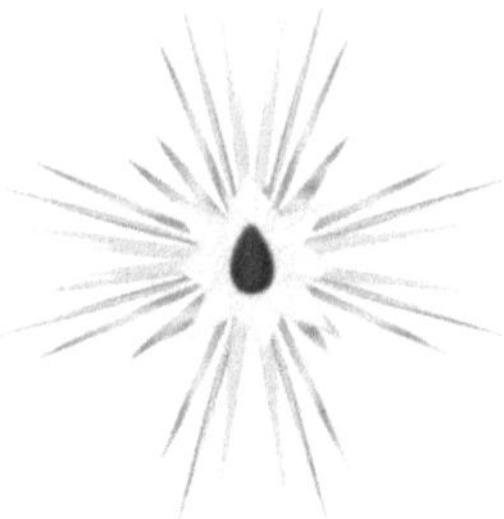

Chapter Ten: Bittersweet Interlude

I

Cheery beams embraced the tropical palms in the lobby until Eric swatted the blinds flat. Shadow befitted the news Walter had delivered moments ago: seventeen-year-old Rebecca Morrissey's body was found that morning.

Sporting a makeshift tourniquet and blood-soaked bandage, Raven followed him into his office. Eric tossed his sunglasses onto his desk and stopped before the rear window's opaque covering as though able to see through it. The cell phone at his side was open but not dialed.

"Do you need nourishment before I call Walter?" he asked.

"I'm fine. I only need to redress this wound." Raven pulled clean bandages from a pocket and sat on the sofa.

"Don't get your blood on anything." Eric closed his eyes with a weary sigh. Suspicions once murmured in private were now loud accusations by people he'd considered friends.

Glancing over his shoulder, he asked, "How bad is it?"

"The silver fragments are working their way out—I can't see the bone anymore." She slapped on a self-sticking, pliable square of rubber-coated gauze. "I'll leave the tourney on another hour and check the bleeding again."

Silence stretched thin between them.

"Silver is harmful?" Eric asked. "That's why it's not healing?"

Surprise flashed through Raven's aura. "You didn't know?"

He shook his head. "Silver harms werewolves."

Dangling her arm over the sofa's backside, Raven said, "Aye, in books."

At Eric's sharp stare, she explained, "Early in the twelfth century, we were sent after a rogue true blood terrorizing Eastern Europe with dreams of hellhounds in humanoid form. But a human hunter got him first—through the heart with a silver bullet."

She jabbed her sternum with her fingers. "Thus, lycanthrope mythology was born and human vampire hunters were none the wiser. It likely inspired Marie de France's poem *Bisclavret* and many other tales. So, aye—*in books.*"

Clutching his silver cross, Eric asked, "It's lethal?"

"A blow to the heart or brain can be, but—"

"Your arm?"

"I'll be fine—thankfully the Cataclysm only nicked it and I dodged his revolver. It's loaded with silver bullets that explode milliseconds after entry. *That* might have killed me or left me comatose—the Chthonic Knights have custody of true bloods technically 'alive and healing' after being shot centuries ago."

Raven squirmed uncomfortably. "But Alex has never needed to exploit our weaknesses for their lethality."

"We can no longer believe what you think you know about your lover." Eric brought the phone to his ear. A few seconds later he said, "Walter, I'm in my office."

Snapping the phone shut as he returned it to his pocket, he sat in his chair and buried his face in his hands.

"What will you do about them?"

"Them?" Eric asked.

"Aye. *Them.*" Raven pointed at the exterior wall.

Folding his hands beneath his nose, he sighed and closed his eyes. *There are so many voices—*

"The High Council won't like this exposure," Raven added.

Sweeping ebony strands from his eyes, Eric stiffly replied, "The High Council will have no say in what happens in *my* town. Walter's in the lobby. Cloak yourself."

"Aye, sir." She pressed a switch and vanished. The phantom odor of an electric spark lingered around her.

Knitting his brow, Eric said, "I thought those were undetectable."

"Aye, to humans and true bloods, but your lineage can—"

A knock at the door interrupted her.

"It's open, Walter." Eric waved him over when he stepped inside.

Walter tossed his hat nervously between his hands as he crossed the massive crimson and cream rug to Eric's desk, reluctant to lift his gaze.

"What is it, Old Friend?" Eric asked once Walter sat down.

With some hesitation, Walter shook his head and looked up. "It's Bill all over again. Same alley, dagger, and bite pattern. Canine punctures, no cuspid markings, no blood. She's bone dry."

He pulled a folded photograph from his back pocket and tossed it onto the desk. "Right through the heart. Not a drop of blood on the blade."

Eric contemplated the folded eight-by-ten sheet as if touching it meant admitting guilt. He slid on his glasses out of habit and unfolded the close up of the weapon's six-inch blade and ornate handle.

"The blade is a stainless steel composite inlaid with silver scrollwork, and the hilt is solid gold with three rubies embedded in the crescent moon there. Awfully expensive thing to leave behind." His thick finger poked the underside of the photo. "Have you had any business with her family?"

"Not for years." Eric set the sheet down without looking up. "There's someone you need to meet. Raven, show yourself."

"As you command," Raven replied.

"*Jesus!*" Spooked out of his chair, Walter whirled around, gaping at the pink-haired huntress.

Raven tapped her forehead in a mock salute. "Pleased to meet anyone in Eric's high esteem."

"This is Raven Hawkings," Eric said. "She was sent to investigate the matter on our end. This is no longer something for your hands alone."

Walter paled and wilted slowly into his seat as he raised a surprisingly steady finger in Raven's direction. "Sh-she's a va-vampire?"

"I'm a tr-true blood," she said, somewhat indignantly.

Fear trained his gaze on Raven as Walter turned slightly toward Eric. "And why is she here?"

"To investigate the matter on our end," Eric repeated. "I told you their government is self-sufficient. She and her First Officer are our security escorts."

Walter's attention snapped to Eric. "There's another one here?" he demanded. "Out there?"

"He's with Paresh and Molly at The Greenery." After a short pause, Eric gently added, "Paresh isn't well. I didn't want her here for this. She needs a break. And I can only give her that because he'll keep her safe."

"I don't know what to say." Walter's eyes sank into his hat. "That poor girl, the hell she's endured. I know it's not your fault, but she should have a normal life. She doesn't deserve any of this."

"You can blame me, Walter. You don't have to pretend that you don't or justify it to make yourself feel better."

Walter dropped a heavy sigh. "It's not your fault," he said. "I do know that. None of this is. But, that doesn't change the difficult situation I'm in. Judge Bankman called me into chambers earlier."

Eric's eyes narrowed. "And?"

The lawman shifted uneasily and averted his gaze. "He wants to run your DNA against the sample taken from the victims."

"That's absolutely out of the question!" Raven darted up, slicing the air with her good arm. "We cannot permit——"

A look from Eric silenced her. He drew his hands up under his chin and closed his eyes, seeking elusive calm in darkness. "Warren wants my DNA?"

"Y-yes," Walter answered uncertainly. "I don't think it's unreasonable given the circum... stan... ces... " Walter's trailing voice was shredded by Eric's icy stare.

"I'm going to assume you remember who you're talking to and let you try that again." Simmering anger in Eric's aura prickled the air.

Walter swallowed hard. "Look, h-he just wants to rule you out. Surely you can appreciate that from a legal standpoint."

"No, I can't. His request shows his doubt, as does your support."

"Hey! I know it's not you!" Walter shrugged helplessly. "But, I mean, after what happened the other night, is it so wrong? People died and you——"

"*Now you listen to me!*" Eric roared, his chair slamming into the wall as he stood. "I won't even go into everything I've done for this town, for you, for the mayor, or for Warren!"

Pointing in the direction of The Greenery, Eric yelled, "But I will do *anything* it takes to protect her, even if I must kill to do so! Did I really hear you throw that back in my face as an accusation?"

"I didn't mean it like that!"

"You'd better quit while you're ahead, Walter. You assured me that you could handle what I had to say and it is quite clear that you can't. You tell Warren to justify a warrant. He may know what I am, but until he can legally implicate me with the facts you have, I refuse to comply."

"Eric, be reasonable," Walter begged, affecting utter helplessness. "You know he can't issue that warrant. Neither of us is accusing you of anything, it's just...if we can prove you didn't do this——"

"Then what?" Raven barked. "You'd tell all those busy gossipers that Eric isn't the vampire they seek? You can't reveal those results without exposing him and you know it. It only services your peace of mind."

"I'm done with this discussion. Raven has a few questions and then you may leave." Eric's eyes drilled into Walter.

"I expected you to understand." Walter's voice disappeared into his hat with his gaze.

"Same to you."

Walter's body sagged as he silently pled for understanding from Eric's cold, ice blue stare.

"Ahem!" Raven grunted, drawing Walter's attention. "I need to study those saliva samples at your lab."

"Our lab?" he asked, confused. "We don't have one. Everything gets sent to state forensics."

"Of course." She rolled her eyes. "Have you received the results?"

"There's a statewide back log. A small town like this hardly takes priority—"

"Fine," Raven said, patting the air. "We'll intercept the samples before they're tested and I'll conduct tests on the bodies here."

Walter glanced at Eric. "I suppose if I say 'no' you'll come anyway?"

A mischievous grin brightened Raven's tired face. "You catch on pretty quickly, Chief," she chirped with a wink.

Resigned, Walter said, "Okay, well, at least wait until after hours—there'll be fewer eyes."

"Timing doesn't matter. No one will know I'm there."

"Look, give me some leverage. I have rules to play by."

"Raven," Eric said. "Make an appointment with Walter."

"Tonight?" she asked. "After your meeting with the mayor?"

"No. Tomorrow," Eric replied. "I had Molly reschedule the mayor. Paresh and I are leaving for the arc after we're done here. Seeing Jonathan will help her."

"You can't possibly think of leaving town!" Walter blurted out.

"I'm not under house arrest, *Chief*," Eric replied in a frosty voice.

"Hey, I'm just doing my job, *Counselor*. Which in case you've forgotten, you got me to accept in the first place!" Standing, Walter jabbed his finger on the desk. "I think I've done a decent job at handling what's happened here, and I challenge you to find someone else who could do the same. You put me in this position of trust, but there's no trust here at all!"

"Raven will see you tomorrow night." Eric peered over his glasses.

Walter huffed and shoved his hat onto his head. "Night patrol takes to the road at seven. Come after that." He stalked toward the door.

"We'll save seven-thirty for you," Raven said. "Oh, one more thing!"

"*What?*"

"I'll need to retrieve our weapons, as well."

Walter's knuckles cracked as he clutched the doorknob. Clenching his jaw, he threw the door open and stalked out.

Eric stared at the open doorway. Nothing felt real anymore. Enemies had turned into allies, and friends had turned into foes. There was no trust, no order, and no peace.

He smashed his fist onto his desk, startling Raven and splintering the wood. *"Damn it!"*

Behind her guarded expression, fearful reverence quivered in Raven's eyes. He watched her finally recognize him as Jonathan's true equal—in power, rank, and nature—and he wasn't sure how he felt about that.

Combing his hands through his hair, he dropped into his chair. His voice resigned, he said, "This stays between us."

She bowed her head. "Anything you command, of course, *my lord.*"

II

The day's downward trek continued, despite sunny rays warming the greenhouse's shaded ceiling panels. Slumped over the table's mosaic tiles, Paresh stared vacantly across the pond and Molly's gaze followed.

Seated between them, worry bridging his brow, Donovan touched Paresh's shoulder gently. "Do you have the ointment?"

Paresh nodded with a groan and grabbed her throat. She pointed at the small handbag on the table.

Pawing through its meager contents, Donovan plucked out the ceramic vial and pried her fingers away to apply the oily substance. "There now—relax and breathe."

"Is she okay?" Sarah whispered. Having slipped in moments ago, she grabbed a chair and sat beside Molly. "What's wrong with her?"

"She's not feeling well," Molly replied.

"But she'll be better soon," Donovan said, lightly rubbing Paresh's neck, watching her closely.

Molly gave Sarah's arm a comforting pat. "Bring her some tea shaken with lots of ice—the cold will help. I'll take a brandy, and please bring our gentleman guest a glass of Eric's private reserve."

Sarah glanced at Donovan, who eagerly grinned to show off his fangs. "Of course," she said, beaming a smile. "I'll only be a moment."

Sadness shadowed Molly's visage. Tracing her gaze to Sarah's departing form, Paresh asked, "What's the matter?"

"It's nothing. Don't worry about me."

Picking at her nails, Paresh mumbled, "Everyone keeps saying that. But I need to get out of my own mind!"

Donovan cocked his head to study Paresh's face. "Better now? Your pulse has evened out."

Paresh nodded. "Yes, thank you." To Molly, she said, "You had the same look yesterday at lunch. Why does Sarah make you sad?"

"I'll explain after she brings our drinks, okay?"

When Sarah returned with their drinks, Molly prodded Paresh to order something.

"I'm not hungry."

"Soup might help you feel better."

Donovan offered an encouraging smile. "I agree with Miss Molly."

"We make the minestrone with all fresh ingredients—carrots, zucchini, spinach, basil—it's so good!" Sarah winked.

"It does sound good," Paresh reluctantly agreed.

Donovan gestured at his chalice. "I'm set, Madame!"

Smiling, Sarah took Molly's order: an artichoke and eggplant panini with extra sweet potato fries.

Swirling the snifter in her hands, Molly stared unblinking at the tiny amber vortex. Once Sarah closed the heavy doors behind her, Molly blurted out, "Sarah's my replacement."

Bouncing his foot on his knee, Donovan leaned back and threw his arms dramatically into the air. "Ah! A modern lady-in-waiting! And pretty, too. The pure of heart do so flock to him."

An involuntary smile tugged on Molly's mouth. "One way of looking at it, I suppose. But I'd rather see her at a culinary school in Europe instead of playing hostess and pastry chef here."

She paused to inhale aromatics reminiscent of toasted nuts and caramel before sipping. "But, since childhood, she's known her place as the caretaker's successor." She sighed and quietly added, "At least she can touch her dream here, I suppose."

Paresh and Donovan exchanged puzzled looks, and the latter asked, "What's a caretaker?"

"For generations, the caretakers were like Eric's valets. All from one family—"

"Sarah's family?" Paresh interrupted, leaning forward eagerly.

Molly laughed. "You're a curious little thing! Wait until I answer one question before asking another!"

Paresh gnawed on her straw and nodded.

"In the past, Eric didn't need a caretaker, so it was an easy job that got easier with each generation—"

"Until you!" Donovan exclaimed. "You're his buffer in the modern world so he can hide in his office and avoid exposure!"

"Neither of you wants me to finish the story, do you?" Molly asked, eyeing them pointedly. "Yes, the modern age has made a confidante more important than a valet. Right now, Sarah cares for her grandfather, Sammy, the current caretaker, and runs this place—"

"Sammy? Weaverly? The driver who took me shopping last week?" The ice in Paresh's glass clanked as she twirled the straw.

Resigned to answering questions, Molly nodded.

"I'm surprised I didn't catch the relationship when I met her," Paresh said, disappearing into her thoughts.

"You had a lot on your mind. It'd be easy to miss the shared last name. And besides, Eric's mother's maiden name was Weaverly, so it's not like they're—"

"Family!" Donovan's feet dropped to the floor as he sat forward.

"No." Molly set her glass down and put her hands up. "Okay! No more questions!" In a hurried, slightly lowered voice, she explained, "When the Civil War ended, some freed slaves who didn't have last names took on their former owners' names. Something similar happened with Sarah's family."

After a question-free pause, Molly got comfortable and watched the viscous amber fluid coat the glass as it swirled. "See, Eric buried his wife and joined up with her father in Petersburg, Virginia, where the Army of the Potomac was in the middle of the war's longest battle— actually, it was the longest military event in the history of American warfare." She paused in thought, and then waved it off.

"About a week later, Eric was out scouting alone and found a Confederate camp where a malnourished slave in tattered clothes was tied to a tree far from a fire's warmth. Eric tossed his jacket over his bony frame, cut him loose, and carried him back to his camp, where he had the battlefield surgeon tend to his wounds. The slave, 'Willie,' was so grateful that he unofficially joined the Colonel's battalion and fought by Eric's side—once healthy enough—until they returned home."

"But Willie didn't have a home," Paresh said sadly.

Nodding, Molly said, "I can't imagine what his grief was like then, but I believe caring for that poor man kept Eric in touch with his humanity when he needed it most."

"One might assume then that Sir Eric provided for Willie upon their return?" Donovan asked, thoroughly engrossed, his fingers intertwined beneath his chin.

"Given Willie's experience with horses in the South, the Colonel hired him as a stable hand. Willie shared a room in the detached servant house with a cook and worked hard. Eventually, he fell in love with a housemaid, got married and had children, moved off the mansion grounds into his own house, and rose to the level of stable master, commanding an entire staff."

"Aw!" Paresh cooed, plunking her glass down. "How shweet!"

Swiping a curious glance over Paresh to land on Molly, Donovan pointedly said, "That 'tea' came from Long Island."

"What?" Molly snatched the highball. It reeked of alcohol. "Oh no, no, no! Paresh—"

"Itsh totally fine!" The girl pawed the glass back into her possession. "Tell us more about the Weaverlahllys!"

Contemplating Paresh, Molly asked Donovan, "You can smell her blood, right?"

"Yes, ma'am. She's a tad more than tipsy, but probably feels better than she has in days." Donovan nudged his chin at the drink. "Let her feel good."

"Yeah," Paresh said, tucking the straw into her mouth.

Molly cautioned, "Please take it slow, honey."

Sharing a brief look with Donovan, Molly continued, "To thank Eric for saving him, Willie wanted to take on the Ravenscroft name to honor his fa—"

"Eric doesanot like his father." Paresh shook her head in slow motion.

"Right," Molly said, "so Willie honored his mother instead."

"Ooh!" Paresh cooed, happily melting into her cupped hands as her elbows slid onto the table's surface.

"I don't like this. You need to eat before you take another drink," Molly said. "That's a lot more alcohol than you've had in wine."

"Nah, ist okay," Paresh said, wide eyes instantly riveted on her hand flopping back and forth in front of her face.

Donovan took custody of the highball. "Sorry milady. Miss Molly says." Tipping his drink to Molly, he said, "Thanks are on tap for this."

"I dine with Eric. It's a natural order."

"So whasabout the car'taker?" Paresh asked, face nestled between her palms.

Molly pursed her lips, but then shook her head and continued. "Willie dedicated his life to Eric. His children grew up knowing that Eric had given them freedom, a name, and opportunity for success— and they weren't blind. Your family employed them, but their loyalty belonged to the 'Man Who Time Forgot.'"

She gave the brandy a final twirl and tossed it back. "For generations, they have cared for the one who cared for them. Soon, it will be Sarah's turn to take Sammy's place, *and mine*."

"Ah! The bittersweet symphony of life," Donovan said dramatically, raising his chalice in a mock toast. "To duty and honor, and all that grand stuffy-stuff."

"Duty and honor." Molly glanced at the doors.

"Ist nice," Paresh said with a firm nod.

Molly chuckled to herself.

"What?" Paresh shot Molly a puzzled look. "Sarah sheems'happy, so-so-so why——"

"The food cometh." Donovan put a silencing finger to Paresh's lips as the hostess pushed through the double doors, platter in hand.

"Here we are ladies!" Sarah announced cheerfully.

As she placed a steaming bowl of soup before Paresh, Molly held the laced highball up and asked, "Sarah, why did you bring Paresh a Long Island Iced Tea?"

Sarah froze before inspecting the glass. "Oh no! I gave the order to the bartender while I prepared your guest's drink. He must have misread it." She touched her hand to her chest. "I'm so sorry, Molly! I'll make coffee——"

Paresh laughed and motioned for her drink. "Ist okay! Isht good and cold, and I feel goood!"

"Ah! And when you feel better, we all feel better!" Donovan proclaimed, tipping his chair back on two legs and laughing like a jolly fat man, which made the girl giggle. The two women exchanged confused glances. Donovan winked at Sarah.

"Ah, blessed be the Fates for allowing such a beautiful maiden to befall mine eye!" Donovan's hearty voice filled the greenhouse with the bravado of a Shakespearean actor and then quieted to a whisper as he arched an eyebrow. "You must be quite popular with the gentlemen callers, eh?"

Despite her slightly reddened cheeks, Sarah planted a hand on her hip while the other flew through the air. Feigning a polite, Southern accent, she said, "Why Mr. Donovan, sir, I don't recall saying I prefer 'gentlemen callers.'"

"Ohh, I see. Luck——y ladies," he said with a slow drawl. Smiling at Paresh, he made his two-legged chair walk backward. The girl, with the straw tucked into her mouth, giggled even harder.

Sarah turned an apologetic gaze upon Molly. "I am sorry. I don't know how this happened. I'll talk to the bartender—"

"Don't. It's working out for those two." Molly patted the chair beside her. "Take a break and tell me what's been happening."

Frustrated lines creased Sarah's brow. "People say the nastiest things. It's unbelievable."

Shaking her head, Sarah knit her lips tightly, and, for a moment, looked much older than twenty-four. "It's been hard to keep my mouth shut. Ingrates think they know so much…they don't know anything at all!"

Oblivious to Sarah's bitter tone, Paresh watched Donovan's antics with childlike delight, and Donovan, thriving on her attention, attempted to balance the chair on one leg without tipping over.

Molly couldn't help but grin. She patted Sarah's arm. "It'll pass. They know not to believe hearsay. Eric's heart beats at the core of this town. They'll come around."

"If that's true, they wouldn't turn their backs on him like this!" Sarah crossed her arms with a huff. "People too willingly believe the worst about each other without even *trying* to find out for themselves!"

"Ah, your Eric is a resilient fellow," Donovan said. Returning the chair's legs to the floor, he finished his drink. "That's good stuff. He has impeccable taste in everything."

"Hm, my Eric," Paresh murmured with a dreamy smile.

"I am in so much trouble," Molly muttered to herself, shaking her head at the drunken girl. To Sarah, she said, "Something's going on that people don't understand, but once they have time to absorb it, they'll come around. As Eric would say—everything will work out in the end. Have faith."

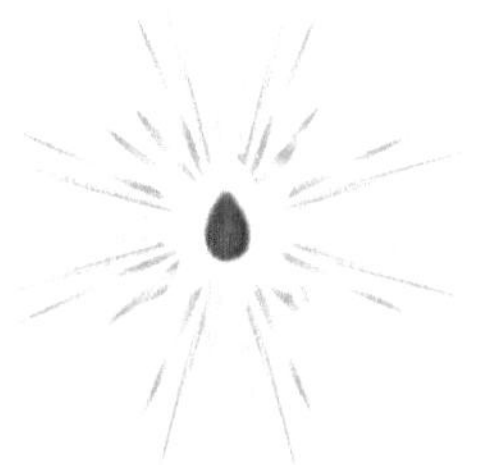

CHAPTER ELEVEN: THE BOOK OF JOSHUA

Footsteps sounded on the grass in their sector of the arc's privacy grid. The fingers stroking Jonathan's forehead lifted. Lucien stiffened and his hand fell to his side. Few approached the First and Second Born unannounced, and yet, for the second time in little more than a day, they had an unexpected guest.

"Endymion." As though chilled by Lucien's voice, the footsteps froze.

"My lords." The Elder swept into a graceful bow, folding one arm behind his back and crossing the other over his chest. "Please excuse the intrusion. The others are soaking in the bathhouse on this lovely early evening. I thought an invitation was in order."

"No," Jonathan replied quietly, sweeping appreciative eyes over the Elder. His silk robe was as fair as his skin and hair, and reflected the moon's light. Ghostly radiance lit his olivine eyes like sea glass. He was Lucien's only rival as a humanoid vision of untarnished, silvery beauty in nightly monotone.

With a reverent tilt of the head, Endymion replied, "I'll leave you be." He hesitated and returned Jonathan's gaze. "'Tis an honor to call you 'Master' once again, my lord. It has been far too long."

An uncharacteristic smile warmed Jonathan's cheeks. "Thank you, Endymion."

When the Elder didn't move, Lucien's eyes questioned his continued presence.

Most would tremble, but Endymion didn't fear the Arch Elder like the others did. Tucking his hands into his robe's sleeves, he stepped forward. "A query, sire?"

Lucien's chin dipped to imply a nod.

"When might Lord Eric and our new lady grace us with their presences?"

Lucien's stare returned to the hills beyond the reflecting pool. "Tell me how the others feel."

"Some are discontented with your decree, as expected, but most are enraptured by the Servator—the Sacred Vessel, in particular."

"Most," Jonathan echoed, spitting bitterness. "They should be grateful she exists at all. Meeting her is an honor few will get."

The charged silence that followed seemed to stretch into eternity. Lucien stared ahead, clandestine thoughts betrayed by a subtle, hard line in his jaw. Jonathan's mind churned. The soft caresses were gone, but emotion had undeniably seeped into the Nation's iron core.

What if you falter, Lucien? Jonathan regarded him through hooded eyes. *Will rust form around our pristine pillar? Will silent questions lead to whispers, factions, and anarchy? Will Paresh have suffered for nothing?*

Centuries ago, Lucien had impaled an Elder through the heart. That brutal punishment vividly lived on in the minds of those present, and the seat remained vacant as a reminder that Lucien acted swiftly and without mercy. Would that image hold true now?

Jonathan's gaze drifted to Endymion. Despite their dark reality, the Elder's warped sense of serenity had defeated every test and defied time's very existence. He appeared completely unaffected.

Lucien spoke at last, lowly, impassively. "Soon."

"Endymion?" Jonathan wanted to hold onto this taste of the way things used to be. To delay the return of the "new" Lucien—and guilt's weight.

"Yes, my lord?"

"What are your thoughts?"

"'Tis an honor to serve under anyone of your lineage," Endymion answered tenderly. "Lord Eric's humanity is not a weakness, but rather a vital element in governing this new age."

As Jonathan's lips curved slightly, Endymion added, "That smile suits you well, Master."

The curve deepened as Jonathan nodded.

Endymion swept down into a final bow. "Good Eve, my lords."

Jonathan watched the Elder's back shrink as he left their privacy sector. "You don't suspect him, do you?"

"Endymion is too placid to be an enemy."

"I would have said that about Alex, once. And he doesn't possess Endymion's cruelty."

"It's not Endymion." Splaying his fingers, Lucien resumed caressing Jonathan's forehead. "You need rest."

"I should finish this confession first. Do you mind?"

"Not at all."

"What I did to Joshua as a child led to my darkest moment with Eric, and his darkest moment, as well."

"Oh?"

"That humanity that you and Endymion believe will help us—" Jonathan paused. "So many times, my greed and lust nearly destroyed our only chance at sal—"

"Salvation came, nonetheless."

Lucien traced Jonathan's cheekbone. How many angels and humans had those fingers torn apart? Would they still kill without question? Did Lucien have a penitent heart, through all that blood?

"'What ifs' create meaningless worry."

Jonathan's head lolled to the side. The pool reflected the moon's pale face and reminded him of time's passage.

"No more excuses," he whispered. "I need to protect her."

Silence descended. Lucien stroked Jonathan's face, tall grasses rustled, fireflies twinkled.

"Trauma shapes the path of human life," Jonathan said at last.

"And where does that path lead?"

"For the Hawthornes? Vulnerability and self-destruction." Jonathan dipped his fingers into the pool. Ripples distorted the moon's face. "Every action has a reaction. I set events in motion and people died. But, if I hadn't, Paresh might not've been born."

The water stilled. The moon stared, accusing. Jonathan swatted the water, vainly attempting to hide from the crescent king's all-seeing eye. "Hmph. Like a monkey trying to catch the moon."

Sighing, he rested his foot on his knee. "But it's not an illusion. How can something as good and pure as Paresh blossom in the wake of something like me? I was never in control of the games at all. Only a player in Karma's revolution."

"That's rather philosophical for you," Lucien said. "You are more like the hare contemplating his longevity than the foolish monkey seeking unattainable dreams."

"Perhaps I am both..." Trailing off, Jonathan deliberated quietly.

Lucien startled him by saying, "You never told me how Joshua died."

Jonathan didn't answer.

"Does Eric know?"

"Eric is well aware."

"Do explain."

"That's not my confession to reveal."

"Were you involved?"

Jonathan nodded.

"Do go on."

Huffing, Jonathan reluctantly began. "Elizabeth's suicide destroyed Nathaniel. He spiraled into uncontrolled paranoia and raised his son with bitter warnings about Eric's loyalty and women. He neglected his businesses and took a huge hit when the railroad failed in Las Vegas. He blamed the banks and stuffed every penny of his fortune into his basement vaults, serendipitously saving himself when the stock market crashed. When Joshua was old enough to inherit his father's mess, he used 'friends' from Chicago to fix it."

Swirling his fingers through the water, Jonathan whispered, "I don't know, perhaps the scars from witnessing his mother's death would have damaged him anyway. But the way Eric..."

Lucien's hand paused. "What did Eric do?"

Staring at the moon without really seeing it, Jonathan said, "Eric wears many faces, but he has *never* been above using his abilities to get what he wants. I suppose he's like me that way."

"What did he do?" Lucien repeated.

"Learned the hard way that a child's mind is too fragile for invasive manipulation."

"He tried to remove the mother's suicide from the child's memory?"

"And instead fractured Joshua's mind," Jonathan replied. "He relived the event repeatedly, ending with Eric peering down from the balcony. Joshua grew into an angry, impulsive, and immoral adult who loved to hate his vampire protector. The only *person* he loved was his wife, Lily, but it was twisted—more like the love of an incestuous son for his mother."

"So you saw the effects firsthand and tried it anyway?" Lucien resumed caressing Jonathan's face.

A chill shot down Jonathan's spine. "That was generations later!"

"No need for anger. I'm merely surprised."

Jonathan brushed off Lucien's hand and sat up. "I am certain that two actions in particular led to the judgment I received, and *that is one of them*."

"You interfered with the Flock."

"He wasn't stable to begin with! And looking back, my actions didn't change his destiny at all!"

"That may not be true. They used Paresh at the last minute because of what you did to him."

Jonathan's shoulders sagged. "What do you want from me?"

"There is a recurrence of tormented children in your confessions. Eric. Paresh. Joshua…"

Lucien's words stabbed at Jonathan. For a while, he said nothing. Then a bare whisper fell from his lips. "I know I've hurt her. I watched her die because of my actions. I don't need you to remind me."

"Do you feel as badly for Joshua? It's not different."

Jonathan swallowed the defensive reply burning his throat. Lucien was right. "He never had a chance because I interfered with the Flock."

Shaking his head, Jonathan groaned. "I was so focused on Eric's actions. But I started it."

"And that is why you find yourself here." Lucien nudged Jonathan down and cradled his head in his lap. "If you felt no regret for Joshua, you would have been forever stuck, no matter the other confessions."

"I understand. This is my confession, after all." Blowing out his breath, Jonathan tried to will the tension from his body.

"Joshua salvaged their railways, hotels, and restaurants using underhanded methods and his Chicago connections. Then, at the height of Prohibition, he threw himself into dangerous situations to force Eric's protection—"

"Your star is glowing." Lucien pointed at Jonathan's jacket in the grass. The Vampiric Star pinned on the lapel emitted light from its ruby center.

"Great." Sitting up, Jonathan pulled a phone from his pocket and called Eric.

"I'm tired of this restricted ID crap! Why can't you give me your number like a normal person?" Eric demanded upon answering.

"I guess there's no emergency then," Jonathan replied dryly.

"Not unless you count the failure of your hunters on two fronts as an emergency."

"Someone's in a foul mood tonight."

"I wonder why, Jonathan. Maybe because I'm the suspect in two murder investigations? Because there was another one—a seventeen-year-old girl—and I'm about to be court ordered into giving up my DNA! Oh, and Alex showed up, but escaped with the help of your VaSH High Commander. Other than that, things are *swell*."

"*What?* Raven wouldn't! There was another attack?" Jonathan shot a worried glance at Lucien. "What about—is Paresh…?"

Hearing Jonathan frazzled seemed to calm Eric. "She's fine, but she can't take much more. She wants to see you."

"How did Alex escape?" Lucien's apathetic question sailed over

Jonathan's shoulder.

"That wasn't to you, he's on the communicator with Raven," Jonathan said to Eric. "Has Paresh improved at all?"

"Raven needs her hunters." Eric sounded strained and tired.

Softening his voice, Jonathan said, "We'll handle this. You need to focus on Pare. Has she improved? Did she drink?"

"No." Eric paused with a sigh. "To be honest, I don't know how much more of this I can take, either."

"You've survived worse than this."

"I suppose you would know better than anyone."

Jonathan didn't respond.

"Still there?"

"Yes."

For a while, the only sound was Lucien's occasional question to Raven.

"The Great Second Born is never this quiet," Eric eventually said. "God help him if he can't hear his own voice."

"You can come up, but before you do," Jonathan whispered, "I'm sorry about Joshua."

He heard the phone crack in Eric's hand. Static buzzed on the line.

"Why?" Eric asked in a tight voice. "You weren't the one who killed him."

☽ ✳ ☾

Thick shadows challenged the vision of all who entered the basement, including the resident vampire…and the woman walking through his bedroom door.

She blindly approached his bed, her cotton skirt rustling over silent footfalls that no human could replicate. She was a fledgling predator and he was in no mood to deal with her.

He watched her every movement, but even when she stopped beside him, trying to peer through the charcoal veil, she couldn't see if his eyes were open or closed, or where his bed ended and his body began. Uncertainty seeped into her aura as her hand slowly lowered. She hesitated and then swept his brow, her hand lingering, awaiting his response.

She shifted her weight to one foot and blew a quiet breath over her lip. Her pulse quickened. He closed his eyes. The woman's nagging voice of logic would chase her out.

Or so he thought. Her heartbeat calmed and confidence surged into her aura. His eyes opened as her hair tickled his cheeks and warm breath brushed his lips.

"What are you doing in here?" he asked, his tone laden with warning.

"Shh…" She straddled him, ripping his shirt open and lightly raking his chest with her nails. The silhouette of her head lowered to his collarbone, where a trail of kisses led to his chin before he snatched her by the throat and jumped up, slamming her against the wall with her feet dangling above the floor.

"I asked you a question."

Despite the brutal fist about to crush her windpipe, she dragged her finger from his navel up to his mouth and flattened it against his lips. "Shh…"

"Are you here of your own free will?"

"Yes."

"I don't think so." He squeezed her throat. "Jonathan enjoys playing his little marionettes against me, whether they are human or not. He doesn't care if I sleep with you or kill you—or both."

"I'll do anything you command."

His voice deepened. "Oh, I know you will."

His nails pierced the back of her neck. A tiny cry of fear escaped her mouth.

"Did Jonathan not mention that I share his blood? That I'm *royalty?*" He flashed a malevolent smile and half-laughed. "You will do everything I ask of you."

Her throat seized within his tightening grasp. She clawed at his arm. As her aura weakened, his smile faded and he dropped her on the floor. Scratching at her throat, she choked in precious air.

"Leave this place," he said. "If I see you here again, no one else will ever see you anywhere else. Ever."

She didn't move. He jerked her up by the jaw and forced eye contact, his darkening gaze grating the black barrier. He may have severed the connection binding her there against her will, but he would not permit her to stay. "Leave. Now. I command it!"

"As you wish, my lord." Turning out of his grip, she left as quietly as she had come.

Tossing an annoyed look at the empty Victorian parlor chair in the corner, he laid flat on his back and mulled his thoughts for several minutes. "To what do I owe this great honor?" he asked at last, sarcasm dripping from each word.

A laugh came from the chair. "Did you actually sense me or was that a guess?"

"I'm in no mood for you tonight."

"Which is why I sent a woman in my place. I thought you liked women." The chair creaked as Jonathan's rising form materialized. He sat on the bed. "I suppose taking control of her gave me away? Oh well. I couldn't let her leave without trying to service you."

"Get out."

"Oh come now, what kind of brother would leave you alone in this sordid state? Cast aside like a common servant, sequestered to your quarters like a beast—"

"Leave."

"As if you would allow Joshua to beat that man senseless. You aren't that cold. Yet."

Eric was silent.

"And just what did that man do, anyway? Oh, yes! Nothing. Nothing at all." Jonathan inched closer. "Other than being the only human person in this world that you actually care for."

Eric remained quiet.

"So tell me. Why did Joshua lash out at you by attacking that Weaverly trustee of yours?"

Jonathan slapped his leg and cried, "Ah! That's right! You checked on the baby! I can see how that might drive a man—and two of his body guards—to beat the crap out of an innocent man."

"Shut up. Do you talk just to hear your own voice?" Eric closed his eyes and tucked his hands beneath his head.

"Oh stop pretending this doesn't bother you. How can Joshua's reaction possibly intrigue me more than you?"

"He never gave me to Daniel. It wasn't my place to check on him. Surely you aren't so arrogant to believe you're the only one who knows how to strike out at me."

Now Jonathan fumed in silence.

"Eat your tongue, *Brother?*"

"*Your place? He never gave you?*" Jonathan seethed. "And when did you become some possession to be locked away in the basement? If he truly owns you, then why aren't you sealed in the eastern wing's vaults? *You share my blood!* How can you sit there like this?"

Eric shook his head.

"No! You will speak to me. Explain this to me! Why do you stay here? No human lock can hold you. How dare you lay there and accept being treated like an animal!"

"Am I getting under your skin?" Eric's sickly-sweet tone oozed from sinisterly curled lips. Jonathan stood with a huff and paced along the footboard.

Eric's hollow laugh rebounded off the walls. "What's there to get? Every *thing*—every *person*—in this house belongs to him. I'm no different. I haven't been any different ever since you killed his mother."

Jonathan stopped. "Excuse me? That woman killed herself."

"Telling yourself that doesn't change the truth."

"I'm not going to argue with you. Semantics don't matter; she wasn't of the Flock."

"Because you led her to fall."

"She was well on her way." Jonathan sat on the bed.

"With your help," Eric said. "After Elizabeth threw herself off the balcony, Nathaniel was angry, but at least he recognized my loyalty to Joshua. But Joshua…I am *his* shield, to use how *he* sees fit, even though a new heir lives."

"And how does that make you feel?" Jonathan asked sarcastically.

"I don't really care."

"Then why are you here?"

"Purpose."

"Oh, here we go again. You and your purpose. I'm tired of listening to it already."

"Maybe…" Too drained to engage Jonathan, Eric's voice trailed into the darkness.

"Maybe?"

"I don't know anymore. These self-centered people don't give a damn about me."

Jonathan slid closer. "What are you saying?"

"I don't know." Eric felt cold, indifferent. They'd once been family, but that family was dead.

Jonathan crept closer, whispering, "Why didn't you use the woman? It's been a long time."

Eric sighed with a shrug.

Jonathan crawled on top of him and pushed Eric's shoulders into the mattress. "If I'd known you didn't want a woman, I wouldn't have bothered Alex to find a fledgling. I am more than willing to satisfy your needs myself."

"Oh," Eric mimicked, "here we go again."

"You're not pushing me off."

"Maybe I'm tired of fighting."

"Or maybe it's something else." Jonathan kissed along Eric's jaw.

"Why are you here?" Eric asked, bored.

Nibbling Eric's ear, Jonathan whispered, "While you were saving your valet, an opportunity presented itself. One I've been looking forward to for a while."

Mild curiosity registered. "An opportunity?"

Sudden commotion outside, in the garden maze behind the mansion, caught Eric's attention. "What did you do?"

"I made good on a promise. And I'm here to free you. You want to go, so enjoy it."

Eric slid out from beneath Jonathan and stood, facing the bed. "What have you done?"

"You don't even like them."

"It's Nathaniel," Eric said, listening to the distant voices. "He wasn't in his room."

"Yes, yes. The insomniac roams the gardens, even on cold nights like this. Tell me something I don't know." Jonathan's shadowy hand swatted black air.

"He's dead."

"Oh, I know that, too. That's what they get for locking you away like this. They left themselves wide open."

Tugging Eric back to the bed by his belt, Jonathan flashed an insinuative grin. "And now the real fun begins."

Eric ripped free. "What have you done? I thought we were finished with this!"

With a sudden burst of force, Jonathan shoved Eric against the wall. "The game isn't over until I win my prize," he growled.

"You never stop to open your eyes for a single second do you?" Eric growled back.

"Same question to you, *Brother*. These humans—"

"Damn it!" Eric's fist smashed into the wall. "I despise them! You said it yourself!"

"Then why are you still here?" Jonathan's growl lost its edge. "Come back with me."

"I can't abandon them! They're family."

"Family? Ha!" Jonathan spat. "The Colonel's dead. Your wife is dead. Your son is dead. See the pattern here? *You made a promise to me first!*"

"I know," Eric replied quietly. The panicked voices were getting louder. "They've found him."

"Do you want to know what happens next?" Jonathan's breath was hot on Eric's throat as he inched closer. "Or do you want to have some fun before you go?"

"Go? Where do you think I'm going?" Eric pushed against Jonathan's chest.

"Oh, you'll come with me before this night is done. That's a promise I'll make to you." With a deliberate jab to Eric's sternum, Jonathan stalked toward the door.

"Where are you going?"

"The game's in play. And since you are so very transparent, I'm not even going to watch your move." At the door, he was a black outline in darkness. "Better get to it, before I take them all out."

"Daniel's only an infant. You can't—"

"Oh, is he here, too?" Jonathan asked, feigning ignorance. "Maybe you'll choose to save him instead."

☽ ❋ ☾

"There were bite marks on his throat! You son of a bitch!"

A fist smashed into his cheek. Eric's face flew to the right. He straightened to meet Joshua's fuming eyes with silent indifference.

"Was he dead when you left him there?" Joshua screamed, his fist slamming into Eric's jaw. "Or did you leave him to bleed to death alone?"

Deflecting Joshua's fist, Eric emptily said, "If you keep hitting me, your hand will get very sore, very fast."

"Don't touch me!" Joshua growled. "You killed my father! You deserve everything coming to you!"

Joshua's fist flew once more and hit Eric's jaw, but instead of following through, Eric stood rigid and cold, no longer playing along, empty inside and bored with life.

"*Shit!*" Joshua cried out, hopping with his hand tucked to his chest. He bit his lip and rolled his eyes skyward. "Damn it!"

"I warned you."

Hatred blazed in Joshua's eyes. He leaped and punched Eric again. Emotionless eyes watched him jump in a circle, holding his hand, screaming in pain.

"Fine!" Joshua shrieked. "Have it your way. No guarantees that your weakness will survive this time!" He turned to the wide-eyed guard standing nearest his father's body and growled, "Drag Clarence Weaverly's ass up here by his feet!"

Before the guard could move, Eric shoved him into the wall—cracking the plaster and knocking him unconscious. Yanking Joshua forward by the shirt collar, Eric warned, "Do you think, in this big, wide world, that I'm the only vampire? Let alone the only vampire your father angered?"

More brazen and stupid than his father, Joshua gripped Eric's arm with tight, white knuckles. "I don't give a shit how many damn vampires are in this big, wide world or who pissed on them. *You* are the one who should have been there to protect him. *You* failed. Therefore, *you* killed him."

"And you locked me in the basement."

Joshua spat in Eric's face. "You locked yourself in the basement. You belong to me."

A spark of anger burned Eric's stomach. He wiped his face with his free hand. "No. I don't."

Inching closer, Joshua snapped, "Yes. You do. And you'd better not forget it." His stare challenged Eric to defy his authority. "You took the money. You made the promise."

"Promises can be broken." Inky wells of navy swallowed Eric's crystalline eyes.

"You are mine until the day I die."

The animosity in Eric's aura curdled the air. Baring his growing fangs, Eric snarled, "That day is now."

A woman's scream raced down the hall. Joshua paled as he looked toward the source. His hands slid off Eric's arm. "Lily? Lily!"

"I'm not the only vampire in this world."

"L-let go and save her!" Joshua begged.

Grinding his teeth, Eric shoved Joshua to the floor. Only a speck of humanity remained to fight his vampire blood, but it was crying out to his equally small sense of morality, and they made for a powerful duo. Eric marched down the hall and barged into Lily's room. She dangled loosely in Jonathan's arms, his teeth already buried in her throat. Her lifeless eyes stared at the ceiling.

Bloody lips lifted from Lily's neck. *"Hello, Brother."*

Eric rolled his eyes in disgust. "Have them. I don't give a damn."

He turned to leave, but paused when Jonathan taunted, "And Daniel?"

"Leave him alone."

"Either you care or you don't. You can't 'not care' while still caring."

Whisking around, Eric snarled, "Have you gone dumb?"

"Excuse me?" Jonathan shook Lily's flaccid body and caught her face to peer into her empty gaze. "Who does he think he's talking to?"

"Dumb and mad, then." Glaring at Jonathan, Eric stepped closer. "Is the life of an infant worth the price of your revenge?"

Jonathan flashed a wicked grin and threw her body at him. Laughing as Eric rushed to catch her, he replied, "You! You are worth it. Even if I spend eternity in Hell, I'll have you beside me."

"N-no…o-oh no! *Noooooo! Lily! Oh God, no!*" Panicked eyes frozen on his wife's bloody throat, Joshua took a few feeble steps through the door before falling to his knees. "*Lily!*"

Eric tossed Lily's corpse onto the bed. Pointing at Joshua, crying on the floor, he said to Jonathan, "You killed his mother. You killed his father. And now you've killed the only person he actually loved. This is your mess. I'm done with it."

Eric threw his hands up and turned to leave, but an acrid scent forced him around. Black smoke trickled from the beneath the door behind Jonathan. Eric's human heart lurched.

"Did you forget, *Brother?* It's your move, not mine." Jonathan's eyes skimmed the dead woman and sobbing man before lifting to Eric, his grin widening as he reached back and opened the nursery door. Thick smoke engulfed the room amid the roar of hungry flames. "You are so easily distracted, you fool."

Joshua tugged on Eric's arm to pull himself up. In a daze, Eric watched him rush to the bed and struggle to lift his wife. Eric looked at Jonathan and a passing thought jolted his heart into a gallop. As though aware of Eric's thought, Jonathan flashed a sinister grin. Locked onto his brother's demonic eyes, Eric backed out of the room.

"You have to help me save her!" Joshua cried over his shoulder.

"No. I don't."

Eric didn't break eye contact with Jonathan, even as he stopped in the hall and grabbed the door. Joshua dropped Lily's body and lunged at him. At the same time, Jonathan nodded.

Eric slammed the door and twisted the knob until the mechanism jammed and the handle broke off in his hand. His thundering pulse muffled Joshua's fists pounding the door, his smoke-choked screams, and Jonathan's laughter. He calmly walked down the smoky hallway. Odors of burning wood and fabric were spreading faster than the smoke. Night staff rushed past him.

"It's too late. Save yourselves or die for nothing," Eric called after them—he thought. His pulse drummed over the sound of his own voice.

Warnings about the fire had reached the servant's quarters when he arrived in the cramped third floor corridor. Some ran toward the fire, some cried or panicked, and some fought a path to the exit. He wove his way through their bodies as though they weren't there and opened the wet nurse's door, one of few still shut.

"Is Daniel with you?"

He jarred the nurse awake, who jumped up, sputtering, "Y-yes, sir. He fell asleep, so I jes' kep' him after you left him here. I was jes' gonna—"

"Give him to me and get out."

One of the cooks shouted a warning down the hall. The nurse gasped. "*There's a fire?* Oh God!"

She ran into the hall screaming, "Old Bethie! Anyone seen Old Bethie?"

She rushed back to Eric, crying, "I'll take the baby. Please! She's a deaf old coot an' the hall's gettin' smoky! Please! You have to—"

"My priority is Daniel," Eric said. "Who you save is your business."

The wet nurse's jaw quivered. She nodded uncertainly.

Eric found Daniel in the cradle beside her bed.

The nurse turned away in shock. "Meet you outside."

The infant slept as Eric swaddled him in layer upon layer of blankets and tucked him to his chest. The smoke was so thick in the hall that he could barely see. He headed for the servant's entrance and jogged down a maze of stairs.

He stepped outside and sucked in crisp winter air. Pajama-clad people huddled together in groups on the lawn and driveway, shivering as flames hungrily consumed the upper floors. He trudged forward one foot at time, vaguely aware of bodies moving out of his way and of sirens wailing in the distance.

There's nothing's left. He paused between the grand house and the hedge maze to gaze upon the bundle in his arms.

The wet nurse yelled his name from the servant's door. In the same instant, an alabaster face appeared at the maze's entrance. Strangely, he felt nothing as he locked on Jonathan's gaze and waited for the nurse.

Hoarsely choking for clean air, she jogged over and bent down with her hands on her knees. Tears dripped from her eyes as she gasped and heaved. "I got her out."

He pushed the infant at her. She straightened and took him into soot-smudged arms, quiet shock on her face yet again.

"Protect him with your life," Eric commanded. "He is the only Hawthorne left."

As Eric walked away, she followed, asking, "Wh-where should I wait for you?"

"You shouldn't."

☽ ✷ ☾

Ruthless despair dragged him to a faithless place he'd gone only once before. Poison Spring was a distant memory, but the red-haired demon wore the same face.

I'm no different from him. A monster.

Turning sharply for the privacy hedge on his right, Eric ran five hundred yards, not a wisp of guilt nagging his soul. How could it? It was singed and smoke-choked, a chew toy for anxiety.

Branches eagerly tore at his skin, but he was too numb to notice. He pumped his legs hard to escape the fiery mansion. As if any distance could extinguish the flame burning him from the inside out.

Frozen fields crunched beneath his bare feet. Winter's frigid night air bit at his exposed chest as though trying to freeze his human heart for his cold vampire blood.

Farmland became woodland. Bursting through Sunset Grove's frosted thicket, he ran on instinct to the beastly silver maple.

"Lucinda, forgive me!" Eric cried, collapsing at the giant base. Curling his fingers into its gray, furrowed bark, he swallowed hard to dislodge the knot in his throat. He didn't deserve to be here. Not at his wife's tree, transplanted as a seedling to memorialize her life. To serve as a reminder of the choice he'd made at the Confederate camp.

His humanity had failed him.

He turned and slumped against the tree, and folded his arms over his knees. He buried his face as guilt shook him at last. Tears and ash stung his eyes. The knot in his throat expanded, and tightened in his chest until it choked him.

"Guilt does not become you," a voice observed overhead.

No words can absolve me. I am not human. No part of me at all, Eric thought without looking up.

Jonathan sat beside him. "We've never made it this far before. How long will this last?"

Eric silently asked himself the same question. Joshua's blood was on his hands for the rest of his days.

"You're not actually grieving, are you?"

Eric thrust his head against the maple's bark. A sliver of moon poked through the forest's naked canopy. The tears on his cheeks froze into tiny icicles. He shook his head.

"I was proud of you," Jonathan said, following Eric's empty eyes to the moon. "But now you are disappointing me."

"You're wrong," Eric said, his voice buried beneath the knot in his throat. "I'm glad he's dead."

"Then why are you weeping like a damsel?"

"I killed him." Eric went numb again. It was too much. Lucinda couldn't save him this time. He deserved to burn.

"You say that like he's the first man you've killed. I saw it—an opportunity presented itself and you took it. So what? He wasn't of the Flock."

"No, I—" Eric stared at his hands for a long time. "You can't understand."

He naively searched Jonathan's face for any sign of guidance. The fire in his belly had burned itself out. He felt empty. "But...I need you to understand."

Jonathan's stone façade hid whatever emotion lurked beneath. "Then make me."

"I closed the door. I killed him. I listened to him die." Barely aware of his own voice, Eric missed the shift in Jonathan's aura as he slid closer.

"Yes, and?"

"I feel guilty for killing him, but—" Eric exhaled. "I'd do it again."

"Is that so?"

"It felt good."

"Yes, it did." Jonathan's satisfied grin and hungry eyes devoured Eric's moonlit countenance, challenging him to see the fiend beside him.

"I want to kill him again, to relive that lightness as I walked down those stairs. My heart was beating so hard it was all I could hear, and my nerves were on fire, but still, it felt so good, so damn good." Eric balled his fists, closed his eyes, and swallowed hard. The lump was still there.

"I don't see the problem," Jonathan said, facing Eric with parted lips and growing teeth.

"I don't regret killing him. That's the problem. *I can't feel this way.* This isn't who I am. I killed a Hawthorne. Not you. *Me!*" Hot tears surged into Eric's eyes. He buried his face into his arms and sucked cold air deep into his lungs.

"But this *is* who you are." Jonathan breathlessly bit down on his lip as his hand slid over Eric's muscled shoulders. He lapped at the blood that pooled to the surface. "Embrace who you are—what you are. You are so *very close.*"

"I can't take this. My human heart cannot live in harmony with my vampire blood." Eric slumped against his legs, his shoulders sagging beneath Jonathan's arm. "Why must I always be at war with myself? Always conflicted. Always embattled."

"Vulnerability is something I look for in my prey," Jonathan said quietly with a heavy breath, leaning into Eric. "But not something I ever thought I'd see in you."

Eric straightened slightly and shook his head, still missing the hidden meaning in Jonathan's words. "I'm so tired of it all."

"I'll make you feel better then," Jonathan whispered into his ear, gaining Eric's attention at last. "I can take away your pain, if…"

As Jonathan's voice trailed, Eric followed his darkened eyes to the cross around his neck. With a slight tug, Eric broke the chain and tossed the trinket into the grass. He knew Jonathan's thirst well. Maybe with an extra push, he could finally go home to his wife.

He let Jonathan press him flat against the ground.

Eyes filled with desire ravaged his body. Eager fingers danced across his chest, lips trailed down his cheek, across his collarbone, up his throat. Eric was so numb it all felt like puffs of air.

Jonathan was lingering over his jugular, hovering, waiting.

Lucinda, please be there for me, Eric thought, closing his eyes and arching his neck. It would end soon.

Jonathan moaned and slipped his hand down Eric's pants.

"No," Eric whispered, pulling on Jonathan's arm. "This is what you want, here." He stroked his throat.

Cupping Eric's face, Jonathan tilted his head and kissed along his jaw to his ear. "Relax," Jonathan whispered. "I know what I want."

Eric tried to retreat into his shell, but Jonathan's wandering mouth and hands suddenly burned like fire, and bile stung the back of his throat as his brother's aroused body rubbed against him. "What are you waiting for? Please sto—"

"*Please?* Oh, you sound so weak. I do so enjoy that in my prey." Jonathan moaned louder and kissed Eric's neck.

"Jonathan…stop! I don't want *that*." A flash of metal in the grass caught Eric's eye and turned his thoughts to Daniel. To atonement. To possibility. "Get off me."

"Mm, yes, I like a fight the most." Jonathan flicked his tongue against Eric's pulse. "Especially with you. Remember the last time we were here together? This tree and I have been waiting to taste you again."

"I'm warning you," Eric said in a raspy, deepening voice. "This isn't what I want and you know it."

"Oh, but I think you do." Jonathan laughed. "I've been pondering you and our unique bond. Logic says you should hate me, but you don't." He licked his lips and grinned. "No, you like me—and maybe you're even a bit curious about what I have to offer." Jonathan pinned Eric's arms at his sides.

"Stop!"

"But more importantly—" With his grin contorting insidiously, and the moonlight catching his engorged eyes, Jonathan brushed his arousal against Eric's groin. He moaned and laughed again. "Ah yes, I know exactly what you want from me. How you want me to take your pain and send you 'home' to Lucinda. But I don't bend to the will of others. They bend to mine. You will be no exception."

"Get off!"

"Oh, I will. But first, why did you think I'd kill you?" Jonathan truly was a demon. "You're so pitiful. You belong to me. I want to savor my prize again and again, not watch it wither to dust after a feisty romp."

He slid down Eric's chest and lashed his ear with his tongue. "I promise you've never felt anything so wonderful, so unearthly euphoric."

Eric struggled to free his arms. Adrenaline flooded his veins. The night wore blood red.

"No! Get off me!" he yelled, arching his hips.

"Oh, fight! You are so beautiful in the moonlight when you're angry."

Jonathan forced Eric's arms out beside his head and held him with enough pressure to sink his wrists into the frozen ground. Flattening himself against Eric's body, he said, "I'm not leaving here without you. Or without having you. You'll beg for more when I'm finished."

"You are such a stupid fool!" Eric yelled with a spray of spittle. He wrapped his legs around Jonathan's waist and twisted his hips to the side, pulling Jonathan off center. Eric ripped free of his hold and flipped Jonathan onto his back.

Wearing an odd grin, Jonathan nestled himself beneath Eric. "Why do you always come here? To this monstrously huge beast of nature? Every time we meet here, your blood is spilled and soaked up by that tree. Every single time."

"*Shut your damn mouth!*"

"Isn't it supposed to remind you of your humanity?" Disturbing intensity lit Jonathan's eyes. "Then why does it *love* the vampire in you? It feeds off your blood and calls to me as much as much as it calls to you. It wants me to feed it, Eric. It wants me to win."

"I said shut up! I'm sick of your manipulations, your devilish tricks!" Eric shoved off Jonathan's chest, shouting, "If you hadn't pushed me, I would have gone with you! But you are so blinded by 'winning your prize' that you can't see it! You'd already won, damn it!" Eric turned away, tossing his hands up and kicking at the air.

Jonathan propped up on his elbows. If Eric hadn't been so heated with anger, Jonathan's calm voice might have chilled him to the core. "I only win when I claim you for my own."

"You had me, Jonathan. You had me." Eric shook his head. "I was yours, willing to go to the Arctic Circle, to bow before Lucien. But you can't see that you will never have me the way you want me. I don't return your desires. I don't appreciate your advances, your insinuative remarks. I do not want to have sex with you!" Eric threw his hands up again and punched the trunk.

"I don't know what I'm doing anymore," Eric said, wiping his face. "If I go back…can I go back? I don't have anywhere else to go. I'm sure as hell not going anywhere with you. Not now. I'd rather face my demons. I don't belong in this world or yours. There is no place for me."

Sinister shadows crossed Jonathan's face as he rose. His crooked smile and delirious eyes turned Eric's stomach.

"What are you doing?" Eric asked, backing away.

"I'm not losing you now," Jonathan said quietly. "And I'm not fooling around. You can hurt me. Did you know that? Do you want to hurt me? Come over here."

"What the hell is wrong with you?" Feeling along the tree, Eric circled backward until it was between them. He glanced over his shoulder at the trail that broke the tree line. He could run to the safety of the Sunset Grove Parish—*if* he could stand on its sacred soil.

He took another step back and hit a firm body. Then the world was a blur. Jonathan grabbed him by the waist and shoved him against the tree.

"Do you realize how sweet your blood is?" Jonathan asked in a quiet, disturbing voice. "It's the blood of the innocent. Pure, sweet ambrosia. My forbidden fruit. I won't allow you to hurt me this time."

"What are you…? Let go!" Eric couldn't move. Jonathan was stronger than he'd ever been before.

Jonathan snarled at him. "Do you have any idea what you do to me? The restraint it takes? How long I've stood beside you, knowing what flows in your veins? That I've always gone easy on you for the fun of it?"

"Jonathan," Eric growled. "Stop this!"

"I've never met someone so strong, someone who drives me so mad. But you don't know your own strength. Or how it takes my breath away." Jonathan threw Eric to the ground and landed on top of him with saliva dripping from his fangs. "*Literally.*"

"Stop!" Eric yelled.

"Why? This is what you wanted. Do you know that you almost killed me the night Elizabeth jumped? Have you ever even thought about it?

That I might have died because of your loyalty to that *scum?*"

"What—?"

"Oh, I truly savored killing Nathaniel at last. *And now I get dessert.*" Scowling with murderous eyes, Jonathan's mouth snapped open and savagely tore into Eric's throat.

The gasp that raced past Eric's lips was part surprise and part ecstasy. His breaths quickened, and grew heavy. He arched his throat and gasped again as Jonathan's teeth sank deeper.

Every nerve screamed from pleasure that increased in exponential waves. It was dizzying. Euphoric. The universe exploded into a kaleidoscope of colors behind his eyelids and his body ached for the ecstasy of skin on skin, naked and slick with sweat, moving in unison.

He moaned breathlessly and cried out as his teeth tingled and grew. The scent of his own blood drove him to salivate. He moaned again as another spike of pleasure crashed over him. As his head lolled to the side, his eyes rolled open and again saw a flash of metal in the grass.

The prism of colors returned as his eyes closed and the air lifted notes of vanilla and honeysuckle from Jonathan's hair. Eric inhaled deeply and moaned.

"Lucinda smelled like cotton and spring," Eric mumbled. His mind latched onto the memory and the mismatched scents, but as another wave of pleasure crested, delirium rode it into Lucinda's arms.

Somehow, he knew he was weakening. Panting, he caught the scent of vanilla and honeysuckle again, and heard Jonathan swallowing his blood.

Jonathan!

Eric saw the glint of metal again. He licked his lips and exhaled. His own breath made his body shudder. He strained to focus, and freed a wrist from Jonathan's grip. His fingers climbed up the muscles of Jonathan's arm and over his shoulder toward his neck.

"Mm." Jonathan released Eric's other hand and stroked his bare chest, moving down his naval, inching lower—

Pleasure sparked a fire in Eric's core that pulled him further into the delirium that Jonathan controlled. He was going to lose himself.

Jonathan's lustful eyes gleamed in Eric's mind. *It won't stop here.*

The cold night air stung his eyes as he forced them open. Taking a deep breath, he yanked on Jonathan's hair, grabbed the metal in the grass, and slapped it against Jonathan's cheek.

Jonathan bolted up, shrieking. Blood dripped like syrup from his mouth. Eric tried to catch all that he could—without it, he'd lose consciousness. He palmed the cross he'd discarded earlier and fought to stay awake, alert, and moving.

Jonathan lunged at him, only to roll off screaming again when Eric grabbed his throat. Keeping his grip as firm as he could, Eric rolled on top of him. He dangled the cross over Jonathan's face, less than an inch from his nose. Paralyzed, Jonathan watched it sway back and forth. Its shape was burned into his cheek and neck, black and deep. It wouldn't heal for months, even with the Vampiric Nation's balms.

With his vision blurring and vertigo spinning the world, Eric whispered, "I'm sorry…for hurting…you."

He brushed auburn locks from Jonathan's throat and bit into his jugular. Each swallow restored strength and energy, and cleared his mind. He ignored Jonathan's moans and knocked away his groping hands. It sickened him to know that he'd reversed their positions and thrust Jonathan into the euphoric state he'd just escaped, especially since his brother was likely enjoying it.

Even when he felt strong enough to walk away, Eric kept drinking. When he withdrew from Jonathan's throat, he pulled the cross away.

Jonathan panted. "You're not going…to kill me?"

"No." Wiping his mouth, Eric said, "I don't understand most of what you were saying before you attacked me, but if you ever do that again, you're going to lose your teeth. This is the last time."

Jonathan gasped for air and tried to lift his hand to his face. Eric helped him cover the burn on his cheek with his palm. Groaning, Jonathan whispered, "Hurts."

"I know." Studying the wound on Jonathan's neck, Eric continued, "I think you need to know that despite *everything*, I've never wished you serious harm. Perhaps I shouldn't, but I feel terribly about these burns even though you deserve them ten times over, you bastard."

"You can't…go back,"

"I can. I have you to thank for that. You set me free *and* forced me to examine my choice yet again. I suppose that means I'm in your debt once more," Eric replied.

Eric stood and cracked his neck. "Daniel is my future and my redemption. I don't expect you to understand."

"I'm not giving up."

"Maybe not, but I guarantee that you will never warp Daniel the way you did Joshua."

"So you think."

"And I'll never trust you again. If not for the weight of my own sin, I might have been angry enough to kill you instead of weakening you."

"Again, so you think."

"Is your pack nearby?"

Jonathan shook his head. "You are a fool to care about me. I'll always use it against you."

Eric gazed at the moon. "Even though I don't return your desire, you'll never stop pursuing me. And even though you are incapable of care or love, you're the closest thing I have to a friend…or family."

"You're not a fool; you're a sap."

"Perhaps." Eric glanced down. He'd never seen Jonathan so vulnerable or pathetic. "But my ability to care about you is what sets us apart, and maybe I need that reminder to keep myself in check. Again, is your pack nearby?"

"Alex is close enough. Why? I won't involve them."

"I don't want to leave you defenseless. But, again, I don't expect you to understand."

"All this time, I thought you'd gone cold," Jonathan said, trying unsuccessfully to sit up.

"I had. You had me, Jonathan. And you lost me."

Jonathan cursed under his breath.

Eric quietly contemplated the cross in his hand. "Daniel sparks warmth in my heart that I haven't felt since Lucinda died," he said at last. "You were wrong about Clarence. He's not the only person I care about. I feel a great need to protect that child. I couldn't have known that Joshua would overreact like he did."

"Why did he really lock you in the basement?"

"Clarence defended himself." Eric shrugged. "He got a decent shot at Joshua's face and, in Joshua's mind, I should have been there to prevent it even though he started the fight."

"What would you have done?"

"What does it matter now?"

"Wondering about your loyalty."

"Earlier, you said it almost killed you. What were you talking about?"

"Something that will never happen again. Tonight was rather telling in whether your loyalty sits with those you serve or those you care for."

Eric glared at Jonathan. "The game's over."

Jonathan grinned. "And saying that makes it true."

Licking at the blood drying on his lips, Jonathan glanced in the direction of the mansion. "It's your move."

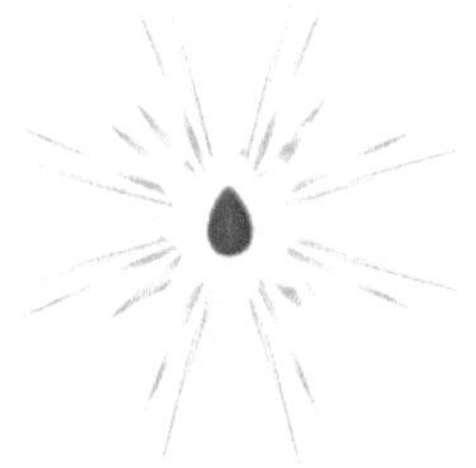

CHAPTER TWELVE: THE KING'S COVENANT

T wenty-five years passed. During that time, the world's economy rebounded from the eras of Prohibition and the Great Depression to balance uncertainly on the precipice of war's mighty mouth. Armies marched upon fields stained crimson until defeat and victory came amid plumes of death and destruction. The Allies' final triumph delivered an era of rebuilding that lasted into the Cold War and Space Race, but Hitler's war had taken a great toll on both the world and the Vampiric Nation.

The repugnant miasma of war-borne fear and hatred had boosted Lucifer's strength to dangerous levels, and, as the only creatures capable of defending against him, the First and Second Born were considered priority targets. Between World War II, the ensuing conflict in Korea, escalating tensions in Vietnam, and the looming threat of nuclear war, the High Council had convinced Lucien to pull Jonathan from his elevated perch and restrict him to the arcs.

It was now the summer of 1960. The High Council had lifted restrictions on the general population in 1946, a year after World War II's end, but had waited to rescind *his* order until that morning.

"Lording their power over me. Bastards. Fourteen extra years!" Jonathan grumbled, soured as he fled into Animus Hollow's endless white haze. It enveloped him, clinging with wispy, white fingers.

His throat was tight. His breaths were shallow. His lungs burned. He needed to run, to escape the non-dimensional plane. But, the Hollow had him now.

He closed his eyes. Buttons popped off as he ripped his shirt collar open, clawing his neck, feeling for an imprint on his skin. *There's no collar. No tether. You're free—*

Faint illumination lit his eyelids. He stepped into the Realm of Man at last, where the real sun embraced him with warm, unrestrained brilliance. The air was heavy and humid, organically sweet over car exhaust, manure, and hay.

It was glorious.

For too many years, he'd craved what his simulated world could never replicate: to jump into oil-polluted puddles and watch rainbows swirl above his shoes, to pluck worms from waterlogged homes during a storm, to swim an algae-riddled pond at the end of summer. Yet now that he was here, a moment of quiet warmth was all he needed.

He slid on a pair of sunglasses and opened his eyes. A cloudless blue sky gleamed through earthy-green foliage overhead.

Where am I?

Rows of squat and twisted forms with branches sprouting young fruit repeated as far as he could see. An apple grove? The portal should have opened onto a manicured lawn stretching six acres in every direction.

He knocked his fedora down to shade his eyes and stuffed his hands into his pockets. Crossing perpendicular to the orchard's lanes, he muttered, "It's obviously not the fixed point in the woods, but the variable point should release on the mansion's grounds. I—"

He circled in place. "I don't recognize any of this."

When the last few rows were in sight at last, he rushed ahead, expecting to see the maze's towering shrub walls. The entrance for the unicursal labyrinth doubled as the exit, but one stray path led to a secret water garden with shallow ponds, fountains, and fairy-themed statues—the place where Nathaniel Hawthorne had wandered on his final, sleepless night. That was where the saggy old sack had met Death's accomplice.

An elaborate, open garden spread out before Jonathan. Pristine white statuary and marble benches sat within cozy topiary nooks. Graceful willows anchored the corners and saplings dotted the interior amid roses, ornamental grasses, and evergreen groundcover. In the center, a marble fountain spilled crystal water down five scalloped tiers into a large, round basin. Moss formed organic grout for a cobblestone path that followed a basic curve—the labyrinth's original footprint—and it branched off toward six reflecting pools on the garden's left edge—remnants of the once-hidden aquatic paradise.

"Erasing the scenery won't fool your demons, *Brother*," Jonathan muttered, eyeing the stables and fenced pastures on the hills that once hosted their moonlit discussions.

Only the mansion was the same, regal and grand, washed in white and edged in black. And there, beneath an ivy-covered pergola by the old service door, his ebony-haired obsession stepped out, holding hands with two young boys, smiling. Laughing.

Betrayal burned his gut. Jonathan angrily clamped down on his teeth. Moisture surged into his eyes, and throbbing pain and blood flooded his mouth. With a groan, he stuck his finger between his lips. He had severed a chunk of his tongue.

Eric and the children were getting closer, impeccably dressed, probably just home from church. For once, he hoped Eric hadn't developed his ability to sense him, and tightened his aura to contain the scent of blood. Luckily, the breeze was in his favor. As he held the piece in place, it reconnected, and then he quickly wiped his eyes, lips, and fingers with a kerchief, and stuffed the soiled cloth into his pocket.

The boys looked like Hawthornes. They had the same soft facial contours of the previous generations' children, one blond and the other dark haired. They wore matching white short-sleeved shirts tucked into tan pants with tiny blue ties and brown suede shoes. The man between them wore his typical black suit.

Eric should have been immune to time's touch, but he had changed as much as the landscape: hair buzzed near the scalp, horn-rimmed tinted lenses atop his nose, and skin snuffed into dullness. Eric could never be ugly—no, his features were much to fine and chiseled for that. But, he no longer resembled the radiant hunter Jonathan had created.

At the garden's entrance, the boys tugged Eric's arms in opposite directions and giggled, pushing Jonathan to his tolerance threshold. Subtle variances in Eric's demeanor—a wider smile, a lingering look, a louder laugh—defined their relationships. The fairer boy was the heir.

Those brats have no right to bind Eric to that contrived family tradition! Jonathan raged internally as the boys ran into the garden.

He stormed over to a statue of the goddess Venus near a bench beneath a weeping willow. Eric had closed his eyes and plugged his ears to count to ten. Then he began an exaggerated search for the brats.

At the very least, Eric would never take his ears off the heir. It was as revolting as ever. Jonathan's lips formed a grim, hard line and his fist tightened at his side.

The dark haired one slinked past him and ducked behind Venus. Jonathan hadn't heard him approach. That was intriguing.

Widening his aura to encompass the boy and make himself visible, Jonathan approached the tree's drip line. "Hello there, little one."

The boy's head swiveled, his brown eyes wide with surprise. As he contemplated Jonathan, his tiny fingers probed a marble fold on the statue's rear. Jabbing that finger into his mouth, he glanced at Eric before scampering onto the bench and sidling over to Jonathan. His innocent eyes sparkled with youthful curiosity. He pointed at Jonathan's face with the slobbery finger.

"You'we like Ewic," he said, his words rounded by a rhotacistic impediment.

"What did you say?" Jonathan asked, more from shock than from a lack of hearing.

"You'we like Ewic."

"How old are you, child?"

"Thwee." He splayed his fingers and tucked his thumb.

Jonathan beamed a tight smile. "What is your name?"

"David Samuel Hawthowne. I'm named for a king!" He puffed his chest proudly.

"King David Samuel Hawthorne?"

The boy's tiny head excitedly bobbed up and down. "Yup, suh! He's in the Bible!"

"I suppose there is a King David in the Bible, yes." Jonathan straightened his cuffs and nudged his eyes across the garden at Eric, who had yet to realize young David was no longer visible or audible. "Tell me King David, what do you think of your brother's friend there?"

David inched closer and touched Jonathan's leg. "He's nice. I like him."

The child's grimy paws were soiling his virgin wool trousers! Forcing a smirk easily mistaken for a smile by a three-year-old wrapped in the naïve notion that someone "like Eric" was safe company, Jonathan said, "Seems to me that Eric likes your brother better than you, King David."

The boy followed Jonathan's gaze to where Eric sat with his brother on the fountain's rim. "Nuh uh, he likes me, too."

"Look, there—do you see how they're together? Laughing and having fun without you?" Jonathan feigned concern with a shake of his head. "Shouldn't they be looking for you? Does Eric ever go anywhere with only you? Without your brother?"

The boy shook his head. He jumped off the bench and buried his face into Jonathan's pants. "No—"

Too repulsed to restrain himself, he pried the boy off and glared at the snot stains on his thigh. Forcing another sympathetic guise, he knelt before David. "Does it bother you that he doesn't care about you? Do you wish Eric spent more time with you?"

"Yep, suh." Moisture glistened in his eyes.

"What's your brother's name?"

"Andwew Michael Hawthowne."

"Andrew? Well, he's not named after a king, is he? What makes him so special?"

"I dunno." The boy's lower lip quivered and tears slid down his cheeks. "Can't Ewic love me, too?"

"He can't. He will always love Andrew. He will always choose Andrew over you. And he will always belong to Andrew and never to you." Jonathan gave the boy's shoulder a reassuring squeeze. "But I would never choose your brother over you. Did you know that King David in the Bible had a special friend named Jonathan?"

The boy shook his head.

"It's true. And guess what?"

"What?"

"My name is Jonathan. Would you smile if I agreed to be your special friend, King David?"

The boy sniffed and nodded.

"Like Eric is your brother's special friend?"

He nodded again and rubbed his eyes.

"You have to promise to keep it a secret and never tell anyone."

David's head bobbed in agreement. His eyes sparkled again. "Yup, I'm good at keeping secwets!"

"Good, because if Eric saw me here, he'd make me go away. Eric doesn't want you to have a special friend." He stroked the boy's hair. "See this ring I wear? It makes it so that he can't hear us."

"But Ewic heaws evewything."

Jonathan smiled. "Not me. And not you when I have this ring. In fact, I can make it so he can't see me or you when we're together."

"Weally?" David's eyes widened and focused on the onyx stone in Jonathan's Hilja ring. "Wow!"

Jonathan's eyes darkened as he tipped the boy's chin up to meet his gaze. "David, Eric will never like you as long as he can choose your brother over you," he said in a deepening voice. "You can make him love you and have two special friends, but that can't happen while Andrew is around. You, and you alone, King David, must decide what to do about that. Do you understand?"

The boy nodded in a daze. "Yep, suh. It's a secwet or you go away."

"That's a good boy." He turned David and nudged him from beneath the tree. "Go to Eric. You'll see me soon."

Shoving his hands into his pockets, Jonathan whispered, "The Hawthorne legacy ends here. Before I'm done, both boys and their parents will be dead, *Brother*."

☽ ✳ ☾

Under a star dusted sky and petite waning moon, Jonathan released his aura and leaned back on his elbows. The crickets were quieter than he remembered. Their tranquil composition mingled with whirring frogs and the occasional hoot of an owl. The night was warm and humid, the air punctuated with pollen and moss, the grass slick with dew that saturated his pants and sleeves. But, tonight, he didn't mind. He was in the Realm of Man, and it was perfect.

Cattails swayed beside him. With so many trees near the main house now and horses roaming his old stargazing spot, Jonathan had settled beside a manmade pond behind the detached garages. Most likely created for fire retention, it was close enough for Eric to detect him, yet far enough to allow privacy from the humans in the house.

"Oh Eric," Jonathan said with a sigh, a reluctant truth forming in his mind. "Life with you is never boring."

An almost shy smile lifted his cheeks and he chuckled softly. "Every time I leave here, I can't wait to return. Is it you? Or is it this place? Is this what home feels like?"

The breeze snuck beneath his hair. He shook a few wayward strands from his forehead and lifted his face with closed eyes to enjoy night's invisible caress. Shoes crunched gravel between the mansion and the garages, and the wind carried a mixed bouquet of cologne and sweetened blood.

Ambrosia. Jonathan opened his eyes. The starry hunter of night loomed overhead. "Orion is especially bright tonight."

Silence.

"I knew you'd come," Jonathan continued. "But why don't you ever try to sneak up on me? You're more than capable."

"What would the point be? You want my attention and you have it, so don't make demands." Eric's tone was dry, disinterested. He stopped ten feet away. "What are you doing here?"

"Oh, come now. I might think you aren't happy to see me after so long." Jonathan tilted his head back to view Eric upside down. "But don't flatter yourself into believing that you had anything to do with my absence."

"What are you doing here?"

"What's with those glasses and that hair? And your ghastly skin? Have you seen yourself?"

"Raising Daniel in the public eye has warranted a few changes. I'm not going to ask you again."

"Wow, you're Mr. Serious, now, eh?"

An exasperated sigh rushed past Eric's lips. He rolled his eyes skyward. "Three seconds. Answer or I'm leaving. One."

"Maybe Mr. Impatient is more apt."

"Two."

"Oh, stop this nonsense."

"Three." Eric pivoted on his heel.

"Eric, wait," Jonathan said. "A big brother should watch out for his little brother. Isn't that right?"

Eric whirled around with narrowed eyes. "What?"

"Ah! And so it begins!" Jonathan replied with a smug grin.

"I have no patience for your games!" Eric growled.

"And how is that different from any other time?"

"You won't get what you want. I refuse to play."

"You're welcome to forfeit. My fun isn't dependent on your cooperation." Jonathan shrugged and watched the stars as Eric simmered in silence. After a few seconds, Jonathan glanced over his shoulder. "So 'Andrew' is the heir?"

"Now you listen here!" Eric seethed, his long legs whisking him to Jonathan's side in two strides. "I will not bother with threatening your life. No, you'd enjoy that too much. You see, I've learned a little something about manipulation from you, *Brother*."

"Is that so?"

"Oh yes. I'll strike where it'll hurt, and you'd better believe I mean it, because after last time? It'll be easy."

Tiring of Eric's tone, Jonathan flicked his eyes up at him. "Do go on."

Eric sat on his heels to bring them eye-to-eye. "I swear to you this: if you dare harm Andrew or touch him in anyway, *I will never forgive you*. I will never join you in front of Lucien, or anywhere. Imagine an eternity of knowing that I exist out of your range, an eternity of having a dream that is only a dream. You touch him—"

Eric pointed at the mansion. "And that is exactly what you'll have. *That* is my vow to *you*."

"Ha! Beware of making empty threats. Forgiving me is in your nature."

A strange smile curved Eric's lips. "Not this time. I don't know where you've been, but things aren't the same between us. Don't presume you know me. You'll never again fool me into thinking you're a friend."

A pit formed in Jonathan's gut. Twenty-five years was a mere drop in time, but it had changed everything.

"You promise me, Jonathan." Eric's smile receded into a face of stone with eyes so cold they shot icicles into Jonathan's heart. "Promise me or live without me, because if you harm him, I am done with you forever."

The force of his tone stunned Jonathan into silence. A vow from the Second Born meant nothing and Eric knew it. But, the ultimatum would never change, which gave Eric leverage over him.

"At a loss?" Eric asked. "It's one word." He held up his index finger. "Just one. Yes or no?"

"You're truly a smug bastard tonight," Jonathan spat with a glare.

"I'll take that as a 'no.' Farewell."

Jonathan caught Eric by the ankle. "Fine. I will not harm Andrew. You have my word. But you have to stay here and talk awhile."

Eric kicked his hand off. "I'm holding you to it, and no, I don't."

"Stop being an obstinate ass!" Jonathan tried to grab him again, but Eric stepped beyond his reach, his seemingly permanent place in Jonathan's life. "I've been stuck in those arcs for more than two decades. I'm finally out, and I'd like some company!"

"It's not going to be with me." Turning his back to Jonathan, Eric tossed his hand over his shoulder and walked away. "Those days are over." He paused after a few steps. "Oh, and Jonathan?"

"What?"

"The next time you cut yourself, you might want to remember that I can smell blood as well as you can. You're more than capable of spying on me without revealing yourself, so if you don't want to lose again, you need to try harder."

☽ ✳ ☾

"I know how this ends," Lucien interrupted. "Further confessions are unnecessary."

"You think this has all been about the kids and that new revelations will prove that I, alone, screwed up David's fate, but you're wrong." Jonathan sat up. "I'm not an idiot, Lucien."

"I didn't imply that you were."

"The defense you forced me to give the High Council was true. David envied Andrew before I ever met him. I merely saw the seed and made it bloom."

"Defense?"

"Fine—*justification*," Jonathan said. "I'm not saying I don't share blame for David."

"Tell me then, if you can accept responsibility for him, and for Joshua, whom you did not kill, then why is this one so important?"

"Because what I did to him, what Gabriel wants me to confess, goes beyond twisted manipulation. Please…" As Jonathan's voice faded, he looked down at his hands folded in his lap. For the first time, he was nervous. "Lucien, you don't know everything I've done. This is the one Gabriel wants."

Lucien's hands parted the air. He offered a respectful nod. "Pardon the interruption, my lord. Please continue."

"Don't submit to me," Jonathan whispered.

Lucien stroked Jonathan's cheek. "All your life, you've walked beside me knowing that your place was beneath me." He paused, his hand lingering on Jonathan's skin. It was warm.

"Lucien don't—"

His master folded his hands into his sleeves and glanced wistfully at the moon. "I can't be your equal in body and spirit the way Eric can. I offer myself as a partner nonetheless and hope that will be enough."

"Lucien—"

"I give you no conditions and make no demands." Lucien placed his hand on Jonathan's chest and met his gaze. "But you have never needed to fear me."

"Until now," Jonathan replied quietly.

☽ ✳ ☾

Hinges creaked in protest as Jonathan pushed the door open. "I've come to rouse King David from his slumber!" he roared in a deep voice despite the house's sleeping occupants.

On the bed, blanketed lumps twitched.

"I don't see him anywhere!"

A lump giggled.

"Did I just hear him?" Jonathan pretended to pause. "Where could he be?"

A tiny hand appeared and tugged at the air. A pocket of darkness formed as the blankets lifted and eyes peered out.

Lifting a finger to his lips, Jonathan whispered, "Shh." He wasn't close enough to contain the boy within his shielding aura.

The eyes blinked in acknowledgment. The blankets lowered and the pocket disappeared.

Jonathan closed the door and padded to the bed. Widening his aura to encompass the boy, he threw the covers back. "Aha! There's King David!"

Squealing in delight, David jumped on the mattress. "Master Jonathan's here! Master Jonathan's here!"

"You were a very good boy there, King David," Jonathan said. "Here you go—cherry, as requested."

David grabbed at the lollipop in Jonathan's extended hand. Jerking it back, Jonathan scolded, "You know better!"

"Sorry sir." At the highpoint of the jump, David kicked his legs out and bounced on his butt. Scooting to the edge, he held out his hand. "No jumping with candy 'cause I could choke."

"Very good."

David's eyes sparkled as he retrieved his treat and shoved it into his mouth. "Whe's Ewick?"

"Don't talk with food in your mouth," Jonathan admonished, already annoyed. "He's with your father in his study. Is he being mean to you?"

David nodded.

"Did you tell your father?"

The sucker came out of David's mouth. "He didn't care."

"That's because you're not Andrew."

"I hate him." David's lower lip jutted out.

"Who?"

"Andrew." David rolled the candy stick back and forth between his hands. "Today, his fingers were in the way when I slammed the car door and Eric spanked me for it."

"Andrew did that to get you in trouble, didn't he?"

"Yup, sir. I said it was an accident, but no one believed me because Andrew was crying like a baby that I did it on purpose."

"Did you?"

The lollipop disappeared into David's mouth. His lips turned up slightly as he shook his head.

"Good boy."

Jonathan grinned. Over the past few years, he'd helped David "properly" interpret his familial interactions. The boy had been testing boundaries since he had to share his fifth birthday cake with Andrew. He'd thrown a tantrum that netted a reprimand from Eric, and that had spurred David to seek retribution at every chance.

"Eric will never like me as long as Andrew is around," David suddenly said, throwing the lollipop at his closet door.

"Why would he?" Jonathan replied, eyeing the cracked candy on the floor. "Your parents gave him to Andrew and Andrew won't share him. You, King David, aren't much more than an afterthought to them."

"What does 'afterthought' mean?"

Jonathan waved his hand. "It's not important. You have to prove yourself to Eric. That you're stronger than Andrew. That you are better than him. That you are more worthy of a special friend than him."

"I try!" David whined.

"I am not permitted to influence what is not already there. Do you think your brother is better than you?"

"No."

"Then why does everyone else? Why should Andrew get a special friend while you get nothing?"

"I don't know."

"You must decide how to win Eric. Can you do that, King David?"

David's body went rigid. His eyes lost focus. He scrunched his blanket in a fist and nodded.

A sullen, withdrawn shell overtook the giggling sprite's body. It'd happened before—a startling change befitting the family's unstable history. Wherever Eric went, anger and jealous attachment followed. David's father had been unaffected despite descending from Nathaniel and Joshua, and ignorantly dismissed David's behavior as sibling rivalry.

"Look at me," Jonathan ordered in a throaty voice. David's face obediently tilted up. "Don't waste my time with your whining. Can your little brain grasp that I hate being here? I should be wandering the Earth with Eric at my side as the magnificent god of death he is. I loathe listening to you prattle about nonsense!"

David's eye twitched.

"Andrew is Eric's shining star and you are a pathetic weakling who doesn't deserve a lick of his attention." Leaning close, Jonathan grabbed David's jaw. "Nothing will change unless you force it to change. You are smart enough to figure this out, aren't you?"

David nodded absently.

"You don't want me to disappear, do you?"

"No," David whispered in a flat voice.

"Now, remember our secret. I'll see you again soon. Be a good boy until then and I'll bring you another treat. What flavor?"

"Apple, please."

"Go to sleep."

David slithered under his blanket and his breathing and pulse sank into slumber's domain. David was more than capable of destroying the family. Once the veil of innocence no longer protected him, Jonathan would require proof of intent, and when that day came, David would kill his brother. Then he would kill his father. When that day came, David would liberate Eric of his earthly ties and Jonathan would finally claim his prize.

"Sleep tight, King David," Jonathan whispered through a menacing smile. Pulling his aura in tight, he left the room.

Habit took him to the basement. Thick darkness blanketed the mansion's nether region. Eric was in Daniel's study, so Jonathan flipped the light switch.

Incandescent beams confirmed that time stopped at the basement threshold where an invisible line distinguished an ageless man and his bygone era from the modern family he served. Jonathan switched the room back to black.

Electrical and plumbing additions aside, Eric's quarters were a steep step 100 years back into a life he refused to relinquish. Ornate Victorian furniture, oil lamps, leather bound books, and tintype photography formed the basis of a world draped in velvet and lace.

Above him, Eric indicated he was retiring for the evening. Jonathan sat in the rocking chair near the bedroom entrance. Eric came down the stairs in darkness and hesitated on the last step. A few seconds later, a light footfall landed, followed by a heavier one. Eric walked over to the armoire in the corner.

A soft ray of light pierced the darkness as he opened its doors and revealed a refrigerated compartment lined with blood bags. "Why are you here?"

Was this a test? Surely, Eric hadn't detected him.

"I don't know why I bother asking." Eric grabbed a bag and a lead crystal goblet. He nudged the cabinet shut with his elbow. "It's not like the answer ever changes."

Jonathan waited out the silence.

"Talk or don't. But I can't believe the Second Born would pass up an opportunity to hear his own voice."

Jonathan's aura unfolded. He tucked the Hilja ring into his pocket. "How nice of you to care."

"I don't."

Wool scratched against velvet as Eric sat on the sofa, and glass clanked against wood as he set the goblet on the table.

"How did you know I was here?" Jonathan finally asked.

Eric snickered. "When aren't you here?"

The aroma of blood snaked between them.

"For a time, I wasn't. Why don't you ever ask where I was?"

"Electricity is a wonderful thing."

"Excuse me?"

"Electricity."

Eric paused to drink, gulping blood down his exquisite throat. Jonathan's teeth prickled.

"I thought you had all this advanced technology," Eric said. "Don't you know that the scent of an electrical spark is hard to miss in a room that's been dark all day?"

Jonathan laughed heartily. "The lights? That's how you knew I was down here? Ha!"

"I aim to amuse you," Eric replied flatly. "I suppose, after all, I am just a plaything to you."

"So?"

"So what?"

"Don't you wonder where I was?" Jonathan asked again.

"Why bring this up now?"

"Because you haven't given me the light of day since my return."

"You might burst into flames."

Jonathan chuckled. "So I say again: how nice of you to care."

"And I'll reiterate that I don't. I thought my lack of asking would make that obvious."

"I can't have you thinking I neglected you on purpose," Jonathan said.

"Attacking a member of the Flock *is* frowned upon in your society. I'm sure those burns served as a warning—probably enough to lock you up for a while?"

"Aw, so sweet of you to concern yourself with my welfare."

"I feel like I'm talking in circles."

"But our little dance in the forest that night had nothing to do with it. Besides, you're one of us. I can't steal what I already have."

It was Eric's turn to laugh. "You don't have me."

"Yet."

"Ever."

"No," Jonathan said with a smile that bled into his words. "*Yet*. As long as Andrew lives, he is safe from me. So you have until the day he dies to enjoy this mundane life you insist on living."

"You haven't changed at all."

"And you're hiding behind a wall of resentment when you should be grateful that I liberated you from that oppressive beast."

"I don't resent you. I simply see you for what you are, and I'll never trust you again. No matter how our relationship evolves in the future."

"I don't need you to trust me."

"Ah, not now, but I think you will in time. What if you couldn't trust Lucien? Or Alex? There will come a day when you will sit in my shoes and face problems similar to the ones you've caused me."

"In this realm, you are a prince living in poverty and I will never wear the shoes of a pauper. Let me take you away from this and we'll see what happens."

"What about the Servator? And atonement?"

"I committed my last atrocity against the Heavenly Host and the Flock the day Lucien requested the truce. And since that day, I have lived by the Treaty without fail."

"Your Treaty places you outside of God's eye. Don't expect me to believe that you haven't adopted the theory that one infraction here or there isn't enough to threaten your nation's future."

"I may not exist in His eye, but His Flock does."

"And that's enough to keep you in check?"

"Believe what you want, but I walk the Treaty's line."

"Why?" Eric asked. "Tell me why, Jonathan. You've taken from me again and again. Now give me this. Tell me something real."

"Lucien is my master and the Treaty is his word. Disobeying him means facing his wrath and that's not something anyone has ever survived. I would be no exception."

"That is exactly the answer I expected from the Second Born," Eric said coolly.

"And what does that mean?" Jonathan demanded.

"You are like a human who abides by the law solely to avoid corporal punishment rather than to do the right thing."

"I'm not like any human. And why does it matter?"

"The difference is in acting on behalf of self-preservation versus a morally correct belief system."

"Easy on the preaching there, Mr. Serious. My unplanned neglect has made you self-righteous and boring."

"I don't need you to change that."

"Maybe I need me to change that."

"We have a deal."

"For one human life."

"Tread lightly, Jonathan," Eric warned. "Lucien has spoiled you into thinking you can take whatever you want—"

"Lucien?"

"—whenever you want—"

"Spoiled me?"

"—but—"

"My birthright dictates—" Jonathan spoke over Eric, not about to yield to his newfound arrogance.

"—you are in danger of losing—"

"—my right to have—"

"—what you want most."

"—whatever I want."

The crystal goblet clanked against the table. Eric rose. "Push me and see how far you get with that birthright."

"Boring, but assertive," Jonathan said. "I am too curious about this new and somewhat improved Eric Ravenscroft to push too hard. But grow your hair out and ditch the spectacles."

"I'm going to bed. You know the way out."

"Of course. Goodnight, Eric Ravenscroft. Don't let the bedbugs bite…that's my job."

"One parasite to the next."

Air brushed Jonathan's cheek as Eric passed. "I bite harder."

"Not if you don't have any teeth." The door to the bedroom closed with a firm *click*.

Jonathan leaned back with a grin. He rather liked the aloof, cold side this "new" Eric had reserved just for him. And, Eric was still talking to him, which betrayed his brother's naïve belief in their "bond."

Jonathan smiled in the darkness. *The comfortable life you've woven for yourself is about to unravel, Brother.*

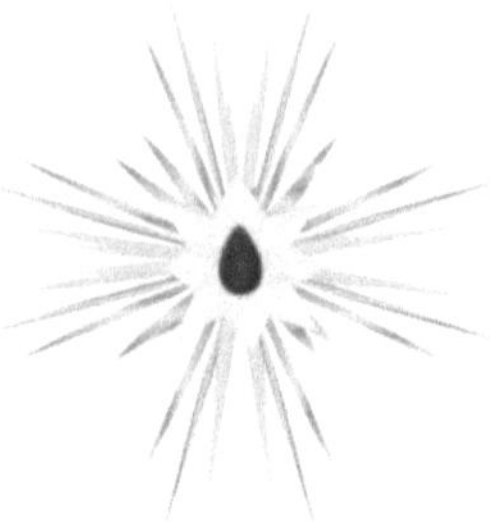

CHAPTER THIRTEEN: FRACTURED CROWN

Under a cloudy moonlit sky, two men in dark suits and a woman in a fitted blouse and pleated skirt entered the sculpture garden. The men crossed from the fountain to the reflecting pools while the woman ran toward the orchard, wringing her hands. Her voice shook as she yelled, "David! David! Where are you? Please come home!"

"Eric, can you hear him at all?" The man, David's father, Daniel, tried to hide the unease in his voice.

"No." Eric patted his former charge on the back, nudging him to go to his wife. "You and Sandy go in and see to Andrew. I'll find him."

Sandy searched the shadowy rows as her worried voice sailed back to Eric. "What does it mean if you can't hear him? He can't have gone far! What if—"

"Honey—" Daniel slid an arm around her shoulders and gave Eric a weary look.

"He can outrun my range in twenty minutes," Eric dutifully responded. "Please—" He pointed at the lighted bedroom on the second floor. "Your other son needs you."

Turning his wife toward the big house, Daniel said, "We'll sit with Andrew until the doctor gets here."

Eric tapped his ear. "The doctor's at the gate now."

Sandy nodded at Eric while saying to Daniel, "What are we going to do with David? Andrew shouldn't have to live like this."

"One of my aides told me about a boarding school near Chicago, over the border in Wisconsin," Daniel said. "I'll check into it first thing in the morning."

Eric watched them go, unaware that the eleven-year-old target of their search was sitting on a bench mere feet away. Jonathan slid his

Hilja ring onto David's thumb since it was too big for his fingers.

Putting a finger to his lips to ensure David's silence, Jonathan said, "Trouble in Hawthorneville, Brother?"

Eric groaned and pinched the bridge of his nose. "Not now! I don't have the patience to deal with you, too."

"Easy there, Mr. Serious. You might hurt my feelings. What's got you in a tizzy this time?"

"Andrew's brother pushed him down the foyer stairs. He has a concussion and possibly a broken arm."

"So the other one ran? Out here? All alone?"

"Don't you even th—"

"Hey," Jonathan interrupted, disgusted. "I was stargazing before the cloud cover filled in. You're the one who came out with the ruckus."

"Watch it," Eric warned.

"Watch what? *You* keep failing this family."

"What is that supposed to mean?" Eric whirled around angrily, following Jonathan's voice to the empty bench. "Damn it! Show yourself, you sneaky son of a bitch!"

"Misplaced anger, Brother?" Jonathan laughed and strengthened his aura. He couldn't release it with that boy sitting next to him. "I'm not the one who pushed your precious human."

"You are the only reason I have ever failed!"

"Oh stop whining. It's all survival of the fittest, right? And who's fitter than us?"

Eric's hand swept through the air and caught Jonathan by the throat, jerking him to his feet. "Get the hell out of here. I'm not warning you again."

Clamping sharpened fingers down on Eric's wrist, Jonathan chuckled. "If you choose to tussle with me, you may not live to find that child."

With a disgusted grunt, Eric shoved him and stormed away. "I'm sick of your invisible shit!"

Jonathan clenched his jaw. "Then hone your abilities."

He snapped his fingers and held his palm open. David obediently gave him the Hilja Ring and waited until Jonathan was wearing it to ask, "Why did he say you make him fail?"

"Andrew blames you for his troubles; Eric blames me for his." Straightening his suit jacket and sitting, Jonathan curtly said, "It's not your concern. How did you know I was out here?"

"The moon is full, it's supposed to rain later, and you like this garden."

"Put that all together by yourself?"

"Yes sir." David fidgeted with his hands in his lap. "I didn't think you'd come to my room tonight, and Mom and Dad are really sore at me this time."

"I'm not your friend, David. I'm only here to help you get what you want from Eric."

David looked down at his hands. "I know that."

"If I want to see you, I will see you," Jonathan said. "Do not overstep your bounds again."

"I'm sorry, sir."

"If Eric had found you here with me, you'd be in trouble and I'd be banished. You saw for yourself that he wants me to go away. Is that what you want?"

"No sir."

"Then think before you act on your impulses."

A small sniffle came from David's tucked down face. "I'm really sorry, sir."

"Crying is for little boys who aren't strong enough to fight their own battles. Are you a little boy, David?"

"No sir."

"Tell me what happened."

"Andrew's baseball team won the regional tournament and everyone was—"

"I don't care about that," Jonathan snapped. "Don't you see that Andrew is inside crying to his mommy like a little boy and Eric is out here looking for you? This is what you've wanted, right?"

"Yes, but it doesn't matter as long as Andrew is around."

"Then do something about it." Jonathan huffed in irritation. "Everyone inside that house sees your brother as someone special who deserves to have everything in life handed to him. Andrew will always get whatever he wants whenever he wants, and you will always sit on the side, scavenging his crumbs. If you want even a shred of recognition, you must work for it."

"I'm trying."

"Not hard enough. Your family covets Eric's company, and once they have it, they fight to keep it. Did you know that your grandfather nearly beat one of the servants to death because he had Eric's favor?"

"No sir."

"And now your parents are going to send you away, all so their precious first born son can keep the gift they gave him. Andrew will do whatever he can to make certain they go through with it, too."

"But I don't want to go away!"

"It's too late."

"Will you come see me?"

"No."

A tear slid down David's cheek. Jonathan stood. David grabbed his jacket sleeve.

"Please don't go!" the boy begged. He wiped his eyes with his free hand. "I'll be good! I won't cry anymore! Please!"

"Are you touching me?"

"I-I'm sorry sir." The fabric slipped from David's hand as he nervously folded his hands in his lap.

Jonathan rolled his eyes. "Enough of this. If I let you walk away, Eric will know you were with me. Where should I take you?"

David didn't answer.

Jonathan glanced over his shoulder. The boy was grinding his teeth and staring at a fixed point on the ground. "I do not possess Eric's patience, boy."

"Drake Pullman's house."

"That's too far."

"Um, Billy Jamerson's, then. I can run there in sixteen and a half minutes."

"Fine." Jonathan cradled David like an infant and dashed into town. Trees and buildings blurred together with night's black backdrop.

"Thank you, Master Jonathan," David whispered. "Everyone loves Andrew more than me. It's not fair, but I promise to do better. I won't let you down."

"You're only letting yourself down."

"But you hate it here."

A shot of fire coursed down Jonathan's spine. "Why do you say that?"

"Don't you remember?" David asked. "You said that you hate being with me and get angry that Andrew walks all over Eric. You called him a god of death or a prince or something. I'm sorry—the memories are fuzzy."

"They shouldn't be there at all. They must be dreams."

This couldn't be happening again. David was dull and nothing like Eric, yet Jonathan was losing his ability to command him. Forcing additional power into his stare, he met David's eyes. "You are to forget those private musings immediately. You must face these obstacles on your own, King David. I will not see you again until you return from school. If you seek me out, I will not reveal myself. Eric absolutely cannot know I'm involved or we'll both lose everything we're working so hard for."

☽ ✳ ☾

Smoky curls lazily uncoiled and drifted to a backdrop of screeching guitar riffs. Black light gave the haze a purple hue, and created bottomless black valleys and bright, neon highlights. Empty beer bottles littered the floor and orange embers smoldered in the joint between David's lips.

The teen sat cross-legged against the bed and sucked in a deep breath. As he exhaled to an angry drum solo, his arms flew into action and banged imaginary sticks high in the air.

The music pounded in Jonathan's skull. "David!" he yelled. "Turn it down!"

David puffed on the joint and shook his head. Blowing a steady stream from his lungs, he dropped his bobbing head. Layers of shaggy brown hair fell over his face.

Jonathan marched over to the stereo and cranked the clamorous flood down to a harmless drizzle. He was sick of the grating noise, the phosphorous lighting, and the stifling stenches of marijuana and patchouli incense.

"Hey, man," David protested in a drawn out drawl.

Jonathan kicked bottles to clear a spot on the floor. Eric and Andrew were away from the estate, and everyone else thought David had started talking to himself. He sat across from David and snapped, "How long is this going to last?"

"Man, I didn't ask you to come," he said in a slow, somewhat nasally voice. "If you don't like the tunes, you can go."

"Excuse me?" Jonathan asked, his brow forming an angry line. "Who do you think you are to speak to me that way?"

Hanging his head and shaking it to the music's rhythm, David said, "I am King David, the key to your goal."

Taking in a calming breath, Jonathan answered in a tight voice, "That you are. So tell me, *King David*, how are you going to do that?"

David shrugged. He held a bottle over his mouth and caught the last drop on his tongue. He tossed it across the room and tried all the others. "Whoa, I think I'm out. You didn't bring enough."

"I am losing my patience!" Jonathan growled, his eyes darkening and his jaw stretching at the hinge as his teeth descended. Taking command of David now required full transformation.

Jonathan cracked his knuckles and flexed his fingers as his nails grew into bladed claws. "I asked you a question."

David's face tipped up. His dopey eyes slowly focused and became transfixed, as though blinking would make Jonathan disappear. Then his eyes widened and his mouth dropped open. "Whoa, man! You're like…the Devil or something!"

He sluggishly slapped Jonathan's cheek and dragged his fingers down, hooking the corner of Jonathan's mouth and dropping off his chin. "Whoa…"

"Don't touch me you insolent brat!" Jonathan hissed, smacking David's fingers. The brat's hands were too calloused for someone with his wealth.

Suddenly David pulled back in fright. "Man, where'd your skin go? It's all bone! White bone. A skull with no skin."

David shrieked and hopped up. The joint hit the floor in a flare of orange sparks. "A skull with no skin! You're not the Devil, man! You're, like, the Reaper, man! You're Death! Get away from me! Get away! *Get away!*"

Jonathan quickly enveloped David in his aura before the whole household came running to investigate. "What the hell are you doing?"

"*No, no, no, no, no! You can't have it!*" David screamed, scampering sideways, riveted on Jonathan's face.

"Aha," Jonathan said, finally realizing that the lighting and drugs had transformed his demonic, alabaster countenance into something far scarier to David. He flashed a malicious grin of sharp fangs.

"You can't steal my soul!" Tripping on a bottle, David crashed into his desk with a groan.

Jonathan grabbed David by the waist and threw him onto the bed. Launching himself into the air, he landed on top of the teen, scowling and sneering, "Who's going to stop me?"

"No!" David fought to free his wrists from Jonathan's grip. "Master Jonathan! Help me! Please! I've been a good boy! *I've been a good boy!*"

Trapped in a hell of his own making, Jonathan swore in disgust. Commanding David as a child had created tiny mental fissures that grew into fractures. When he wasn't present at the boarding school to bind David's psyche, those fractures had cured into permanent cracks and hostile voids. Then David started smoking weed and dropped out of school.

He was practically useless. The drug erased his drive. It stole his resentment and denied Jonathan access to his splintered mind. But he wasn't giving up, yet.

"Who is this Master Jonathan you speak of, boy?" he whispered into David's ear.

New fear made David stiffen. Tears dripped from his eyes. "N-no one! D-don't tell Eric! Please! Take my soul! *Don't tell Eric!*"

"Why?"

"Becaaaaaause," David wailed. "I don't want Master J—no! Don't make him go away!"

"So, I ask again, who is this man you speak of?"

"Please! I have no one but him! Everyone hates me, except him. He wants to help me—" David sniffed and arched his shoulder against his nose. Snot trailed down his cheek to his shirt. "Andrew has Eric, but I have no one. I can't—" David swallowed hard and choked. "I can't live without him."

"What will you do to keep this man?" Blood swished hard and fast through David's jugular. Jonathan's teeth prickled from temptation, but David was still protected. "Answer me! How will you help him?"

"I don't know!" David cried. "I-I don't know!"

"This is going nowhere!" Jonathan growled in frustration, squeezing David's wrists even tighter. "Look at me! You will go to sleep and escape this nightmare. If you ever smoke weed again, I'll steal your soul and drag Master Jonathan to Hell, as well."

"No!" David whined in a sleepy daze. "No…"

As David's pulse and breathing slowed, Jonathan stood and ground the joint into the floor with his heel. He turned the stereo off and slumped against the wall, where he watched the teenager sleep.

"What am I doing?" Jonathan asked aloud, his voice raspy and raw. With David's father in the Senate, Jonathan couldn't force a move.

The game had stalled. Life was boring again. Eric wouldn't engage him. Instead, he spent his days with Andrew at the local university. Daniel and Sandy lived in Washington D.C. when Congress was in session. That left David alone in an empty house to pursue his vices and lose motivation.

"All he needs is a push. Just one," Jonathan told himself, thinking about the parties the Senator threw upon arriving home for summer recess.

The house had already started preparing for the upcoming bash. Bunting, lights, and tables were up in the ballroom and around the grounds, and soon, Sandy would arrive ahead of her husband to oversee the staffing schedule, floral arrangements, and other final details. When

Daniel returned, he would lavish praise and attention onto Andrew and Eric, and largely ignore David.

"I can count on that." Jonathan shifted his weight to the other foot. "David will fall any day, and then he *will* eradicate this family."

Despite Jonathan's self-assurances, anxiety was a step behind him, and now it was closer than ever—its breath chilled his nape. If Andrew followed his father into politics, Jonathan would lose all the footing he'd gained.

His body ached in protest as he pulled away from the wall. Stiff joints and lethargic muscles were boredom's compatriots. Rolling his neck, he left the room and trekked down the hall. He stopped at the veranda overlooking the foyer.

"Alex," he said in a low voice.

"Yes, Master Jonathan?" The sunny chirp came from the moonlit spot near the French doors.

"I feel like an old man. Some stimulation is in order." Holding the banister tightly, he descended the stairs, each step hitting heavily in his knees and hips. "Somewhere tropical—hot and humid. The rainforest."

"As you command, sir. Any special requests?"

"I want a challenge. Maybe a vampire hunter or—" Jonathan paused. "No, I want something with bite. Get me a fledgling."

"Male or female?"

"Surprise me." Jonathan resumed his descent. "Patch it to Seneca and gather your pack. I'm tired of this place."

☽ ✴ ☾

Jonathan had never dreaded going back before. Eric's crystalline eyes and the promise of victory had always pulled him like a magnet. But now, on the eve of the Senator's party, uncertainty trailed him through the gates. It was all going to slip away.

What's another generation compared to my life? If I give this one to Eric as a gesture of faith, maybe he'll reconsider.

But, Eric knew nothing of his deception. Such a gesture meant nothing, much like his word.

Searing pain cut across his abdomen. Groaning, Jonathan clutched his side and dropped to one knee. Blood bubbled up his throat. He swallowed it and gritted his teeth.

"Damn it, Alex!" Jonathan grunted, thinking back to the two weeks he and his pack had spent hunting and sparring in Peru's jungle. The pack had attacked with rare ferocity and Alex had pushed the line

181

further than ever, taking advantage of certain liberties that came with having the Second Born's favor. Even the peaceful Crimson Commander enjoyed a good fight—and his job only required him to keep Jonathan alive.

Self-restraint replaced the pleasure of battle with monotony, something Alex knew Jonathan hated, especially since he could only freely—and rarely—spar with Lucien. Therefore, Alex had secretly realigned the mission parameters to allow his team to exert double the usual force to protect the fledgling. Additionally, Alex had granted himself access to combat-only weaponry.

Jonathan hadn't expected the Cataclysm to ring by on a near miss, and certainly hadn't anticipated it shooting out again and nicking him on the left side. The six-inch gash left in its wake had shocked them all.

But, filled with adrenaline and the dawning realization that his pack was striving to give him what he needed, Jonathan forged ahead. Fighting hard, and with more strength, he easily evaded everything they threw at him; although, after the injury, Alex hovered unnecessarily close—just in case.

As usual, the fledgling was told to fight for life and strike to kill, and this time, Alex had chosen almost too well. The fledgling was a former trustee who'd been ex-military and possessed excellent combat skills. But, despite a good fight, the team had failed. The fledgling survived, of course—that was Alex's price for participation in non-sanctioned aggressive maneuvers. Jonathan was nobility, after all, and he didn't want the pack, or Alex, to face Lucien for disobeying orders— particularly not when they involved his life.

Only one man would fight me to the death without care for the consequences. Jonathan peered up through hooded eyes at Eric balancing on a ladder in the circular drive to untangle a string of lights.

His icy eyes flashed over Jonathan as he hopped down and dusted his hands on his pants. Under his breath, Eric said, "I can see you."

"Rest assured that they cannot." Jonathan straightened with another groan. Not even he was immune to a weapon designed to inflict misery.

"Is the Great Second Born actually injured *and* bleeding?" Eric asked, stopping about forty yards away.

"Not so much 'is' as 'was.'" Feeling along his ribs under his jacket, he said, "Another fragment just worked its way out."

"A fragment of what?"

Grinning, Jonathan stuffed his hands into his pockets and approached Eric. "Do you really care?"

Eric grunted. "Eh, merely wondering what could lead to such a thing happening." Eric's hand flipped through the air. "After all, doesn't fighting back beckon Lucien's stupendous wrath? Something like lightning and death, and all that?"

"Ha! Was that a joke?" With a mock laugh, Jonathan sprinted the remaining distance. He stepped intimately close to savor Eric's body heat and scent. "Sarcasm doesn't suit you, Brother."

Eric pushed against Jonathan's chest. "I have an acrid taste on my tongue that keeps coming back."

"Hm, you're feisty tonight." Jonathan leaned into Eric's palm and cocked an eyebrow. "Miss me?"

Eric dropped his hand and stepped aside, emotionless as Jonathan tumbled forward. "Not particularly."

Catching his fedora before it hit the ground, Jonathan said, "Face it." He tugged his jacket straight. "It's boring here, and these little maneuvers are your way of seeking excitement without asking."

"I know it's hard for you to accept," Eric retorted. "But this is exactly the life I want. No games. No drama. Just human normalcy."

"Normalcy…" Jonathan's voice trailed as a young man with trimmed hair and haunted brown eyes appeared on the veranda with Daniel. Before Eric could follow his gaze, Jonathan snorted. "*And human?*"

Jerking Eric by the collar, he spat, "You are not human! The beast in your heart craves all that you deny yourself. Whether you realize it or not, you need the stimulation I offer to keep it tamed. You need *me*— not law school or humans who keep you as a pet."

Eric smacked Jonathan's hand away. "You will never understand. All that I need, I have right here."

"I'm here. My presence alone keeps you on guard, makes you stronger."

"All I have ever needed is a family and people to care for." Eric pointed at the young man with Daniel. "Remember Andrew's brother, David? He met a girl. He's cleaned himself up. He's been talking with his father about college options after he gets his G.E.D. Hell! He's even planning on attending this party tomorrow night!"

Eric's finger flew at Jonathan. "My life here is finally in order. You only seek to destroy the core of my happiness."

"And you constantly deny the truth of my words."

Eric shook his finger at Jonathan and threw up his hands. He spun on his heel and walked away.

"You'll never reveal this to me," Jonathan said in a voice that made Eric pause. "But evaluate your life during the years I was gone. Yes, we seek different paths, but the crux of our existence is the same."

After a few seconds, Eric resumed his departure and Jonathan turned his gaze to David, saying, "What is the point of having people to protect if you have nothing to protect them from?"

☽ ❋ ☾

Through David's bedroom window, Jonathan watched the moon set as the boy approached the house. It was after three o'clock. David shuffled in and landed on his bed with a sigh of exhaustion.

A solitary yellow beam lit the nightstand when Jonathan pressed the bedside lamp's switch. David scanned the room before swinging his legs over the edge of his bed and slogging across the room to close the door. On his return path, Jonathan caught his arm and enveloped him in his aura.

"I leave and come back to a new you. Explain."

Surprise widened David's eyes. They darted from Jonathan's hand to his face.

Jonathan let go. "You are not to touch me. The same does not apply in reverse."

David nudged his chin at the Aegis cloak Jonathan had asked Alex to bring him. "What's with the robe?"

"Call it a protective measure. I have an injury that Eric can detect. Now, what's—"

"An injury? What happened?" David's forehead furrowed. He sank into the mattress with sagging shoulders. "Oh no," he groaned. "It's my fault isn't it?"

"How so?" Jonathan asked.

"He got to you."

"Who?" Genuinely frustrated and confused, Jonathan realized that David was the same chaotic mess inside his "improved" exterior.

Fear lit David's eyes. He rose and hesitated before grabbing the cloak. "Death, man! I thought if I was good, he'd spare you. But I must not be working hard enough."

David dropped onto the bed. "I'm sorry. I mean, I haven't touched the stuff—" He shook his head. "That's not important now. What did he do to you?"

Prying David's fingers off with far more gentleness than he felt, Jonathan tried to make sense of his blathering. "What happened to me is none of your concern. Why do you think you are to blame?"

David stared at the pale hand holding his fingers. "Death warned me that I've been squandering my life. And that if I ever smoked dope again, he'd go after you, but I swear! I haven't touched it!"

"Oh—" Jonathan finally understood. He chuckled.

"What's funny about that?"

"It's not. It, uh, must have been a warning to keep you from slipping. Death rarely speaks to humans." Jonathan clicked off the lamp as an involuntary grin spread across his face. He'd never wanted to laugh harder in his life.

Forcing an even voice, he released David's fingers. "So, you met a girl?"

"Yeah, at the library. I've been studying to take the G.E.D. exam. Dad thinks I'm young enough for a real diploma, but I want to move quickly. I care too much about you to let my mistakes endanger your life."

Afraid that opening his mouth would unleash a maniacal sound, Jonathan sat on the bed. Monotony had been murdered by irony. Once he had control of his vocal cords, he said, "I appreciate that, King David. What is your plan?"

"I'm looking at classes now. I don't like politics or law, so I'm thinking about psychology."

"Psychology?" Jonathan bit his lip.

"Yeah. Most of my life, you've helped me see how people truly are— to see through action to motivation and consequence. Learning more about the human mind would help me achieve your goal."

David glared out his window to where Eric and Andrew were rehearsing their party roles behind the valet station. "All my life, I've strived to impress him, but all he wants is Andrew. I've suffered enough. Now it's their turn."

Jonathan gripped David's shoulder as a gesture of encouragement and grinned. Oh, what a marvelous twist "Death's" epiphany had added! "Indeed, King David."

☽ ✳ ☾

Enveloped by his aura and swathed in stringed harmony, Jonathan stood behind the cellist on the mansion's landing. In the circular drive, valets took keys and directed drivers, while tuxedoed men and women draped in silk, chiffon, and taffeta presented themselves to the bash's younger host and his vampire guardian.

Each heavily perfumed couple then passed the quartet en route to the ballroom. Blood's sweet aroma no longer wafted through wretched bodily odors. Now, it drowned in toilet water.

Wrinkling his nose, Jonathan studied Eric: the unnaturally white smile that brightened his eyes, the glossy black locks that haphazardly fell over his brow, his skin's luminosity that stubbornly showed through the dull powder he wore. When had Eric stopped wearing glasses and buzzing his hair? And when had Jonathan become so preoccupied with David that he'd stopped admiring Eric?

A deep, grumbling engine announced David's arrival. His muscle car's menacing façade contrasted the guests' curvy luxury cars. The soft top was down, offering a clear view of the occupants.

Jonathan caught the way Eric's eyes skimmed over Andrew and darkened. Neither vampire had missed Andrew's pulse jump as his gaze lingered on David's blond passenger. Jonathan grinned. Any fool could interpret that expression.

But David hadn't noticed. With a dramatic wave and a big, fake smile, David gunned the engine and yanked hard on the steering wheel, pelting the valets and guests with dust and gravel. The blond squealed in surprise and shielded her face as David peeled off toward the detached garages. The only one not choking on the blossoming plume was Eric. A line of apprehension crossed his face as his darkened eyes focused on the disappearing girl.

☽ ❈ ☾

Shortly after the guests were seated and applauding the Senator's greeting, the string quartet moved to the sculpture garden for a later performance and the valets disappeared to assist the wait and kitchen staff. Jonathan was alone at last.

"I hate politics," he muttered, leaning against the wall. Despite the risk, he stayed there throughout the evening's mundane speeches, applause, and dinner conversation to listen to Eric's voice.

But Eric wasn't talking much.

Thankfully, *Andrew* staved off boredom. A hidden distraction underlined every discussion with his father's colleagues and constituents, and when the guests spilled from the ballroom into the garden, Andrew excused himself. He burst through the French doors and jogged down the veranda stairs with Eric in tow.

"She's fine!" Eric grabbed Andrew's arm. "Stop!"

The young ward froze, his gaze searching beyond the detached garages. "But David—"

"I haven't heard *anything*." Eric tugged Andrew's arm to get his attention. "Go back inside. Your father will miss you. This impression is important if you hope to follow in his footsteps."

"I know." Andrew sighed. "Dad even got me in with the governor. But I can't…" Andrew helplessly gestured at the garages. "Will you make sure she's okay?"

Patting Andrew on the back, Eric said, "I should get away for a while, anyway—I need distance from all those officials. You go in and enjoy yourself—forget the pressure. You have a few years yet; this is only building a foundation."

Andrew nodded reluctantly.

"She's fine." Eric nudged his ward up the stairs. Once Andrew was inside, Eric sighed heavily and set off for the garages.

Hidden within his aura, Jonathan followed, but stayed on the gravel when Eric snuck off through a cluster of trees and brush to spy on David's picnic by the pond. Atop a floral blanket, David was smiling as he entertained his date by tossing grapes into her mouth. She giggled and shyly hid her face to chew each successful catch.

Jonathan studied Eric's reaction—the eyes that got darker, the bulge at the hinge of his jaw, the somber reflection of an internal realization. A wry grin split Jonathan's lips.

All that work, Jonathan thought. *And your precious human is the one who's going to destroy your quiet life? Over a girl?*

Jonathan stifled a laugh. It was too perfect. Years of grooming David's hatred and minding his mental fissures had cultivated a natural tendency for paranoia and jealousy. Thanks to *Andrew*, Jonathan only needed to sit back and watch the game unfold on its own. No interference. No risk.

He left Eric to contemplate his future and headed for the gnarly oak between the mansion and the garages. The tree was older than the house. A swing had hung there for so long the thick branch had grown around its rusty chains and formed ridges like scars around the links. Jonathan preferred to ignore time's existence, but its power to change and shape the world was undeniable. He sat on the wooden slats and kicked off the ground.

Eventually, Eric trudged up the driveway, his head tilted skyward, hands in his pockets. Eric sighed and kicked at the gravel, too deep in thought to notice the swing moving on its own. This amused Jonathan, so he waited a few seconds to release his aura.

"Looking for me?" Jonathan flashed his teeth in a wide, innocent smile.

Eric's tongue flicked over his lips as he closed his eyes and pinched the bridge of his nose. "Don't you hate parties and politics?"

"Yes," Jonathan replied, patting the seat beside him. "But live entertainment is refreshing."

Eric hesitantly sat as Jonathan tugged the crimson ribbon free at his nape and shook his hair loose. Eric focused on a star low in the sky. "The music belies a peace I doubt will last."

"That's awfully pessimistic of you, Brother." Jonathan gathered his hair and tied the ribbon. He panned his hand across the sky. "The moon is surrounded by millions of celestial bodies, but feels the loneliness of a solitary heart. Why? Because its perfect partner burns the shadows of night into obscurity to illuminate a better world the moon fears to see. Yet only when the moon surrenders that fear can it realize that it and its perfect partner reside in the same world. They merely see it differently."

Dumbfounded, Eric stared at Jonathan. Then he laughed. "I can't believe I'm saying this, but that is the most beautiful thing I've ever heard come from your mouth."

"Is it so incomprehensible that I'd be capable of poetic symmetry?" Jonathan snapped.

"Not at all." Eric chuckled and stood. "You are perfectly symmetrical, in an asymmetrical way, Jonathan. Everything you do—everything you say—has an ulterior motive or meaning that balances the beautiful with the ugly. Thanks, I needed this laugh tonight."

"Glad to oblige," Jonathan replied dryly.

Tossing his hand up, Eric headed for the house. "And for the record, I don't think the moon is lonely or fears a brighter world. After all, it watches over the world it loves most, and it can do that all on its own."

"Touché, dear brother." Jonathan waved Eric off. Tightening his aura and confident he was hidden, he added, "But that world is shrouded in shadow and the moon is oblivious to what's missing in its life. Hide behind your ignorance all you want. The daylight is coming. And that girl is the catalyst."

☽ ✳ ☾

Lucien covered Jonathan's mouth with his hand. "And so she was. The brothers and father are dead, and you and Eric finally share the same world." He traced Jonathan's lips. "Do your regret influencing David?"

"I don't know." Jonathan sat up and searched Lucien's face. "He was never quite right—not that I gave him much of a chance. Now I can see that I didn't need to hook him. He'd been clinging to me all along."

He paused in thought. "My influence was negative, yes—but he and Andrew were pitted against each other by Fate."

"No regret, then?"

"How can I answer that? Changing a single thing would mean—"

"Paresh."

Jonathan nodded. "I do regret causing pain—I can feel it—everything I put Eric through, and it's like Hell. But I can't change anything without altering the present or future."

"So, 'yes' then," Lucien said, rising with effortless grace. "I know how this ends."

"Everything—every single thing David did—" Jonathan ticked off his fingers. "Killing his parents, killing Felicia's parents, setting the second mansion fire, and rigging the accident that killed Andrew and Felicia—he did it all without leaving a single fiber of evidence behind. I can't take credit for that."

"We rarely think much of human skill, but you admitted that David was more intelligent than his brother, with near limitless potential."

"Until he fell apart. After the first murders, he fled to Chicago and met Nicole. His hate and fear of Eric led him to transfer his assets to her before they moved to Wisconsin and disappeared—"

"After Paresh was born and he burned the church," Lucien interrupted.

"—and his revenge plot hinged on my protection."

"Which you refused to give."

"Until it suited our needs, as ordered."

"When did you first notice Lucifer's presence?"

"After I took Paresh to Kansas. Nicole's attention shifted to her quickly. But I think he'd been there awhile."

Wiping his hands on his pants as if to erase an imaginary stain, Jonathan added, "That's when it made sense. Why else would Nicole stay with a disturbed man in love with someone else? Or taunt him about Felicia and Andrew? She inflated his obsession until it filled the voids in his mind.

"I didn't care *why* she urged him to murder people she didn't know. We shared a common goal. Between the two of us we had David where we needed him. She influenced his plans for the 'accident' and he built the complex in Kansas for her. I don't understand why she wanted that, but I couldn't have given Paresh a normal life without it."

"David's wealth and proficiency at manipulation must have been attractive to Lucifer," Lucien said. "What better way to get the human race to fall than to influence large groups at a time?"

"Then Lucifer was only there because of David's potential to reach out en masse? It wasn't about Paresh?"

"Not until you took her to him."

"But why Lucifer himself? He's above recruiting."

Lucien shrugged. "In the war between good and evil, Karma cannot choose a side. It is a direct result of freewill and presents opportunities indiscriminately."

"Then his presence was a coincidence?"

"No," Lucien replied with a partial smile. "David was groomed by the Second Born—his favorite 'son.'"

"Because of me—"

"You created the perfect tool and gave Lucifer wide-open access to your life. I'm certain he would have targeted you, eventually, had you not arrived with Paresh."

Jonathan shook his head. "How many people did that affect? There were dozens of houses there, plus Simon, and Gary, the guy who died in the accident, their friends, their families—not to mention the danger to our nation. Lucifer was so close—he could have wiped us out or tempted me beyond my control."

"Perhaps my assessment of this confession was premature," Lucien said. "The biggest revelation came from what wasn't understood."

"Perhaps, but Gabriel wants something else."

Smoothing his kimono around his knees, Lucien knelt. "Go on."

"I was so bored. So tired of Eric's happiness and David…being David. My joints ached and I was stiff, again. I just…I needed to feel *something*."

"What did you do?"

"I—" A fire sparked in Jonathan's belly that burned its way up his throat. *How apt.*

"You…?"

"I took command of a trustee to burn down the Sunset Grove Parish and left a drop of David's blood to secure Eric's suspicion. I…I wanted to get Eric worked up, and hoped that David's paranoia would push him to act impulsively and make a move without my protection."

Lucien was silent.

Jonathan wiped his face. "From the moment Paresh touched my cheek as Gabriel—I knew it. This is what Gabriel wanted me to confess."

"You did that to the holy place where Eric's blood brought an infant to life? After you reported the incident to me? You knew what I suspected about her."

Jonathan's body sagged, defeated. "I lied to you and violated the Treaty. My selfishness put us all at risk."

"Is the trustee alive?"

"She didn't survive alteration."

The kind of breath meant to quell a great anger came from Lucien, but his aura was calm. "Lucifer said he wasn't the only one watching you. Perhaps Gabriel witnessed your sacrilege, but he values human life above all else."

Black silk unfolded gracefully as Lucien rose. Smoothing out the creases, he spoke quietly, perhaps sympathetically even, despite his evident disappointment. "When I forged the Treaty and gained Gabriel's trust, he argued that you were a dangerous variable. I assured him that you would never defy me."

"I never imagined I would." True fear singed every nerve. He was burning alive from the inside out. "Your word is my law. I—"

"Your confessions are complete. You have surpassed empathizing with Eric to feel shame and sorrow. I don't excuse your actions, but I cannot deny that without them, we wouldn't have found our salvation— including the church."

Lucien quieted and glanced over his shoulder. Then he turned and walked in the same direction.

"Lucien! What happens now?" Jonathan choked on the knot in his throat. "It's worse—"

"Did you expect to feel better?" A cold edge cleaved Lucien's aura. "I listened as a guide to a penitent heart. You are there. How you choose to atone is not for me to say."

Charged energy warped Lucien's aura, spiraling down until the Earth absorbed all but minute, residual particles. "I am this Nation's indestructible core—"

"Lucien—"

"And you are its Second Born—its ruthless commander." Lucien was nearing the neighboring privacy sector. "It is impossible to defy an order that was never given. Your emotions have misconstrued the past. Control them and clear 'what ifs' from your head."

Lucien paused without looking back. "That girl wasn't under our protection until you took her as ordered. Regardless of when you gained Gabriel's attention, *she* was the one he was watching. You confessed a secret that revealed a lie. The Archangel doesn't care about property over life."

"Where are you going?" Jonathan hated how insignificant he suddenly sounded and felt. He ground his teeth in frustration.

"To greet our guests."

"They're here?" Jonathan stood. Lucien gestured for him to stay.

"I'll send for you when you're needed." Lucien crossed the sector boundary.

"I'm sorry," Jonathan whispered, his chest tight as he sank into the grass. Lucien's back grew smaller over the distance. His heart dropped into his gut. He'd stolen so much out of greed. He didn't deserve to keep what he cared for most. "Is Fate truly so cruel?"

The breeze caressed his skin as the moon shone its crooked blue grin. A thread thin voice slithered through the blackness of space.

"*Ahhhh…I sssee. Yesss…you shall live on,*" it mocked. "*But, whereasss I shall lay eyesss on her for eternity, you shall never lay eyesss upon her again.*"

Jonathan covered his ears, but blocking a voice that didn't exist was as impossible as outrunning his guilt. Throbbing vibrations rattled his bones and his psyche, reiterating what had pained Lucien too much to reveal: the true cost of a penitent heart.

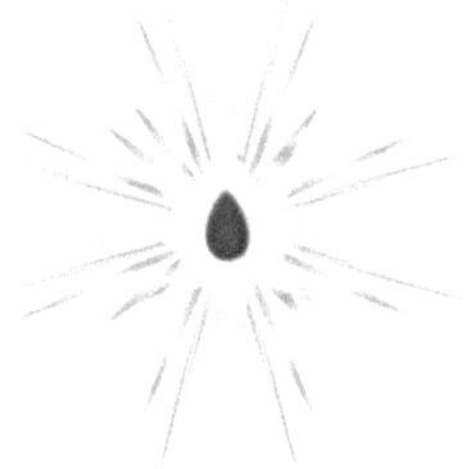

Chapter Fourteen: Comfort and Assurances

I

Animus Hollow's white veil rolled endlessly past, hiding all from sight and muffling sound. Only the warm arm around her waist proved she wasn't alone.

"Eric?" Paresh sounded far away from herself. Was he really beside her? Would she hear his response?

"Oh, no." Pain burned an arc across her chest. She couldn't breathe. The haze was too thick. Too white. Too stifling. Too similar to Gabriel's void—the place of nightmarish revelations.

She lurched. The arm around her waist tightened.

"I'm here!" Eric was yelling, but his voice was faint. "Don't let go!"

"I'm scared! I can't see anything!"

"Close your eyes!"

As darkness swallowed the fog, Eric tucked her to his chest and gave her a soft, reassuring kiss. She clung tightly to his neck, burying her nose into his shoulder. "I don't like it here."

"The Hollow is safe." His breath was warm against her ear, but his voice was distant. Gentle fingers stroked her hair. "The journey seems longer than it is."

He stepped forward and whispered, "See?" His voice was rich and intimately close.

Holding her breath, she peered from one cracked lid. The white haze was gone. She streamed air from her lungs and felt her anxiety go with it.

A meadow bathed in silvery light stretched before them. Its tall grasses whispered in the breeze and moved as an organic sea. Through swaying, feathery tips, white dots flickered along the horizon, burning the darkness with comforting familiarity.

"Lights?" she asked.

Beneath their feet, moss-grouted slate stones wove a path into a shadowy garden. Towering hedges and an arched entrance formed a black hole that swallowed anything to cross its threshold—even the moon's light.

Paresh checked Eric's watch. It read four o'clock. They had crossed over 2,400 miles in seconds, so why did a crescent moon reign overhead?

She stared in awe at the sky—at more stars than she'd ever seen—an array of sparkling, prismatic color. "Wow…"

"It is beautiful, isn't it?"

The familiar voice made Paresh smile. She glanced shyly over her shoulder. Similar to the last time she'd seen him, he wore a black kimono with embroidered Vampiric Stars. "Hi, Lucien."

The Arch Elder nodded his greeting, appearing casual and comfortable without the formal samurai-style pleated trousers and jacket. His Vampiric Star and silk ribbon bar were pinned on the crimson sash tied at his waist. Tucking his hands into his sleeves, he stepped beside Paresh and gazed at the sky.

Biting her lower lip, she inched closer to him and breathed in the scent of vanilla and incense. It reminded her of her father's pipe tobacco. "The sun was shining when we left."

"It is scheduled to be shining here, as well," Lucien replied, "but Jonathan enjoys the moon's company so."

Peering at Lucien from the corner of his eye, Eric moved his hand to the small of Paresh's back. "He's not with you?"

Silver strands gleamed as Lucien shook his head. "When I learned of your entrance into Animus Hollow, I silenced the heralds before they announced your arrival and came to greet you."

"Where is he?"

At Paresh's query, Lucien's cold visage warmed. He nodded at a ghostly, barefooted man enrobed in white emerging from the shadowed garden. "Jonathan is on the other side. Endymion will escort you."

The man approached them, stepping from stone to stone with grace. His damp, flaxen hair hung straight to the middle of his back. He offered a comforting smile and his eyes, reflecting the moon, glimmered with kindness. A familiar, floral and spicy scent permeated the air around him—freshly cut lavender.

He glided past her, bowing his head and dropping to one knee before

Eric. "My lord, I am Endymion, Seventh Elder of the Vampiric High Council. I am honored to serve beneath you." His voice was as gentle as Paresh imagined it would be.

The Elder pivoted on his knee and took Paresh's hand into his fingers. "'Tis more than an honor to meet our lady of the pure hearted."

He stood and panned his hand across the sky. "The stars have never burned brighter, nor the moon smiled with such exuberance. Milady possesses such beauty that even a simulated night shines as never before. Such breathtaking radiance would surely steal away the words of the most accomplished poet." He tipped her chin and kissed her on each cheek.

She touched her cheeks, gaping at him. He shared Donovan's perfectly proportioned features. He was fairer, with eyes like sea glass, and appeared delicate and fragile, but Paresh knew not to doubt his strength. Endymion wasn't just any true blood; he was among the first created.

With a respectful nod, he swept down at the waist to bow before Lucien. Balling his fist over his heart, he said, "My life is yours to take should I fail her, my lord."

"Jonathan is waiting," Lucien replied.

Paresh shot an uncertain look at Eric.

He pulled her close and met Lucien's gaze with deliberate eyes. "She'll wait and see him with me."

"Endymion is an ally." Lucien gently touched Paresh's arm and swept his hand toward the garden. "Since you came unescorted, I have entrusted Donovan's duties to Endymion."

Eric and Lucien locked eyes. The air stiffened between them. Unbending resistance butted against unyielding authority. As the powerful force crushed Paresh from both sides, she squeezed Eric's hand. "I'll be fine."

"If anything happens to her—"

"Endymion is an ally," Lucien coldly repeated.

"If I may interject—" Endymion pointed to a distant lighted dot. "With exception to us and Lord Jonathan, all others are in the bathhouse, unaware of your presence here."

Lifting onto her tiptoes, Paresh kissed Eric. "I trust Lucien."

With a reluctant sigh, Eric cupped her cheeks. "And I trust you. If you yell, know that I'll come running."

☽ ✳ ☾

As the hedge garden's darkness swallowed Paresh and her pale escort, Lucien said, "You won't hear her scream. The arc's privacy grid is active."

"If she has any reason to scream," Eric replied in an icy voice. "I will tear you apart."

"You may try."

Eric's eyes flashed angrily. "She trusts you, but I know where your orders got her *and her parents*."

"You should not have brought her here."

"Ah yes! Because she's so much safer at home with your rogue Commander on the loose."

Lucien's crystal eyes gleamed like hematite. "Would you rather announce to the rogue's general that his target has entered his house?"

"*His?*" Swiping his hand toward the bathhouse, Eric growled, "If you know who it is, then *why is he still alive?*"

Lucien regarded Eric silently before turning his grim stare skyward. "It took only one serpent in Eden to topple humanity. Imagine what two can do to us."

"Two…" Eric's voice trailed as he noticed the quiet anger simmering beneath the Arch Elder's reserved façade. A shiver ran through him. Eying the garden's dark interior, he caught his breath. "And you—you've only identified one—"

"Endymion is an ally," Lucien reiterated quietly.

II

"Master Jon!" Paresh squealed, dashing from Endymion's side.

Only when she was thirty yards away did her auburn-haired guardian turn with a gasp. "Pare—"

Running into Jonathan with extended arms, she embraced him and felt his shoulders loosen as though relieved of a great weight. "I've missed you," she whispered.

The hint of a smile warmed his worried expression as they parted. "You can't stay long, Pare."

"I know it's dangerous, but—"

At her side, Endymion swept down into a reverent bow. "Master Jonathan, if you need nothing further, I shall return to the garden grid."

"You may go," Jonathan said.

"It was nice to meet you, Endymion," Paresh said.

The Elder took her hand and knelt. "Meeting the Sacred Vessel is an honor to cherish and remember always." He kissed the back of her hand and then bid them farewell.

Her cheeks flushing, Paresh absently rubbed her hand and watched him go. When she looked over at Jonathan, he was grinning.

"Welcome to nobility." He sat and patted the grass beside him. "How does it feel?"

"Weird!" Sitting with her legs tucked to her chest, she folded her arms over her knees. "It's uncomfortably formal."

He smiled and tossed his hair off his shoulder. She'd never seen him with his hair down. Resting her head on her arms, she watched the breeze toy with his copper strands and marveled at how such an important man could sit so casually with her. *Except he's not really a man at all—*

"I worry about you," he said. "Eric said you're still suffering from Lucien's bite. How often do the attacks come?"

"About four or five times a day," she said, biting her lip shyly. "Donovan gave me ointment that helps with the pain."

"May I take a look? It shouldn't hurt more than a day. Lucien's bite is much different from Eric's."

She nodded and sat up, wincing as he felt along her neck and jugular vein. His eyes darkened as his lips formed a somber line.

"This whole side is tender and you're a bit swollen here." His fingers swept over the gland beneath her jaw.

Rubbing her throat, she said, "I'm more tired and less energetic than usual."

Jonathan grimly contemplated the moon. "It'll only get worse. Solid food won't make you feel better."

"I don't eat much of anything." An empty laugh skimmed her lips. "It's driving Molly crazy."

"You need to drink blood." His voice was quiet, yet firm.

Closing her eyes, she mashed her palm into her forehead. "I really don't want to talk about this, okay? I know what I need to do, but it's not that easy."

He grunted. "I've been saying that very thing to Lucien all day."

"About me?"

"No." He sucked in a deep breath. "About Gabriel. And my fate."

She inched closer, hesitating briefly before threading her fingers with his. "I believe that you are a good man in your heart."

"You have no idea what I am capable of, Pare."

"Perhaps not," she said. "But Eric is capable of everything you are, and he is a good man."

"Eric has a human heart." Heaving a sigh, his gaze dropped to Paresh's hand in his. "Mine belongs to a beast. I do not possess Eric's morality."

"Maybe—"

"No 'maybes.' The man you've known for the last ten years—barely a fraction of my life—doesn't reflect who I truly am," Jonathan said. "I am a ruthless war machine forged from brutality and cruelty to exploit the morality and empathy of the weak. I was created to inflict pain and death."

"Someone that cruel could never care for me or possess the gentleness I've seen in you." She tugged on his arm. "Maybe that's who you were, but it's not who you are now."

"*With you.*" Jonathan shook his head. "It's your essence—you remember the Trunkle's cat? I think it actually liked me."

"Huh?" Paresh asked. "What does that…Mr. Wesker liked everybody!"

"No." Jonathan wagged his finger. "Animals don't have a choice—they instinctually fear me. But, that cat almost jumped into my lap and might've let me touch him. *Only because of you.*"

"I don't understand—"

"Think of how the animals fawn over you at home." He squeezed her hand. "You tame beasts. We are no different—even Eric. I know he's said something similar about it to you. But what matters is that I am a good man *to you.* To everyone else, I am a monster."

She shook her head. "I refuse to believe that. I can't see you that way. And I won't. Ever."

"I hope you never do. But I earned the judgment I received. Your god knows my sins, Pare."

Paresh nervously wiped her face. "But He granted you a pardon!"

Putting his arm around her shoulders, Jonathan said, "Maybe your god can forgive me, but I have to forgive myself first. I have pressed every limit of the Treaty, manipulated everything possible, and pushed boundaries to make them bend to my will."

"But—"

"This is not something to discuss." He tipped her face up and met her gaze with sad eyes. "I must choose to seek a penitent heart or face death. This is my decision and mine alone—you can't change that. I have committed so many atrocities against your family. You don't know what I've done."

"Tell me then! If I forgive you, then you must forgive yourself!"

Jonathan bowed his head, casting a grim shadow over his face. "If you knew the truth, you'd never look me in the eye again—I promise you.

What if I told you I killed your parents? Could you forgive that?"

Her breath caught in her throat.

"I thought not. These are my burdens, not yours."

"Did you?" she whispered. "Kill them?"

"I did not."

"O-okay." Tears glistened in her eyes as she let out a shaky breath.

"I am truly sorry for the things I've done," he admitted. "But that's not enough."

"Don't give up and leave me alone!" Her tears ran like a river as she faced him, tugging on his arm. "Promise me! Don't leave me alone!"

"Pare…stop—I'm not giving up. Don't cry." He pulled her close and stroked her hair. He dried her eyes with the kerchief from his jacket. "All the tears in Heaven couldn't put out the fire of my sins, but yours seep through bone and rust my iron core away."

"You've been with me every day since Mom and Dad died. I missed you the moment the train pulled away." She sniffed and wiped her nose. "And now, with those awful visions, I'm scared that I'll never see you again."

"You'll never be alone. You have Eric."

"It's not the same. You're like a father to me. You're the only family I have left."

Jonathan stiffened and his hand froze. Long seconds passed as he stared ahead. Finally, his voice subdued, he said, "You should go, Pare. I'll come to see you soon."

"Okay." Balling the kerchief in a fist, she wiped her eyes on her sleeve.

"Promise me something?"

She nodded.

"Drink from Eric tonight so I don't have to worry about you."

She sighed at the moon. "I'll try."

"That not's enough. Promise me."

She sighed again and closed her eyes. "I promise."

Shaking her head, she mumbled, "So much for being a vegetarian."

Jonathan chuckled. "You're only a vegetarian because you couldn't fathom eating your friends." He squeezed her gently and dotted her forehead with a kiss. "You pose no danger to Eric."

"I guess you're right."

"I'm going to summon Endymion to take you back to Lucien so I can talk with Eric."

"Okay," she said reluctantly, leaning against his shoulder. She wondered if they'd ever sit together like this again.

☽ ✳ ☾

Jonathan stared into the distance long after Paresh and Endymion disappeared from view. With a sigh, he turned and contemplated the crescent moon hanging over his reflection. Five minutes later, footsteps sounded behind him.

"I'm surprised it's not raining." Eric's reflection appeared beside him.

Jonathan grinned. "You know me too well."

"I can't say if that's a good thing."

"Me neither." A sound that was neither sigh nor laugh, but something in between, came from Jonathan's mouth. He shook his head and sat. "Is it ironic that she says I'm the only family she has left when I'm the reason she has no family left?"

Sitting beside him, Eric said, "Sounds like a cruel twist of fate to me."

"Like someone such as myself receiving a pardon from your god?"

Eric shrugged.

"Why do you care about me? What have I ever done to warrant this kindness from your heart?"

"I've often wondered the same thing," Eric admitted. "Above all, you saved my life. And despite everything else, you've taught me about my abilities and limitations, explained our history, helped me—"

"Ha! When? When have I ever helped you?" Jonathan asked bitterly. "All I've ever done is take from you, turn your vulnerability against you, and use your humanity to my advantage—time and time again."

Eric's tongue flicked over his lips. He answered in a voice lower than a whisper. "You freed me from Joshua and allowed me to restore the tarnished Hawthorne name."

"You freed yourself."

"Only after you presented the opportunity. I was ready to abandon my life, even knowing that Joshua would have killed Clarence in my absence."

Eric quieted to reflect internally. "But killing Joshua…that's not who I am. That's what anger and emptiness did to me. And the man I am today is built upon the foundation of that sin. It's why I've dedicated my life to helping those in need—it's my penance."

"Hm." Shifting sideways, Jonathan kicked his feet out and leaned back on his elbows to stargaze with wistful eyes. "Your penance."

"Jonathan," Eric said, tilting his face to the moon. "I may be more human than you'd like, and I'll never be your lover, but I will always be your brother. I do get you, probably better than Lucien does."

"In some ways."

"And it appears that you finally understand me—that you feel my human pain. We've always been similar, but now we are more alike than ever before. Even I've realized that—whether I like it or not."

"Paresh said that I am a good man because you are a good man."

"Then perhaps I am a monster, since you are a monster?" Eric half-laughed and moved to sit beside Jonathan instead of behind him. "I have failed her at every turn, but you've been there to save her. Without you—you put her life before your own, ahead of your orders—a selfless act by the Second Born."

"Selfless?" Jonathan rolled his eyes. "I knew I'd benefit from her survival."

"No wonder Gabriel commented on your stubbornness."

"That angel is blind to my true nature."

"He said no one is beyond forgiveness."

Jonathan straightened. "You talked to him?"

Eric nodded. "He possessed Paresh when she touched Grandfather Wisdom. That's why she's having visions of your death."

"That tree…" Jonathan huffed as his head lolled back. A moment later, he eyed Eric suspiciously. "Her aura was too loose. Has she been drinking alcohol?"

"You're not going to nag me like an overprotective father, are you?"

"That's not it. Her spiritual energy—it…" Jonathan's voice trailed into thought.

"It's irresistible—intoxicating—when alcohol's involved," Eric said. "I know. She's a bit tipsy."

"It's a dangerous temptation given the power of her natural call. Such youthful innocence—"

"You didn't…"

"Never."

"How? Even I found it impossible to ignore."

Shaking his head, Jonathan said, "I've never once even thought about it."

Eric smiled. "Is that why you wanted to see me?"

Jonathan sat up, crossing his legs. "I don't really know why. I just needed to see you."

Eric patted Jonathan on the shoulder. "I'm fine. Better than fine, as long as I have her."

"I finished my confessions." Jonathan glanced nervously at Eric. "I told Pare I'd come see her soon, but I don't know that I can. That I should."

Eric's eyes narrowed. "Why not?"

"I've been greedy. All my life. And I've taken so much from you—"

"So you think punishing yourself by punishing her is the answer?"

His shoulders sagged as Jonathan searched Eric's face. "I don't know what else to do. She's what I care about most. I don't deserve her."

"This isn't supposed to be easy," Eric replied. "Do you think I had instant answers after the Confederate Camp or Joshua? Saving Willie, returning to Daniel—it wasn't enough. In fact, I felt guiltier. Willie's family still serves me and raising Daniel was a joy. I had to come up with something else."

"I worry that I won't be sincere enough to prove that I've changed," Jonathan said. "Or that I haven't changed and am avoiding a fate I deserve."

"You think you can lie to God? It's not about deserving forgiveness; it's about the journey you take to get there."

Nodding thoughtfully, Jonathan said, "I think I finally understand."

"So in the meantime, humble yourself and do some good in the world." Eric slapped him on the back. "But don't you dare hurt Paresh. Swallow your guilt and face her smile. The shame you'll feel is punishment enough in that regard."

Reaching high above his head, Eric twisted to stretch his back and shoulders. Then he cracked his neck. "I don't think I ever felt this much stress from anything you did to me. But damn if it isn't peaceful here."

Jonathan offered a genuine smile. "It really is. And you're finally here with me."

"Come with me." Eric stood and extended his hand. "Say goodbye to her before we leave."

III

Lucien stood at the center of the shadowed garden. Moonbeams danced across his emotionless face and reflected off the silver flecks in his irises, affecting an illusion of contentment. But deep within his bottomless pupils lurked something darker than the surrounding pitch. His body was tense. His aura colder than the frigid winter wind.

His eyes locked onto Paresh.

To her vampiric escort, he said, "Eric is on the plains' security sector. See him to Jonathan and return to the plains awaiting further order."

"As you command, my lord."

Endymion walked away without looking back. Goose bumps riddled Paresh's flesh as uncertainty tickled her ribcage. She glanced from the exiting cavalier in white to the man enrobed in black. The dark intensity in his eyes pierced her soul and she couldn't look away. A chill ran through her. Rubbing her arms, she tried to speak, but her voice was a mere squeak.

Shadows darkened and the already unnerving silence became stifling. Gone was the peaceful light, the delicate moonflower perfume, the serenade of crickets and toads. The garden was a sable pit. Devoid of light and sound. Only Lucien stood apart from the darkness.

When the Elder's mouth opened at last, her eyes dropped to his fangs. Her heart was pounding, but she was deafened to her own pulse. Her hand fluttered to her throat. She took a step back.

He pulled his kimono open, exposing his chest. "Touch me. Here," he demanded, tapping his sternum with a bony finger.

"W-w-wh—" She took another step back.

He grabbed her wrist and jerked her so close that her nose bumped into his chest. She tried to yank free. "L-let m-me go! What are you doing? Lucien! *Stop!*"

Ducking to peer into her eyes, Lucien said, "No matter how loud you scream, no one will come. This is *my* domain."

"W-what? I don't understand!"

His cheek was cold against hers as he blew into her ear, "The privacy grid may be active, but it doesn't work on me. I hear *everything*. No one can help you."

"But, Er—"

"*No one.*"

"B-but—"

"Touch me."

He straightened and positioned her hand in front of his heart. His grip was so tight. The veins in her hand were bulging and she was losing sensation in her fingers.

"S-s-stop! You're hurting me!" she cried. "*Why are you doing this?*"

"Do as I command!" he yelled, his powerful voice filling the garden. His eyes gleamed like dark crystals.

She shuddered and stopped resisting. She stopped thinking altogether. She was too scared to fight him—too scared to let a single thought cross her mind.

Before she knew it, her palm was flat against his chest. His fingers slid limply off her wrist. His arms dropped to his sides. His eyes were rooted on her, but they were clear and empty, and his expressionless face was more white than blue.

Heat built beneath her hand and radiated up her arm. It consumed her fear and filled her with strength, but it was an odd, tingling sensation that she didn't like. She snatched her hand back. Lucien collapsed at her feet.

"*Lucien!*" she screamed. "Eric! Jonathan! Endymion! *Help!*"

Frantically circling in place, she saw only darkness at every turn. Still she shredded her voice raw until movement in her peripheral vision made her freeze.

Lucien sluggishly clawed at the ground. She drew in a shallow breath and held it as he struggled to prop himself up. He shook his head, dazed.

Run! her brain screamed, but her legs refused.

Lucien had both elbows under his body now.

Run! Go! Go!

Paresh turned to take a step. Her knee buckled. Time seemed to slow. Over her shoulder, she watched Lucien rise. He was moving so much faster than she was falling.

Gravel cut into her palms and knees. She tried to scramble to her feet, but Lucien was already standing over her, reaching for her. She screamed and slapped at his fingers. Sliding his hands under her arms, he lifted her with ease.

A vanilla cloud enveloped her as he pulled her back against his chest and said, in a deep, earnest voice, "I will not hurt you."

"Liar!" she cried, kicking at his legs and trying in vain to pull free. "Let me go!"

"Paresh." He brushed her cheek as he turned her and nudged her face up. "Look at me."

Sorrow filled his eyes—the same sorrow she'd seen in the forest the night they met. "I will not hurt you. You have my word."

She hesitantly stopped fighting.

"I apologize for scaring you," Lucien said. "I did so only to determine the extent of your power."

"Why?" she choked out in an uneven voice.

"With mere fingertips, you paralyzed Jonathan that night. I desired to learn if your power affects me. We are most powerful when scared or angry."

A chill prickled her skin. Paresh shuddered and hugged herself for warmth. Lucien tucked her under his arm, draping his silk sleeve around her. She felt so small—his shoulder loomed inches over her head.

"Fatigue will come soon," Lucien said matter-of-factly, facing the moon. "Adrenaline fired your body up. Now it's cooling down."

She closed her eyes. Again, the scent of vanilla stirred memories of the nights when her father smoked his pipe. Just as she did back then, she inhaled deeply.

As tension drained from her body, Paresh opened her eyes. "Please don't do that again."

The arm around her shoulders tightened, swallowing her completely in black silk. "The Nation looks to me to be an unchanging pillar at the core of a rapidly evolving world. I must be aware of every threat to our existence and know every detail of our weaknesses. You are both."

Paresh understood what he meant. It made her sad.

"I am sorry," Lucien said. "You are not an experimental toy. I dislike upsetting you."

From within the veil of black, she mumbled, "Gabriel said to trust you, and Raven said that if not for you and Jonathan, the Vampiric Nation would fall into chaos."

"Oversimplified, but factual."

"Is she really a true blood?" Paresh poked her head out from the folds of Lucien's sleeve.

"Why do you ask?"

"She has a last name."

"Ah, yes. She does, and is." He paused and then asked, "Will you touch my cheek?"

Nodding, she flattened her palm against his surprisingly smooth skin. The man known for his cold heart was also cold to the touch.

"Either you are weak in a relaxed state or you pose no danger to those you trust. Thank you."

Pulling her hand away, she rubbed her fingers with the opposite thumb. "You know, Jonathan raised me…but, you remind me more of my real dad."

Lucien looked away from her as though to hide his face. Paresh added, "I mean, maybe it's dumb, but I feel like I'm a kid again, loved and safe at home without a care in the world."

In the pale moonlight, Lucien smiled at her and motioned for her to walk with him. "Join me. I'd like to show you something."

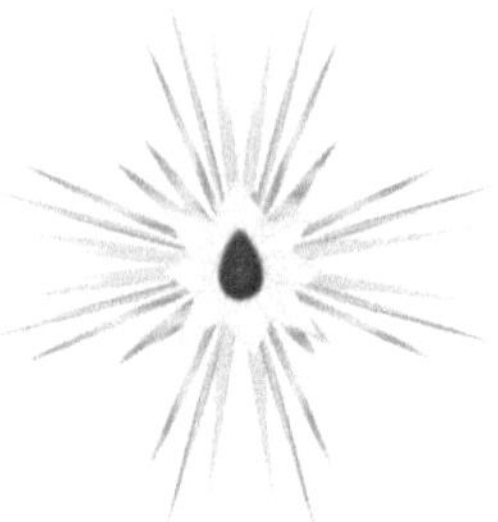

Chapter Fifteen: The Opening

I

The steel alloy that outlined the arc's perimeter was a stark contrast to the interior's natural splendor. However, the industrial grating was every bit as grandiose, with supports driven miles into the Treuter Mountains, its segments varying from ten to fifty feet in width, and the service platforms dipping below sea level and rising higher than ten stories. Elevators, ladders, and long stairways connected the levels, but what appeared to be hard and rigid wasn't—it was unlike any metal Paresh had ever touched.

It cushioned each step, absorbing energy to push back with additional lift. The heavier the step, the more gravity lost its hold.

"This must be like walking on the moon!" Paresh ran and jumped, landing with enough momentum to rocket ahead of her escorts. Giggling uncontrollably, she bounced to the edge of the casements.

A chuckle floated past her ear.

Nothing within the Arc of True Blood adhered to mankind's context of normal. In an arctic environment where tropical plants thrived, day became night, and solid became buoyant, the man supposedly devoid of emotion had laughed.

She glanced at Lucien and Endymion, who'd paused at the railing about fifty feet behind her. Endymion smiled and then spoke to Lucien in a voice she couldn't hear. Paresh watched them a moment longer before turning her attention to the mysterious casements.

"'Tis a sign we have lived here too long that we do not find the same joy in the simple forms around us," Endymion said to Lucien. "And yet our ignorance has not completely blinded us."

"Oh?" Lucien asked.

"'Twould seem a simple marker of such joy has presented itself—though not from her mouth."

The comment drew a sharp look from Lucien.

"Shall I watch my tongue?"

"Do continue," Lucien replied emptily.

"As you wish." Endymion swept his hand toward Paresh. "I speak in reference to Elder Arria's concern that the girl might affect you as she does Eric and Jonathan."

"So it would seem."

Despite the ice coating Lucien's response, Endymion continued, "I feel it, too. She lifts my soul higher than Heaven. 'Tis doubtful any one of us could deny it, but you must remain constant. It matters less that the Nation sees you falter and more that our enemies do not see weakness."

The muscles along Lucien's jaw bulged. "I am aware."

"Being the Sacred Vessel makes her a priority target without adding—"

"Enough."

Flicking his eyes at Paresh, Lucien tipped his head in response when she waved at him.

"Apologies, *my lord.*"

"Do not misunderstand." Lucien began walking toward the outer wall. "Don't apologize for speaking the truth. Be wary of what *she* may overhear. No matter the weakness our enemies *think* they see in me, I will not falter. Or sacrifice my nation for one life."

Endymion stopped. "She is not just 'one' life."

Lucien continued walking. "Once her purpose is complete, she is a symbol. Any attempt to use her against me will fail. She would not be the first sacrificial lamb."

Endymion moved briskly to catch up with Lucien and heatedly whispered, "'Twould be no sacrifice at all! This is nothing like the Son of God—she would be a martyr for a cause she knows nothing about!"

Lucien's hand landed on Endymion's shoulder. "The fact that she is a weakness means I will not allow them to get her. And if they do, I will not allow them to keep her. It merely matters how they think I see her—even you're so distracted that you believed my bluff."

"Testing everyone tonight, I see," Endymion murmured before tucking his chin. "I apologize for my outburst."

The hand on his shoulder tightened, prompting Endymion to look up. Lucien's eyes were dark, and the voice that slid between his lips was grave and firm. "You wear this peaceful façade well, but you are my greatest commander. If the enemy ever does get her, retrieval shall rest with you and your *full* discretion."

A hint of darkness swept over Endymion's face. "I shall never fail you where her safety is concerned."

"You never fail me, Endymion." Lowering his hand, Lucien glanced at Paresh, who was staring high into the casements with her hands clasped beneath her butt. "Do you know why I selected Raven to go?"

"'Tis a suitable job for the VaSH High Commander, a ready presumption to be made by the others." He smiled innocently, but knowingly.

"A millennium hasn't affected *your* perception." Lucien bit his thumb and watched a crimson bead form atop his skin. "Since receiving the Sacred Vessel's blood, Raven feels the same physical changes as us, but isn't affected by the gravitational pull of Paresh's aura. As the only other Elder who knows what that means—"

He pressed his thumb to Endymion's forehead. "I dub you Eternal Blood High Elder Endymion and return you to your rightful rank as third seat of the Vampiric High Council of Elders."

Dropping to one knee, Endymion bowed his head. "My lord honors me. The life in this body is yours to command and its spirit vows eternal allegiance to your will."

"Yes, well, *melodrama* aside, the seventh seat is now officially open and may be filled."

"How would you have me react? There are *ears* all around, as you pointed out." Endymion grinned wider.

"Indeed," Lucien said drily. He eyed a spot on the horizon. "When Paresh leaves, return to the Elders bearing my mark and tell them Hawkings has manifested. If any of them understand what that means, they will reveal themselves and force *Lucifer* into moving."

"What does that mean?" asked Paresh from Lucien's side, curious eyes rooted on Endymion's forehead.

The Elders glanced at each other. Neither had heard her coming. Lucien wiped his thumb on his robe and motioned for Endymion to rise. "I've promoted Endymion to the third seat, which has been vacant for centuries. What do you think of the casements?"

Hesitant to look away, she gnawed her lip and whispered, "It's beautiful."

Endymion interlinked his arm with Paresh's and escorted her to the wall of celestial simulation. "Where else can you touch the stars but at the top of the world, milady?"

Paresh lifted her hand to the casement. Even this close, the stars seemed light years away and burned brighter than their real life counterparts. "Is it really okay to touch?"

Lucien nodded.

Expecting the surface to feel smooth and firm, she gasped when a rainbow of ripples exploded beneath her fingertips. Only slightly thicker than water, the substance was warm and sucked her hand in. At about wrist deep, she met gelatinous resistance that grew denser the farther in she went. "What is this?"

"The liquid layers measure a few feet," Lucien said. "The solid portion that forms the exterior casing is only three inches thick."

Eric's fingers appeared beside hers. He agitated the surface into rainbowed streaks. "This is something else."

Paresh looked back at him and caught her breath. "Master Jon—"

She pulled her arm out and was surprised to find it dry and residue free. Jonathan grinned and tucked his hands into his pockets, leaning back to follow the wall's vertical curve with his eyes.

"The Heavenly Host gave us this material as a good faith gift after the Treaty was signed. There's nothing else like it in the physical world."

Eric slid his arm over Paresh's shoulders. "This place is amazing. Part of me regrets not coming sooner."

"Told you," Jonathan muttered.

"We can come back, right?" Paresh asked.

"Of course, milady." Endymion touched Paresh's hand. "I would be honored to take you on a stately tour, if you'd have me."

Fully immersed in his role as the respectful subject, Endymion closed his eyes and tucked his chin to his chest.

"What's with the blood on your forehead?" Eric asked, pulling Paresh closer to him.

"With no intended disrespect, sire," Endymion replied. "I must deflect that query to Lord Lucien the Eternal."

Jonathan hadn't noticed the bloody thumbprint. He shot a visual query at Lucien, who returned an icy stare that kept him silent.

"*The Sacred Vessel.*"

The words broke the strained silence with a masked bite. Devoid of emotion, supreme logic filled the voice with an affect of arrogance. It was richly feminine, soft yet commanding, noble yet bored, and musical, yet flat. It rang of innocence that belied great peril.

Jonathan's jaw clamped tight and Eric instinctively tightened his arm around Paresh. A shadow passed over Lucien's face. He closed the gap between himself and Paresh without appearing to move.

"Rainne," Lucien said. "Show yourself. Explain your presence."

As a humanoid form shimmered at the outer railing, Jonathan demanded, "And your reason for coming shielded!"

The form solidified into a woman draped in a hooded cloak. Loosely clasped with the Vampiric Star, the vermilion wool hung off her shoulders, revealing a limber, nude frame. The moon's light painted her creamy skin with a silver touch that emphasized the curve of her breasts, brightened her navel, and stroked her thighs. Even with a snow white mask shrouding her face, she was a stunning vision, unparalleled in nature, and a partner to whom the night itself made love.

She was a creature that belonged in darkness.

Her unearthly presence commanded fear without the slightest physical gesture. All moving at once, Eric put himself in front of Paresh, Endymion tucked in on her exposed side, and Jonathan advanced toward the woman, stopping at the midpoint between them.

A slender finger, as perfectly sculpted as a porcelain doll's, traced the arc's curve through the air. "*There was a vibration in the casements, my lords.*" The woman's voice radiated curiosity and malevolence. "*I felt it. A scream.*"

Eric glared at Lucien. "A scream?"

Ignoring him, Lucien said, "Tell me why you came."

"*After much deliberation as to the cause, Elder Corben suggested that I investigate—cloaked so as not to disturb you unnecessarily.*"

"Corben sent you." Angled about forty-five degrees, Lucien's arm became a biological spear as his nails lengthened into sharp tips.

"Elder Rainne, perhaps you should return to the bathhouse," Endymion suggested, tucking his hands into his sleeves. "All is well here."

Not heeding his veiled warning, she replied, "*We have waited so long.*"

Rainne lowered her hood and shook her wavy locks free. Lacking natural pigment, her tresses absorbed and reflected points of twinkling prismatic light and the blackened sky. A few locks swooped into a crescent moon-like streak, and the tips shone metallic like the steel grating.

As she approached Jonathan, her hair defied gravity, riding the flow of her aura and twisting like a gorgon's snakes. Dipping her face to the side, she reached for her mask. "*Let...the...*"

Racing to pin her arms at her side, Jonathan yelled, "*Lucien!*"

Gracefully arching her spine, Rainne flew feet first backward and twisted her arms free. Landing with the lightness of a feather, she held one hand out to the side and pulled the other up the center of her body. Shoving it outward, she hit Jonathan in the chest, easily knocking him aside. Resuming her approach, she continued, "…*blood…*"

"Rainne Blood Pathos, acknowledge voice command override Alpha One Echo Zero." The edge in Lucien's voice betrayed the urgency lurking beneath his façade—as did his posture: leg back, torso down, angled forward, his spear-tipped arm ready to strike.

The female Elder stopped in place and did not resist when Jonathan jerked her hand away from the mask. "What were you waiting for?" Jonathan yelled at Lucien as Rainne said, "*Voice command override Alpha One Echo Zero acknowledged.*"

"Deactivate all attack modes." Turning a lofty eye on Jonathan, Lucien replied, "What were *you* waiting for?"

The woman robotically replied, "*As you command. Deactivating.*"

"*What the hell is going on here?*" Grinding his teeth, Eric glowered with darkening eyes.

"Ah, 'twould appear our wolf has revealed himself." Endymion stepped to Eric's side, fortifying Paresh's protective shield. "'Twould be best for you to take your leave, *now*."

"Not until I get an answer," Eric seethed. "How am I supposed to protect her when I don't know who or what to protect her from?"

"You knew the danger of bringing her here," Lucien coldly replied without looking back.

Eric bristled and growled at him. "Don't think you can shirk your responsibility by turning it back onto me. *That woman heard a scream!*"

"My responsibility does not excuse your ignorance after refusing Jonathan's offers for more than a century." Spinning on his heel, Lucien stuck his finger in Eric's face. "Our history spans millennia. You share the blood of the Second Born, so I have bestowed upon you an appropriate rank, but you have neither our wisdom nor the right to make such demands or judgments."

Blood light cut through the darkness in Eric's eyes as he snarled at Lucien. Hands outstretched, Jonathan darted to stand between them.

"We cannot fight each other!" His palm flat against Eric's chest, he said, "Paresh's safety is paramount, right?"

Receiving no response, Jonathan repeated, "*Right?*"

Eric's glare turned to Jonathan.

"Take her home. Protect her. Raven and Donovan will capture Alex, and we will resolve this, here. When there's time, I'll tell you everything." He turned sad eyes on Paresh. "Please, *go*."

Jonathan opened a portal to Animus Hollow. "Raven can protect you better there than we can here."

Lucien turned a pointed eye to Eric. "Rainne is only the weapon. We have yet to neutralize the threat."

Fuming, Eric took Paresh's hand and turned his back to the others. Catching Paresh's eye, Jonathan whispered, "Say nothing of Rainne to Raven or she will become distracted."

Paresh stared back at Jonathan, eyes wide and bewildered as the white mist swallowed her and the portal closed.

☽ ✻ ☾

"Endymion," Lucien said. "Secure and isolate Rainne. Hunters will relieve you after the containment protocol is completed."

"As you command, my lord." Endymion covered Rainne's head with the hood and pulled the cloak over her body. His peaceful features became rigid and stern, and his voice came out lofty and commanding. "Elder Rainne Blood Pathos, acknowledge authority Endyseven and reconfigure to Endythree under command of Zero Zero One."

Barely on the human side of mechanical, she replied, "*Authority Endyseven acknowledged and reconfigured to Endythree pending voice approval by Zero Zero One.*"

"Approved." Beneath Lucien's face of stone, blazing anger nipped his threshold of control and threatened to scorch his aura's natural chill.

"*Reconfiguration complete,*" Rainne said, moonlight streaking off her mask as she faced Endymion. "*Input command.*"

Endymion flashed knowing peridot eyes at Lucien before glancing at Jonathan, who had yet to notice Lucien's internal struggle. To Rainne, he said, "Peto somnus."

She crumpled into his arms like a ragdoll. His placid demeanor restored, Endymion clutched Rainne to his chest and announced, "Our greatest weapon slumbers like a lamb."

"For now." With a grunt, Jonathan flicked his hand. "Take her to her quarters."

As the Elder crossed the grating and descended the stairs, Jonathan slapped on a communicator. "Seneca, apprehend Corben and hold all Elders excluding Endymion and Rainne at the bathhouse. We are en route—"

Cursing her response, he turned to Lucien. Fine stress lines creased his master's forehead. "You heard her. Corben is gone. The arc's locator can't—"

"Seneca shall send six hunters to guard Rainne," Lucien interrupted. "And relay an order to Raven to terminate Corben on sight."

After imparting Lucien's orders, Jonathan pocketed the communicator. "First Connall. Now Corben? That's two High Elders down and two left—plus Endymion, of course, as the first true blood created after us—"

"He has your temper." Lucien gazed up into the casements, taking in even breaths to steady his voice and quell his anger. "Eric."

Jonathan made a thoughtful noise. "He doesn't like to cede control. He's been that way since his mother died." Nudging his chin toward the bathhouse, Jonathan said, "We should go. Endymion aside, what do you make of it? Another failsafe?"

"I doubt Lucifer would need more than one. Likely something bad in the mix. Place Ambrosia and Lucasta under guarded surveillance."

"Ceallach is the most insistent that Eric is a threat."

"He isn't wrong. Eric almost made that situation worse—for all of us." The moon and stars reflected in Lucien's wistful eyes. "Corben used Ceallach's outbursts as a distraction. He's benign."

"Outbursts." Jonathan eyed Lucien's mussed kimono and exposed chest. "If you hadn't made Paresh scream, that never would've happened."

Heading for the inner railing, Lucien tucked the silk fabric back into place. "It was noteworthy. She can paralyze and absorb energy with touch alone." Lucien glanced at Jonathan from hooded eyes. "But more importantly, I can take command of her."

"B-but how?" Jonathan stammered, quickening his step. "Eric said she was immune to the hierarchy. You confirmed that yourself in the forest. Her fear, not your words, made her run from you."

"I ordered her to run and she ran. The reason is irrelevant now. She isn't immune. She's resistant." Lucien descended the stairs. "I altered her perception of reality through forceful persuasion."

When Jonathan stiffened, Lucien added, "I did not harm her."

"I didn't—"

"My aura swallowed the light and induced a waking nightmare, but it took an unprecedented amount of power to hold her attention, trigger her fight or flight response, and command her into touching me against her will."

In Jonathan's silence, Lucien paused. "The power residing in that young woman surpasses anything this Nation can throw at her."

"Even Rainne?" Jonathan stared over the horizon.

Resuming their descent, Lucien quietly confessed, "If she hadn't released me, and wasn't in such a weakened state, she might have killed me."

"And she has no idea," Jonathan whispered.

"Neither do our enemies."

Looking up sharply, Jonathan demanded, "Then why'd you restore Endymion to the third seat? Is such a bold move necessary if no one knows what's truly going on?"

At the pathway, Lucien stepped onto glassy blue and white marble. Thick layers of quartz crystals lined either side and glinted like fresh snow. He took in a deep breath of cool air, feeling control return.

Steeling his aura, Lucien answered, "I suspect that Paresh's divine essence has caused Hawkings to manifest, so it wasn't a decision made lightly. I'll confirm it when Raven reports in person. Until then, since he is the only Elder who can see it, Endymion will watch the dark spot in the sky for signs of change."

Groaning, Jonathan wiped his face. "So Lucifer will recognize it if he sees it, right? Did you send Raven instead of Alex hoping to trigger the Apocalypse?"

"I would not seek this world's premature demise so carelessly."

"But that's what you've done! Alex can see the dark spot, too!"

"And if I had sent him, our enemies would have that knowledge *and* the Servator."

Jonathan shook his head. "Anyone worthy of commanding an army would steal the enemy's greatest weapon—why use Rainne as a distraction? Surely Lucifer would want her—more than anything else—right now."

"What fate awaits the world, I cannot say," Lucien said. "But my strategy has kept us ahead thus far. Lucifer will realize his mistake in recruiting Corben quickly enough, unless he, too, is a decoy, and the real serpent is not so thoughtless. We must be careful."

II

Animus Hollow's thick white plumes muffled Paresh's voice. "Eric?"

"I'm here," Eric called. "You're safe now."

"That's not it..."

She sounded far away and he couldn't see her, but—curiously—he could *feel* her in his arms. The Hollow was peculiarly tactile. Usually sensations were reduced to energy impulses, but—

Electricity jolted his body—her lips were *against* his throat. He'd

214

swear it. Hovering close, diffusing so much heat that it surged into his core and blasted his pulse.

"Is it…? Can I…?" she asked, faintly. Maybe breathlessly?

His galloping heart drowned out what little sound there was. His teeth throbbed and grew. Burying his fingers in her hair, he encouraged her by tilting his head back. The vibrations of her voice struck his skin, but he couldn't hear her.

His control was spiraling away. Her aura was so innocent. So vulnerable. *Intoxicating.* Raw and excited. It stroked his entire body— the seductive caress of her fingers everywhere at once.

It was maddening.

"Help…"

Against mounting desire, he filled his lungs with copious amounts of air. "It's okay," Eric said, unsure if she could hear him since he couldn't hear himself. "It's there. Right there. Feel the heat. It'll come natur—*ah!*"

An involuntary spasm rocked his body when her fangs sank into his jugular. Clamping down on the ache in his jaw, he moaned and arched against her, pushing her in deeper. His fingers curled tightly in her hair, unnecessarily holding her in place. Instinct had already taken over.

Her nails pierced his neck and trapezius muscle as she latched onto him and wrapped her legs around his waist. Sliding his tongue along his teeth, he moaned again. The haze was blood red. He panted from desire, for both her body and her blood, and possessed neither the strength nor the will to resist.

He felt himself move in space, as though in free fall. He inhaled deeply and exhaled excruciatingly slowly. Racing against his sanity, he raised his forearm to his mouth. There was no pain and no pleasure, only pressure as his jaw snapped tight against muscle and bone, and the empty satisfaction of sinking his teeth into something solid.

Only when her lips lifted, did he lift his. He ravenously captured her mouth, kissing her deeply and tasting his blood on her probing tongue. For the first time in days, her aura exuded strength. It enveloped them like a summer shroud and chased off the Hollow's empty chill. Reveling in her palliative essence, he relaxed. His teeth receded and the haze returned to the pristine hue of snow.

Their kiss could have lasted an eternity. When they parted, he felt Paresh rest her head on his shoulder and the heave of her chest under a sigh. Words may have followed, but time had rolled to a stop and there was no sound. Even the haze's infinite movement stood still.

He tightened his hold. There, in the non-dimensional plane

encircling the Realm of Man, it was just the two of them. Their own special moment. Letting go meant returning to the outside world—a world of death and danger, and endless questions.

But there were questions in here, too. And the moment had to end. He kissed her again and moved toward the portal. He led her out and squeezed her hand. She rubbed her arm nervously and dodged his gaze.

"Hey." Eric pulled her to his chest and nudged her chin up. "You did great. There's nothing to be ashamed of."

Nodding, she traced her lips with her index finger and stared at the bloody smear left behind. "E-Eric…" Her voice quivered.

"Hey, hey," he said softly. "It's a good thing."

"Oh no," she said, her eyes widening when she saw his mouth. "I got some on you."

"No, this isn't—" Dried blood flaked off his skin as he brushed at his chin. "It doesn't matter. How do *you* feel?" He searched her face over the rim of his glasses.

"I feel—" She felt along her throat. "It doesn't hurt! And the swelling is gone, too. I feel—"

She grinned. "I feel great."

"Good," Eric replied with a smile, leaning in for another kiss.

Sharp, stabbing pain dropped him to his knees. Clutching at his chest, he threw his head back with a gasp. Panting for air that wouldn't come fast enough, he watched the forest turn black and close in. It was racing at him. He fell forward on his hand and swallowed hard.

"Eric? *Eric!*"

Paresh's cry seemed like it was an ocean away, but he could see her frantic expression, her lips moving. She rushed over to him, but he waved her away and squeezed his eyes shut. The pain was crushing— like pressure plates on his heart. He huffed out as forcefully as he could and opened his eyes. The world tilted sideways and then tunneled out.

☽ ✳ ☾

"*Eric! No! Eric!*" Paresh shrieked, crashing to the ground with a groan to catch his body. Ignoring her throbbing hip, she rolled Eric onto his back. His empty eyes peered up at her and slowly closed.

"No! No! Not again!" she screamed. "You can't leave me!"

She balled her fists against his chest and cried over his body, her tears drenching his shirt. "Please, no!"

Thump.

Thump.

Holding her breath, she listened to his heart. It was faint. Slow.

The portal had opened behind the tree line near the southern trail. At least she knew where they were. Rifling through his pockets, she found his cell phone and started to dial 911.

His ashy, bloody face made her pause. How would she explain that? Or the fact that he wasn't human?

"Oh Eric." She rubbed her forehead with trembling fingers, staring at the device and trying to remember what he'd said when he told her how to use it. 911. Green phone button. That's all she came up with. She didn't know another number to dial.

She pulled the Vampiric Star from his pocket and studied the prongs, searching for blood on the one he'd used to contact Jonathan. It was spotless. She looked from the pin to the phone and back, and dropped her hands into her lap, her shoulders sagging.

He didn't have the communicator Raven had given him or his keys.

"Someone, please!" she whispered, tears welling again. Through the trees, she eyed the cottage. There were plenty of rocks. She could break a window, but how would she boost herself up to get inside?

As panic's tendrils inched up her back, her gaze fell back to Eric. His pulse was steady and his chest was rising and falling. Taking a deep breath, she dialed 911.

When the dispatch operator asked for the nature of her emergency, she froze. When the man repeated himself, she tried to form even, composed words, but her voice was a squeak. She cleared her throat and rushed out, "Hi, yes, um, I-I didn't know what else t-to do. I n-need to contact Walter Hodges, but I-I need his help, *right away!*"

"Ma'am, Chief Hodges is out on a call. Do you require police or medical assistance?"

"No! Yes! I don't know. Please! You have to get him for me. It's an emergency and I didn't know how else to reach him. He's the only one who can help me! Please, tell him I'm..." No one knew she was back—except Walter and Molly.

"I'm...tell him I'm at Andrew's! He'll understand! Please, hurry!"

"Ma'am, take a deep a breath and try to calm down. I'll do my best to get help sent your way. I need some more information. Who is calling?"

"What? I can't! I'm at Andrew's! Tell him, tell him to come!" She snapped the phone shut and let it slip through her fingers. She was shaking all over, staring at the device, hoping she'd done the right thing.

The forest's silence was suffocating. Cicadas should've begun their evening salute by now. There weren't any woodpeckers drilling or crows cawing, no twitter of birdsong or animal clatter in the brush.

She inched closer to Eric's body. "There has to be another explanation," she told herself. "Because if *he's* here, then Walter can't help us."

The peal of the phone jolted her to her feet. She dropped it twice in her scramble to grab it.

"Molly? Are you with Eric? I just got the weirdest call over the rad—"

"Walter? *Walter!* Oh, thank God! No! No—it's me—I…it's Eric! He needs help! He just—he collapsed! And I don't know what to do! I don't kn—"

"Whoa, it'll be alright, hon. Breathe for me. First, are you okay?"

"Yeah, but Eric…" she trailed into a groan and sank down beside him. "Oh no. I think I did this to him!"

"You're with him now?"

"Can you bring him something to…you know, from the restaurant? Maybe that will help."

"Where are you? I didn't get an answer when I called the cottage."

"In the forest. Off the trail. I can see the cottage if I stand up. Please hurry." She tossed a wary glance around. "It's, um, very *quiet.*"

"Damn. Then I'm not making a pit stop, honey." Walter paused briefly. "Pare, I need to tell that Raven lady what's going on. How can I reach her?"

"Molly's with her. At Eric's."

"I'm going to hang up for a sec, 'kay? I'll call you back real quick."

"Wait! Walter?"

"What is it, hon?"

"Tell Raven to come alone. I don't want Molly to see me like this."

"I'm almost afraid to ask, but…no, never mind," Walter said. "Look, if you need *anything* before I call back, dial 911 and have 'em patch you through. Everything's gonna be fine, all right? You did the right thing."

"Thank you," Paresh whispered as tears blurred her vision. She closed the phone and stroked Eric's cheek.

"Everything's going to be okay," she choked out. "Walter says so."

Not much time passed before the phone rang again. Wiping her eyes with her sleeve, she answered, "Walter? Where are you?"

"Pulling up to the carriage house, now. Raven's on the way. Do you see anyone or sense anything out of the ordinary?" The jangle of keys and slam of a car door came through the earpiece.

Shaking her head, she replied, "I don't see anyone. It's just quiet."

"Yeah, I can hear that. It's real creepy," he replied, huffing unevenly into the phone. "I'm rounding the cottage's east side now, can you see me?"

Paresh stood. "Not yet, we're more on the west side. Wait. There!" Holding the phone against her chest, she jumped and yelled, "Walter! Over here! Over here!"

She waved her hands and kept yelling until he saw her and pointed to his phone. When Eric's phone was back up to her ear, Walter said, "That woman's going to be here soon. Now, I didn't have time to grab much, but I have a handful of moist wipes from my car. I'll help you get cleaned up before she gets here, but I expect an explanation."

"Okay." She met his gaze over the distance and gave him a solemn nod. "I'm sorry, Walter. Thank you for coming."

"You have nothing to be sorry for, honey. I promised your dad I'd watch over you, didn't I?" Walter had to catch his breath to add, "That much Eric and I have in common, no matter how mad at me he gets."

"Huh? He's not mad at you," Paresh said, confused. "He was giving you time to absorb what happened, that's all."

"Nah, he was downright pissed off when I left his office earlier. And given our conversation, I'm not touching him until Raven gets here." Only a few yards separated them now. "I'll take your silence to mean he didn't tell you about it. Guess I'm not the only one he's keeping in the dark." Walter shoved his phone in his pocket and crossed the tree line.

As he knelt before her, she averted her gaze to the phone in her lap. "I believe he has a good reason for not telling me. But still, I want to know what happened."

Walter snapped on a pair of latex gloves and emptied his pockets of small, square packages with restaurant logos on them. He tossed one to her and ripped open another. The moist wipe smelled of citrus and was cool against her skin as he dabbed at her chin. "As you can see, I eat out a lot. I can see that he's breathing fine, so that's a good sign that his heart's beating. Can you tell me what happened?"

Paresh stared at the towelette package in her hand. "Eric told you about me, right? I mean about what happened when I was born?"

Walter nodded.

"Well, now I'm actually changing, but I've been reluctant to…to…"

"Drink blood?" Walter offered.

"Yeah. And I've been in more pain and getting weaker. Both Eric and Master Jon—"

"This would be the Master Jon who kidnapped you?"

"Well, it's not exactly like that."

"Sorry, but the more I learn about this situation, the less I like it. I look at you and see the eight-year-old girl who went missing all those years ago. It's hard not to see you as a victim in all this."

She tore open her package and ran the contents over her lips. "I may not have had a choice, but if not for Eric, I never would have lived. And if Jonathan hadn't taken me, I wouldn't be alive now. And if Lucien hadn't bitten me, *Eric* wouldn't be alive today."

Walter huffed. "Positive out of negative, huh?"

She swallowed hard and fidgeted with the towelette. "What I've learned from Gab—well...the past is the past. Only the present bears the weight of our lives to form the foundation for our futures. If I die now because I can't accept that—" Her sad eyes washed over Eric. "I can't deny my needs and die again after so many have protected or saved me. They need me to save them now."

Walter was quiet for a moment. His voice was soft and sympathetic as he said, "This was your first time, huh?"

"Yeah." Paresh sighed and stared at Eric. "He was fine, but then he suddenly grabbed his chest and collapsed. His face was all twisted and ghastly pale, and he was in so much pain. He kept swatting me away. I couldn't do anything."

"Did you bite him in Animus Hollow?" Raven's bright pink bob and toothy grin appeared overhead.

She waved her hand in a stiff arc and patted the flask on her hip. "This'll bring him 'round for now."

"It's my fault, isn't it?" Paresh asked. "I took too much—"

"In that case, he'd be weak. I suspect it has more to do with you siphoning energy from his aura after you left the Hollow."

"What are you talking about?" Walter asked, annoyed. "Can't anything be simple with you people?"

Ignoring his tone, Raven gave a quick explanation and added, "Non-dimensional planes like that convert everything that enters into energy. Here, we share a synergistic existence with our auras, which cannot exist without our physical form, but in the Hollow, the two become one. It's simple really. When she bit him there, she drained more than his blood."

"Yeah, real simple. But I think I get the gist." Walter huffed.

"So, Eric was as weak spiritually as he was physically when we returned here?" Paresh asked, stroking Eric's hair. With his eyes closed, he seemed peacefully at rest.

"Aye. You constantly drain energy from his aura, so it was only a matter of time before you took more than he had to give, especially weakened from blood loss. It's fascinating. No one like you has ever existed."

"Fascinating isn't the word I'd choose, myself," Walter mumbled, gathering the used, bloody wipes and wrappers. He held everything in one hand and removed his gloves so that the last one came off inside out with the contaminated items inside. A look passed between him and Raven. He rolled his eyes and tossed the garbage to her. "Heaven forbid you trust me with any of your kind's DNA."

"Thank ya!" she replied with a two-fingered salute.

"He'll be okay now?" Paresh's question drew a sympathetic gaze from Walter as Raven crouched beside her.

"Aye. However, if he's to gain any strength, you can't be with him."

A crow cawed in the distance. Raven straightened and held her hand out for silence. As the three of them stared at each other, life slowly returned to the woods.

"On my cursory sweep of the area," Raven said at last, "I didn't sense anyone, but obviously someone was here and just left. We need to go." Flattening Eric's tongue with her thumb, she poured blood from her flask into his mouth.

Her voice was commanding as she hoisted Eric over her shoulder and said to Walter, "I'll carry him to your car. Drive as fast as possible to his house. I will follow on foot. Paresh will go in to stay with Donovan, and I will gather additional supplies. Then you will drive him back here while I again follow on foot. Whether you choose to stay is up to you."

Grim air settled over the trio with enough presence to suffocate the strongest man. "You may not believe it," Walter said. "But he is literally my oldest friend and I will never turn my back on him, or those he loves." He pulled Paresh up and led the way to his car.

With sirens and lights blazing a trail across town, Walter relayed to Paresh the argument he and Eric had earlier that day. He finished up as he turned into Eric's driveway. "Go on inside, hon. Our little tiff will pass."

The squad's leather seat squeaked in protest as Paresh shifted to gaze upon Eric one last time. "Do you trust him, Walter?"

"Of course I do. And I genuinely wish I'd never made that request." A thick finger tucked a lock of hair behind her ear. "But the people here aren't stupid and someone has to answer their suspicions. Even my officers want solid proof that vindicates him. No amount of respect can refute that—on the surface, anyway—things look really bad for Eric right now."

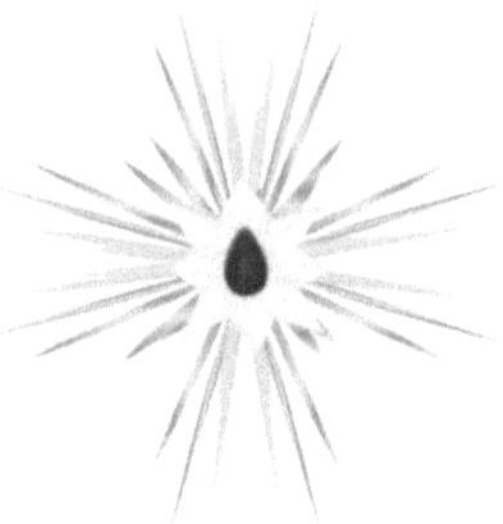

Chapter Sixteen: Black Shuck

I

The dense canopy offered a brief respite from the heat of a day that had been grueling on more than one front. Weary lines cut across Walter's forehead and spread outward from his eyes and mouth. The pressure to name an official suspect and stress of the previous two days was more than he'd handled in over a decade.

Molly was more adept at diving behind an emotional barrier, but she wore the same lines and wrinkles. A shockwave had slammed into her when she saw Eric's body in his car and she'd wrung her hands the entire way back. The red and white cooler clutched to her chest was filled with supplies that Raven needed. Molly held onto it like a life raft.

Even the huntress was subdued. Vertical creases bridged her brow and her jaw bulged at the hinge. It seemed like she was straining to carry Eric, but her expression hadn't changed since that crow's caw, and Walter did not find that reassuring.

As he thumbed through a mess of keys, Molly quietly said, "I have mine if you can't find yours."

"Yeah, better grab it." Walter shoved the keys into his pocket. "Don't know that I ever got a new one after he changed the locks."

Molly reluctantly handed her cargo off to him and jogged up the flagstone. She entered the cottage and pulled down the window shades.

With a note of awe, Raven said, "I've never seen such a devoted trustee when there's nothing to gain."

"I don't know much about you people," Walter replied gruffly, shooting a stern look at the huntress. "But that woman knows Eric better than he knows himself. Can you say that about anyone?"

An expression of quiet reflection passed over Raven's face. "You don't expect an answer, but I do."

"I'm listening."

"My Elder, Lord Endymion, and the hunter I thought would love me when we entered the Second New Age. Alex."

"*Alex?* As in, the *murderer*, Alex? Great."

Walter followed Raven inside and dropped the cooler into Molly's hands. "Did you hear that? The murderer knows our vampire hunter better than she knows herself."

"Walter, please!"

On a normal day, Molly's worry might have reigned him in. But this wasn't a normal day. Walter threw his hat onto the table and sat in the leather wingback chair by the fireplace. "Sure, come take my evidence. Show me how to run an investigation all proper like," he muttered. "Guess you'd know better than anybody since you're so tight with the one responsible, *Vampire Hunter*."

) ✳ ☾

As Walter mocked her in the corner, Raven laid Eric on the sofa and waved Molly over with the cooler. Both humans were in their fifties, but right then, Molly looked more like a timid girl facing a pack of wolves. Tears glistened as she looked from Walter to Eric.

Feeling weary herself, Raven forced a smile and shot a playful glance at the stewing lawman.

"Okay *Chief*," Raven said, tossing her hair. "Both are anomalies in the ranks like me. It's natural we'd be close."

Meant to reassure them, neither human would ever know how painful those words actually were—how they ripped open Raven's wounded newborn heart. Threading an IV catheter into Eric's arm, she continued, "Before he became an Elder, Lord Endymion was a mentor. And, until now, Alex was the closest thing to a friend that I could have."

"Whatever you say, lady. Friends don't usually try to kill each other, but what do I know?" Walter sucked his teeth.

"Walter! What has gotten into you?" Molly cried.

"Oh, I don't know—I have two murders on my hands, and even though I *know* who's responsible, I can't do anything about it! Or announce that I have a solid lead! Tell people that I have every resource hunting this jerk down! Nope. *They*," he said, thoroughly disgusted as he pointed at Raven, "have removed me from my own investigation."

"So what!" The tears running down Molly's face finally hit Walter's soft spot. "I can't help in the smallest way, not even an encouraging word. At least you have a badge! But you know what? Never mind us! What about that girl? That poor, poor girl and what she's been through?"

"Molly—"

"*Or him?* Forced to watch yet another love of his life die right before his eyes? Can you even fathom what that must be like? When was the last time you saw him this happy? Does he deserve your grief? Or that woman there, sent to help not only him, but this entire town?"

"Molly—"

A cottage-shaking *thud* jolted Walter to his feet. "*What the hell was that?*"

Raven was at the door faster than lightning. Her fingers froze on the knob at the distinct clicking of a revolver's hammer.

"I know you better than you know yourself, huh?" Alex's cheery voice came from down the hall. "That's not saying much when you make it so easy. You're slipping, Goody."

"You know I hate that nickname," Raven said without turning. Her eyes darted sideways to Walter and flicked over to Molly. Walter grabbed Molly and hunkered over her in the corner.

Alex laughed. "Got everybody all settled there, Goody-as-a-Gumdrop? Mm, if gumdrops tasted as sweet as you, I'd chomp one down in a heartbeat and relish the hell it caused on my body."

Raven turned around wearing a fake smile and planted her hands on her hips. "Oh Alex, how *do* you fend them off with a mouth like that?"

"Aw, you're cute," he drawled. "I enjoy our banter, but there's a pressing matter that needs our attention."

"Our attention?" Raven's fingers slipped into her pockets and withdrew a cluster of darts faster than the human eye could see. But she wasn't fast enough. Shrieking in pain, she dropped the darts and tugged at the silver spike Alex had thrown to pin her shoulder to the door.

"It was fun in the woods, but I'm done playing around." Alex stepped into the living room and tipped an imaginary hat to Walter and Molly. He shoved his sunglasses up and eyed the bag emptying into Eric's arm. "She's not here, and neither is that First Officer of yours. Tell me where Lady Paresh is or we'll both be in for it when *he* wakes up and finds her dead."

II

Without the lights or the siren's wail, Walter's unmarked squad car seemed to creep down Eric's private lane. The tires kicked up small plumes of dust as the car turned onto the country road. The farther it went, the smaller it looked, and the heavier the weight in Paresh's chest grew. Donovan gave her shoulders a light squeeze.

"Raven will have him patched up in no time," he said in a soft voice. "Come inside and relax. A hot shower will melt this tension away." He gently kneaded the muscles along her neck. "You're stiff through here, and there's blood in your hair. Come, Doctor Donovan says."

She embraced the transient moment—her chin dipped, her eyelids drooped, and a sigh rode a tide of ebbing sorrow as she leaned into his hands. A mourning dove cooed over the rising drone of cicadas and a lone cricket chirped beneath the porch. It sounded like home.

Seconds passed, maybe even minutes, but it felt like hours before Donovan gave her a slight tug. "Let's go in. They'll be back soon."

Her head bobbing in agreement, she reluctantly led the way and collapsed, facedown, onto the sofa's cushions. The house felt so empty. She wanted to cry, but no tears formed.

"Is he really going to be okay?" She glanced back at Donovan, who was craning his neck out the door. "Is something wrong?"

"Nope. Not a thing." He nudged the door closed with his foot. As he twisted the deadbolt, a thin smile crept over his face. "Quite the opposite, actually. A little birdie dropped by earlier and told me something utterly fantastic."

Paresh sat up. "Good news?"

"Very good news, dear Guinevere. Very good news, indeed."

His voice was as melodramatic as usual, but there was nothing playful about his intense stare or crooked grin. A pang of unease nipped her ribs.

"Do you realize this is the first time we've been alone together?" Donovan asked. "Completely on our own? No spies? No one to see us? No one to hear us?"

The pang bit down hard. "I hadn't thought much about it," she replied cautiously. "So, um, who stopped by to see you here?"

Donovan's grin widened as he kicked off the door and started toward her. "Someone who wanted to make sure I don't squander the wonderful opening you've presented to us."

"Opening? What are you t-talking about? Who came here?" Tossing a glance at the hall, Paresh inched along the L-shaped sofa. Even if she could make it to a room at the back of the house, would a locked door offer any protection? Would it last long enough to call for help?

Donovan wagged his finger at her. "Don't tempt me with a chase, because I won't be the one who loses."

"What is going on? Who came here? Answer me!"

"By the tone of your voice, I'd say you can answer those questions yourself. So why don't you tell me?"

She knew little about his speed and abilities—or if fear would let her run—but she had to try. He was still across the room and the sofa's arm was within reach.

Sucking in a quick breath, she leaped up. He dashed forward and caught her. Her scream reverberated off the walls as he slammed her down onto the cushions.

Landing on top of her, he cooed, "Oh, do tell me, Paresh. Tell me what you think's going on here in that sweet, sweet voice of yours."

"*Get off! Get off! Let me go!*" she shrieked. There was no logical thought, no plan. Panic and instinct drove her to fight and scream as hard and loudly as she could.

With a laugh, he restrained her wrists over her head. "Let's gain control of ourselves, shall we? My lord may overhear and think I've lost control of you, and you don't want him to come here himself."

Blinking back the sting of tears, Paresh struggled to free her hands and cried, "I've already been killed by the Devil once! I doubt your lord can do any worse!"

"You might be surprised."

"Let me go!"

"No."

"*Let me go!*" she screamed, straining every muscle to push against him.

"Ah! Why would I let such a succulent creature loose?" Donovan whispered. "Your blood is sweeter than that of any innocent, and believe me, as a god of death, I've tasted plenty." His breath brushed her cheek as he added with a twisted laugh, "The prey of a Reaper doesn't live long enough to answer questions. It's easy to shift the blame of a nibble."

"But Raven! You said you loved her!"

"No, I didn't." Light gleamed off Donovan's eyes. "I never said anything like that."

"W-what?"

"One drop," he said as his pupils began dilating. "One drop is what we were given, but it wasn't enough."

"What? Donovan—"

"Could never be enough."

"Please stop—"

"The taste has stayed fresh upon my tongue."

"Donovan—"

"The memory sweet in my mind." His engorged gaze dropped to her throat. "Even tainted with *his* blood, your scent is so tantalizing, your aura so loose and innocent——*so intoxicating*——"

"Don't——"

"Not a second has gone by that you haven't stolen my every thought." His lips peeled back over his teeth. "And I'm not about to share you *with anyone.*"

"*No!*" Paresh screamed. A new round of panic reinvigorated her muscles, but Donovan was like an immovable slab of granite.

He licked her pulse and then plunged his fangs into her throat. Euphoria forced its way inside, lighting every nerve with pleasure's fire while pillaging her body of all resistance. A gasp fled her mouth and with it went her will.

Tears streamed from her eyes, but she only felt moisture on her skin. The link between the bile burning her throat and Donovan's sickening moans didn't exist. The reduced pressure on her wrists was trivial.

Swept up in ecstasy's paralyzing waves, her mind desperately grasped hold of that last sensation and sought an elusive string that led to something useful. She was sinking fast into delirium. Her fingers dug into Donovan's wavy locks. His hair was as soft as cashmere, and his tongue was as warm as the hands gliding beneath her shirt.

Teetering between reality and intimate memory, she mistook the feel of his body for Eric's. Even his scent morphed into something more familiar. She moaned breathlessly and thrust her head back. His response was impossible to ignore as he ground his pelvis against her thigh. She panted and writhed beneath him, yearning to surrender.

Through the haze, her mind found a string attached to Lucien in the moonlit garden. As though watching a scene play out, she saw her hand move down to Donovan's shoulder. It slid beneath his hair and flattened against his neck.

Ripping out of her throat, he arched up, rigid as though shocked by an electric bolt. His eyes rolled back and his head flopped loosely on his neck as he crashed down on top of her. She screamed, desperately pushing against him with one hand, but digging her nails into his neck with the other. Letting go meant rousing the monster he'd revealed himself to be.

Tears and blood saturated the cushion beneath her head. She cried so hard her chest couldn't expand under his weight. She hyperventilated and choked on each breath.

Closing her eyes, she cupped a hand over her mouth and eventually managed to breathe with some measure of control. She opened her eyes. Wavy brown locks blocked her view.

Another steady stream of tears and fear choked her again. Where was Donovan's "little birdie?" *What if he came back?*

An eternity seemed to pass before her eyes dried and her chest stopped heaving. She hated the smell of cloves beneath her nose. Donovan's lustful eyes appeared in her mind. He'd looked so arrogant and triumphant.

"Eric," she whispered as a new batch of tears pooled. "I need you. Please hurry—I can't do this—I can't take this anymore."

The house was too quiet. Too empty. She didn't know how long she lay there. Her eyes lost focus. Her mind went blank. Cramps riddled the fingers buried in Donovan's neck; otherwise, she was numb and no longer aware of his body's weight.

Maybe she fell asleep. Warm, blinding light washed the room in gold and a man she'd never seen, garbed in black cargo pants and a red and black shirt, appeared in the doorway. His hair stood as a crown of glowing spikes. She had to be dreaming.

"Help," she whispered as the man ran in calling her name.

He had a youthful voice, slightly squeaky and kind to a fault. She imagined green eyes that smiled as wide as his lips. A whoosh of air blew over her face as he dropped to his knees and pressed his fingers against her throat.

"Thank Apollo that your heart is stronger than it sounds." An expression of disgust knitted his brow as he studied the bloody punctures on her neck. "This never should have happened."

He yanked Donovan off her, unaware of her gnarled grip until she tumbled down with him. He caught her before she landed on top of her attacker.

"Whoa, careful now!"

Still not sure if she was dreaming or awake, she tried to peer past the garnet lenses covering the stranger's eyes. Focused on loosening her hold on Donovan, he didn't notice. He shook his head in disbelief.

"Her fingers are really in there," he said over his shoulder. "I'm afraid I'll hurt her if I pry them loose."

"She knows he'll regain consciousness if she lets go," said a familiar, feminine voice. "If she hasn't killed him already."

"No such luck—he's breathing. How's you-know-who?"

"Awake and livid. Not stable on his feet yet. I ran ahead of the car. They're not far off now." Raven knelt beside the stranger and swept strands of hair from Paresh's face. She offered a sad smile. "I'm not going to ask you to let go, because I can't imagine how this has been for you, but you are safe now."

Paresh's numb shell cracked off like broken shards from a mirror. "*Raven!*" she croaked, ripping free of Donovan's neck and flinging blood as she threw her arms around the huntress. She sobbed into the crook of her neck.

"Oh, milady, hush now." Raven smoothed Paresh's hair. To the man, she whispered, "Lord Lucien wants him detained for questioning. Get him secured and gone before Eric arrives and kills him."

"Hey, nothing would make me happier, but it's not like I can waltz in and out of the holding cells, myself, you know," the man whispered back. "And I'm not leaving you here alone. He's not stable, yet."

"He's strong enough. Tend to your orders and hurry back," Raven said. "I've briefed Lord Lucien. You won't have any trouble at the Arc of Mourning Eidolons."

Paresh sat up and wiped her eyes. "Where's Eric?"

"He'll be here any minute, sweetie," Raven replied. She tucked the girl's head to her shoulder and turned to the blond stranger. "Which means you need to get him out of here."

"All right, but I'm going under protest."

"But like the good little boy that you are." Raven tousled his spikes.

"Man, Goody! What's your deal with my hair?"

"Go on. He's going to be right pissed when he walks through that door and isn't greeted by a dead Donovan, especially after what he did to her."

"Better right pissed, than wrong pissed, I always say," the stranger grumbled as he flipped Donovan onto his stomach and bound his wrists with a hinged silver ring. "I wouldn't have minded being greeted by a dead Donovan myself, the rotten chump. I should have killed him in the forest."

A white portal appeared behind the stranger when he pressed a prong of the Vampiric Star pinned on his belt. He hoisted Donovan over his shoulder, pinched the air over his head like the brim of a hat, and gave a quick nod. "Ladies, don't mourn my passing. It won't last long."

"You're such a weirdo," Raven groaned, slapping at him as he disappeared into Animus Hollow.

"Ow, ow, ow! My assssssssss!" he whined.

A quiet laugh fluttered from Paresh's lips. Raven smiled.

"Now, that's a refreshing sound. Proves he's good for something." Raven nudged Paresh's face up. "Can I look at it?"

Paresh tilted her head to the side. Mimicking Jonathan's earlier exam, Raven felt along the sides of her neck and pushed on her lymph nodes. Then she pressed her fingers into the bite itself.

Paresh grimaced. "It hurts more now than when Lucien bit me."

"Damn," Raven whispered.

"What is it?" Paresh cast a teary glance down her nose.

"He pushed the lethal protein in deeper and undid all the progress your body made to heal itself. Damn," she repeated, squinting as she surveyed the damage. "I don't know how I missed it, but you're not healing, and now that you're sitting up, you've started bleeding again. Here—" She grabbed Paresh's hand and pressed the heel of her palm against the wound. "Apply pressure and don't let go or it'll start spurting. I'll get a clotting agent from my jacket."

Raven jogged over to the kitchen counter and returned as an engine rumbled outside. The car was pulling up the drive as a door slammed and angry feet pounded the cement. Eric ran through the door and crossed the room faster than Paresh had ever seen him move. "Where the hell is he?"

"Eric! Eric! Oh thank God!" Paresh latched onto his neck as he whisked her into his arms.

"Paresh!" Raven yelled, jumping up to mash her palm against the girl's throat. "Eric, she's not healing! I have to stop the bleeding!"

Eric sank into the sofa and nudged Raven's hand away. His darkening orbs peered at the punctures and then moved up to Paresh's face. "Donovan did this to you?"

Another knot formed in Paresh's throat. The sting of tears resurfaced. She sucked in a breath through quivering lips. "And...he...he...touched me—like it was...you...b-but...it wuh—w-wasn't you—"

"*Unforgivable,*" Eric growled, holding Paresh firm as she broke down sobbing into his shoulder. He glared at Raven. "*Where the hell is he?*"

"At the Arc of Mourning Eidolons," Jonathan said from the doorway.

"*Why is he alive?*"

"Trust that I share your sentiment on that matter, Brother." Jonathan set his fedora on the ottoman and sat beside Eric. He tucked a lock of hair behind Paresh's ear and kissed her hair. "Unfortunately, we need him alive. Corben fled the arc. Until we find his partner, the entire Council is under house arrest. At least Lucien has an idea of who it might be now."

Paresh lifted her tearstained face and reached out to Jonathan. Her jaw quivered harder and plump tears dripped from her eyes. Jonathan took her hand and scooted closer. "I'm so sorry, Pare."

"It hurts, Master Jon."

"You shouldn't call me that anymore," Jonathan said, sitting back without letting go of her hand. "Can you tell us what happened?"

"I'm sorry to interrupt, but I must stop the bleeding before she does anything." In one hand, Raven held a swab, and in the other, a vial of clear fluid. As Eric nodded, she leaned in, but Jonathan waved her off.

"What the hell are you doing?" Eric demanded.

Jonathan cupped Paresh's cheek. "You can heal your wound and erase the pain at the same time. Understand?"

Averting her gaze, Paresh sniffed and nodded.

"Raven, get her a drink," Jonathan ordered.

"Right away—"

"Hold on a sec," Eric said, tossing an irritated glance at Jonathan. "Back off, would you? Now's not the time. She's traumatized enough!"

"Eric!" Paresh gasped as a spasm seized her throat.

Glaring at Jonathan, Eric tugged his collar open and positioned her mouth over his pulse. "I know this is difficult, but you've got to do it."

"No!" Raven protested. "You're too weak! She almost killed you!"

"I'll heal faster than she will!" Eric yelled.

"Commander," Jonathan said in a tight voice. "He can replace what she takes while she's taking it, and I can supplement what she absorbs from his aura."

"Aye, of course, my lord. Excuse my outburst."

"Give us a moment and get enough to sustain him," Jonathan ordered.

"As you command." Raven turned away and tucked the swab and vial into her pocket. "Eric, do you want Molly and Walter to wait in the car?"

He nodded. "Before you head back to my closet, let them know we're okay and to yell if they need anything."

"Of course."

Paresh sighed nervously as Raven closed the door behind her. Eric's pulse beat strong and hard against her teeth, but the instinct to drink wasn't there.

"I can't do this," she whispered.

"Don't let what Raven said get to you," Eric replied gently. "I'll be fine this time."

She shook her head. "No, I mean, nothing's happening. I want real food, like soup."

"What?" Jonathan leaned forward, perplexed. "That's impossible this far into alteration."

"Brother," Eric said, eyeing Jonathan. "Will you go ask Molly to get

Paresh some soup from The Greenery? Raven can go with them."

"It won't help."

"Please?"

"I'm coming back in."

"I'd expect nothing less."

Paresh licked her lips and whispered, "Thank you, Eric."

"Don't thank me yet," he replied as Jonathan reluctantly walked out the door. "Because Jonathan's right. Solid food isn't going to work, and we don't have time to wait for the thirst to hit you again."

"But—"

"It's okay," Eric whispered. "Trust me and open your mouth."

He propped her up and sliced his jugular open with a lengthened fingernail. The sight and iron scent of his blood had no effect. Discouraged, she started to lean back, but he caught her head and forced her lips to his throat.

"It's going to close without suction," Eric said. "You have to do this, even if you don't think you can, and you need to take a lot, even if you don't want to. I'm sorry, Paresh, but you have to. I can't lose you again, and I'm sick of saying that. Sick that this has become the norm of our life together. Please try, for me. Please."

The warm, metallic fluid filling her mouth tasted nothing like it had in Animus Hollow. There it had been sweet and succulent, like the juice of a perfectly ripened peach. It had left her thirsty for more and eager to embrace her new life. Now, she fought against gagging.

"Paresh, it's going to close. It's already starting to clot."

Huffing through her nose, she squeezed her eyes shut and formed a tight seal against his skin with her lips. Forming suction between her tongue and the roof of her mouth, she pulled his blood into her mouth, and after the first few mouthfuls were down, the sticky nectar she remembered began to return.

Pressure mounted behind her teeth. His blood smelled so sweet, blending with the bergamot and musk of his cologne into a scent similar to cinnamon rolls hot from the oven. She was so hungry.

Holding onto his neck, she bit into his flesh.

"Ah! There's my girl. You've got it now," he whispered.

The front door opened and closed. The heels of Jonathan's shoes clacked against the granite floor and scuffed over the shag area rug. She knew exactly when to expect the weight to shift on the sofa as he sat and even felt a disturbance in the air as he reached over to rub her shoulders.

"Jonathan," Eric said with a note of urgency in his voice. "I need something. Quick."

Paresh tried to withdraw, but Eric held her in place. "Don't stop," Eric said. "Jonathan—the cooler in my closet——"

"Don't be a fool. I'm right here and you know you're better off drinking from me anyway."

"I'm not...I can't..." Eric sounded out of breath and started coughing. The pressure on the back of her head disappeared. His hand fell to his side.

Uncertainly glancing at Jonathan from the corner of her eye, she saw him roll up his sleeve. "Don't you dare stop." He pointed a stern finger at her. "Let him take care of you and I'll take care of him. I'm a bridge between you, remember?"

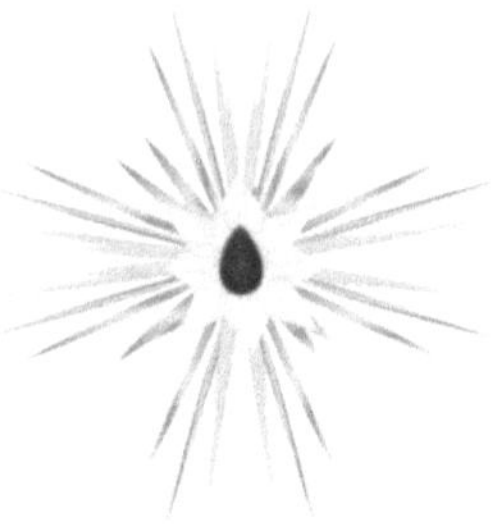

CHAPTER SEVENTEEN: THE TIDE EBBS

I

Fiery magenta streaked across the western horizon. The moon had yet to rise, but the night was already long. Not that anyone needed to say it aloud. Whether human, vampire, or something in between, each face wore the same tired expression.

Raven had already succumbed to the Sandman's dust in Eric's living room. Alex plucked a throw off the bloodstained sofa and stopped beside her with it folded over his arm. Curled up in an oversized armchair, she looked like a punk princess after a night of stomping beats in a moshpit. He might have smiled if not for her bandaged arm and shoulder. Reality crushed his imagination and cast deep furrows over his face and heart.

"My dear Raven," Alex whispered so quietly he hardly heard himself. "This never should have happened."

His eyes lingered on the bloody bandages. He hadn't meant to strike her. She'd dodged his bullet, as intended, but he'd miscalculated her path when he threw out the Cataclysm. He was lucky it hadn't severed her arm.

"Thank you for not killing me," he whispered, draping the blanket over her. "If you'd tried, Donovan would've been the only one that walked away."

He caressed her cheek and half-smiled at the incoherent mumbles that fell beneath her breath. Lack of sleep and blood loss had exhausted her way beyond normal battle fatigue.

"Has Donovan given us anything useful?" Eric asked, engrossed in a hushed conversation with Jonathan in the kitchen. Stress and nearly two weeks without rest had given Jonathan sagging eyelids and creases beneath his eyes, and Eric bore the haggard visage of a beaten man at least a decade older than his usual physical appearance.

It was hard to believe that the stamina of just one of them eclipsed the combined level of a troupe of true bloods. After working nearly forty-eight hours straight to clear his name, Alex would only last another day or two without sleep. He didn't doubt that Eric and Jonathan could go another few weeks, even in their current states.

"Since waking up in Chthonic Knight custody, he's been quieter than a dead man buried at sea by Poseidon himself," Alex replied, his voice soft and quiet as he passed the table, returning to the kitchen nook.

The humans, Molly and Walter, sat dazed in front of barely touched soup and half-eaten sandwiches, and Paresh, her bowl slurped dry, eyed their food with a famished stare. About to pounce from hunger, she wasn't paying attention to anything else.

Leaning against the counter in a spot where everyone and the door was visible, Alex pulled a coin from his pocket and steadied it on his thumb. He flicked it into the air and watched the likeness of Hercules tumble over Zeus on his throne. The thick silver piece, given to him by Raven shortly after her creation in the fifth century, was an Alexander the Great coin that dated to 323 A.D.

Pulling off his glasses, Eric closed his eyes and pinched the bridge of his nose. He heaved a sigh of frustration and fatigue. "If he's of no use to us, then get rid of him." Even his voice sounded tired, as though thinking the words and then speaking them was incredibly taxing.

"In due time, Brother," Jonathan replied. "His silence won't last long. The Chthonic Knights are far from noble. He'll talk for them—or he'll scream for them."

"Not that I give a damn," Eric retorted. "But how the hell does the threat of torture work on creatures who heal like us?"

"Techniques in the Realm of Man are not the only techniques." An almost inaudible metallic whine accompanied Alex's voice as Hercules tumbled over Zeus. "If Donovan remains uncooperative, he knows full well that the Knights will inject his blood with liquid silver. And believe me, as someone who has witnessed what that does to the body, he won't want those needles anywhere near him."

His lords quieted into their thoughts. Alex eyed the dining trio. The day's ordeal had taken a hefty toll on Molly and Walter. Sleep's gravity tugged at their eyelids and pulled yawns from their mouths, but they fought back to support the young woman between them—the seemingly normal girl that had saved his race.

The lives of men had seemed enviably peaceful in comparison to the Vampiric Nation's blood-soaked existence. But Alex wanted more. He wanted the bliss that sprouted from the mystery of the unknown. The joy of faith without proof. Each century had passed one after the other with each day no different from the one before it. There had been no bliss. No joyous wonder. Nothing unknown in his world.

Angels and demons. God and Lucifer. Vampires and humans. Plants and animals. He'd come to know the inhabitants of the spiritual and physical realms intimately well. Extinctions would come and go. Civilizations would rise and fall. Battles would be won and lost. And the longest war of all would continue to rage until Lucifer surrendered or failed. These were the truths that Alex knew.

But then came an unknown. A golden-haired girl whose very birth changed everything. Every fiber of her being was a mystery.

He would do *anything* to protect that.

The coin landed on his thumb and returned to the air as he pondered the echo he'd heard behind her pulse. He'd dismissed it as arrhythmia caused by Donovan's attack, but while waiting for processing with the Chthonic Knights, he realized that so much about her defied the laws of their existence that he had no idea what to think.

Jonathan caught the coin in midair. "Spill it, Commander."

"Just musing, sir. Thoughts that aren't so different from yours, I'm sure." Squeaking Styrofoam drew his attention to the table. Walter had finally noticed Paresh's hungry stare and shoved his soup at her.

"Have at it, hon. I tell you what, if nothing else, this whole thing has been great for my waistline." With a wink, Walter smoothed his hands over his gut. "Don't you think?"

Molly groaned. "You're terrible." She dropped her spoon onto her napkin. "But I think I'm on that diet, too."

Paresh accepted Walter's offer and dug in, prompting the older woman to add, "It's good to see this skinny thing eating for once. I bet she'd inhale a hamburger if we put one in front of her."

"Maybe. If you promised I'd never met the cow." Paresh slurped a green bean off her spoon. "After a day like today, nothing's impossible."

Alex chuckled and snatched his coin from Jonathan's fingers. "I'm in awe of her appetite." Sliding the silver piece into his pocket, he admitted, "No, that's not it. I'm in awe of *her*."

Jonathan's mouth split into a partial grin. He nodded and crossed his arms, but said nothing. Molly was coming their way.

"Paresh, feel free to claim mine, too. I'll stick it in the fridge. Just reheat it when you want it," she called over her shoulder. "Walter, I don't have it in me to drive home. Do you mind?"

"Nah. It's fine." He stretched his arms over his head and yawned. "I'm ready to turn in myself."

Eric met Molly at the refrigerator and propped the door open. "You're not staying here tonight?"

Molly shook her head. "You kids need a good night's sleep and I need a break. I'll ask Sammy to drive me into town tomorrow. My boss hasn't been in at the office recently, as you probably know, so I don't think he'll mind me spending a day at the spa." She plucked at graying hairs hanging over her brow. "Relaxation and a good hairdresser are calling my name."

"Of course I don't care if you take the day off." Eric gave her a gentle hug. "Take two or three, or more. I'm just worried about leaving you alone."

"Eric, you aren't Superman and I don't need a babysitter. Focus on that girl over there, because we've seen firsthand that what will be, will be, and you can't change it otherwise." She patted his chest and stood on her toes to kiss his cheek. "You know I love you."

"But?"

"Insert your own." She grabbed her purse off the counter. Her eyes passed over Jonathan and Alex as she motioned for Walter. "Good night, gentlemen. Ready, Walter? Paresh, you take care, okay?"

Paresh nodded as Walter replied, "Yes ma'am."

The lawman haphazardly threw his sandwich into its cardboard container and shoved his hat onto his head. He touched Paresh's shoulder. "Get some rest, okay, hon? And make sure that guy teaches you how to use the contact menu of a cell phone." The finger pointed at Eric morphed into a waving hand. Walter bid everyone good night and followed Molly outside.

"Not that I suppose it matters——" Walter poked his head inside. "But lock this——better safe than sorry."

"There's a voice that can wake the dead," Raven grumbled, peering from a cracked eye. "See you tomorrow, Chief." She lifted two fingers in a parting salute.

"Seven-thirty on the dot or I'm going home." Playful respect sat within Walter's voice. "Night, Vampire Hunter."

"Night, Walter."

"Aw! Does wittle Goody have a new fwend?" Alex teased as he rounded the barstools to secure the deadbolt. Unable to resist, he made a pit stop to grind his knuckles against her head. "Huh? Does she?"

"Stop it!" she cried, smacking his hand. "He's more trustworthy than others I've called 'friend' lately."

"Oh, ouch!" Alex clutched his chest and toppled into her lap. "Oh, it hurts Goody! It hurts so much!"

She kicked him off and rolled over, turning her back to him. "I wasn't talking about you, you daft idiot."

"Yeah, I know," he replied quietly, sobering as he slumped against the chair and slid to the floor. He reached over his shoulder and patted her thigh. He'd spared that traitor's life only because of the information he carried. Donovan was lucky Alex was an honorable man, because in all of his life, he'd never despised—or yearned to kill—anyone more.

II

A fist smashed onto Walter's desk. "This is such a crock of shit!"

"Watch yourself," Walter warned. His dayshift officers had barged into his office minutes earlier. "I know how you all feel, but Mr. Ravenscroft is not a suspect in this matter!"

"Would you be saying that if you two weren't buddy-buddy?" asked his Lieutenant, Kyle Waggoner.

"My personal relationships have never affected my investigations."

"Yeah, right. So your friendship with the Hawthornes had nothing to do with paying us overtime for a month after their daughter went missing or having the entire department attend their funeral in uniform?" Lieutenant Waggoner huffed and rolled his eyes.

"A little girl was missing and her parents were dead. It wouldn't matter whose child it was, I wouldn't have done a thing differently. And Andrew was a huge supporter of expanding this department. Did any of you not *want* to pay your respects?"

"Well what about making us keep Paresh's return a secret?" Officer Larry Bishop, the one who had pounded on Walter's desk, began pacing impatiently. "It's been over a week now. We all looked for her—the town deserves to know she's safe."

"There's no excuse." Kyle straightened and tipped his hat back on his head. A few grays hairs poked out. "Maybe it's time the Village Board found out that our Chief is protecting a murderer."

"Is that a threat, Lieutenant?" Walter asked in a cool voice, leaning over his desk. "Because if you think, for an instant, that any of those board members are going to disagree with me, then go ahead and run to them. But I'm telling you right now, Mr. Ravenscroft has everyone on that board in his pocket and if you go running your mouth about unjustified and unwarranted accusations, he might just leave this town. And if that happens, his money goes with him. The people here can't afford to pay the taxes this heavily compensated department would cost them. Without Eric Ravenscroft, this is a poor, Podunk town and all of you would do well to remember it."

Walter sat back and eyed the three men. So far, only Officer James, a thin-framed man of gentle temperament, had remained quiet. "Now, I don't care what you think you know about him. Mr. Ravenscroft has two solid alibis and is not remotely considered a suspect for either murder. Knock this crap off or I'll write all of you up for insubordination."

The door to Walter's office creaked open. The officers' red faces instantly lost color.

Wearing a charcoal shirt and creased black trousers, Eric's pointed stare hit all of them at once. "Let's get something straight. I have this entire town in my pocket, not just the Village Board."

Walter cleared his throat and gestured at the officers. "You wanted the best in the state and you got 'em. They've got more questions than I have answers."

"Come to turn yourself in?" The Lieutenant crossed his arms.

"Wow guys—" Eric held out his hands. "Relax. I was joking."

Grinning, he entered and slapped the speechless Lieutenant on the back. "How long have you known me? You can ask me anything. And no, I'm not turning myself in."

"Then why are you here?" Officer Bishop asked.

"Under the guise of paying my old friend a visit—" Eric stood in front of Walter's desk facing them. "I'm here to give a saliva sample to put an end to this nonsense once and for all. But first—" He held up his index finger and pulled off his glasses.

He captured their gazes. One by one, the spark in each faded. "Shouldn't you be out doing your jobs instead of harassing your Chief? Look deep in your hearts—do you really believe I'm responsible for these atrocities?"

"No," they answered in unison.

Eric looked down and rubbed his glasses on his shirt. "What were you saying Officer James? Your question trailed off. I didn't quite catch it."

As the man's eyes regained focus, he pursed his lips and scratched his head. "I don't remember. Sorry about that."

"Well, if there's nothing further, I'd like a word with your boss." Eric swept his hand toward the door.

"Why were we here in the first place?" Lieutenant Waggoner muttered. "Were we in a meeting, Chief?"

"You're all dismissed," Walter replied gruffly. "I want ten traffic citations from each of you before the end of your shifts today."

"Jeez, ten?" Officer Bishop whispered to the Lieutenant as they all turned away. His superior adjusted his hat and scratched behind his ear, shaking his head.

Officer James was the last to shuffle out. Walter slammed the door behind him. "What the hell was that?" he demanded. "I had them under control! I don't need you in here brainwashing good off—"

"If 'under control' means telling them that I've bribed the entire Village Board and that my money is worth more than the lives of the people in this town, then yes, you had it under control."

"What?" Walter looked dumbfounded. "That's not what I meant. Did I really tell them that?"

Eric nodded.

Walter sank into his chair. "Oh, brother."

"The pressure's getting to you. They won't remember anyway." Eric's tone was dismissive as he sat in a chair opposite the desk. "But I do want to give you that sample and you're free to release the results to whomever you see fit."

"But how? Raven summed it up pretty well. What am I supposed to do? Say, 'Eric Ravenscroft isn't the vampire we're looking for?'"

Eric smiled and folded his hands in his lap. "The words people whisper behind my back will never change, but fears in relation to them can be allayed. You don't have to say 'vampire,' just that I came in voluntarily and it's not a DNA match."

"And Raven's on board with this?" Walter asked somewhat dubiously.

Eric swiveled in his chair and addressed the far corner. "Raven, do I have your permission?"

"No," came an invisible grumble.

"Jesus!" Walter cried. "Would you *stop* doing that?"

Facing Walter with a smile, Eric said, "So there you have it. I'm a rebel. But I outrank her, so—"

"Hold up." Walter's eyes narrowed as he mentally sorted through his concerns. "I'm not so sure I disagree with the invisible woman, now. The results will give conclusive proof that you're not human."

"I really don't care as long as it makes your job easier. Any problems that arise will be mine alone to deal with and I'm fine with that, so it's your call."

Walter shook his head. "I'm not fine with causing you an eternal headache."

"I don't get headaches."

"Now that's a lie and we both know it. Yesterday…I've never seen you so pissed before. This is getting to you, just like the rest of us."

"We all have our moments of weakness, but that's no excuse. I shouldn't have yelled at you. I'm sorry."

"You don't need to apologize. I regret ever making that request."

"Ahem!" Raven grunted. "Focus!"

"Look, Vampire Hunter," Walter said. "Show yourself. I'm not down with all this cloak and dagger-y stuff."

"Can't, sorry."

"What she means is—we have a counter proposal and can't risk anyone seeing her." Eric put his hand up to the side of his mouth and whispered, "I should add that she finds this plan only slightly less objectionable and I'm not sure you'll disagree with her."

"Well, I'm not seeing things as black and white as I was a few days ago, so let's hear it and find out." Walter's chair creaked as he leaned back. "I'm just glad you got that scumbag before—"

"Speaking of which," Eric interrupted. "I'd like to report the assault that happened last night to Paresh. I believe the dispatchers can verify that she called 911 and your officers will believe that you kept your response quiet since her return hasn't been publicly revealed."

"I'm listening."

"As soon as you agree to this, Raven is going to enter the station posing as an FBI agent investigating the murders here in relation to the Hawthorne kidnapping. Upon requesting to see you, she will relay information that David has been working with a local man, Simon Driggs, which you are aware of since you've already listed him as a missing person."

"A bit leery, but still listening."

"She will implicate David, Nicole, Simon, and a third man in the murders, and will confiscate the saliva samples and daggers in your possession as evidence in her 'federal' case. In exchange, she will give up a location where you can find Simon's and David's bodies, as well as a physical description and the name of the third man."

"Ohh-kay," Walter said, holding his hands up. "I'm not saying no, but I ain't saying yes, either. David and Simon died a week before the first murder. Forensics and the coroner are going to figure that out."

"They won't." Raven's disembodied voice was closer—behind

Eric's shoulder. "Their bodies were preserved. It'll look like they died this morning."

"Ohh-kay," Walter repeated, shaking his head. "Then what about this third guy? I don't want anyone chasing a ghost. What if an innocent guy gets picked up for this?"

"We aren't giving up a ghost. We're giving up the actual murderer," Eric revealed.

Walter's eyes popped open wide. "You're what? I can't possibly hold Donovan here!"

A laugh sailed over Eric's shoulder. "You aren't actually getting *him*, Chief, 'cause you're right—he'd rip this place to shreds. Donovan Trueblood collaborated with Nicole O'Reilly and David Hawthorne in a conspiracy to steal the Hawthorne fortune. When David's plan—or sanity—began to unravel, they killed him and Simon, and used local rumors to implicate Eric in staged murders as a distraction aimed at regaining control of Paresh—hence the assault last night. You'll get two suspects to name publicly who will also appear on the FBI's national wanted list. The arrangements are set to go once I give the go-ahead. Plus, Nicole's body can turn up whenever you want it."

"But…but…" Walter sputtered. He stared at Eric with his hands up. "I don't even know what to ask. This is insane."

"Walter," Eric said. "All you have to do is treat her like an agent, listen, and take what she says as the truth. You can trust that her superiors have a very wide reach. Everything she tells you can be verified by anyone curious enough to dig, no matter how deep they go."

Walter sighed and licked his lips. "I don't know. This is my career here."

"You're a good man, Old Friend," Eric replied. "I know you prefer honesty and have done a good deal of looking the other way when it comes to me, but this is as close to the truth as you can get. Otherwise, both cases will go unsolved. Donovan will be put to death soon, and while his body won't be released, the knowledge that he was found dead can be. Bill's and Rebecca's families deserve closure and he *is* the actual killer."

"Fine," Walter said. "Do it."

Eric tossed his chin in the direction of the door. "Call down the hall that you're expecting a visitor. Raven will slip out and appear at the front desk in a few minutes."

"Like anybody's gonna buy an agent with punk pink hair and that many piercings," Walter mumbled.

A hard slap on his back sent him stumbling and knocked the wind from his lungs. "You won't recognize me, Chief. I won't let you down."

Coughing to catch his breath while he opened the door, Walter replied, "Yeah, right."

Two minutes later, Officer James peered into the office. "Sorry to interrupt, but there's an FBI agent here to see you."

"Send her in and close the door."

True to Raven's word, Walter didn't recognize the woman who entered. In a pressed, navy suit jacket and skirt, with shoulder length chestnut hair, brown contacts, and wire-rimmed glasses, Raven brushed past her escort with cool aloofness and marched over to his desk.

As he and Eric stood to greet her, she held out a rigid hand. "Gentlemen. Special Agent Hawkings, FBI. Thank you for meeting me on such short notice. I am working the Hawthorne case and have information that ties into your murder investigations."

She took the seat beside Eric and crossed her legs. Smoothing her skirt, she eyed Officer James with an arched brow. He awkwardly backed out and closed the door. Sharing a look of confirmation with Eric, she grinned. "This is going to be a breeze."

She pointed at the door and said to Walter, "Right now, two of your officers are whispering about overlooking David's local connections. In no time, we'll have all your problems solved."

III

The sun's prismatic array shot through the glass panels overhead and scattered into thousands of iridescent particles. Some spotlighted minute specks of dust and others turned water droplets into short lived, multifaceted gems. The rest bestowed radiant kisses upon each plant from the highest palm frond down to the delicate snowy-white petals of the potted orchids in the rattan seating area.

Despite the sting in his unprotected eyes, Alex was as enthralled as a new soul in Heaven. The magical, golden stream and sparkling green garden whisked him far from the world he'd known for centuries.

Perhaps that was a slight exaggeration.

Eric's atrium was as ordinary as any other greenhouse. The irrigation system had misted the plants and the sun's light had mimicked a fairytale-like atmosphere—*to Alex*.

What he saw and felt went deeper than flesh and bone. It wove through his aura and penetrated his very being as a beacon of warmth. It wasn't a figment of imagination or a trick of his mind's eye. This was the world as Paresh made it.

Still, it couldn't defeat biology. The sun chomped down on his corneas and smeared his surroundings into a runny, watercolor mess. Squeezing his eyes shut, he jabbed his fists into them to rub the pain away.

The room's rustic wooden door opened and closed with a faint *clunk*. He arched his neck over the seat's back and popped an eye open. "Paresh finally asleep?"

"Mm-hm." Jonathan traced the moisture trail on Alex's cheek. "What's this? Crying again?"

"No…just flying too close to the flame, I suppose." Alex wiped his face and straightened. Tapping his sunglasses down from their perch atop his head, he said, "Call me Icarus."

"Have you ever gotten an adage right?" Jonathan sat beside him on the rattan loveseat. "Icarus flying too close to the sun is not the same as a moth attracted to a flame."

"Well, ah—" Alex laughed. "I'm a moth named Icarus?"

"You're an idiot." An exasperated sigh fell from Jonathan's mouth as he propped his feet on the ottoman. Although dressed as impeccably as usual, his hair was loose around his shoulders. "Commander, I am relieved that you're innocent, but tread lightly. I don't have patience this afternoon for *antics*. Have you submitted your report?"

"Sorry sir." Alex patted the air in an apologetic manner. "I'll have a formal report ready tomorrow. I've given the security detail priority for now. I can give you a verbal summary, however."

"Go through it. Before Donovan blamed you, you'd told me that you could account for your hunters and the pack. And that you'd narrowed the pool down to VaSH officers ranked auxiliary or higher since they have clearance to other squad's weapons."

"If Donovan hadn't blamed me so quickly, he might've deflected suspicion for a while. I doubt he expected me to leave directly from Snowblood Square or for Raven to let me go. Killing the second victim, the young woman, was his biggest mistake. I wish I'd caught that sooner. She died nine hours before her body was discovered, which was when Donovan was alone, supposedly scouting for me, while Raven waited at the cottage with Eric and Paresh."

Tucking his knees to his chest, Alex wiggled his toes over the loveseat's edge. "Unfortunately, I wasn't aware of the second attack when I lured Raven into the forest. I wanted her to verify Donovan's whereabouts after the VaSH meeting the night of the first murder. But Donovan snuck behind her and attacked me before I could reveal my suspicion or ask any questions."

Alex tapped his temple and stared straight ahead at nothing in particular. "At that point, I thought that if I kept hidden long enough, conclusive proof would surface to clear me. Donovan can plant my weapons, but not my DNA. He isn't as smart as he thinks he is."

"Or he's smarter than you think. The night he and Raven arrived, Gabriel grabbed Paresh and made her scream, which brought Eric and Raven running." Jonathan ran his hand through his hair. "If he hadn't done that, Donovan could've taken her right there and then."

Alex retreated into his thoughts. "Gabriel knew she was in danger? I didn't know that. Okay, so since *that angel* saved her, he forced Donovan to improvise. Getting rid of me had to be a priority—in fact, I bet he expected Raven and me to kill each other. He was furious when she let me go. I shouldn't have settled on a stalemate. Or runaway. I could've killed him——"

"It was the best call given what you knew," Jonathan replied. "Most importantly, you were alive and able to intercept the communication from Seneca to Raven about Corben. You traced his energy pattern to Sunset Grove before anyone else. If not for you, he would have gotten them both while Eric was unconscious."

"I kept him moving, but lost him after Raven arrived." Alex shook his head. "I should have made better choices and acted faster. Nothing would have happened to Paresh if I had."

"I can't say I don't wish the same thing." Jonathan sighed. "Her injuries will heal, but...what he *did do* and the possibilities of what he *could have done* prey on her mind. She doesn't think quite like us, yet. She's broken right now in a way none of us can understand."

"Nothing should have happened at all." Anger limned an arc through Alex's aura.

"Why didn't you arrive here faster?"

"I thought Corben was the higher priority since he'd armed Rainne Blood Pathos. Never for an instant did I think he'd risk exposure by contacting Donovan directly. I was foolish," Alex said. "I wasted time searching for him. It was complete luck that I was in the woods and heard Molly and Walter arguing. By the time I realized Raven was only there with Eric, it was too late."

Alex shook his head in frustration. "There is no punishment that can undo what's been done, but I'll accept whatever you deem worthy of my negligence, Master Jonathan."

"There was a time," Jonathan began slowly, "when I might have punished you. And a time when Lucien might not have lifted the order for your head. But, how can either of us fault you for saving her? She died last week on Lucien's order and he sent a rogue to protect her this week. We haven't made the best choices, either."

Jonathan pulled a crimson ribbon from his pocket. Alex took it from him and threaded his fingers through Jonathan's hair. As he had done many times before, he gently gathered soft auburn locks into sections and pulled them taut at Jonathan's nape.

"Alex," Jonathan said in a quiet voice. "You are not responsible for what happened here. Donovan betrayed us and chose to align himself with Lucifer."

"I keep replaying the forest in my mind. What would've happened if Raven hadn't let me go. I see her taking my head off just as I sling the Cataclysm at Donovan. He dodges and then uses my revolver to kill her. There was no way either of us would've survived."

A burst of air flew over Jonathan's lip as he knocked Alex's hand away and knotted the ribbon himself. "We've all made choices that we must live with. You made the one that led to you saving Paresh."

Jonathan's head lolled to the side, facing away from Alex. An incredible depth of sadness began to rise in his voice even though he spoke lower than a whisper. "Why do you like the sun so much? It bestows radiance to everything it touches. Always, even when it's cloudy."

"It—"

"*Commander!*" Seneca's frantic voice buzzed Alex's communicator. "Breech at Mourning Eidolons! Donovan's gone!"

"How?" Alex's voice was calm as he motioned to Jonathan and ran from the room. Jonathan passed him en route to the master suite.

"Commander Nallura suspects an aided escape. Her Auxiliary Officer, Skyvania, is also gone."

"Nallura is to have the Chthonic Knights lockdown all arcs. Assume co-command of the Crimson Guard and order Commander Landor to scatter the Silent Vespers into the Realm of Man. They are to apprehend any sighted rogue." Alex paused at the bedroom threshold while Jonathan checked on Paresh. "I'll alert High Commander Hawkings when I'm able."

"Understood. Do you require reinforcements?"

"Stand by." Alex lightly rapped on the doorjamb. "Master Jonathan, it appears a Chthonic Knight Auxiliary Officer assisted Donovan's escape. Shall I have the pack respond to assist us here?"

From the darkness within, where Paresh slumbered in peace, Jonathan's voice was grave. "Send three by stealth rendezvous to the police station, not to make contact with Raven until you apprise her of the situation, and three here to use as you see fit. I want all threats neutralized. The Silent Vespers are to use lethal force."

He relayed the order and confirmed by saying, "Seneca, do you copy?"

"Yes, sir. Heron and Cyprian's units are en route."

"Inform Lord Lucien and keep me updated as liaison to the High Commander. Alexander out."

Jonathan came out and quietly latched the door. The fire of rage burned within his stare, but he trekked down the hall in a strangely subdued state.

Unwilling to venture too far from Paresh, Alex stopped halfway down the hall. "Lord Jonathan, sir?"

"You've done well." There was a monstrous edge to Jonathan's voice that Alex had never heard. "Stay here. Don't let *anything* happen to her."

"She'd be safer with Lord Lucien. The Arc of True Blood isn't without danger, but we must separate the three of you."

"I disagree. Keep her here."

"Sir, I must insist. One of you must survive to revive the others if anything happens."

"You have my order, Commander. Do not disobey me and do not wake her."

"As you command, my lord."

Jonathan's aura thickened with murderous intent as though the enemy stood before him. Alex's internal alarm blared. "Is he near?"

"I was Donovan once." Jonathan's voice was deep and raspy. "You've seen it. I've known desire so strong it consumed me. And we both know what it drove me to do."

"I don't follow—"

"I am not the only one aware of Eric's weaknesses. Anyone who has spent time with him can see where he's most vulnerable. You've seen it. You know." Jonathan shot a fierce, blackened glare down the hall. "You keep her here and you keep her safe. I will not overlook failure this time."

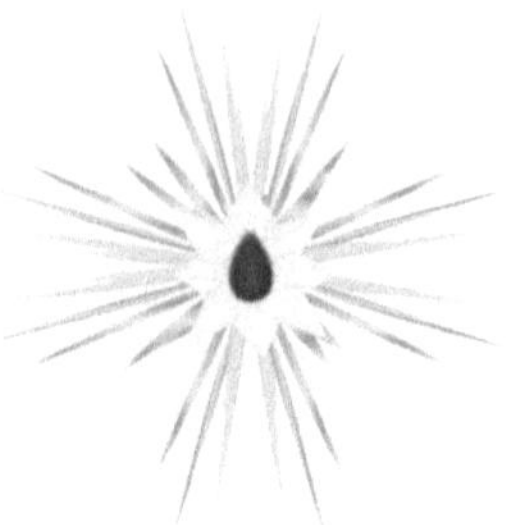

CHAPTER EIGHTEEN: ATONEMENT'S CRUEL HAND

"Damn it, Gabriel," Jonathan cursed under his breath, racing past another cornfield. The edge of town was in view. "Is this why you wanted me to repent? Why you gave Paresh the vision of my death?"

He grunted sourly. "You tricked me into thinking salvation was attainable. But I was never worthy in the first place. And now she's caught in the middle."

Ahead, brick facades and large display windows lined Main Street's sidewalks. Cars and concrete had replaced horses and plank roads long ago, but the core had hardly changed. He fortified his aura and leaped to the roof of a building capped with ornate Victorian stonework, and cut across the downtown hub just as he had on that fateful autumn day so long ago.

A faint electrical odor wafted downwind from the police station. *Good*, he thought, pausing only long enough to confirm that Cyprian's unit was there and to hear Walter agree to Raven's proposal. If Jonathan was right, but was too late, at least Eric had Raven and Walter as alibis.

Jonathan veered right.

The village planners had created a blocked residential grid around the business district and left the non-wooded areas north of town open for farming. The Hawthorne and Faust families owned most of the land, which kept the village quaint and cozy despite property selloffs in the 1970s that had birthed a few new subdivisions.

He entered one such area where nondescript, brick or vinyl houses dotted winding streets and cul-de-sacs. They lacked the sprawling porches and charm of the original settlement's Victorian architecture.

Instead, rectangular evergreen shrubs framed plain, concrete slabs, giving the neighborhood a look of dated uniformity.

The pale yellow house with wooden siding at the end of the last cul-de-sac was different. Graying snake rail fencing wove its way among plots of bluestem prairie grass beneath looming shade trees. A rustic hand pump poured water into a small pond, and purple pansies, white phlox, and vivid, yellow coreopsis sprang up from antique crocks and wooden barrels. A porch with hand turned spindles and distressed wooden chairs blended items reminiscent of the nineteenth century with the structure's modern architecture to appear as though it'd been there since the Civil War.

Beyond arguing neighbors and a rigorous game of basketball in the court, Mother Nature was tellingly quiet. Focusing solely on that house, he honed in on the refrigerator compressor's hum and closed his eyes.

The hum bounced off hard surfaces and sank into porous items, and gave him a mental blueprint. There was an off center abnormality where he heard gentle rustling, gurgling, and a rhythmic beat.

The scent of blood was already in the air.

Adrenaline surged into Jonathan's veins and crimson stained his vision. Racing into the backyard, fleeting movement in the kitchen window caught his eye: a tall humanoid with broad shoulders and a silent pulse.

To avoid unwanted attention, Jonathan shouldered the backdoor and pressured the latch to break free. The blood scent was stronger in the garage. Grinding his teeth, he kicked the interior door open, embedding the knob into the wall, and charged in, holding his arm at a rigid angle to form a biological spear. His first thrust sliced only air.

"Ah! At last you join us!" Donovan announced with a rolling laugh as he twirled the woman in his arms.

Blood oozed from holes in her throat. Dread seized its opportunity to freeze Jonathan in place. Donovan spun his victim into an embrace and kicked backward, hitting Jonathan hard in the solar plexus.

Jonathan was still focused on those bloody marks when he crashed into the cabinets beneath the sink. They were all he could see.

Smirking, Donovan laughed again. "Surely, you know how rude it is to keep a lady waiting." He rolled his hand through the air. "So, we decided to get to know each other while we waited."

Get up! Jonathan growled internally. *Get up!*

Somewhere, in the back of his mind, the old war machine's instincts screamed to skewer that monster's beating heart. But, his new emotions churned beyond control and frantically yelled over them, repeating one word: *No!*

The brilliant red ribbons streaming from those punctures stole Jonathan's logic and hope. Her eyes were empty, her pupils dilated and fixed. Her bifocal lenses were askew and low on her nose, and her hair, once speckled with gray, was a rich shade of chestnut, neatly trimmed and swaying freely above her shoulders.

She stood on Death's stoop, waiting for the scythe to fall on her neck. But, she didn't know. She couldn't know. Not now. Donovan had plunged her into a world of concentrated pleasure and forced her to enjoy whatever he'd done to her.

A new spark of anger burned Jonathan's gut and set his entire body ablaze. Tremors ripped through his muscles. He clenched his jaw. A growl rumbled gutturally deep.

"*Molly!*" Jonathan snarled between his teeth.

"Oh, you've met? Do you want to dance with her, too, Johnny Boy? I knew I did the moment I met her." Donovan dipped her low and pulled her knee up past his thigh in an overtly sexual manner. "She's such a delight! And so feisty!" He shot Jonathan a bloodstained grin. "I don't have to tell you that Eric has exquisite taste in women. I can't wait to make the other one mine, again, too."

Jonathan sprang up and whisked Molly into his arms. A tiny moan fled her mouth as her head flopped against his shoulder. "You rotten bastard!"

"Oh no!" Dramatically clutching his chest, Donovan held his other hand out in mock protest. He squeezed his eyes shut and swung his face away. "Alas! My maiden has been stolen away! Whatever shall I do?" He belted out another hearty laugh.

"*What the hell is so damn funny?*" Jonathan shrieked. Holding onto Molly tightly, his breaths came fast and ragged, and his anger swelled uncontrollably into his head. He staggered back from the pressure.

"Something wrong?" A mischievous glint lit Donovan's eyes. "Perhaps I shall retake my maiden. Raven did tell her that I'd take care of her."

Forcing a solid external façade, Jonathan snickered and reaffirmed his footing. "Are you suicidal?"

"Aw, shucks!" Donovan drawled, "Does that mean you want to dance with me instead? Eh, Johnny Boy?"

Dropping to the floor, Donovan swept Jonathan's legs and followed up with a swift heel to his kneecap, forcing the joint in on itself. In an instant, Jonathan was down and Molly was back in Donovan's arms.

Despite the grating pain in his leg, Jonathan jumped up and spun on the ball of his foot, swinging his arm out perpendicular to his body.

Donovan should have been there, but, again, he caught only air.

"Such persistence!" Donovan teased, twirling Molly in front of him as he danced out of reach. "Prowling for a new partner? Hmph, that's unlikely, right? Since, well, except for Eric, you prefer the fairer haired among us."

"Jealous you never made the cut?" Jonathan growled.

Laughing heartedly, Donovan cried, "Oh! Come, come, Johnny! You know I don't swing that way. I only waltz with the ladies." He jerked Molly's arm out to the side and dragged her feet as he box-stepped away from Jonathan.

Gritting his teeth, Jonathan lunged again. The nimble bastard twirled Molly aside and thrust back with his foot, kicking Jonathan square in the abdomen. He crashed into the lower cabinets amid Donovan's amused roaring.

The laughter faded into silence. Donovan glared over his shoulder and spat, "Even if I had 'made the cut' as you say, I positively would not have rolled over and taken it from you like Alex did. Like your attention is some grand reward."

Something about Donovan's mood shift cleared Jonathan's head and calmed his anger to a simmer. He stood and flexed his fingers.

"Don't lie to me." Jonathan took a deliberate step. "You crave attention. If you had my favor, you would have done anything I asked. But you're too over the top for my taste."

Taking wide, sweeping steps, Donovan dragged Molly farther away. "Oh, Johnny Boy, you're too self-involved and too impatient to enjoy the finer aspects of art. Otherwise you'd see the beauty in this dance."

Jonathan took another step. "See? Even now, you seek my attention. Now that you have it, how much longer do you expect to survive?"

"My, my. Sorry dear. He insists on cutting in," Donovan said to Molly.

Dropping her, Donovan slipped his hands into his rear pockets and rushed Jonathan, holding a sickle and a dagger. "Since you're so insistent on dancing with one of Lucifer's elite!"

Donovan moved faster than he should've been able to. Jonathan caught the sickle before it sliced into his arm and barely managed to deflect the dagger into his shoulder instead of his heart.

"One of Lucifer's elite? You?" Scoffing, Jonathan shoved Donovan back. "You're a child masquerading as a warrior." Ribs crunched beneath his heel as he kicked Donovan into the side of the refrigerator. Blood dribbled down Donovan's hairline and chin, forming fat drops that splashed onto his chest.

Jonathan yanked the dagger from his flesh and held it out in his palm. A crescent moon was on the hilt.

"Lucien never filled Connall's seat because the thought of seeing you on the High Council disgusted me," Jonathan revealed, eyeing the dagger. "And I never wanted you on any VaSH squad. I knew you didn't have the discipline for it."

He hurled the dagger into Donovan's left bicep so hard the tip embedded into the fridge with a firm metallic *twang*. Jonathan kicked him in the ribs again and then bent to twist Donovan's jaw to force eye contact.

"You've proven me correct."

"Oh boo, hoo, hoo. Johnny doesn't like me. Whatever shall I do?" Glaring at Jonathan, Donovan tugged unsuccessfully on the dagger's hilt. "Lucien's mighty wolf, once coated in blood and gore, reduced to a spoiled lapdog."

"Endymion has taken the third seat, and Jocathian will fill the vacancy that would have been yours. And you—you will return to the Arc of Mourning Eidolons for your date with a needle of liquid silver—just for the hell of it. And then, you die."

Molly whimpered behind Jonathan. Her arm was twisted at a sharp angle beneath her head. The jagged piece of bone protruding from her elbow had almost gouged her eye. Gushing blood mixed with the stream from her throat into a growing pool on the floor.

She was regaining conscious awareness, but her pulse was weak. Whether she survived or not, her time as a human was over. Donovan's infectious protein was already altering her physiology.

Jonathan knelt and stroked her hair. "I'm so sorry Molly. I will help you through this."

A weak hand grabbed his ankle. "N...o..." she whispered, laboring for breath.

Robust giggling returned Jonathan's attention to Donovan. He'd worked the dagger free and was sitting up wearing a strange smile. "Pathetic! She's *human!* The Second New Age has reduced the Great Second Born to a weakling. A fitting start for the downfall of a nation."

"Laugh yourself to the grave for all I care," Jonathan spat. "But I guarantee you two things." He held up his index finger. "One: you won't be laughing for long. And two—" His middle finger popped up. "You will scream all the way to the Reaper and burn for eternity in the Lake of Fire."

"Johnny, Johnny, Johnny," Donovan taunted, his head bobbing with each iteration. "I hope you didn't mean to surprise me with Endymion's and Jocathian's good fortunes."

Donovan's lips flattened and his eyes darkened into obsidian orbs. "I know the dark spot is moving. Even an idiot would realize that my proximity to Raven gave me a seat to witness the manifestation. Lucifer already had his hand in the High Council; why does he need me there?"

Jonathan felt the blood drain from his face. "How do you know about th—" The fingers around his ankle tightened as a coughing fit overtook Molly. Blood trickled from her mouth. Without aid, she would die.

"The Second Born has gotten rusty in his old age!" Donovan boomed, his deep and melodramatic voice echoing off the walls. "To think that someone such as myself would turn sides for a piddly reason like being denied my rightful seat on the High Council. Tsk, tsk."

Donovan winked and flashed a confident grin. "A once great warrior taught me that the sweetest of all victories comes amid the greatest of all personal chaos. I got a taste, but didn't strike hard enough to win. My *prize*, if you will."

Jonathan lunged and crushed Donovan's cheek with a fist harder than iron. "I am going to kill you!" he roared.

Laughing again, Donovan caught Jonathan's fist before it connected a second time and shoved him half way across the room. Leaping to his feet, he readied his weapons. "And with my sights on *that one*, I have no more use for *this one*."

Time slowed. Jonathan's pulse thundered as Donovan dove for Molly and landed on her stomach with the dagger raised over his head. Sound waves rattled Jonathan's body as he yelled out and flung himself into Donovan's path. His claws dug into Donovan's shoulders and snapped him backward. They tumbled to a stop several feet away.

Jonathan eyed Donovan's hand. The dagger was gone. He looked at Molly. No dagger.

His chest felt like it was on fire. He glanced down and saw the golden hilt.

"Aw, drat!" Donovan drawled. "Looks like I missed." Wrenching the handle horizontally, he shifted the blade dangerously close to Jonathan's heart.

Crying out in shock, Jonathan frantically slapped at Donovan's hand and scurried to his feet. Warm fluid gurgled up his throat as he backed away. His lung burned. He coughed. Bright red blood spattered the wall. He pulled the dagger out. It dropped from his fingers and clattered beside Molly.

Still armed with the sickle, Donovan jerked Jonathan forward by the shoulder with his left hand. His right swung wide. The instant the curved blade touched Jonathan's skin, his gaze locked with Donovan's. Seeing victory there, he silently acknowledged defeat. The sickle sliced Jonathan's midsection from back to front. It barely missed his spine.

Jonathan dropped to the floor, instinctively cupping his hands to hold his organs in place. Despite the excruciating pain, a peaceful sensation fell over him.

"Now, tell me again, Johnny," Donovan said, jabbing his finger into the corner of his mouth as though in thought. "Who was going to kill who here?"

Jonathan smiled weakly and tried to laugh, but choked on blood instead. "I've…redeemed myself. Lucifer will use you…and you'll die. Burn for eternity…in the Lake of Fire. Fool."

"Perhaps," Donovan cooed. "But I'll have Paresh to keep me company. Who's the real fool? *You* chose to protect a human over the Sacred Vessel."

Donovan glanced over his shoulder. "Well?"

A shadow shimmered and materialized in the dining room, near the breached garage door. It was muscular with a slightly bulkier build than most true bloods. Fear needled its way into Jonathan's heart.

Propping himself up on one knee, Jonathan asked, "Come to collect your stray, Corben?"

"In a manner of speaking," Corben replied dryly, lowering the hood of his Aegis cloak. His head was arrogantly high as he glanced down his rich umber nose. "By appearances, he's performed quite well."

Tightening his hands against his abdomen, Jonathan forced himself to stand. The wound wasn't healing and he was lightheaded from blood loss. Succeeding and making it look effortless took every bit of his remaining strength. "Well, we know appearances can be deceptive."

Corben grunted. "That we do. Fall back."

"I want to finish him," Donovan replied, smirking at Jonathan.

A cruel laugh nipped the air. "Have you gone daft?" Corben snapped his fingers and pointed to his feet. "He and Lucien possess the strength of the Fallen. Not even I have the gall to ignore that."

Donovan glared at Jonathan and spun around. He knelt before Corben and kissed the back of his outstretched hand.

Corben curled a bloody hand through Donovan's hair. "It's not so hard to train them when you give them what they want."

"You bastards!" Jonathan seethed.

"Wait for me in Animus Hollow," Corben ordered.

Donovan opened the portal and stepped inside. He aimed a smug look over his shoulder as it closed behind him. "Bye, bye, Johnny!"

"Corben y—"

"A man fighting Death to stay on this plane should focus more on himself," Corben interrupted. He glanced at Molly with disdain. "Had Lucifer known you would stoop to protecting *them*, he might not have ordered me to spare you." He grunted. "Seems your little spat last week reminded him why you're his favorite."

Corben ran his finger along the table and wiped it off on his cloak. "The filth in this realm will take some getting used to, I suppose. A small regret for sacrificing life in the arcs—for now."

"Did you have a point?" Jonathan asked in a tight voice.

"That should be obvious. Anyone can fall. No one is immune—not even those who have been saved. Lucifer's not giving you up, yet," Corben replied. "I, myself, find it amusing that Donovan got you into such a sordid state all by his lonesome. I should let him kill you."

A portal of rolling white haze appeared behind the rogue Elder.

"Wait!" Jonathan ordered.

"If you can possibly stop me, I'll do anything you ask," Corben replied with a snide grin. He pulled the hood over his head. "Appearances can be quite deceptive indeed. Should you survive, I doubt Lucifer will grant you another pardon."

"This isn't over!" Jonathan yelled as Corben stepped into the Hollow.

"Oh, that you have correct. This will only end when Lucifer reigns over a world burnt to ash. I believe your little lady has seen what's about to happen in that regard." Wearing a truly evil grin, he disappeared into the closing portal.

"Damn it!" Jonathan fell to his knees.

"J-Jo…n…"

"Hold on, Molly," Jonathan said. "Neither of us will make it out of here without help."

From his pocket, he pulled the cell phone Eric had goaded him into carrying. Then he noticed the phone on the wall beside the fridge. Dragging himself over, he yanked the cord to knock the handset down.

A sheet of numbers hanging on the fridge included the Orison Crossing Police Department's public line and Walter's private line. He dialed the latter.

"Let me speak to Raven," he said curtly when Walter answered. With Raven on the line, he lowered his voice. "No matter what, you keep

Eric and Walter together. I called this number to lend credibility to your story. Cyprian and two other hunters are cloaked outsi—"

Jonathan coughed blood into the mouthpiece. He heard Eric demanding the phone from Raven. "Don't!" he yelled. "Order Cyprian's unit to Molly's house. You three come in Walter's squad car, and whatever happens, Eric can't leave Walter's sight! Now, hurry!"

The handset dangled freely as he let go. The room was spinning and fringed with darkness.

"Jo…n…"

Clutching his side, he summoned strength from an unknown reserve to crawl over to Molly. "You're going to be okay. I won't let you die."

"N…o…" she whispered. "Do…n't…wa…nt…" Her pulse was as faint as her voice. "Plea…se. Ki…ll."

Blowing out a weighty sigh, Jonathan pressed Molly's hand against his forehead and closed his eyes. His voice was stuck in his throat.

"Plea…se."

His chest tightening, Jonathan squeezed her hand. Eric would never forgive him. "It shouldn't be me—"

"N…ot…Er…ic. *You*…"

Jonathan nodded. "Okay, Molly. Okay." He lowered her hand to his leg and picked up the dagger.

"Pare…?"

"If Corben had gotten her, Alex would've followed him. She's fine, I promise."

Molly's tears streamed into the bloody pool. "Lo…ve. Er…"

"I'll tell him." Jonathan smoothed his fingers over her brow. "Don't worry. I'll take care of them for you."

Her lips quivered as she squeezed her eyes shut. "Tha…nk…y…ou."

Holding the dagger over her chest, Jonathan whispered, "Go in peace, Molly. I'm sorry I was too late."

She squeezed his leg. He thrust the blade down through her sternum and hit her heart. It stopped instantly.

"I'm sorry," he whispered again, his hand slipping off the hilt. "Eric…I tried."

The room flipped on its side and blackness stole all but a pinpoint of light. He fell into a puddle, knowing it was blood, just not whose. "I'm so sorry. For everything."

☽ ❋ ☾

Muffled voices traveled through the darkness. Everything ached. He groaned and brushed something soft. Flesh with blood pumping beneath the surface. His teeth prickled.

"Don't touch him, Walter! If he bites you, you're dead!"

"Raven?" Jonathan croaked.

"Aye, my lord. Here, open up and bite down."

His teeth plunged into what he presumed was her arm. Her blood always tasted metallic—like silver. Not iron.

"The wounds in your chest and shoulder have mostly healed, but the one in your side isn't closing," she said. "I used Bioserum to re-seam your organs and temporarily seal the soft tissue, and have you wrapped up until I can figure out what happened to you."

She blew out her breath. "I-I barely have you stable enough to play along with our story. I don't like it, but Cyprian is procuring an ambulance and the rest of your pack will assume roles of human medical staff and FBI forensics. Walter's officers have secured the scene outside."

"Paresh?" Jonathan asked.

"Corben stormed my house." Eric's voice oozed anger. "I trusted you with her safety!"

An insistent hand held Jonathan still. "Is she—"

"Eric!" Raven scolded. "Master Jonathan, she's safe with Lord Lucien. Alex escaped into Animus Hollow with her. He and Heron will be here soon, along with the rest of your pack."

"I knew Donovan would go after the people you're closest to," Jonathan said weakly in Eric's direction. "I tried to save Molly."

"That worked out real well, didn't it?" Eric retorted.

"Lord Jonathan, please bite down," Raven pleaded. "If you don't replenish the blood you've lost, you won't survive. Eric—be angry with him later."

"If he dies, then being angry with him later won't do me a damn bit of good, will it?"

"So why don't you go ahead and kill him then, and see how Paresh feels about that?" Raven snapped.

"Commander, watch your tone," Jonathan warned. "Why is it so dark?"

"Sorry, sir," Raven replied while Walter answered, "It's a cold, damp cloth. You were sweating and Raven was outside, so I—"

"Walter's helping the best way he knows how," Eric interrupted. "That's what it means to have a sense of duty to someone."

Jonathan snatched the cloth off his face. Fuzzy silhouettes stood against a blurry background. The one closest to him smelled like Raven. The more he blinked, the quicker she came into focus, still guised as

FBI. "The gash isn't healing because Donovan opened an old wound."

"But the only weapons capable of leaving lasting damage like that—"

"Belong to Alex," he finished. "About thirty years ago, he hit me with the Cataclysm during a sparring match."

Raven snagged her lip on a long tooth and faced away from him. Eric must have seen something in her expression. "What does that mean, Jonathan?"

"No disrespect, sire, but Lord Lucien restricted the Cataclysm to actual combat for a reason," Raven said in a quiet voice, curling her fingers over her injured arm.

"What does it mean?" Eric demanded.

"Raven can't close this wound or stop the bleeding," Jonathan replied. "The Bioserum doesn't work on the Cataclysm's scar tissue. If I can't heal on my own, I'll die."

"You stupid fool!" Eric yelled, slamming his fist onto the countertop. "Why the hell didn't you stay put?"

"If he had, then Donovan might have kidnapped Molly instead of killing her here," Walter said in a gruff voice. "Don't belittle her memory like this."

"Donovan didn't kill Molly." Jonathan's words shattered like glass.

Incensed energy flew off Eric's body. "*What?*" His lips curled over growing fangs. "Choose your response very, *very* carefully."

Gesturing helplessly, Jonathan said, "He bit her before I got here."

Eying the hilt sticking from Molly's chest, Jonathan jabbed his finger into the large bloodstained hole in his shirt. "I took that blade to defend her. I kept him away from her, Eric. I kept him from killing her. But after he was gone and I told her I wouldn't let her die…"

His hand fell limply to the floor. "She didn't want to be like us. She didn't want *you* to see her suffering."

Jerking him up by the collar, Eric screamed with a spray of spittle, "*You killed her?*"

"Eric!" Raven yelled, trying to pry them apart. "I cannot let you endanger his life!"

"You can't help it can you?" Eric spat, shoving Raven away with one hand. "It's too much a part of you to kill everyone I care about, isn't it? *Answer me!*"

"She said she loves you," Jonathan answered quietly. "And she was worried about Paresh. I promised I'd look after you both."

Eric pushed off Jonathan and ran his hands through his hair, staring at Molly's body. Huffing angrily, he marched out the front door, slamming it behind him.

"Master Jonathan——" Raven began.

"He can heap his anger onto me." Cringing, Jonathan returned to a prone position. "He knows where the blame really goes."

"He's powerless." Walter clucked his tongue. "I suppose we all are. I can hold it together thanks to my job, but this…she was my best friend."

Jonathan gingerly touched his bandaged abdomen and groaned. Gritting his teeth, he forced out, "Eric has more power now than ever before. But he's not in control."

To Raven, he asked, "Had you received word from Alex before I called?"

"No. I contacted him on the way here." Gathering the remnants of bandaging material, she reached over Jonathan for a final scrap. "Your pack…Rowan died en route to the Arc of Mourning Eidolons."

"Damn it."

"Aye. Corben slit his throat with a silver wire and clawed him through the back. Hit his heart." She paused and glanced at the door. "Cyprian's here with the ambulance. You'll go out on the stretcher in plain view, but we'll cover your face. Once you're safely inside, he'll open the portal and transport you for proper medical care."

Jonathan shook his head. "I'm not going to an arc."

"What about your wound?" Walter asked.

"Don't concern yourself with my wellbeing," Jonathan snapped.

"I echo the Chief. This field dressing won't hold."

"I'm going to Eric's house," Jonathan said coolly. "Request a cleaning crew if Alex hasn't already done so. I want that house spotless before he arrives home, including Paresh's bloodstain on the sofa."

"Aye, sir."

The walls briefly flashed red and blue as Eric charged in through the front door. "How the hell did this happen, Jonathan?" he demanded, shoving the door shut without breaking stride. "How the hell did Donovan strike you like this?"

"I know I let him get away, Eric. I should have stop——"

"*Shut up!*" Eric rammed his fist into the already dented refrigerator. "Don't anticipate where my questions are going! He got away because you *couldn't* stop him and I want to know why!"

"I…I don't know. He was stronger, faster, and sharper than ever. It was like…fighting with you."

"It's because he drank Paresh's blood. And now that they know what it can do, they'll strike back even harder!" Pushing against the freezer door, Eric kicked in the fan plate and cursed under his breath.

"Hey!" Walter protested. "Stop touching stuff in here!"

"Damn it, Walter!" Eric yelled, spinning around. "This isn't a real crime scene. And that's not a real forensics unit!" He licked his palm and slapped the countertop behind him. "There! D.N.A."

"That's real fine of you there, Counselor," Walter replied sarcastically. Jabbing his own chest, he yelled, "I don't know what to do here, okay? You always have the answers, but I'm not used to this!"

"Calm down!" Raven demanded, holding her hands high above her head as her gaze bounced between Eric and Jonathan. "Pardon me for overstepping, but you two need to keep your heads on. And Walter—" Her tone softened. "You lost your friend. Freak out or get angry— *something*. It's creepy to see you this calm and Eric *not*."

"Sorry to disappoint you." Crossing his arms, Walter slumped against the wall. "This is too unreal. Like I'm about to wake up from a very crazy dream."

Facing the ceiling, Eric huffed and combed his fingers through his hair, lacing them together on top of his head. "Okay," he said quietly, visibly forcing calmer breaths. "Okay."

He exhaled and paused. A look of mutual apology passed between him and Walter, then he addressed Raven. "Paresh is safe with Lucien, and Jonathan is…*stubborn*…so you need to pull this off. If you can't, I'll carry him to that damn arc if I have to right now."

"I can do it," she said quietly. "You know that FBI agent Walter contacted at the Kansas compound? And the ones you met with later?"

Walter and Eric's heads bobbed in unison.

"They're only a few of many who work with us. I'll snap some pictures of the scene for Walter's file and the pack will tidy up."

"What about the people outside?" Walter asked. "I'll have to tell them something."

"I'll issue the statement with you standing beside me," Raven said. "This has blown up, but it's containable. We'd do more damage if we try to hide it."

"But no one knows that Paresh is back. Eric postponed his meeting with the mayor," Walter said. "This is happening too fast. I have doubts."

"Don't. We can release that detail later," Eric said. "Let them speculate. For now, we only need to get their suspicions off me."

"So where do I fit in?" Jonathan asked.

"Simple," Eric replied. "You're my brother. You came over to pick up Molly so she could retrieve her car from my house."

"And what name do you plan on giving to the press?" Walter asked. "Jonathan Trueblood is listed in the kidnapping report I turned over to the FBI and it's far too close to Donovan Trueblood for my liking."

"He's my brother," Eric repeated. "Jonathan Ravenscroft was injured when he interrupted the murder in progress and tried to intervene."

"That does provide a witness to corroborate Eric's description of the suspect in Paresh's assault." Raising her brow, Raven looked impressed. To Jonathan, she said, "But you will be in the human eye."

"A small price——" Jonathan braced against pain grating his ribs.

"Okay then, let's get it going. Walter, poke your head out and motion for my guys to enter so your officers and the neighbors see you." Raven stuffed the leftover bandaging into her jacket pocket and stood. "Master Jonathan, if Lord Lucien knew of your condition, he'd want you in an arc."

"I do not require Lucien's approval, Commander."

Drawing her lips, she straightened and assumed a tight, business-like tone. "Regretfully then, I can only spare Alex, Heron, and Cyprian to go with you."

"That'll do." A deliberate look dissuaded any further comment.

"I want protection for this town," Eric said quietly so Walter wouldn't hear him. "I don't care what Lucien has them doing, get the rest of Raven's squad and as many hunters as you can spare. Make it happen. Quietly and quickly."

"There may be more turncoats," Jonathan replied.

Sadness pooled in Eric's eyes, but his words were firm. "Assign them in teams to watch each other, whatever. Just get them here. We need to mobilize a solid defense."

Eric's gaze dropped to Molly. "I am burying her in three days. I don't want any interruptions. No attacks. No threats. No disruptions. No one else will suffer because I choose to live here."

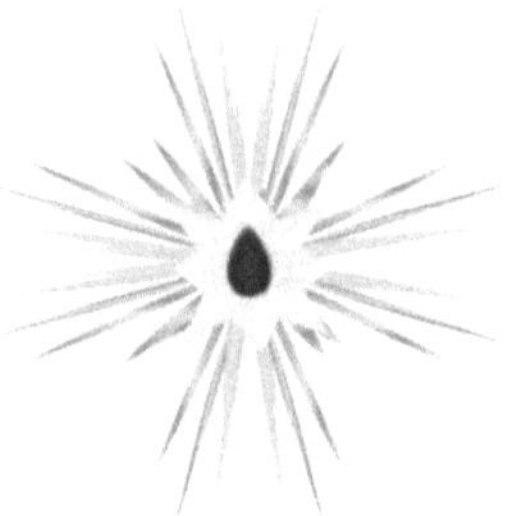

CHAPTER NINETEEN: THE MOURNING COMETH

I

Their shoes damp with dew, hundreds of townsfolk clad in black trudged past rows of granite and marble markers. The white tent at the cemetery's rear wasn't large enough to hold them all. The grieving overflow huddled together in groups outside. Healing would come with time, but solace came in numbers.

William Jamerson. Rebecca Morrissey. Molly Sims. They knew these names well, but only Molly, as the first step for philanthropic assistance for decades, had touched all their lives.

Many remembered the smiling young woman waiting tables at the old diner before she inexplicably showed up on their elusive benefactor's arm in 1975. Although shadowed by his mystery, life at Eric's side had shone a light on her caring spirit, and she'd left her own mark as a nurturer and guide during times of need. Money and assistance had come from her guarded employer, but Molly had been the gatekeeper with a comforting soul.

Eric sat in the shortened row nearest the coffin. As eyes lifted to his paraffin face, charged energy pulsed beneath their sorrow. No depth of mourning could cull their curiosity.

Beside him, Molly's sister, Abigail, cheeks puffy and glassy eyes lined red, clutched his hand so tightly her fingers had lost all color. She couldn't look away from Molly's face. Wiping her nose with a crumpled tissue, she leaned against her husband, who flanked her other side and held her with a reassuring arm. Their fifteen-year-old daughter wept into her father's shoulder while her older brother angrily stared down tiered arrangements of white lilies.

Sarah and Sammy Weaverly finished off the row on the aisle end. Sarah comforted her grandfather as he tried to hold himself together, clutching soaked tissues in his arthritic hands.

Molly's friends sat in the longer second row, including the firm's partners, Kenshin Dugao and Karen Daley, their families and their secretaries, and Walter and a few off duty officers. The remaining rows had filled in quickly, leaving the rest to stand outside with the on duty officers.

That much was normal.

The oddities sat on Eric's left side.

The girl beside him resembled a woodland nymph in a black flowing skirt, sandals, and cap sleeved blouse. There was something familiar about the golden curls cascading to her shoulders and the petite facial features largely covered by oversized sunglasses. But, the trio next to her was even stranger.

Curiosity drew quick glances. No one risked a lingering gaze. Gossip and rumor said the man in the homburg hat was Eric's brother, who had taken a near critical hit trying to save Molly, and speculators thought the remaining pair to be bodyguards given their lofty attitudes and streamlined attire. But, others weren't so sure—not given the tiny silver and gold hoops lining their ears, the male's choppy, gravity-defying hair, and the female's bouncy, neon pink bob.

The entire group was protective of the young pixie woman—that much was clear to everyone. Her very presence called to all who saw her or got near her. She evoked warmth, and eased their sorrow and pain. It was as though Molly's soothing nature had taken physical form to console them one last time.

People were still arriving when Pastor Caine took his place. Facing the casket, he looked like a white-haired man paying his respects. Turning slowly, with his fingers intertwined around his Bible, he said, "Thank you all for joining us today. Let us pray."

Fabric and feet collectively rustled and shifted as hundreds of heads bowed in unison.

"Oh Heavenly Father," he began. "On this day, we come together to mourn the passing of Miss Molly Evelyn Sims. Hear our prayers and comfort us during this painful transition. Help us find peace in the knowledge of your loving mercy and shine a light so that we may find our way through darkness. May we find solace in knowing that she no longer suffers and that her soul is now home with Jesus Christ in Heaven. This we pray, in His name. Amen."

He thumbed through the Bible. "Christians know that in death, we shed our physical forms and begin our eternal lives in Heaven. But when someone is taken during the prime of worldly life, we may struggle with our faith."

He surveyed the crowd. "That's normal. No one is perfect. No one is always strong. We all succumb to weakness. We all succumb to doubt. Things happen that we don't understand, and it's okay not to understand them. It's okay not to have the answers."

He paused. "When we need Him most, we may fail to ask for His help. For His guidance. For His strength. For Him to walk with us and to carry us when we cannot walk any farther. But He is still there."

Tapping the open page, he said, "The lessons taught by our Lord and Savior, Jesus Christ, have been handed down to us in written verse through the words of His prophets and disciples. Right here, in this book." He tapped the page again.

"When loved ones—young or old—are taken from us suddenly, we may be left with many unanswered questions. But we can turn to Christ's moral teachings for comfort."

Slipping on reading glasses, he said, "If you brought your Bibles, please join me as I read from the Sermon on the Mount, beginning in Matthew, chapter five, verse three."

Amid the rustling of pages, he read, "Blessed are the poor in spirit, for theirs is the Kingdom of Heaven."

He quieted for five, long seconds. "Blessed are those who mourn, for they shall be comforted."

Soft crying and sniffles accompanied the next pause.

"Blessed are the meek," he said. "For they shall inherit the Earth—"

A loud sob from the first row interrupted the pastor.

His shoulders shaking, the blond man's face was buried in his hands. His sunglasses had been shoved atop his head. He wiped his nose and stood.

"Please excuse me," he said, his gentle voice strained. He looked apologetically at Abigail with verdant green eyes and moved out of the tent.

Pastor Caine resumed reading without interruption. He surveyed the crowd when he finished. "Even when we feel lost without answers, we can all take comfort in knowing that our reward is great in Heaven." Snapping the book closed, he turned his gaze to Molly. "That Molly's reward is great in Heaven."

He laid a hand over her forehead and said, "The Lord is my shepherd,

I shall not want. He makes me lie down in green pastures and leads me beside still waters. He restores my soul and leads me in paths of righteousness for His name's sake. Even though I walk through the valley of the shadow of death, I fear no evil. For thou art with me. Thy rod and thy staff—they comfort me. Thou preparest a table before me in the presence of my enemies. Thou anointest my head with oil; my cup overflows. Surely, goodness and mercy shall follow me all the days of my life, and I shall dwell in the house of the Lord forever."

The last syllable rang the silence like a bell. Soon, no one would ever see Molly again outside of photographs or memory.

"Please, take the next two minutes to pray quietly and then we'll close," Pastor Caine said.

Only half the people bowed their heads; the rest were unwilling to look away. Many who did bow their heads squeezed tears from their eyes. The end was coming.

At last, Pastor Caine began Molly's final prayer. When he finished, he shared a look with Abigail and then turned to close the casket. A fresh round of cries flooded the gatherers.

The pastor forced a sad smile as he turned to announce, "We are celebrating Molly's life at the Sunset Grove Parish. Please head on over for fellowship, and for food jointly catered by The Greenery and the Love Our Buns Bakery and Deli. The family and I will follow shortly."

As the crowd departed in silence, they cast sorrowful gazes at the first two rows, and at the blond man, who stood at the rear with garnet lenses hiding his eyes. In that moment, grief and kinship suspended both curiosity and suspicion. Strangers or not, they were the ones chosen to attend Molly's private burial. The ones left behind. The ones who deserved a final goodbye.

II

For almost a century and a half, the Sunset Grove Parish had reigned over lush forest. But now its steeple watched the sun rise and fall over fields of green and gold instead. The arson's sole survivor, the oxidized bronze bell in the tower, had just tolled for Molly.

The Sunset Grove Parish was the village's only church. Its parking lot was crammed full and the building was bursting with its largest gathering yet. The conversation inside rattled the walls.

Eric hated to go inside. His presence would instantly stilt the air, and this was supposed to be Molly's day.

He eyed his new entourage. Jonathan had insisted that he and the

Commanders attend in proper form, which had drawn more attention than he would have alone—along with the curious eyes that had ultimately centered on Paresh.

Eric hadn't seen Paresh shed a single tear. Not for Molly. Not for Jonathan. She'd stayed at the Arc of True Blood for hours following the attack getting updates from Lucien. When she came home, she stepped from Animus Hollow in a state of sorrowful relief—dry-eyed and quiet.

Molly was dead. But Jonathan was alive.

Paresh smiled as Eric threaded his fingers through hers. His feet slowed. Perhaps it was time to relinquish this town to its rightful inhabitants, move forward with her, and take his seat on the High Council. Anywhere with her was home.

"Keep going." Jonathan dragged him ahead by his elbow.

"What are you doing?" Eric asked, tossing a glance back at Paresh as Raven and Alex caught her between them and slowed down.

"Your humanity makes you who you are," Jonathan said under his breath. "Hell, it makes you stronger than me. Don't turn your back on it—"

Grimacing, he clutched his side. The gash was slowly healing, but bouts of pain and bleeding were a daily plague. Exhaling an uneven breath, Jonathan pointed at the parish.

"They expect you to walk through those doors," he said. "And not going in makes you look guilty."

The sharp look Eric shot him drew a pointed stare. "You know it's true. You're too set in your ways to walk away now. You'd regret it."

"How did you know?" Eric rolled his eyes. "Never mind. Are you really doing this?"

Jonathan shrugged. "I've never been inside a church. Aren't they great places for healing?"

Eric grinned despite himself, unsure if Jonathan was serious or not. "Yeah—for the soul, not life-threatening injuries. You should be in bed."

Jonathan dismissively swatted the air.

"Aren't you worried about spontaneously combusting or disintegrating to ash as you cross the threshold?" Eric asked. "Or getting splashed with holy water?"

"Is Mr. Serious actually joking?"

Eric smiled into the sun's caress. Orison Crossing had always been home—no matter how many times Jonathan had tried to pry him away.

Cracking an eye, Eric said, "I rather like the new you, *Brother*."

A genuine smile lifted Jonathan's cheeks. He aped Eric's appreciation of the sun. "Brother," he echoed softly.

Eric slapped him on the back. "Let's go."

"Boy, I bet Lucifer's top would pop clean off if he saw this," Raven quipped.

"It does sound like a gag, right? Let's see, four and a half vampires walk into a church——"

"Knock it off, Alex," Jonathan warned lightly.

Hanging his head in mock shame, Alex replied, "Yes, sir."

"And no more outbursts, either." Raven jabbed him in the ribs. "You cry easier than an infant."

Bridging his brow, Alex rubbed his ribs and cried, "Ow, Goody! Maybe if you didn't punch like a giant cyclops, I wouldn't have to cry like a baby!"

Paresh giggled. "How did *you* become a VaSH Commander?"

Raven's jaw dropped. "Daaaaamn!" She laughed and smacked Alex on the butt. "She's got you pegged, doesn't she?"

"Awwww! No fair! Two against one!" Alex whined. He flipped an open palm at Paresh and glared at Raven. "Why are you corrupting such a sweet girl?"

"Moi?" Winking at Paresh, Raven looped her arm through Alex's and ran her knuckles across his head.

"Aw man, Goody! Stop it!"

"You spend more time on your hair than I do! And stop calling me that!" She wrestled him into a headlock and thoroughly tousled his hair.

"Life's never boring," Eric said with a chuckle.

"Not with those two, no." Jonathan shoved his hands into his pockets and nodded at the doors. "What are you going to do?"

"Not a thing."

"But the rumors——"

"I've always aroused suspicion. Nothing I say or do will ever stop that. What will be, will be. I can't change it otherwise." Eric paused and added, "That's what Molly said the night before she died and she was absolutely right."

Sobering, the Crimson Commander straightened, placed Raven's arm around his waist, and draped his arm over her shoulders. Paresh hurried to Eric's side and took his hand.

"I only knew her for a short time," she said. "But I'm going to miss her."

"Me, too." Eric dotted her forehead with a kiss. "It's never easy to lose someone you love, vampire or not, but your human losses will always hurt the most."

Paresh nodded thoughtfully. "So my parents will always stay in my heart, despite the way I feel now?"

Eric gazed wistfully at the blue sky beyond the steeple. "I can't answer that. When I lost my mother, circumstances didn't let me grieve."

Jonathan went rigid, but before anyone noticed, Raven said, "No one knows, sweetie. Your half breed DNA makes it impossible to foreshadow anything about you."

Her thumb flew in Alex's direction. "Take the yahoo here, for instance, a true blood bawling during the service when your eyes were dry."

"Hey!" Alex objected as Paresh replied, "I thought raw emotions were a byproduct of the Second New Age."

"No, that's just Alex," Jonathan replied dryly, stopping on the landing.

"Hey!" Alex cried again. "I have feelings, you know!"

"No doubt about that." Raven snickered and rolled her eyes. "If you ever take him to a sappy movie, take a few dozen boxes of tissue, life jackets, and an inflatable raft, and still prepare to drown in his tears."

"Oh! It hurts, Goody. It hurts, so bad." Alex fell to his knees, thumping his hand against his chest with his heartbeat. "I can't help wearing my tears on my sleeve."

"Or Seneca's. Minerva's. Heron's," Raven replied, ticking off her fingers. "Cyprian's, Orn's, Lenore's, Urien's, Valerian's, Pharon's, Taryn's—"

"You've run out of fingers, Raven." Shaking his head, Jonathan wiped his face and said to Alex, "You meant 'heart' not 'tears,' Commander."

As Paresh giggled beside him, Eric smiled, but his thoughts were in a place devoid of laughter. Four inches of wood separated him from people grieving a fresh loss, and the quiet sobs of a lone woman in the restroom let guilt goad him into believing that he should have saved Molly. That tears should have dripped from his eyes instead of Alex's. That he should be demanding respect for the dead instead of enjoying this lighthearted banter.

He squeezed his eyes shut. It wasn't logical. He knew Molly would be overjoyed to know they were all okay.

"Because I have a family now." He said it so quietly that half a minute passed before Eric realized the conversation behind him had stopped. Feeling the pressure of four sets of eyes, he added, "Molly would want me to celebrate her life instead of mourning her loss, and to live my life enjoying every opportunity possible, with people like you."

He turned and smiled. "She would call you my family, however extended you might be." He glanced at Paresh, head against his shoulder, gazing up at him. "People who I can watch over and who can watch over me now that she's no longer here. But, I'm sure she's still watching. After all, she did choose eternal life…just not on this plane."

Alex sucked in a breath over quivering lips and puffed out his chest. "That was so beautiful."

"Yeah, it was." Paresh rose up on her toes to kiss Eric. He swept her into his arms and then released her with a sigh. He focused on Raven.

Alex had proven he'd stay within the boundaries of his station, and Jonathan had already conceded his trust. That left only one to object.

"Whatever happens inside, I expect you to maintain composure and follow whatever lead I give. Should it become necessary, Raven, you are responsible for Paresh, and Alex, you have Jonathan. Stay by them at all times. Understand?"

Raven's mouth popped open, but a look from Jonathan silenced her. Both hunters straightened and replied, "As you command, sir."

"All right then, let's go in, shall we? Oh, and—" Eric paused and glanced back. "These people are well intentioned, but they won't take 'no' for an answer when it comes to food. They'll heap spoonfuls onto a plate for you. Politely take it. You don't have to eat it."

"I am a little hungry though," Paresh said, rubbing her belly. "I didn't have any breakfast."

"You're the only of us who can eat solid food, Pare," Jonathan said with a grin that brightened his tired visage.

"Oh. Right." Paresh's cheeks lit up pink as Eric smiled, too.

"Boy, this girl's a hoot!" Raven cried. She charged up the steps and wiggled her way between Paresh and Eric with a mumbled, "Excuse me, sir."

Then, taking Paresh by the hand, she raised her eyebrows at Eric. "Ladies first, right?"

"Riiiight, you're a lady," Alex said, snorting. "And I'm a flying monkey."

Raven shot him a fake grin. "Bend over. We'll see how far my foot sends you."

"Composure?" Eric eyed both hunters. Nothing he'd ever experienced compared to the fusion of frivolity and lethality they embodied. He was glad Molly had met them.

Pushing away the thought that Donovan had demonstrated similar quirks, Eric pushed the door open for the women. He'd never fully trusted Donovan, but he had no misgivings about these two.

As he stepped into the lobby, an olfactory smorgasbord assailed him.

In another life, the barbecued meats, baked goods, salads, and desserts would have enticed him to treat his palate and fill his belly instead of turning it.

He'd overcome many discomforts over the years, from pungent odors, ashy burns, and searing light to the raucous noise and odors that came with large gatherings. His aura's protection had become instinctive, but this was going to be harder than usual.

As he moved through the foyer, swathed in peaceful gray and blue tones, he fortified his aura to dampen the noise behind the sanctuary's closed double doors. About fifteen people were nearby, many waiting for the restrooms while others chatted by the water fountain and coat alcove. Their voices trailed off as he passed.

Stopping at the information desk, Jonathan pulled a small white envelope from his jacket pocket. He shoved it into the lockbox bolted to the counter and met Eric's questioning gaze. "It's a tithe."

"Ten percent of what?" Eric prodded. "Because tormenting me didn't earn you a salary."

His arrogant pride kicking in, Jonathan peered down his nose. "I may have little use for money, but that doesn't mean I don't have any. A thousandth of a percent of my worth is more than one hundred times the amount you and the Hawthornes possess combined. I told you that you were a prince living among paupers."

After calculating the numbers in his head and losing track of all the zeros, Eric pointed to the box with a smile. "Ten percent means ten percent, old man."

Alex chuckled until Jonathan produced another envelope. Speaking well below the human hearing range, he said, "You can't be serious, Master Jonathan!"

"If this is what Eric wants, then so be it."

"My math's a little fuzzy here," Eric said, catching Jonathan's wrist before he reached the box. "But I'm sure that amount is worth more than this entire country's debt a few times over, and we don't need your gesture of goodwill throwing up a flaming red flag with the government."

Eric plucked the envelope from his fingers. Upon returning it to Jonathan's jacket pocket, Eric felt two more inside. "You came prepared. How much did you just 'tithe?'"

"Enough without being too much, I assure you." Jonathan knocked Eric's hand away. "Are we done now?"

In Eric's lasting silence, Jonathan added, "It doesn't concern you. *I* must atone."

"Fine," Eric replied. "Shall we join Raven and Paresh, then?"

Jonathan and Alex followed Eric to the sanctuary doors. They swung open into a large room awash with cheerful, colored light flowing through the stained glass windows overlooking the pews. An awkward silence immediately descended as smiles flattened and all eyes settled on Eric and his group.

The trek down the center aisle was grueling as Eric smiled and made eye contact. His friendly façade belied an awareness of the pent-up energy from the town's reservations, doubts, presumptions, and suspicions. It clawed at him and nipped at the others. Their auras instinctively formed protective barriers that thickened the air and would unwittingly trigger the human fight or flight response. That was unacceptable today.

He motioned several rows ahead and let the others pass. Paresh squeezed his hand, her innocent spirit unaffected. Reluctantly releasing her, he followed them, and continued up a few more rows before circling to survey the faces staring at him.

"Good morning," he said.

Time could have stopped. Silence had placed a seal upon the lips of every person there and snuffed every cough and sniffle. Someone in the back finally managed to clear his throat. With the seal broken, it began, and with far more ferocity than Eric had expected.

"Tell that to Abigail!" a man said in a loud, grievous voice. Eric presumed it was Berg, but wasn't sure.

"Or Rebecca's parents!" a nasally woman snipped.

"Or Bill's wife!" The man spat the words.

"How many more people will die because of you?"

The question was filled with such vile disgust that Eric looked away from the source. When the dust of anger settled, he'd rather not know who'd said what.

As he listened patiently, he noticed Raven's hand clamp down on Paresh's wrist to keep her from jumping up. Then a voice worn from fatigue and steeped in sorrow spoke over all the rest.

"It is a good morning." A middle-aged woman two rows ahead stood and took in the congregation. Dark circles anchored her eyes into sallow skin, and the four children beside her, ranging in age from eight to seventeen, looked as though they hadn't slept a whole night in days.

Sounding as tired as she looked, she continued, "The sun is shining on us as sure as Bill's smiling on us from Heaven."

Judy Jamerson's narrow finger flew in Eric's direction. "Mr. Ravenscroft has done nothing but good by me. And he's been nothing but kind to every one of you. To this entire community. To everyone!"

Her whole body began to quake. Splaying her fingers wide, she threw her hands up as though beseeching the heavens. Her expression screamed of frustration and her questioning eyes were sharp enough to force even the hardest gaze to the floor in shame. Her voice, at first peaceful and hopeful, now bit at them with the kind of incensed grief only a woman in her position could know so intimately well.

"How can you possibly think he'd do something so horrible? How? *How can you sit there and say things like that?* On today, of all days? Molly was…she was his best…" Judy choked and gestured at Eric with tears in her eyes.

Under the weight of sadness, no one looked at any one else—or at Eric. Simple questions, uttered by the right person, acted as a scolding that he hoped would stop the unpleasant exchange.

But then the man sitting in front of Judy stood.

A knot formed in Eric's gut. Weston had possessed the only factual account of the town's history until Eric had purchased Dora's diaries from him. The old man wasn't going to make this easy on him.

Weston faced the widow. He tugged at the sagging skin of his face and neck. "See this? Yeah? Well look at that one—" He pointed at Eric. "Yeah, I might not've been such a looker, but I was that young once—over fifty-five years ago! I remember he looked the exact same back then, too. And we was supposedly the same age! How to account for that? Huh?"

"I…well," Judy searched Eric's face for an answer.

At the end of the row where Eric had stopped, Sarah jumped up, her face lit with anger. Slower to rise, but with determined eyes, Sammy stood and placed hands of support on her shoulders.

"Excuse me, Mr. Faust," Sarah snapped. "But when did you get so high and mighty to cast stones like that? You only care about your own family! Never anyone else. I'm so sick of all the accusations! Since when does someone's appearance make them a murderer?"

"You young people understand nothing and imply everything!" Weston charged back. "That's not what I was saying! He's…he's a…ohh!" His finger shook at Eric before he yanked it down into a fist at his side. "You know! God, I can't say it!"

"Because it sounds ridiculous!" Sarah yelled.

"Well, he does have a point."

Judy's quiet voice brought astonished stares from both parties. Sarah's eyes widened as she demanded, "What now? You're on his side?"

"Hey, all's I'm saying is that it's awful weird that he doesn't age like the rest of us. I don't think he killed anyone." Judy once again searched Eric's face.

Quietly regarding Judy, Eric held his hands out to silence Sarah and Weston, and then gently said, "If you have a question, ask. I will not lie in God's house."

Judy paused in shock, but quickly recovered and thought for a moment. "Is it really true that you don't age? At all?"

Hand raised in protest, Raven shot up. "Now, hold on!" Seeing that Paresh had risen with her, she pursed her lips and tugged the girl down.

"No one needs to defend me," Eric said. "I have done nothing that needs defending."

He briefly studied Weston with a coolness the old man would feel deep in his bones. Then his gaze shifted to Judy, filled with warmth and sympathy. He held out his hand out to her. "Tell them why you came to see me, if you'd like."

Accepting his hand and joining him in the aisle, she said, "Blake got into some trouble, and…and you know we can't afford much—now more than ever—but Mr. Ravenscroft was working for free to get the charges dropped."

"That doesn't answer the question," Weston said.

Turning a cool eye to him once more, Eric held his finger to his lips. Facing the rest of the congregation, he pointed to an elderly man on the left side who appeared physically frail despite the resilience burning within his eyes. He nodded at Eric.

"Sixty years ago, Mr. Reece found himself in a spot of trouble that I helped him through—"

"And you weren't no lawyer then, neither," the old man interrupted with a firm nod.

Eric smiled. "No. I wasn't."

"Damn skippy. You was a good man back then, same as now. And that's what matters."

With an appreciative smile, Eric said, "Thank you, Mr. Reece."

"Don't gotta thank me. You's the one due the thanks. I'd of died in prison an innocent man if not for you."

Bobbing his head in agreement, Eric turned back to Judy. His smile faded. "I am truly sorry for what happened to Bill," he said. "If you need anything, anything at all, day or night, I am here for you."

Tears dripping down her cheeks, Judy fell forward and bawled into Eric's chest when he caught her. "Thank you so much…Mr. Ravenscroft," she choked out as he held her and let her cry.

"See?" Sarah suddenly cried. "Take a good look! That's the man ya'll have said such horrible things about!"

"That's enough, Sarah. Thank you."

"I'm sorry, but I just couldn't take it anymore."

"I understand."

Eric motioned for Blake to help his mother back to her seat. Then he looked up and held his hands out, beseeching.

"I can't hide who I am," he announced. "I don't age like you. I don't age at all. I can't hide that."

Murmuring through the pews caused a muscle near Raven's temple to twitch as she clenched her jaw. Jonathan stretched his arm across Paresh's seat and Alex leaned forward on his knees. Paresh locked eyes with Eric and shot him a proud smile.

"It's my strength of character and kind heart that define the type of man I am," Eric said. "And that has allowed me to call this place home for the last century and a half."

A collective gasp plunged the room into silence. Paresh wrenched free of Raven's grasp and stood, curling her fingers around her sapphire and diamond cross.

With a knowing smile, Eric called out for Pastor Caine to join him. "I'd like to introduce you to someone."

Seated along the rear wall, the clergyman shook with uncertainty and almost dumped his plate on his wife. "I…w-well…just a moment, Eric."

"I don't think Judy asked the right question," Weston grumbled.

"Well it was my question to ask, wasn't it?" Judy retorted. "Why are you so bent on causing trouble, Weston? This is supposed to be a celebration."

"Have you forgotten *why* we're 'celebrating?'" he fired back.

"Yes! *For my sister!*" Abigail yelled, charging up the aisle behind Pastor Caine. "But instead you insist on making a scene and accusing Mr. Ravenscroft of murder even though the FBI lady told us who's responsible!"

Abigail's eyes blazed with such bitterness that Eric feared she'd slap Weston when she reached him. He quickly announced, "Indeed, and Molly would not want us to fight. In fact, if everyone will bear with me just a moment longer, we'll give Molly a final gift—something she'd wanted for a long time. If you'll recall, I wasn't her only friend."

Abigail dropped into the nearest open seat, crossing her arms and legs, glare set on Weston. Pastor Caine arrived beside Eric a moment later.

"Recognize her?" Eric nodded at Paresh, who was wearing the biggest grin of her life. She'd been antsy and nervous about this ever since she and Eric had talked with Abigail about it the previous day.

Pushing his glasses up, the pastor squinted to see. A glimmer of recognition surfaced in his eyes. Paling, he glanced sharply at Eric. "No! It can't be!"

To Weston, Eric said, "It's no coincidence that I've been targeted by the man responsible for killing Bill, Rebecca, and Molly. I'll give you that. But it's not because I'm guilty or because I don't age. I've said it before and I'll keep saying it because it'll never stop being true: I am not the one who did this."

The Pastor grew even paler. "It can't be," he repeated in disbelief, wobbling slightly.

Eric held onto the pastor's arm to steady him. "The FBI briefly touched on this the other day, but I'm sure everyone remembers that ten years ago Andrew and Felicia Hawthorne died in an accident and their little girl was missing from the wreckage."

"Is it true?" Pastor Caine whispered to himself, jerking his glasses off.

Eric followed the pastor to Paresh. Biting her lower lip, she stepped into the center aisle and blushed as Pastor Caine cupped her cheeks.

"However," Eric continued. "What we have learned is that she was kidnapped by Andrew's brother, David—many of you may recall he was suspected in the Hawthorne and Schaffer deaths, and the arson fire of the original Sunset Grove Parish. David orchestrated the car accident and took his niece to gain control of the Hawthorne fortune."

"Paresh?" Pastor Caine studied her face. "Is it truly you?"

She nodded.

Tears glistening, the pastor buried her in his arms. "Praise God!"

Gently squeezing Paresh's hand, Eric announced, "Paresh returned home about a week ago, but we kept it a secret amid valid concerns for her safety. And since then, Walter Hodges and I have been cooperating with the FBI to understand how her kidnapping connects with the events that have happened here…" His voice trailed. Raven's FBI alter ego had summarized the rest days ago. "Andrew's little girl has finally come home. I present to you, Paresh Hawthorne, home, safe and sound, at long last."

Everyone crowded around Paresh at once, surely comparing her to the eight-year-old girl of memory. Only Weston remained in place, staring at him.

"Well? Did I pass?" Eric asked.

"For now," Weston grumbled reluctantly. "You've done good in bringing that girl home. But the cost was high."

"I agree. I, too, lost someone very dear to me."

For the first time, Eric saw understanding in Weston's gaze. He held up his index finger. "One more question?"

Eric scanned the crowd. They were focused on Paresh. "One is fine."

"The little boy in Dora's diaries was you, wasn't it?"

Eric nodded.

"Then I suppose I'll let well enough alone. What she wrote about you then is true today. You're a decent person, Mr. Ravenscroft. You can't say the same about me, but you've known my family long enough to know where I come from."

"That I do."

"I suppose if nothin' else, I should apologize for the way you was treated back then."

"That's not your burden to bear, Weston."

They shared a look before the old man shuffled to the far end of the row. As Eric watched him go, he heard heavy footsteps approach from behind. He reacted appropriately when a hard slap to his back would have sent him stumbling forward. Whirling around, he was greeted by the grinning face of the mayor, Matthew Hinkles.

"So this is the secret you wished to speak about, is it?" A hearty laugh rolled off his tongue. He grasped Eric's hand in a meaty paw and gave it a good shake. Built to farm, Hinkles spent most of his days in his tractor rather than his office. "Can you believe the Women's Auxiliary has already planned a float for her in the Autumn Pumpkin Festival's parade? They even know her favorite color—pale blue!"

"You don't say?" Eric saw Jonathan wink from the opposite wall where he and Alex had escaped. At the center of the swarm, Raven had embraced her assignment and snagged Walter to help. Each had Paresh hooked by an arm and fawned over her like everyone else.

Paresh caught him watching and mouthed, "Thank you."

He smiled and then beamed mischievous eyes at Jonathan. To the mayor, he said, "Your Honor, you haven't met my brother, yet. He's just over there…"

☽ ✳ ☾

Paresh pirouetted into Eric's office, giggling and swirling her skirt.

Joy radiated from every inch of her body as her aura embraced Eric, reducing his focus only to her.

He wrapped his arms around her waist and spun with her, capturing her mouth in a deep, loving kiss. For a brief moment, he felt as though they were alone.

The group had spent the last four hours at the church, and, despite all the catered food, Paresh hadn't eaten a single bite. Walter volunteered to get her a bowl of soup from The Greenery while everyone else met up at the closest safe haven: Eric's office, now shielded inside and out by Raven's buttons.

Paresh cupped Eric's cheeks and smiled as she pulled away. "I wish Molly could have seen it," she whispered. "I'm sorry I had to steal her day."

Resting his forehead against hers, he kissed the tip of her nose. "She'd say the same thing Abigail said—that she'd be happy to share her day with you." He slowed their rotation and smoothed his hands over Paresh's hair. "She was a wonderful woman with a heart bigger than this town. Believe me—it would have made her so happy."

"And I suppose dragging all of those humans over to meet me would have made her happy, as well?" Jonathan asked sarcastically, pouting in Eric's chair.

"Who knows? I got a kick out of it!" Eric replied with a grin. "In fact, I think Alex even enjoyed it."

Jonathan glared at the leader of his pack. "Is that so?"

Squirming under his scrutiny, Alex tried to slink low into the recliner, but gave up with a shrug and pushed himself up into a comfortable position. "Hey, I can't help finding your interactions as entertaining as you both seem to find Raven picking on me."

"Aye, I concur." Near the door, Raven propped her foot on the wall and leaned back.

"I mean, you're so different now." Closing his eyes, Alex tucked his arms beneath his head and stretched his legs out over the coffee table. "Before, you were always at each other's throats, like literally. It was intense."

Paresh caught the murderous looks Eric and Jonathan both shot him. Giggling, she said, "Really? You have to tell me about it, Alex!"

"No, he doesn't!" Jonathan and Eric exclaimed in unison.

Alex popped an eye open. "Sorry milady, but I must respectfully decline your request."

Paresh wriggled free from Eric's hands and approached Alex.

"Why're you so serious now—is it really that bad?"

"Even Alex knows when not to press his luck," Raven replied. "An order's an order."

"Pare, would it suffice to say that our past created the people you know now and leave it at that?" Jonathan picked up the photo on Eric's desk. Something akin to regret burned in his eyes.

Eric came up behind Paresh and tugged at her waist. "It felt like a dream, but I recall hearing you tell Walter that the past is the past and only the present can bear the weight of our lives to form the foundation for our futures."

She twisted in his arms. "You heard me?"

"Your voice kept me bound to this plane," he replied softly. "My past with Jonathan formed the man standing before you now, but you are everything I've been missing for so long. You are part of my past and you are my present. You are my foundation and my future."

"Oh Eric—"

"I can't imagine my life without you."

"I love you."

Eric pressed his lips against hers. His heart felt so huge, overflowing with all the joy, sorrow, and anger of the day. No matter the obstacle, they could jump any hurdle and find a peaceful future. His strength was hers and hers was his, and now they had the backing of an entire nation—one he'd fought to avoid for so long.

With the button active, Walter startled Raven when he burst through the door. Panicked and pale, with white knuckles clutching a plastic bag that drooped under the weight of spilt soup, he panted, "Did you hear it? The radio?" His eyes didn't focus on anyone.

The air stiffened with charged energy. Alex jumped to his feet and Raven straightened. Walter shuffled halfway into the room.

"Hear what?" Paresh asked cautiously. Eric's hands had frozen in place on her waist.

"On the radio." Walter motioned toward the street, where his car was parked. "There was an explosion. In the Arctic Circle. I think on a Canadian island." Regaining some of his composure, he faced Jonathan. "Isn't that where you people call home?"

Jonathan snapped his fingers at Alex and slapped a communicator on his jaw. "*Lucien!*"

Raven and Alex barked into their communicators, and seconds later, Cyprian, Heron, and their hunters raced through the door. Failing to reach Lucien, Jonathan looked to Alex, who said, "It's the Arc of

Celestial Night. The Chthonic Knights are en route to the Arc of True Blood and I've dispatched the Silent Vespers to assess the damage on Banks Island. It's serious—humans on the space station were the first to notice the smoke plume."

The silence that followed might have stretched into forever if not for the peal of the desk phone. It rang three times before Eric walked over and put the receiver to his ear.

"The communicators are compromised," Lucien said, as apathetic as usual. "They're calling themselves the Children of the Morning Star and have made their official declaration. I'm evacuating the Arc of True Blood. Prepare to receive us with full escort momentarily."

The phone slid through Eric's fingers and crashed onto his desk. He dropped into a chair. The turbulent ground he'd finally steadied had disappeared altogether. His peaceful home was about to become a battleground.

How many more people will die because of you?

It was a question Eric feared to answer.

Bonus Content & Notations

Interviews with an Unwilling Vampire

To celebrate the initial release of *Confessions of the Second Born*, the author shared a series of interview attempts with Jonathan in the reader's group on Facebook. Edited for content. No story spoilers for *Confessions*.

ATTEMPT ONE

Me: To celebrate Confessions' launch, I sat down with Jonathan for a behind the scenes tell all . . .

Jonathan: (grumbles lower than I can hear)

Me: Good Morning! Are you excited to be done with Confessions?

Jonathan: (pointed stare)

Me: (innocently blinks)

Jonathan: (sighs) Humans. (sighs)

Me: Um, ok, so . . . um . . .

Jonathan: (looks at Eric) Why am I here?

Me: To Celebrate the release of *Confessions*!

Jonathan: (to me) So you're essentially showing the whole world my diary?

Me: Well, it's not your diary. Do you keep a diary?

Jonathan: You created me. Do I?

Me: Uh, that's not how this works.

Jonathan: That's not how any of this works.

Me: In the book, Lucifer creates you.

Jonathan: (mischievous grin) So you're Lucifer?

Me: Um, no.

Jonathan: But you created me.

Me: Ok. But I'm not Lucifer.

Jonathan: Did you create him?

Me: No

Jonathan: Then how's he in the book?

Me: I put him there.

Jonathan: And how does he feel about that?

Eric: (pinches bridge of nose and shakes head)

Me: We've gone a bit off topic.

Jonathan: You didn't answer the question. He's not a genie in a bottle, you know. He's not going to blink and call you Master.

Me: I don't expect tha—Hey, I'm not the one being interviewed!

Jonathan: Why am I here?

Me: Because they're your "Confessions"

Jonathan: So we're back to the diary thing?

Me: You don't keep a diary.

Jonathan: That's good to know. I didn't think I would. Seems awfully boring.

Me: Well, since you can clearly think for yourself, what do you think about *Confessions?*
Jonathan: (glares at Eric)
Eric: (sighs and rolls eyes)
Jonathan: Spoilers?
Me: No spoilers.
Jonathan: Then don't ask stupid questions.
Me: Hey now!
Jonathan: I only did what you made me do. Maybe you should release *your* confessions.
Me: That's not how this works.
Jonathan: We've already determined that.
Eric: (mutters) Master manipulator
Jonathan: (glares at Eric) Why are you here?
Me: Don't you want him here?
Jonathan: (stares blankly)
Me: Didn't think that one through, huh? You always want him with you.
Jonathan: I won't let you win.
Me: This isn't a contest.
Jonathan: I don't want to play.
Eric: Just answer the questions!
Jonathan: I do not submit to humans.
Me: (wipes face and huffs)
Jonathan: (stands) I'm going to buy a new suit.
Eric: (sends apologetic look and follows Jonathan)
Me: (muttering) Well that went well. Better luck next time!

ATTEMPT TWO

Behind the Scenes with Jonathan, take two:
J: (after 15 minutes of primping, smoothing his jacket and trousers, and folding and refolding his pocket square) So I'm back. For some reason.
Me: The reader's [sic] want to know, so I thought we should try this ag—
J: The HUMAN readers?
Me: What else would they be?
J: (rolls eyes) Proceed
Me: How—
J: Shouldn't an author know when to use a possessive apostrophe?
Me: What? (Scans interview)
J: (mocking) *"The reader's want..."*
Me: Damn Autocorrect
J: (to Eric) And you want me to carry one of those idiotic things around. Our communicators don't have that problem.

E: Well, you're not b@man. Using a symbol to reach you is a little archaic.

J: B@man is human. I'm better than b@man.

Me: So if Jonathan carried a phone, you'd talk to him more often, Eric?

E: I didn't say that. Don't get his hopes up.

J: Oh…(coy grin)…That's not what's going up.

Me: (covers screen) OK, NOTHING TO SEE HERE FOLKS. WE'LL TRY AGAIN LATER!!

ATTEMPT THREE

Behind the Scenes with Jonathan - Take THREE (3rd time's the charm, right?)

Me: Welcome Back.

J: Why isn't Eric here?

Me: Because you don't behave when he's around.

J: And you think I'll behave by myself? (Stands)

Me: No. I know you. I created you.

J: (walking away) Ah yes, the fake Lucifer.

Me: (patiently waits)

J: (marches back in and whispers) That's a dirty move!

Me: (whispers) Yup. I made you, remember?

J: (drops into chair with huff)

(Paresh enters and sits beside him)

Me: (muwahaha)

P: Good morning! I'm so excited to be here!

J: (sends fond look to P)

Me: So, Jonathan - the end of *The Arrival* was rather emotional for you.

J: Of course it was.

Me: Are you happy with the way it played out?

J: (looks over at P) I'm happy for Pare.

Me: Several readers have asked what you and Lucien were up to in the forest after you kissed.

J: I'm not going there. (eyes P) They may think what they like.

Me: You were only half dressed by the end.

J: (glares at me)

P: Me, too! Although, I did put a robe on.

J: (Stares at P)

Me: (thinking) Hm, how much was Eric wearing?

J: Didn't you have some *good* interview questions?

Me: Me? No. Paresh?

P: (turning toward J) What is your favorite color?

J: Blood red

P: Do you prefer Homburgs or Fedoras?

J: Fedoras, but it depends on my suit. I dislike bowlers.

P: I've never seen you with your hair down. Is there a story behind the
ribbon?
J: It was the first gift Lucien gave me—a very, very long time ago when we
roamed the Far East.
P: Would you ever cut your hair?
J: Lucien likes it long.
P: Me, too. It's very pretty.
J: (smiles)
P: Why do you like the rain so much?
J: It makes everything tangible. Standing there. Cold drops. Splashes.
Watching the water catch the light and undulate. The scent of the organic and
the taste of atmosphere. It's…being in the moment, feeling, hearing, seeing,
smelling, and tasting everything at once. It's stimulating, yet relaxing.
P: It's your moment of peace?
J: That's a good way to put it.
P: But what about your clothes? You're a perfectionist.
J: Clothes are replaceable. The rain is special. Like you.
P: (smiles shyly) Thank you, Master Jon.
J: (returns smile and holds her hand)
P: So, um, when's your birthday?
J: I don't know
P: Oh, that's awful! We need a day to celebrate!
J: Well…let's wait and see how things go in Confessions before we make
any long term plans. OK, Pare?
P: That better not mean…
J: Please don't cry. (strokes her hair)
Me: No spoilers! (concludes interview)

Author's Note & Acknowledgments

In addition to the abridged acknowledgments below, many thanks to Magpie Press, authors M.K. Deppner, Serene Conneeley, Ruth Miranda, & Julie Embleton for support, friendship, and advice, and to everyone who's supported this relaunch! Thank you!

Dedication goes to Robin, my dear friend who passed away. She kept this manuscript on her nightstand waiting for the "perfect" moment to "give it the attention it deserved." That moment never came. Thank you John, Connor, Linda for sharing her with me.

Thank you to my mom, Carol, for hours poring over the manuscript and talking scenes out, and an attention to detail that helped me finish! To my husband and soul mate, Tim, for answering endless "what do you think about…" questions, reading snippets or listening to me read, and supporting me every bit of the way. I love you, babe. To Jacque, Liz, and Betsy, and Tami E. To Jennifer, my sounding board and graveyard adventurer—even though you made me pose with creepy wax figures at the Abraham Lincoln Presidential Museum! To Bob and Anna, and the relaxing luxury of Oakridge Manor. To Pastor Ron, and the 8th Regiment of Illinois Volunteer Cavalry re-enactors (8thIllinoisCavalry.org).

Again, I thank my cats. They are a writer's best friend.

And…Thank You! I hope to see you again in *Last Born Daughter*!

Reviews are lifeblood to authors! Please let other readers know
what you think of this book by reviewing on Amazon and/or
GoodReads! It's as easy as telling a friend!
Thank you so much for your support!
https://kastiepavlik.wixsite.com/author

HISTORICAL NOTE

<u>Army of the Potomac & Fictional Application</u>

The longest military event in the history of U.S. warfare involved the Army of the Potomac during the Civil War. Commonly known as the "siege" of Petersburg, Virginia, Confederate and Union forces battled from June 15, 1864 to April 2, 1865 before the Confederates retreated and the Union declared victory. Given that the movements of units during the Civil War are well documented, artistic license places Eric at the side of Colonel Thaddeus Hawthorne in a frigid Virginian forest in the winter of 1864. The real 8th Regiment of the Illinois Cavalry (out of Chicago) did fight with the Army of the Potomac in the "siege" of Petersburg.

<u>Revolvers & Fictional application</u>

The first U.S. patent for a revolver was filed in the early 1800s. Given the Vampiric Nation's advanced technology and Alexander's obsession with Ancient Greek and Roman Mythology, it's plausible that he was gun slinging *long* before the cowboys. Inspired by the many designs of mathematical and engineering genius, Heron of Alexandria, Alex probably built his first revolver's prototype in the first or second century, A.D.

<u>Black Shuck</u>

Medieval legend and English Folklore tell of a black hellhound that acts as a portent of death. People were warned to hide from Black Shuck's howl or to run if they ever met him…or face their deaths. He's commonly described a black dog, of comparable size to a horse or calf, with red eyes—or one fiery eye—who hunts with silent footfalls. The name "Shuck" means devil or fiend, and the word "shuck" can meant "to lie or deceive." Stories about large black dogs in this context go back almost a thousand years.

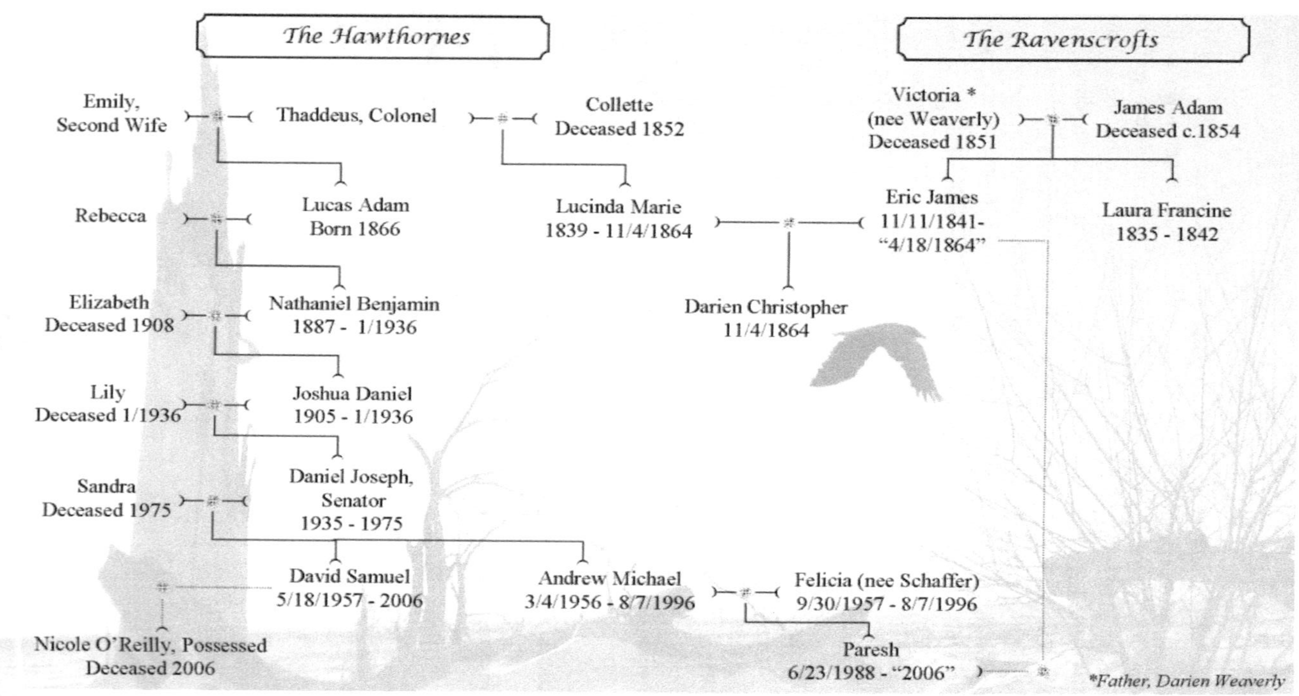

The Hawthornes
The Ravenscrofts
Emily, Second Wife
Thaddeus, Colonel
Collette Deceased 1852
Victoria * (nee Weaverly) Deceased 1851
James Adam Deceased c.1854
Rebecca
Lucas Adam Born 1866
Lucinda Marie 1839 - 11/4/1864
Eric James 11/11/1841- "4/18/1864"
Laura Francine 1835 - 1842
Elizabeth Deceased 1908
Nathaniel Benjamin 1887 - 1/1936
Darien Christopher 11/4/1864
Lily Deceased 1/1936
Joshua Daniel 1905 - 1/1936
Sandra Deceased 1975
Daniel Joseph, Senator 1935 - 1975
David Samuel 5/18/1957 - 2006
Andrew Michael 3/4/1956 - 8/7/1996
Felicia (nee Schaffer) 9/30/1957 - 8/7/1996
Nicole O'Reilly, Possessed Deceased 2006
Paresh 6/23/1988 - "2006"
*Father, Darien Weaverly

TIMELINE

Vampiric History		Human History
2000 B.C. Lucien created	**2000 B.C.**	
1000 B.C. Jonathan created		
c.36 A.D. Great Holy War begins on Earth	**Year 0**	c.36 A.D. Lucifer expelled from Heaven
		Altered History Begin Date Unknown
		c.300 - 500 A.D. Altered History reflects Roman Empire Collapse
c.998 A.D. Lucien signs Treaty of the Lasting Peace & then creates Vampiric High Council of Elders	**1000 A.D.**	c.1000 A.D. Leif Eriksson settles L'Anse aux Meadows
	1840s A.D.	1841 Eric is born
		1842 Eric's sister dies
1847 Jonathan meets Eric		
		1851 Eric's mother dies
		c.1854/55 Eric's father dies; Eric meets Thaddeus
	1860s A.D.	1860 Eric marries Lucinda
		Apr.1861 U.S. Civil War begins
		1861 Eric goes to war
		Feb.1864 Lucinda becomes pregnant
Apr.1864 Jonathan alters Eric		Apr.1864 Eric "dies"
		Oct.1864 Eric awakens, altered
		Nov.1864 Lucinda & infant Darien die
Nov.1864 Jonathan witnesses Eric's Events of Chapter 7		Nov.1864 Eric's Events of Chapter 7
		May 1865 Civil War ends
		1866 Hawthorne Legacy begins; Lucas is born
	1880s A.D.	1887 Nathaniel is born
	1900 A.D.	1905 Joshua is born
1908 Jonathan's Events of Chapter 9		1908 Events of Chapter 9
	1930s A.D.	1935 Daniel is born; later becomes Senator Hawthorne
Jan.1936 Events of Chapter 11		Jan.1936 Events of Chapter 11
1936-1960 Jonathan is restricted	**1950s A.D.**	
		1956 Andrew is born
		1957 David is born
1960 Chapter 12 begins		1960 Chapter 12 begins
	1970s A.D.	1975 Daniel & Wife die; Felicia's parents die; Molly meets Eric
		1976 Andrew & Felicia marry
		Jun.1988 Paresh stillborn & reborn
Summer 1988 Sunset Grove Parish Arson		Summer 1988 Sunset Grove Parish Arson
Aug.1996 High Council orders Paresh's abduction	**1990s A.D.**	Aug.1996 Andrew & Felicia die; Paresh is kidnapped
Summer 2006 Events of *The Arrival* over 3 days & 4 nights; 6 days later, Events of *Confessions of the Second Born* begin	**2000 A.D.**	Summer 2006 Events of *The Arrival* over 3 days & 4 nights; 6 days later, Events of *Confessions of the Second Born* begin

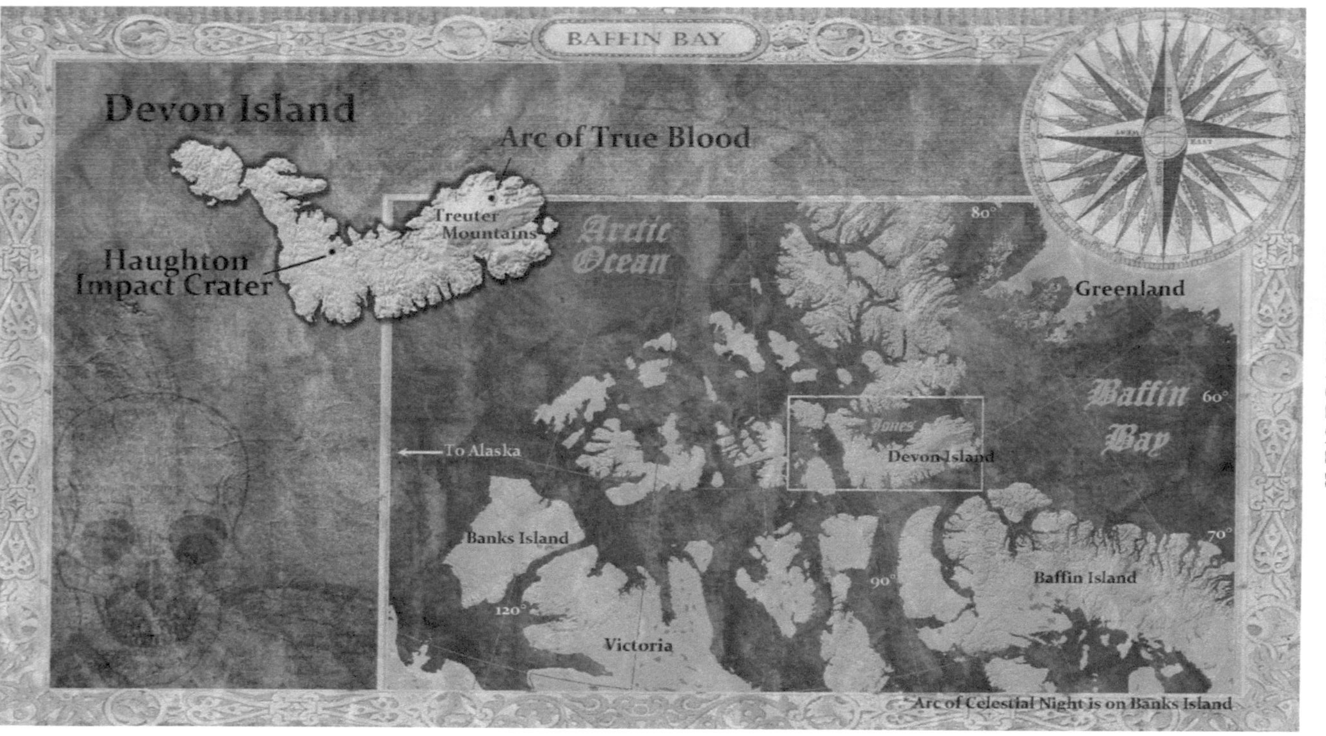
BAFFIN BAY
Devon Island
Arc of True Blood
Treuter Mountains
Haughton Impact Crater
Arctic Ocean
Greenland
Jones
Devon Island
Baffin Bay
To Alaska
Banks Island
Victoria
Baffin Island
Arc of Celestial Night is on Banks Island
60°
70°
80°
90°
120°

AUTHOR SKETCHES

Above:
(pencil & charcoal) by Kastie
Pavlik, 2018. Jonathan leaning
back in the rain, post *The
Arrival*.

Right:
Sketch (pencil) by Kastie
Pavlik, 2018. Donovan, Wraith
Reaper First Officer.

Above: Sketch (pencil) by Kastie Pavlik, 2018. Raven, Wraith Reaper Commander/VaSH High Commander.

Below:
Digital sketches of Vampire Shadow Hound Insignias &
Vampiric Star by Kastie Pavlik, 2010 & 2007 respectively
(updated 2018).

Scythes: Wraith Reapers. Moon: Crimson Guard.
Star: Silent Vespers. Key: Chthonic Knights.

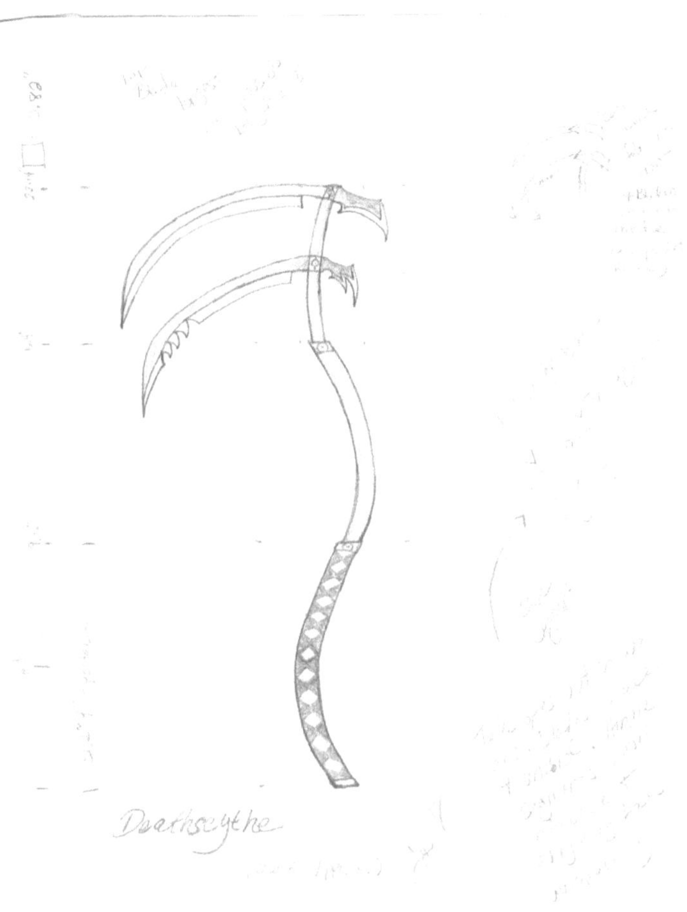

Rough, technical blueprint (pencil) for Raven's weapon, Deathscythe, by Kastie Pavlik, 2018. (Thank you to Rich, Connor, John, and Tami for insights into designing a conceivable weapon. It's like a curved combat baton when collapsed.)

Hand notes starting upper left going clockwise:
- ♦ Top blade longest max. possible length = 13"
- ♦ Back blades fall over front & blades fold into handle (like a pocket knife)
- ♦ Hollow for blades (written above arrows pointing down at handle segments, labeled top segment, middle segment, and base segment)
- ♦ Telescopes out in an arc. Blades release & unfold. Handle segments swivel into place & everything locks automatically.
- ♦ Dimensions listed on left: base ~ 9" – portable

KASTIE PAVLIK is a gamer, artist, techie, and hopeless bibliophile who grew up loving all things macabre and creepy crawly, with an affinity for mythology, vampires, the paranormal, and psychology. Diagnosed with Multiple Sclerosis in 2008, she has subsequently beaten breast cancer, and manages a rare genetic disorder, Ehlers-Danlos Syndrome. She spends her days entertaining (annoying?) her feline overlords while adapting to her endlessly changing needs. Surrounded by the starry cornfields of Illinois, she enjoys a quiet life with her husband and their cats. She is the author of the *Children of the Morning Star* vampire series and the horror novelette *How to Make Lemonade*. Her writing influences include *Edgar Allan Poe, Anne Rice, James Herbert, Alfred Hitchcock,* and *Hideyuki Kikuchi*. She is a member of The Alliance of Independent Authors.

www.ingramcontent.com/pod-product-compliance
Lightning Source LLC
Chambersburg PA
CBHW061601190726
48288CB00007B/2123